KURT AUSTIN ADVENTURES
Novels from the NUMA® Files

Journey of the Pharaohs
(with Graham Brown)

Sea of Greed (with Graham Brown)

The Rising Sea
(with Graham Brown)

Nighthawk (with Graham Brown)

The Pharaoh's Secret
(with Graham Brown)

Ghost Ship (with Graham Brown)

Zero Hour (with Graham Brown)

The Storm (with Graham Brown)

Devil's Gate (with Graham Brown)

Medusa (with Paul Kemprecos)

The Navigator
(with Paul Kemprecos)

Polar Shift (with Paul Kemprecos)

Lost City (with Paul Kemprecos)

White Death (with Paul Kemprecos)

Fire Ice (with Paul Kemprecos)

Blue Gold (with Paul Kemprecos)

Serpent (with Paul Kemprecos)

OREGON® FILES

Final Option (with Boyd Morrison)

Shadow Tyrants
(with Boyd Morrison)

Typhoon Fury (with Boyd Morrison)

The Emperor's Revenge
(with Boyd Morrison)

Piranha (with Boyd Morrison)

Mirage (with Jack Du Brul)

The Jungle (with Jack Du Brul)

The Silent Sea (with Jack Du Brul)

Corsair (with Jack Du Brul)

Plague Ship (with Jack Du Brul)

Skeleton Coast (with Jack Du Brul)

Dark Watch (with Jack Du Brul)

Sacred Stone (with Craig Dirgo)

Golden Buddha (with Craig Dirgo)

NON-FICTION

Built for Adventure: The Classic Automobiles of Clive Cussler and Dirk Pitt

Built to Thrill: More Classic Automobiles from Clive Cussler and Dirk Pitt

The Sea Hunters (with Craig Dirgo)

The Sea Hunters II
(with Craig Dirgo)

Clive Cussler and Dirk Pitt Revealed (with Craig Dirgo)

WRATH
OF
POSEIDON

CLIVE CUSSLER

and Robin Burcell

MICHAEL JOSEPH

an imprint of

PENGUIN BOOKS

MICHAEL JOSEPH

UK | USA | Canada | Ireland | Australia
India | New Zealand | South Africa

Michael Joseph is part of the Penguin Random House group of companies
whose addresses can be found at global.penguinrandomhouse.com

First published in the United States of America by G. P. Putnam's Sons 2020
Published in Great Britain by Michael Joseph 2020
001

Copyright © Sandecker, RLLP, 2020
Map copyright © Denéa Buckingham, 2020

The moral right of the author has been asserted

Book design by Nancy Resnic
Printed and bound in Great Britain by Clays Ltd, Elcograf S.p.A.

A CIP catalogue record for this book is available from the British Library

HARDBACK ISBN: 978–0–241–42465–0
OM PAPERBACK ISBN: 978–0–241–42466–7

www.greenpenguin.co.uk

MIX
Paper from
responsible sources
FSC® C018179

Penguin Random House is committed to a
sustainable future for our business, our readers
and our planet. This book is made from Forest
Stewardship Council® certified paper.

CAST OF CHARACTERS

SARDIA, 546 B.C.

General Mazares—the head of King Cyrus II of Persia's army

Artaban—Mazares's lieutenant

Magos—a soldier

Tabalus—the *satrap*/governor of Sardia, appointed by Cyrus

Pactyes—a Lydian appointed by Cyrus to oversee the treasury of Sardia

POSEIDON'S TRIDENT, 546 B.C.

Xanthos—age fifteen, a Korseai fisherman

Agathos—age ten, Xanthos's brother

Drakon—a Samian pirate

Lampros—a Samian pirate

Alyattes—a Lydian thief

Korax—a Lydian thief

THE FARGOS

Sam Fargo

Remi Fargo—*née* Longstreet

CAST OF CHARACTERS

THEIR FRIENDS

St. Julien Perlmutter

Frank—St. Julien's driver

Rubin "Rube" Haywood—a CIA agent

Blake Thomas—Sam's friend and a real estate agent

Olivia Brady—Remi's post-college roommate

Keith Brady—Olivia's brother

Steve Drake—a retired Navy SEAL

Kate Drake—Steve's wife

Selma Wondrash—the Fargos' researcher

GREECE

FOURNI RESIDENTS

Dimitris Papadopoulos—Remi's college friend

Nikos Papadopoulos—Dimitris's father

Ares—Nikos's nephew

Valerios—Nikos's cousin

Tassos Gianakos—an expert on pirate lore and Zoe's grandfather

Zoe Gianakos—Dimitris's girlfriend

Skavos—owner of Skavos's café

Manos Mitikas—Dimitris's friend, a Fourni Underwater Archeological Preservation Society diver

Denéa Buckingham—Manos's girlfriend, a Fourni Underwater Archeological Preservation Society diver

SAMOS RESIDENTS

Helena—a friend of Tassos

Professor Pallas Alexandris—a classical literature expert at the University of the Aegean

CAST OF CHARACTERS

PATMOS RESIDENTS

Adrian Kyril
Minerva Kyril—Adrian's mother, an olive oil magnate
Phoebe—Adrian Kyril's girlfriend
Leon—the Kyril family's attorney

ADRIAN KYRIL'S GANG

Ilya—Adrian's head of security
Fayez—Ilya's second in command
Giorgo—a guard
Lucas—a guard
Zenos
Gianni
Piers
Kostas
Gregor

INTERPOL

Sergeant Petros Kompouras

Fournoi Korseon
Φούρνοι / Κορσεαί

GREECE
ATHENS
TURKEY
Ikaria   Samos
FOURNOI

Cape Saita /
Ακρ. Σαίτα

Agios Minas /
Άγιος Μηνάς

Fourni / Φούρνοι

Agios Nikolas /
Άγιος Νικόλας

Thimena / Θύμαινα

Kamari /
Καμάρι

Kleftolimano /
Κλεφτολίμανο

Kampi /
Καμπί

N

W   E

Petrokopio /
Πετροκοπιό

S

0.5 KM
1 KM   2 KM

Mikros Anthropofas /
Μικρός Ανθρωποφάς

Alatonisi / Αλατονήσι

Megalos Anthropofas /
Μεγάλος Ανθρωποφάς

Makronisi / Μακρονήσι

WRATH
OF
POSEIDON

PROLOGUE I

The steep acropolis of Sardis loomed against the night sky, while far below at the city's edge, flames consumed the reed-thatched buildings. General Mazares, dispatched by King Cyrus II of Persia the moment he'd learned of the revolt, had ridden through the night, leading a unit of armed heavy cavalry. According to the imperial messenger, the Ionian mercenaries were set to spark the revolt at dawn.

Apparently, they'd gotten an early start.

"Fools," Artaban, his lieutenant, called out over the sound of hooves as the horses neared the gates. A wooden building exploded near the gold-refining works. "Do they not realize that Cyrus will crush them?"

"There is nothing left to crush," Mazares shouted. "I'm surprised that there's anything left to burn."

It was the second time they'd marched upon Sardis. The first was when King Cyrus's army had broken the siege of the wealthy Lydian capital, captured its king, Croesus, then plundered his vast treasury.

If not for this revolt, Mazares would be accompanying the bulk of Croesus's treasure back to Ecbatana.

"The quicker we quell this rebellion, the sooner we get home." He eyed the flames swirling from several structures just outside the gates.

As they neared the inferno, Mazares realized the purpose of the fires. He and his horsemen were almost blinded. Waiting for them, the insurgents, with their backs to the blaze, had the advantage. Within moments, Cyrus's cavalry was attacked by a shadow army of soldiers armed with spears, axes, and swords.

Dividing his men into two flanks, Mazares led the left, Artaban the right. The deafening clash of metal rang through the night as his horsemen, blinded by the flames, battled the unseen enemy. Mazares thrust at an armed silhouette. His blade struck something solid. The rebel's shield. Shouting, Mazares ordered his left flank to close in, while Artaban did the same with the right, sweeping in behind the rebels, who suddenly found themselves sandwiched between both flanks. Spurring his horse to rear, Mazares blocked the thrust of a spear, and drove his blade into his opponent's chest, piercing through the man's inadequate armor.

Pulling his sword free, he wheeled his mount to the right, then swung at the next man, felling him as well.

Within minutes, it was over. The insurrectionists fled. The flames of the wooden structures, no longer being fed, began to die as a smoky dawn in the eastern sky burned along with the embers of the failed revolt.

Mazares surveyed the scattering of bodies—none of them his men. The speed with which they put down the insurrection troubled him as he met up with his second in command. "Tell me, Artaban. Does it not seem suspiciously convenient that the fire was confined to the outer wall? And that the skirmishers dissipated almost the moment we rode in?"

"And why wouldn't they?" Artaban nodded back at their troops, who were awaiting further orders. "If you were a group of outnumbered mercenaries and you beheld Cyrus's immortal cavalry charging?"

Immortal they were not. But the ease with which they'd won this so-called battle would certainly add to their legend.

It did not, however, lessen Mazares's concern.

It was something more than the desertion of the city gates. His unease grew as he led a contingent of horsemen into the city.

"A trap?" asked Artaban.

"I fear something else entirely." He raised his hand. His men halted in the agora, looking down the empty streets on all sides. Before his departure from Sardis, King Cyrus had appointed Tabalus to govern the newly conquered city in his stead. "Tabalus's guards could easily have crushed the insurrection, as small as it was. So why have we not seen any of his guards on the streets?"

"Perhaps the governor is part of it?"

"Let us hope not. Magos, take charge. If there is any evidence that the rebels are regrouping, end it. Artaban, bring back one of those rebels. Alive."

"And where will you be?" Artaban asked.

"I intend to find out whether the king's trust in Tabalus has been misplaced."

As his officers took off in opposite directions, Mazares and a handful of his horsemen rode to the acropolis, only to discover the palace guards sprawled on their backs in front of the great carved cedar doors, both standing wide open.

"Dead," Mazares said. "Find Tabalus." He strode past the guards, down the long hall into the throne room. A few minutes later, two officers returned, escorting the frightened governor between them.

Dressed in nightclothes, Tabalus, attempting to regain his magisterial dignity, scrambled onto the throne. "Well met, General Mazares. I prayed that you would arrive in time," he said.

"Who is behind all this?"

"I cannot say. My spies were thwarted at every turn, one even impaled. I managed to get a messenger out moments before the rebels besieged the acropolis."

One of Mazares's men nodded. "The governor speaks the truth. We found him bound to his bed, and his chamber door barred from the outside. The rest of the palace staff was shut up in the Scroll Room."

"None of this makes sense." Mazares paced across the polished marble floor, trying to fit the pieces together, certain there must be something they were all overlooking. An answer of sorts finally came when Artaban returned, dragging one of the rebels into the palace. He threw him to the ground at the base of the dais. "Tell your governor what took place here tonight."

The man, groveling on hands and knees, lifted his head, swallowing past a lump in his throat as he looked at the disheveled governor. "We were paid—generously—to burn what was left of the buildings near the city gates."

Mazares noted the soot on the man's face and clothing. "Who paid you?"

"I know them not."

Artaban drew his knife and held it to the rebel's neck.

"I swear," he said, his eyes beseeching. "The one thing I can tell you—they were not from Sardis. They were not even Lydian."

"How do you know?" Mazares asked.

"One had a boar's head tattooed on his upper arm."

"A boar's head?" Mazares asked. "Are you certain?"

The man nodded.

Samian pirates. The marauding Samian ships were notorious, not only for their red ocher hulls and scarlet sails, but also for their boar's head prows. "What would Samians be doing in Lydia?"

4

If anything, Tabalus appeared even more shaken. "I fear I may know something about that. But it is best said in private."

Mazares nodded. The guards removed the rebel, leaving Mazares and Artaban alone with the governor.

"Two nights ago," the governor said, "one of my spies informed me that he saw Pactyes meeting with a few Samians."

Pactyes, a Lydian, was the newly appointed Overseer of the Imperial Mint and Gold Refineries, a position bestowed upon him by King Cyrus. Although Mazares had counseled the king against such an appointment, Cyrus insisted that a Lydian figurehead was necessary to prevent the newly conquered Lydians from revolting once the Persian army left. "You're certain of what you saw?"

"I am. I even conducted a surprise inspection at the mint yesterday morning, but I found nothing amiss."

Mazares and Artaban exchanged glances. One of the rebel fires was near the mint.

"Get dressed! Order your grooms to ready your horse," Mazares said.

"For what purpose?" Tabalus asked, descending the throne.

"To confront Pactyes."

"He will only deny everything, as he did with me."

"Then we shall determine what is truth and what is not," Mazares said, a feeling of dread coursing through his veins. "To the Royal Mint."

Less than ten minutes later, Mazares and his men, along with Tabalus, rode down from the acropolis and out of the razed city to confront Pactyes.

In all his years commanding King Cyrus's cavalry, Mazares had never seen anything to match the wealth found in King Croesus's treasury, and he was amazed once again by the vast quantities of gold as he and his men entered to inspect the mint.

Just as Tabalus had said, all seemed in order—except for the fact that Pactyes was not at his post.

"Why set the fires and raise a sham revolt?" Artaban asked.

Mazares turned back to the brass-bound coffers of coins in the treasury, opening the lid of one. The gold Lion's Heads of Croesids gleamed despite the half-light.

He picked up a coin, feeling the weight of it in his hand—alarmed when he realized it could not be solid gold. He rubbed the coin on a nearby touchstone, the gold plating scraping off, revealing a center of lead. He tossed the coin, then plunged both hands deep into the chest, through the golden surface, and came up with handfuls of lead tokens.

He ordered his men to open every chest in the Royal Mint. Each had the same layer of gold Lydian Croesids on top, the coins all lead-filled. And beneath, nothing but lead. Lead coins stamped with Samian boar's heads.

Pactyes had fooled them all.

He turned to Artaban. "Ready the cavalry. We ride for the coast. If fortune smiles upon us, we'll get there before Pactyes flees with the gold."

"At once."

Mazares dumped a handful of lead-filled gold coins in Tabalus's hand. "Find me enough gold for smelting," he ordered as he strode out. "When I find Pactyes, I intend to force open his mouth and pour molten gold down his throat."

PROLOGUE II

Korseai
546 B.C.

The long shadows of the rising sun cast a trembling fear in the two boys as they pushed their small boat into the Aegean Sea. If all went well they'd be back in two days' time.

Xanthos, fifteen, with a final glance back to make sure they hadn't been seen, held the boat steady for his ten-year-old brother, Agathos. "Hurry."

Xanthos took up the oars. Only when the small craft was far enough from shore did he think of his mother and her heartbreak when she found them missing. It had only been a few months since their father had disappeared at sea. He murmured a prayer to Zephyr and raised the sail. It snapped, then billowed, the west wind blowing them out into the deep waters as the dawn-washed sky turned blue.

The sun had almost finished its course by the time the boys caught sight of the forbidden island. It was a monumental pyramid rising out of the sea, with three long sharp rocky pinnacles reaching to the heavens. Silhouetted against the setting sun, they resembled gigantic spires.

Both boys stared in awe. They'd reached it. Poseidon's Trident.

"Do you think it's true?" asked Agathos. "Will Poseidon really hear us?"

"I hope so." Xanthos lowered the sail, took the oars, and rowed toward a breach in the rocks, which concealed a small inlet.

"But where's his ear? I don't see any cave. How do we talk to him?"

The cave, they'd been told, was somewhere on the north side of Poseidon's Trident, and reached only by boat. It was a good thing, too, since setting foot on the sacred island was forbidden. "We'll have to look in the morning. It's too dark now."

When they reached the shallows, Xanthos dragged at the stone-filled net attached to a rope and pitched it over the side to anchor the small vessel near the shore. They ate their supper of olives and cheese, drank from a flagon of water, then settled down for the night, allowing the gentle water to sway them to sleep.

Xanthos awoke to a sudden tilt of their boat and a vise-like grip on his shoulder. A fierce, bronzed face stared directly into his eyes. Before he had time to realize what was happening, two men were hauling him and his brother out of the little boat and into the shallow water. Agathos dug in his heels, his screams piercing as he cried, "No! No! No!"

"By all the gods," came a voice from somewhere on the beach, "silence that shrieking harpy."

One of the men raised his hand to strike the small child. Xanthos darted forward, tried to stop him, and was struck instead. "He's afraid," Xanthos said, ignoring the pain in his jaw. "It's forbidden to set foot on the island."

"Is it?" The burly man picked up Agathos and tossed him onto the gravel in front of the tallest and fiercest of the group.

He looked down at the boy, his dark eyes narrowing. "You're very small for such a loud harpy."

Agathos stilled, his eyes widening as the bare-chested man took a step forward, the morning sun hitting the tattoo of an angry boar's head on his shoulder and the deep scar on his forehead. Someone had branded him with the letter *D*, signifying that he was, at least at one time, a slave. "What're you staring at?" the tattooed man said. His heavily accented Greek frightened the boys even more knowing he must be from the island of Samos.

Agathos looked down, edging his way toward Xanthos, who recognized the lot for what they were. Pirates. Their father—before he was lost at sea—had warned Xanthos about the men who sailed the Aegean in a red ship, plundering and enslaving all they came across. "Please. If you let us go, we won't tell a soul we saw you here."

"To be sure," one of the men said, grabbing Xanthos by the scruff of his neck. "Pactyes will want to see the fish we've caught before we put them on a spit and roast them."

With a roar of laughter, the pirates frog-marched the boys across the beach to a serpentine path that wound its way up to the top of the island and the pinnacles of rock, to Poseidon's Trident.

They reached the peak and stumbled out onto a plateau. The boys looked down to the east side of the island where the Samian corsairs' ship lay at anchor, its scarlet sails furled. The evil eye on its boar's head prow stared out as a warning to others. Xanthos, seeing the rows of oars lining both sides of the red ship, all manned by slaves, reached for his brother's trembling hand. Even he was not big or strong enough to survive that fate.

He turned his gaze from the red ship to the center of the plateau, where several men—some of them clearly Lydian foreigners—were looking down into a dark cavity at the base of the centermost pinnacle rock of Poseidon's Trident. One, wearing a purple tunic of shimmering silk that barely concealed his protruding chest and belly, seemed to be directing two Samians using a wooden hoist and pulley to lower an amphora into a cavern. He looked squarely at them. "What have we here, Drakon?"

The man with the boar's head tattoo said, "Lampros tells me they were sleeping in a boat in the small cove."

The exquisitely dressed foreigner approached, looking them over, then focused on Xanthos. "What are you doing on this island?"

Xanthos, who'd never seen anyone wearing silken trousers, wondered if the man was sent there by the gods to punish them for trespassing on sacred land.

"Speak up!" the tattooed man ordered. "The honorable Pactyes asked what you are doing here."

"Fishing." Even as Xanthos said it, he knew how absurd it sounded. They'd been sleeping long past sunup. True fishermen would've been on their way home by then. "But we were blown off course last night," he added, hoping that would account for their presence.

The foreigner turned his gaze on Agathos. "And what say you?"

Agathos, near tears, looked at Xanthos, then back. "I—I just wanted to whisper in Poseidon's ear. To send our father home."

"Whisper in Poseidon's ear?" Pactyes looked to Drakon for clarification.

He nodded to the cliff's edge. "A shallow cave in the rocks at sea level. Some of the islanders believe if they whisper into it, Poseidon will hear their prayers."

Pactyes scrutinized him for several long seconds, then turned back to the boys. "Perhaps Poseidon would be appeased by a sacrifice?" He nodded to one of the Lydians. "Kill them."

Xanthos tried to throw himself over Agathos to protect him, but one of Pactyes's men caught him and grabbed the back of his tunic, then drew a long knife, pressing the blade against the boy's neck.

Drakon's hand shot out, catching the Lydian by his wrist. "The island is sacred."

"Pactyes is the only one I answer to." He raised his knife.

Heart pounding, Xanthos held his breath, waiting for the death blow. Drakon knocked Xanthos to the ground, drew his *xiphos* from the scabbard under his left shoulder, and brought it crashing down on the pirate's neck.

The man in the shimmering robes halted in his tracks, his piggish eyes taking in first the dead man, then Drakon. "You dare defy my order?"

"To prevent the wrath of Poseidon?" Drakon said. "Yes."

"And yet you killed Alyattes on sacred ground. What difference will two more bodies make? Three if we count yours."

"I will not let you desecrate sacred ground." Drakon held his short sword at the ready, then sidestepped so that he stood between the boys and Pactyes.

"Who would be so simple to believe the island is sacred?"

"You might. Considering that the Persian Cyrus has placed a bounty on your head. You may well need all the help that Poseidon can give."

"Korax," Pactyes said. "Kill him as well."

The mercenaries looked at each other, then split into two factions, those with Drakon, those with Korax. Xanthos, realizing that they'd been momentarily forgotten, looked for a way out. The path to the boat was blocked by the pirates. The only other way down was over the cliff, far too steep for either of them to live. Then he spied the mouth of the cave, giving him hope that they might hide there. Signaling to his brother, he pointed.

As he and Agathos edged toward it, Korax lunged. Drakon blocked him, the boar on his shoulder bristling with the movement of his muscles. The two men circled each other, each feinting, testing each other's mettle. Korax attacked again, his sword clashing with Drakon's. Drakon moved in, but Korax shifted, deflected the blow, then swung his sword against Drakon's upper arm. The silver blade sliced open the tattooed boar's head. The Lydians cheered. Drakon glanced at the blood dripping down his arm, then charged, as did the men behind him. Swords clashed, the metal ringing.

Xanthos peered in the cavern, grateful to see that it wasn't the almost vertical drop that he'd feared. It angled down. The shouts and screams of those fighting echoed into the cave as Xanthos helped Agathos over the edge. They started to climb down, when the earth shook so hard, Xanthos fell back against his brother.

The fighting stopped as the men looked around, fear and confusion on their faces. "Poseidon!" one of them yelled.

As if in answer, a low rumble emanated from deep within the cave, frightening the boys as the earth came alive beneath them. The walls convulsed and Agathos lost his brother's hand, sliding downward in a hail of gravel. "Xanthos!"

Xanthos reached for his younger brother as the earth thundered around them. But when the sunlight beaming into the cave quickly disappeared, he looked up to see one of the towering spires of Poseidon's Trident toppling forward. He scrambled down to his brother, holding tight as the giant rock crashed against the cave's mouth, the echo deafening, the dark near absolute but for a sliver of light high over their heads. As the boys slid to the bottom of the cave, landing on the pirates' bounty of amphorae, rock and dust rained down. They could barely breathe as the air turned to dust.

They clung to each other, their heartbeats pounding in their chests. Slowly silence, then above them, someone shouted, "A ship! A black ship!"

"The Persians." Drakon roared and gave a deep belly laugh. "Perhaps you should have heeded my warning about angering Poseidon. Take him."

"Let go of me," Pactyes called out. "What are you doing?"

"Since the gold is lost, we'll collect the bounty."

"It's not lost. It's all in the amphorae down there. You saw them!"

"And Poseidon took them with his very own trident. You'll not find a man among us that would dare go against such a powerful god, even if we had a way to lift that stone. To the ship, men."

Pactyes's pleas faded, the pirates dragging him away. Soon, again, the only sound was that of Xanthos and Agathos breathing.

"Hear me, Poseidon," Agathos whispered. "Please get us home."

"Quiet," Xanthos said. He moved to his hands and knees, then lowered his head to the floor, listening. "Do you hear that?"

"Hear what?"

"Water. I think it's the sea."

CHAPTER ONE

Georgetown, Washington, D.C.
The present day

I hope this is worth a twenty-two-hundred-dollar bottle of wine."

"For Pete's sake, Sam. Not only did he agree to see us, he invited us to dinner. And he *did* send a car."

"Gourmand or no gourmand," Sam muttered.

"You're mumbling, Sam."

Sam Fargo glanced over at the bottle of 2000 Mouton Rothschild, Pauillac that Remi, his auburn-haired wife, cradled in her arm. The two sat in the back of a sleek black 1936 Packard Twelve 1407 Coupé.

"You know what Rube said," Remi continued. "If we wanted the man's help, we needed to bring a nice bottle. And we do want his help."

Sam eyed the driver, then lowered his voice. "Pretty sure Rube's definition of nice and yours are two different things."

The Packard suddenly veered toward the freeway off-ramp at the last second. Sam looked up, realizing they were still miles from their destination. "Something wrong?"

The driver was focused on the rearview mirror, not watching Sam but the road behind them. "Sorry about that. A car's been following us ever since we left your hotel. It may be nothing, but old habits die hard."

"Old habits?" asked Remi.

"Let's just say that Mr. Perlmutter has an unusual set of friends, which has given me a bit of practice over the years when driving them around."

St. Julien Perlmutter, the soon-to-be recipient of Sam's beloved bottle of wine, had been recommended by their mutual friend, Rubin Haywood, a CIA agent. Perlmutter was a world authority on maritime history and had an extensive library known to be coveted by the Smithsonian. He often helped other government agencies with sensitive cases. That would, undoubtedly, explain his driver's cautious nature.

Since caution was a trait Sam also shared, he craned around, squinting against the glare of headlights coming from the surface street they'd just turned onto. If they were being followed, the man's maneuver had worked—the freeway off-ramp was empty. Relaxing, Sam leaned back in his seat, not too worried. Not only were they in good hands, he doubted anyone knew that he and Remi were in D.C.

With the coast clear, they returned to the freeway, the remainder of their drive uneventful. Twenty minutes later, they turned onto a brick road flanked with massive oaks, the moonlight shining between the branches, casting long shadows on the drive. The car continued past the manor, then stopped in front of the renovated carriage house, which was equally impressive in size.

Once out of the car, the driver said, "Nice to see you again, sir."

"Good to see you, too, Frank. How old are the kids now?"

"Graduated college. Both. Phyllis and me, we're empty nesters."

Sam smiled, saluted, then took the bottle from Remi.

"I swear, Sam, we never go anywhere that you don't know someone from your days at DARPA."

"How did you know?"

"The salute," Remi said, rolling her eyes.

Sam linked her arm through his and the two strolled up the walkway. A weathered brass door knocker in the shape of a ship's anchor adorned the heavy wood door, which opened wide the moment they set foot on the porch.

To say that *the* St. Julien Perlmutter cut an imposing figure would be an understatement. His curly gray hair and beard gave his crimson face a distinguished look, reminiscent of Holbein's iconic portrait of King Henry VIII, but with a longer beard. Perlmutter wore a paisley robe trimmed at the collar, cuffs, and belt with gold brocade, burgundy silk bottoms with matching gold piping at the side seams and the hem, and burgundy loafer slippers with gold crowns embroidered on the top. He stood a couple of inches taller than Sam—six foot four—and weighed nearly four hundred pounds. He carried that weight like a regal redwood, solid and straight. His blue eyes, filled with intelligence and wit, were as welcoming as his words. "Mr. and Mrs. Fargo. I can't tell you what a pleasure it is to finally meet the both of you."

"Please, call me Sam." They shook, Perlmutter's grip strong and sure. "My wife, Remi."

"The enchanting Mrs. Fargo." The older man took her slender fingers in his, kissed the back of her hand, then led her into the house. "I'm honored to make your acquaintance."

Once inside, Sam handed him the bottle. "And wine. I hope it will complement dinner."

Perlmutter read the Rothschild label, his brows rising. "An excellent choice. This will pair nicely with the chateaubriand. A classic recipe, one of my favorites." Waving them in, he led them through a maze of halls to a sitting room stuffed to the gills with books and papers. The far wall was lined with bookshelves filled with models, relics, and books. At one end was a fireplace with a perfectly banked fire and at the opposite a well-appointed bar. In front of the fire was a sofa and two end chairs, a Queen Anne chair and a gentleman's club chair, all set around a coffee table large enough for appetizers and three champagne flutes. "Please, have a seat while I decant this lovely bottle of wine."

Sam walked Remi to the Queen Anne chair, then seated himself.

At the bar, Perlmutter lit a candle and set a glass next to it. After removing the cork, he slowly poured a small amount into the glass, sniffed and took some wine into his mouth, savoring the taste. He raised the glass to the light and, looking through the deep ruby liquid, said, "What a full breadth of flavor, rich and ripe with beautiful tannins. And a long finish. After it has time to breathe it will be the perfect accompaniment to dinner. A beautiful choice. My deepest gratitude."

He slowly poured the remainder of the bottle into a decanter, holding it over the candle, making sure no sediment would pass from the bottle. Then he reached below, opened the wine fridge, brought out a 2008 bottle of Pol Roger Cuvée Sir Winston Churchill brut champagne and joined Sam and Remi at the fire. Settling himself in the sofa he said, "While we wait for the dinner, please let's talk about the reason you're here. Rubin mentioned that this all began shortly after the two of you met at the Lighthouse Cafe in Hermosa Beach?" His blue eyes twinkled as he looked over at Sam. "Love at first sight, was it?"

"I'm still trying to deny it. But . . . there's never been anyone like Remi. She's had my heart from the beginning."

"Sam, you could have fooled me." Remi's green eyes lit up as she smiled.

Sam cleared his throat. "You see. It wasn't easy."

"Hardly a fair assessment."

"Totally fair assessment."

"Do I sense differing views?" Perlmutter asked.

Remi laughed. "Let's just say it wasn't smooth sailing."

"Well, it wasn't typhoon fury."

"Maybe just a few ten-foot swells."

"A few?" Sam said. "Understatement of the year."

Remi gave Perlmutter a sideways glance. "It's a bit complicated."

"As love is," he replied. "But it sounds like you two still enjoy a few waves now and then." This brought a laugh from Sam and Remi.

The champagne poured, Perlmutter continued. "So . . . a chance meeting at the Lighthouse somehow led to this Mediterranean caper, and the *one* treasure that the two of you never found?"

"Exactly," Sam said. "It was the hoard of gold stolen from King Cyrus after he conquered King Croesus in 546 B.C. It kickstarted our love for adventure."

"And for each other?"

Remi placed her hand over Sam's. "I'd say it played a *small* part. And, while we didn't find the fabled hoard, we did find proof it exists."

"But that was what . . . ? Ten or more years ago?" Perlmutter's brows furrowed. "Why now?"

"We'd recently been talking about the treasure and what we might have missed in our search," Remi began.

"But, more importantly," Sam continued, "the man who was obsessed with finding the treasure all those years ago was recently released from prison—far earlier than anyone expected. From what Rube has told us, the man's spent over a decade in confinement consumed with hate and fixated on two things—those who he feels are directly responsible for landing him in prison, and where this treasure might be. I have a feeling that the first obsession might be Remi."

"And you," Remi added.

"The second is that anyone who gets in his way of finding the treasure will not be safe," Sam said.

Perlmutter lowered his glass. "I know we could get straight to the point—search my memory banks and my library for the possible location of this fabled hoard—but I have to admit, I *do* love a good adventure. And Remi being so deeply involved, I don't suppose you'd be willing to tell it? From the beginning?"

"That depends," Sam said. "How much time do you have?"

Perlmutter smiled. "However long it takes."

CHAPTER TWO

Hermosa Beach, California

Sam Fargo gripped the top corner of his bodyboard with his right hand, his left hand on the outside rail, and looked back at the massive wave approaching.

Timing was everything.

He gave a swift kick, his fins propelling him forward. At the crest, momentarily suspended, he teetered, then dropped almost straight down the shimmering wall. Head up, back arched, chest out, he dug the waterside edge of his board into the wave, riding across the smooth, glassy surface as the lip fell, creating a tunnel of blue and gray. In a rush, it was over. The white water crashed, the surge speeding him toward the shore crowded with onlookers who came to watch the expert surfers and bodyboarders riding the giant waves left over from a rare Category 3 hurricane a few days before.

Sam, having been out there all morning, was ready to call it a day. He reached the shallows, pulled off his fins, picked up his board, and waded up to the beach, walking across the wet sand to where his friend Blake Thomas sat. The two were polar opposites, size-wise and coloring. Sam, brown-eyed with light brown hair bleached by the sun, was tall with a lean muscular build. The dark-haired, blue-eyed Blake had a wrestler's build, short and compact. They'd met their freshman year at Caltech when they were assigned adjoining dorm rooms, and had remained friends ever since.

Sam dropped his board on the sand, took a seat next to Blake, and picked up the lunch bag he'd packed earlier that morning. The offshore wind nearly ripped the paper from his hand as he reached in and pulled out a peanut butter and jelly sandwich. "Just like Mom used to make."

Blake, eating a deli sandwich thick with roast beef, eyed the Spartan meal. "Ever thought if you got a real job, instead of working midnights, stocking shelves, you could afford real food?"

"But I wouldn't have time to work on my project." He bit into the soft wheat bread, chewed the stiff peanut butter, and washed it down with water from his thermos.

"Come to think of it, you can afford real food. You know, I don't remember you being such a tightwad."

"I have plans."

"You and your plans. I remember, if Plan A doesn't work, go to Plan B. You need to chill. Loosen up. Relax. If you backed off, you might actually have a life. Maybe even meet a girl."

Sam smiled at Blake's ribbing, then nodded at the Coast Guard cutter as it sped north across the water, lights flashing, siren blaring.

Blake glanced out. "Heard a surfer up in Malibu was killed yesterday."

Sam had seen the news. A forty-year-old man had fallen from his surfboard. By the time anyone could get to him, he'd drowned. "Let's hope whoever they're after is okay."

He watched the boat disappear past the pier, then finished his sandwich. As he got up to toss the bag into the trash, he saw a surfer paddling to catch what promised to be a monster wave. The swell turned into a wall of water, glistening in the sun as the man expertly hopped up onto his board, hands holding either side. He balanced then rose as the tip of the wave curled over, creating a perfect barrel.

Blake stood next to Sam. "Where was that wave when we were out there?"

The surfer emerged from the tube, victorious for several seconds—until an avalanche of water collapsed on top of him.

The crowd on the beach gasped almost collectively as he disappeared from sight. His board shot up, straining against the leash connected to his leg, then jerked back into the water. A moment later, the man surfaced, only to disappear as another wave came crashing down. He didn't rise a second time.

"Call for help!" Sam said as he grabbed his bodyboard and fins. At the water's edge he put on his fins and wrapped the Velcro leash to his arm, and paddled out. With each wave that broke, Sam pressed the front of his board down, ducking his head, diving below the white water. A few surfers to the south tried to reach the fallen man, but the waves, breaking in a southeasterly pattern, made it near impossible.

By the time Sam paddled out there, the man was nowhere in sight. Worried he'd lost him for good, Sam noticed someone waving and shouting from the pier. He glanced up, saw a red-haired woman pointing to his right. He looked, saw the orange surfboard, then a blur of black from a wet suit in the froth just a few yards away. He swam over.

At first, there was nothing but the gray-green of the ocean below and the white storm above. Somehow in the midst of that, he caught a glimpse of the surfer being tossed about, the churning water propelling him downward then upward in a relentless struggle.

Sam darted forward, reached out, scooping his hand beneath the limp man's arm, pulling him toward his bodyboard. There was a gash on the man's temple, and his eyes stared at nothing. Sam put his mouth to the surfer's, forcing air into his lungs. As he rose out of the water to take a second breath, the bright orange surfboard shot toward them like a spinning torpedo. Sam ducked, pulling the man with him, the surfboard skimming over the top of their heads.

He managed to hold tight to the surfer as the next wave crashed down and then the next. After each, he pulled the man's head to him, blew into his lungs, all the while kicking his fins in a desperate attempt to stay surfaced and get closer to shore. His muscles burned, and he wasn't sure how much longer he could hold the man. When he looked up, he saw Blake and another bodyboarder swimming out to help.

Sam gave one last breath to the surfer as Blake pulled the unconscious man up onto his own board. Once they reached the shore, Blake and the other man dragged the surfer onto dry sand, Blake taking over the CPR. Sam, exhausted, dropped his board, then stood there, trying to catch his breath.

A few minutes later, the EMTs arrived and loaded the now semiconscious man onto a gurney.

"Nice job," Blake said, clapping Sam on the back. "But one of these days, that Fargo luck's going to wear off, and you'll wish you'd had the sense to wait for help."

Sam managed a tired smile. "In the meantime, he's going to live."

"You working tonight?"

"Night off."

"We're heading over to the Lighthouse. Have a few beers and watch the game."

"Sure. I'll see you there." Assuming he could walk off the beach.

The strains of a jazz band drifted out as Sam pulled open the door of the Lighthouse Cafe. A popular nightclub, the bar was crowded, the lights dim. He spied Blake standing at the bar with a group watching a muted television, their cheers drowning out the jazz band.

Blake called over to Sam. "Better order now while you have a chance."

Sam, about to tell him that he couldn't stay, caught sight of the same woman he'd seen up on the pier that afternoon. Tall, slim, her wavy red hair swept back into a ponytail, she was dressed in a tailored blue-and-white linen shirt, navy capris, and white sandals. She stood in the doorway, looking around, her face lighting up with a smile as she waved at three other women sitting at a table across from the bar. Instead of joining them, she walked up to the bar not two feet from Sam.

The bartender asked her what she wanted to drink.

She picked up a wine list. "You don't have any red wines from Spain, do you?" she said.

"Sorry. It's California or bust."

Her smile faded. "It would've made the perfect toast."

"Remi!" one of her friends shouted from behind her. "We have wine!"

She glanced at the table, saw her friend holding up a bottle of chardonnay, then returned the menu to the bartender. "Thanks anyway."

He nodded, and moved on to the next customer.

"Earth to Fargo. You realize the game's on?" Blake, seeing the direction of Sam's gaze, clapped him on the back. "Don't even try. The women at that table are blue-blooded East Coasters. Way out of your league. It'll take them about ten seconds to size you up, figure out you're a California boy with a four-wheel Jeep, determine your credit limit, then spit you out. All the Fargo luck in the world won't help you there. Heck. Their shoes cost more than you make in a week."

"And you would know this how?"

"I used to date the blonde. Olivia Brady. It didn't last, and *I'd* just closed a multimillion-dollar real estate deal."

"Ever think it's *you*, not the money?" Sam gave him a cocky grin.

"Word of advice, Fargo. You might want to avoid mentioning where you work—and it will come up. Trust me on this."

"Noted," Sam said. He moved to the end of the bar, picking up the wine menu, scanning the list of California reds, seeing the host of usuals from Napa, all with price tags to match and out of his new lifestyle. He skipped past them and saw a reasonably priced California Spanish wine from the northern San Joaquin Valley. He got the bartender's attention. "I'll take a bottle of the Bokisch Tempranillo and four glasses. Can you send it to the table where the redheaded woman is sitting?"

CHAPTER THREE

Sam watched as the waitress brought over the wine and glasses, setting them on the table.

"I think there's some mistake," the blond woman said. "We didn't order any wine." She pointed to the bottle of chardonnay.

"From the gentleman at the bar."

All four women looked in Sam's direction. One gave a cool smile, then shook her head. "Thank him for us, but we can't accept."

Sam, seeing the waitress reach for the bottle, walked over, saying, "I'm actually on my way out, but I heard you were celebrating. Four of you, four glasses, and a bottle of Spanish Tempranillo. Enjoy."

He started to turn away when the redhead caught his gaze, her green eyes alight with a mixture of curiosity and wariness. "You were at the beach today."

The other women looked at him with renewed interest, the blonde saying, "You're the one who saved that surfer. The hero."

"Hero, no. Right place, right time? Yes."

The brunette looked at her watch. "Speaking of time, we're late." She drained her wineglass, then pushed her chair back. The other two rose with her. She looked at her friend, who hadn't moved. "Are you coming, Remi?"

Remi tapped the stem of her nearly full wineglass. "I'll meet you there as soon as I finish this."

The three hurried out, leaving them alone.

"Dinner reservations," she explained, then nodded at one of the empty chairs. "You're welcome to join me."

"I don't want to keep you from your friends."

"I can miss the appetizers." She lifted the bottle. "I've never heard of this winery."

"The bartender assures me it's very good."

"And how do I know it's not spiked and you're some stalker?"

"I'll take the first sip." He poured a small amount into two glasses, sliding one across to her, then held his aloft. "To whatever it is you're celebrating."

They touched rims. She waited for him to drink first, then followed suit. "That *is* good . . . Black cherry, dark chocolate . . . and a hint of cranberry." She picked up the bottle. "Tempranillo grown in California. I see a wine tasting trip in my future."

"What about your friends? Are you sure you don't want to . . . ?"

"They've probably already forgotten about me. And leave such lovely wine?"

He set his glass on the table and held out his hand. "Sam Fargo."

She took it in hers, shaking with a firm grip. "Remi Longstreet."

"Nice to meet you, Remi." He refilled their glasses. "So, what's worth celebrating with a Spanish varietal?"

"You have to promise not to tell."

"Cross my heart."

Her smile lit up her entire face. "I've been looking into rumors that a Spanish galleon sank off Abalone Cove. This morning, I actually found a reference to the ship in the Rare Books and Special Collections Reading Room at Long Beach State. It's all of two sentences, but considering it took me almost six months just to find that much, I'm ecstatic."

"That definitely deserves a toast," Sam said, lifting his glass once more. "So, what's next? Exploratory diving to find it?"

"Eventually. But that's only part of it. I'm leaving for Greece in two weeks. Fourni, to be exact."

"You should have your pick of shipwrecks. What are there, about fifty surrounding the islands?"

"You're familiar with the area?"

"Read about it, but never been. Underwater archeology's always fascinated me. The lure of being the first person to find something that's been buried for centuries . . ." He smiled. "Is that your job? Archeologist?"

"I wish. I'm a translator for an international shipping company. Sadly, it's not the glamorous globe-trotting job I was hoping for. I sit in a cubicle in Long Beach most of the day, wearing a headset."

"Which language?"

"Whichever one they need. I'm fluent in several, passable in a few more. How about you?"

Recalling Blake's warning, he kept it vague. "Past job, design engineer. Current job, retail."

"Doing what, exactly?"

So much for glossing over the truth. "Would you believe grocery store shelf stocker?"

"That's quite the change in careers."

The truth was a bit complicated. Sam, a Caltech engineering graduate, had been recruited by DARPA, the Defense Advanced Research Projects Agency, to design technology for the Department of Defense. After seven fruitful years, he'd put in his notice, and moved back to California to pursue what had been up until recently a life-long dream. "It is, but I wanted the freedom to work on a project. An argon laser scanner."

Her brows went up, then furrowed slightly. "Which does . . . what?"

"If it ever gets past the paper stage, it'll identify mixed metals and alloys at a distance. Gold, silver, platinum, you name it."

"For real?"

"Not yet, but that's what I'm hoping. My friend," he said, nodding at the bar, where Blake was still camped out in front of the TV, "set up a meeting with a group of investors in a few weeks. If all goes as planned, they'll be funding the project, and I can actually take it from paper to reality. For now, the grocery job keeps a roof over my head and gives me time to work on the project."

"And yet," she said, tapping her glass with her perfectly manicured nails, "you're buying bottles of wine for complete strangers? Not exactly budget friendly."

"So I eat a lot of peanut butter sandwiches for the next week? High in protein and *very* affordable."

She laughed. The next several hours passed in a blur as they talked about anything and everything, most of it nautical. Before Sam knew it, the bartender was crying out, "Last call!"

Remi looked up, her expression mirroring how Sam felt. The night was too short. She'd been discussing her upcoming research trip.

He reached over, tapped her hand, getting her attention. "You were saying? About your trip, why you picked Greece?"

She seemed startled by his touch, but smiled. "Sorry. I don't know where the time went. The trip . . . I spent my junior year abroad. One of the other students' father heads up the Fourni Underwater Archeological Preservation Society, a nonprofit that's working to preserve some of the ancient shipwrecks from looting. He invited me for a summer sabbatical. I couldn't pass up the invite and have a few weeks of vacation coming. Couldn't think of a better thing to do. Especially with this awful job I have."

"So you do have a background in . . ."

"Oh, no. The only thing I know about underwater archeological sites is from school—"

"What'd you major in?"

"I have a master's in history and anthropology, with a focus on ancient trade routes. And," she said with a beaming smile, "you're looking at a newly certified scuba diver—as of yesterday."

"Congratulations."

"Thank you. I figured it's all good training for when I get back here to search for my Spanish galleon."

"So how long will you be in Fourni?"

"Three weeks. Then it's back here, same old, same old. Until, well—" She looked up as the lights flickered on overhead, warning them that time was up. They were the only two left in the bar.

"Here's to a successful trip." The two had switched to water long before that, and he lifted his half-empty glass. They touched rims once again, drained their glasses, then stood. "Walk you to your car?" he said.

"I'd appreciate that."

They walked out into a nearly deserted parking lot, theirs the only two cars remaining. His, a well-used red Jeep Wrangler with a patina of California sun, bleached and sandblasted, and oversized off-road tires complemented her shiny red Porsche 911 GT3. As they neared, she took out her key fob, unlocking it. Trying to ignore Blake's earlier comments, Sam reached over, opening her door, and said, "I'll see you soon."

She tossed her purse onto the front passenger seat, then turned back to him. "You sound pretty sure of yourself. Exactly how will you find me?"

"Do you know anything about constellations?"

Her smile dazzled him. "A bit."

"That star there." He pointed into the black sky. "The one at the end of the Little Dipper."

"The North Star?"

"You find that, you'll find anything." He stared up at it a moment, then looked over at her. "It'll always lead me to you."

"What if we're in the southern hemisphere, where we can't see Polaris?"

He laughed, telling himself he shouldn't be surprised that she knew the actual name of the star. He leaned down, kissing her before he lost his nerve. "Just in case, a phone number works." He stepped back, giving her plenty of space, the cool night air rushing between them.

The next thing Sam knew, Remi was reaching back in her car for her purse, then pulling out a pen. She found a receipt from the grocery store in one of the pockets and jotted down her number. "You're definitely a bad influence on me," she said, handing him the slip of paper. "I'm giving a man I just met—at a bar, no less—my phone number."

She slid into the driver's seat, looking up at him. "I did have an enjoyable evening. Certainly better than dinner with the girls."

"Let's do it again. Tomorrow night. Not the same thing. Something different, but tomorrow night."

"You realize it's already tomorrow?"

"You know what I mean. Oh, wait a minute." Sam fumbled in his pocket as Remi watched with a small smile on her face. Obviously, she was doing something out of character. But, obviously, he looked a little like a fish out of water, too.

"Here, the card is old, but the cell phone number is still mine. I'll call you in the morning."

He closed the door. She started the car, backing up from the space. She started to pull forward, but then the pavement lit up from the glow of her brake lights as she stopped, rolled down her window, and looked back at him. The corner of her eyes crinkled as she laughed. "I accept. Looking forward to today's tomorrow night!"

CHAPTER FOUR

It seemed Remi had only just fallen asleep when her alarm went off, the vibration so loud her teeth felt like they would crack. Wait. Not her alarm. She didn't have to go to work. Finally, Remi's hand reached her cell phone on the nightstand. "What?"

"Good morning."

The voice was far too cheery for this early hour. "Who is this?"

"Guess I didn't leave the impression I had hoped for last night."

"Who is this? Sam?" Remi sat bolt upright. "Sam." She took a deep breath. This was not how it was supposed to go.

"I need to ask you a couple of questions."

"What time is it?" She pulled her phone from her ear, trying to read the time through sleep-blurred eyes.

"It's just after seven. But I need to ask you a couple of questions."

"Now?"

"No time like the present. You said you were leaving in two weeks and planning to dive on wrecks in Greece. Do you have your wreck diving certification?"

"Noooo?"

"That's what I thought. Do you have your own dive gear?"

"No."

"We'll have to remedy that. How do you take your coffee?"

"I take my coffee from the kitchen."

"I'll be over in an hour. We can talk about everything then. I just need your address."

Before she could stop herself, Sam had her address and the line was dead.

An hour later Sam was at the door with two steaming coffees and the most beautiful warm croissants Remi had ever eaten. There she was sitting in her kitchen, watching Sam as he talked about her Spanish galleon and friends he had who could help her with her research. Then there were certificates for wreck diving, deep diving, and drift diving, and something about kelp. And the next thing she knew they were going to see a friend of his that worked in a dive shop in Santa Ana, a Clive something or other. He was going to get her a really good deal on dive equipment. On the way out the door, all Remi could think about was one big question, is this a first date?

In the afternoon, they drove to Newport Beach, had lunch at the Crab Cooker, walked the beach, took the ferry to Balboa Island, and as the sun set, Remi found herself at the smallest, most charming French restaurant, where everyone knew everyone's name, even Sam's.

So, maybe it was a first date. But the next morning there was no alarm ringing at seven. As a matter of fact, the whole morning was deadly silent. And when the phone finally rang late that afternoon, she was so angry with herself for waiting for the phone to actually ring that she almost didn't answer it. After all, she was an independent woman. That thought fled the moment Sam said hello, and she found herself smiling. Of course, dinner would be great and maybe a movie.

They chose the Lighthouse again and there was so much to talk about, the movie never happened. The idea of kelp diving off the island of Catalina fascinated Remi, and Sam was going to arrange for her to get her wreck diving certification. Sam knew someone for everything. Plans were made, and the next day bags were packed, more bags than Sam ever thought necessary.

The ferry ride over was the beginning of amazing.

Meeting them at the dock was Steve Drake, a retired Navy SEAL who ran a charter boat and dive shop. He also happened to be a dive instructor. They stayed with Steve and his wife, Kate, who ran the best bed-and-breakfast on the island.

The next morning Steve, Kate, Sam, and Remi headed out to the kelp fields. The moment they entered the water, Remi found herself enveloped in a world of muted greens and blues below. Above, the afternoon sun lit up the surface, giving an iridescent glow to the ocher-colored leaves and thick stems of the undulating kelp bed. A school of small fish suddenly turned tail, darting away in a flash of silver. Sam began swimming in and out of the kelp. Remi was fascinated as the long ribbons danced in the water. Slowly, she began to turn and twist among the giant kelp, when a dark shadow suddenly stole the sun from her and the water turned. Catching the long dorsal fin from the corner of her eye, she glanced up, startled, certain it was a shark—then breathed a sigh of relief at the sight of the massive sunfish as it slowly turned and faded away.

After watching it a few moments, she continued her descent, catching up to Sam. Together, they swam to the bottom of the kelp bed, where a reddish-orange spiny-headed scorpionfish lurked. Sam reached past it, picking up an empty snail shell rolling along the seafloor, handing it to Remi. She dropped it into her dive bag, thinking it would make a nice reminder of her first successful dive since being certified. Before she knew it, Sam was signaling that it was time to surface.

"That was incredible!" she said, pulling her regulator from her mouth. "I could do this forever."

Sam, treading water next to her, slid his face mask up. He reached out, drawing her close, then kissed her on the lips. "I could do that forever . . ."

They slipped down into the water, and he kissed her again, this time holding her tight. When they surfaced a few seconds later, she nodded. "Me too."

They left Catalina, Remi with wreck certificate in hand and two friends richer.

CHAPTER FIVE

Remi eyed the stacks of carefully folded clothes on her bed, ready to be packed for her trip to Greece, then looked at the full suitcase for her weekend with Sam. "I think I have everything."

Her roommate, Olivia Brady, shook her head. "What's gotten into you?"

"I may be falling in love."

"Are you even listening to yourself? The guy's a stocker in a grocery store."

"For now."

"Right. Like we haven't heard that story before."

"He's an engineer."

"And you know this how?"

"He told me."

"I can't find anything about him on the internet. And you know I'm good at that."

Remi looked up from her suitcase. "Why would he lie?"

"Why do you think guys lie about that stuff? How naive can you be?"

"He's not like that—"

"Says the girl who's never been out on her own before. College doesn't count. He picked you up in a bar, for heaven's sake. You can't possibly think it's okay to go away with him."

"You sound like my mother."

"For good reason."

Remi zipped up her suitcase, then took a second look in her closet to see if she'd missed anything. "I wonder if I should pack a coat."

"You know nothing about this guy."

"I've dated him for almost two weeks. Every day. If he was going to do something shady, he'd have done it by now."

"Are you even listening to yourself? You can't just run off for the weekend with someone you don't know."

"I have before."

"I wasn't here then, but now I am, and I need to put a little sense back into you. You have a plan. This," she said, nodding at Remi's suitcase, "does not fit with this." She swept her hand toward a corkboard hanging on Remi's bedroom wall. There were articles of the Fourni archipelago shipwrecks pinned to it, notes from research, and timelines she'd mapped out on how she planned to proceed with that venture. Another board showed the Spanish galleon notes.

Remi had always known from an early age what it was she wanted to do. Working as a translator was a very small step in her overarching goal of one day heading up a team to explore some of the areas she was researching. From there she planned to write a book, then produce a documentary. "You worry too much."

"Do I? What, exactly, do you know about him?"

"Besides that he saved a man's life at risk of his own?"

"Emphasis on the risk. He recklessly jumped into the water without waiting for help."

"He loves the ocean. He's nice. And he's a dreamer."

"Which is code for poor."

"So . . . ?"

"Money? That stuff we need to keep us in the lifestyles we're ac-customed to? The clothes in your luggage are worth more than his car."

"There's nothing wrong with being poor."

"Until *you* become poor. And you might if you continue down this road. At the very least, take your car. That way if you end up on the bottom of the ocean, his prints will be all over it."

Remi dragged her full-to-the-hilt suitcase off the bed and rolled it into the front room, leaving it next to her dive gear bag. "I have a good sense for people."

"Who are you and what have you done with my roommate?"

"It's just a weekend."

"This from the girl who's plotted out her entire life like detectives plot out crime scenes for court. Need I remind you that you're leav-ing for Greece on Monday?"

"And I'll be back Sunday."

The doorbell rang.

"Do not do this, Remi."

"It's a date. Nothing permanent."

Remi walked to the door and opened it.

Sam stood there, looking as carefree and handsome as he had the night before when they'd sat at the beachside grill before he left for work. A moment of uncertainty hovered at the back of her con-sciousness, but it quickly evaporated when he smiled at her. "Good morning," he said.

"Good morning."

He looked past her to see her roommate standing in the kitchen. This being the first time Sam had actually been to their apartment when Olivia was home, the two had never really met. "Sam Fargo," he said, holding out his hand.

Olivia lifted an empty glass, an innocent smile on her face. "Would you like some water before you go?"

Remi crossed her arms. "Seriously?"

Sam glanced at Olivia, then Remi. "Do I sense a little tension here?"

"She wants to get your prints."

He laughed, then walked over, taking the glass from Olivia, holding it firmly, then setting it on the counter. "I assure you, I'm harmless."

"Which," Olivia said, "is what all the serial killers probably say."

He picked up Remi's suitcase and gear bag. "Ready?"

She nodded, then turned to her roommate. "Have fun while I'm gone."

"I'll be doing an internet search the moment you leave." Olivia stood in the doorway, watching as they started down the stairs toward the parking lot.

Sam opened the tailgate of his Jeep. Remi glanced into the cab, then into the cargo area. "A backpack?"

"I tend to be a light packer," he said, moving everything aside to make room for her full-size suitcase. "I noticed you aren't."

"I like to be prepared for every eventuality."

"Nothing wrong with being prepared." As he closed the tailgate, his eyes strayed up to the balcony, where her roommate stood, holding her camera out, very obviously taking a photograph of his car. He waved to Olivia, then opened the door for Remi.

"Sorry," Remi said. "She's a bit overprotective."

"Good friends worry." He closed the door once she was seated, then walked around to the driver's side, getting in behind the wheel. "I have to admit, I thought I might get a pass on being a serial killer since I'm a friend of Blake. They used to date, didn't they?"

"I . . . sort of didn't mention his name."

"Yikes. That bad?"

"Let's just say she's relegated him to the category of someone she used to know."

"Used to know? That's sort of harsh." He turned the key and looked over at her. "Bad breakup?"

"She doesn't talk about it. The only thing she'll say is that everything with him was about dollar signs. In her opinion, he was . . . a bit shallow."

"A bit?" He laughed. "He grew up dirt poor, worked hard to get where he is, and wants everyone to know it. Still, he's got a heart of gold. He'd write you a check for the balance in his bank account if he thought it would help. Being humble? Not his strong suit. Being kind is."

"What's your strong suit?"

"Good question. I suppose if you asked Blake, he'd tell you my strong suit is also my greatest weakness. Jumping in headfirst and shooting from the hip." He backed from the space, then pulled out toward the street. "What about you?"

"If you were to ask Olivia, I'm an expert planner."

"Ah. Polar opposites."

"Guess you could say I'm a navigator, always laying out the plans."

"That must make me the pilot."

CHAPTER SIX

The day was beautiful, sunny and warm, and the two-hour drive along the coast to La Jolla passed too quickly. Saturday was gone and soon Sunday evening was all that was left. Sam suggested a walk on the beach before the drive home.

The shadows were growing long and Remi's internal clock was telling her it was time for them to leave. But Sam seemed determined to reach a certain spot on the beach.

"Don't you think it's time to head back?"

"In a little bit. I've got something I want to show you."

As they strolled hand in hand, the sunlight shimmered, its deep orange hues contrasting against the beauty of the blues and purples of the Pacific Ocean.

She sighed. "It really is beautiful."

"I know," he said.

But he wasn't looking at the sunset. He was looking at her and the way the offshore breeze played at her hair. He'd pictured her like this, almost at this very spot.

Apparently, she noticed his attention. "We're not looking at the sunset, are we?"

"Not the sunset. That." He pointed to the bluffs, where the setting sun turned the folds of earth jutting from the ocean a warm gold. Seagulls flew overhead, then disappeared to the north. "That's where we're going to build our home."

Remi stilled.

"You own that?"

"Yes. Even a pilot can have plans."

For a few moments, she let herself imagine that life was that easy. Buy a piece of land, and everything would simply fall into place. But she knew it was not the way life worked. Now she understood. Buy a cliff top, eat peanut butter.

The walk back to the hotel was quiet. Remi could feel a sense of calm in Sam. She was certain he could feel a sense of disquiet in her. Perhaps he wanted to test the waters. Almost to the hotel he wrapped his arm around her shoulders and turned her toward him. The kiss was natural, warm and meaningful. And neither felt the need to let go. Then just as suddenly, reality returned and it was time to get into the Jeep and head back.

Sam cranked the engine over. Nothing happened. He tried several more times before opening the hood.

It was after dark when they'd managed to find a local mechanic, who confirmed the extent of the problem. "Sorry," the man said, wiping his hands on a rag. "No one's going anywhere until the alternator gets replaced. And that won't happen until tomorrow afternoon."

Remi watched them working, her unease growing as time ticked away. They were at least two hours from Long Beach, but it was getting later and later. "Maybe we can rent a car?" she asked.

"You could," the mechanic said. "If you can find someplace that's open this late on a Sunday." He tossed the rag into his toolbox, then slammed the hood shut. Noticing the worry in Remi's eyes, he said, "You don't have somewhere you have to be, do you?"

"Just an early-morning flight."

"Can't help you there." He looked at Sam. "Want me to order the part? Or do you want to wait for a tow truck?"

"Order the part."

Before she had a chance to voice her concern, Sam was on the phone, explaining the situation to whoever was on the other end. "Nothing to worry about," he told her.

"Easy for you to say."

"Trust me?"

"When I'm on my way to the airport, then yes."

He gave a nod, finished his call, then settled up with the mechanic.

Less than an hour later, the sound of rotor blades from an airborne helicopter grew louder. Sam looked up. "I think your ride's here."

"You hired a helicopter?" But it wasn't just any helicopter, it was a big, no, a very big, double-rotor Marine helicopter.

"Not exactly. I called a buddy of mine. He owes me a favor."

Twenty minutes later, they were in Long Beach. They caught a cab, and ten minutes later, they were at her apartment. Sam unloaded her suitcase, then walked her to her apartment.

Their goodbye kiss was cut short when Olivia opened the door. "About time," she said. "You were supposed to be home hours ago."

Sam smiled at Olivia as she stepped out and rolled Remi's suitcase inside. Turning back to Remi, he kissed her once more. "Have a safe trip."

"I will," she said. "And good luck with your investor meeting."

"Thanks," he said, and headed down the stairs. When he got to the bottom, he looked up at her. "I'll be pining away until you get back."

She stopped to look back at him. "You don't strike me as the pining type."

"I've never had anything to pine over before now."

Remi laughed. "See you in three weeks, Sam Fargo."

CHAPTER SEVEN

Fourni Korseon, Greece
Three days later . . .

Adrian Kyril moved to the mouth of the near-vertical cavern, looking down as Fayez lowered himself into the dark depths, the glow of his headlamp disappearing from view. "You're sure this is the right cave?" Adrian asked Tassos Gianakos, the resident expert on pirate lore.

The gray-haired man nodded. "I don't know of any other cave on the island that fits the description you gave me. *Votzos.* Straight down. With bones."

The cave wasn't exactly what Adrian had read about, but it was the closest that he'd found. And he'd spent a veritable fortune searching for it in hopes that it contained the legendary Sardi treasure, stolen from Cyrus the Great.

After years of meticulous research, most of which turned out to be false leads, this possible location was discovered by accident. An overheard conversation between two archeologists about an inscription found in a cave attributed to a man who'd hidden there to escape hanging for piracy. That discovery had led to an obscure reference in another book about another cave that led them to Fourni and eventually to Tassos.

Unfortunately, Fourni was a very small island with a little over a thousand inhabitants. While Adrian had gone to great pains to make sure his name wasn't associated with this search, he worried constantly about word getting out. "Who else knows about Poseidon's Trident?"

Tassos drew his gaze from the cave and looked over at him. "On Fourni? Everyone. Some of the islanders claim to be related to the very pirates who hid the treasure."

Eventually, Fayez emerged. As he pulled himself over the top, the loose limestone rock crumbled beneath his weight, showering down into the cavern below. "There are definitely bones in there. I took photos if you want to see them."

The news of the bones was encouraging. That, at least, fit with the history. Adrian glanced at Tassos. "You've certainly earned your money." Again, he asked, "You haven't told anyone about my interest here, have you?"

He shook his head. "No. I made a promise."

Adrian moved next to the old man, clasping his thin shoulder. "Good," he said, then shoved.

Tassos tumbled into the opening. His scream echoed as he fell.

"Adrian . . ." Ilya, one of Adrian's oldest and most trusted friends—and in charge of his security team—stood a few feet away, looking through a set of binoculars.

"What is it?"

"At the top of the hill, over there." He pointed to the northwest, then handed Adrian his binoculars. "Two people just walked up. One is taking pictures with a telephoto lens."

Adrian focused, seeing a red-haired woman with a camera

talking to a man standing next to her. "What are the chances her lens could capture anything here?"

"Hard to say without actually seeing it. It looks big enough."

Adrian returned the field glasses to Ilya. "Make sure it didn't. We don't need any more witnesses."

CHAPTER EIGHT

A flock of gray-and-black hooded crows swooped from below, then arced skyward. Remi lifted her camera—heavy from the telephoto lens borrowed from the archeological society—to capture their flight, then realized there were three people standing on the hill below them. No doubt that's what sent the birds flying, she thought, pressing the shutter as the flock twisted into a magnificent pattern against the blue sky.

Instead of the familiar click, nothing happened.

"Did you get the shot of the murder?" Dimitris, a young man in his twenties with an affable smile, olive complexion, and a head of dark hair, stood next to her, staring up at the sky, his hand covering his eyes against the bright sun.

"Murder?"

"Yes, that's what a group of crows is called. You can thank Homer for the name."

"Wow." Remi shook her head. "I've heard of a flock, a skein, even a parliament of owls. Never . . ." She looked at the screen on the back of the camera, dismayed to see a MEMORY FULL notification. "Darn it. No."

"There'll be others. Fourni is full of beauty."

47

Pulling out the memory card, she stuffed it in her pocket, then took out a new card, inserting it into the slot. "Just my luck. Probably could've won a *National Geographic* photo contest with that shot."

"But you know what you saw." He tapped his temple, smiling as she took more photos of the sea that shimmered in hues of light to dark turquoise in the early-morning sun.

"You're right. It was worth the hike up." The vista, overlooking the Aegean, was—to use a clichéd phrase—picture postcard perfect. To the right, she could see the small village of Chrysomilia. To the left, a partial view of the main village of Fourni, its classic white houses trimmed in blue, terraced on the hills overlooking the port. "The view is amazing."

"The best in all of Fourni. My friend Denéa always says gods and grapes have the best view." He pointed. "You can see the island of Thimena over there, and on the other side, Samos, where you took the ferry to get here. When it's very clear, you can even see Turkey."

They continued hiking up the steep hill, then stopped in front of a sheer rock face. Dimitris pointed out a carving. It looked like a wreath or a sun about a foot in diameter. Beneath it was an inscription.

"Do you know what it says?" Remi asked.

"I don't think anyone knows. It's centuries old."

Remi took pictures from every angle. Finally, she looked back to where the birds had flown from and saw three men standing there. She distinctly remembered seeing four men and wondered where the other had gone.

After several minutes, Dimitris looked at his watch. "We should get going. I need to drop something off at the post office before we head out."

They picked their way along a worn goat path of exposed stone that created natural steps down the steep hillside. The melodic tinkling of goat bells carried across in the wind, the animals hidden behind the dense brush of junipers growing in the area. Eventually, they reached the dirt road where Dimitris had left his scooter. Remi slung her tote over her shoulder, then climbed on behind him, holding tight as he drove up to the gate, a trail of dust kicking up behind them, until they reached the paved serpentine road that led back to Fourni.

They parked near the port, then walked along the dock to the *Asteri*, a twenty-three-meter shallow draft survey boat, where Dimitris had left his satchel. It was only a short stroll from there to the post office, so Remi decided to leave the camera bag on the boat. From the port, the two crossed the street to the narrow, gray-flagstone street, surrounded on both sides with shops, some still closed at the early hour. Many of the shopkeepers sat in chairs out front, some watching over young children running up and down the street, others chatting with their neighbors or simply enjoying the warmth of the sun.

At the post office, a young woman with deep brown hair worn in loose curls about her shoulders looked up as they entered. The moment she saw Dimitris, her dark eyes lit up, and a shy smile played at her mouth.

Curious, Remi glanced at Dimitris, who was busy pulling a large manila envelope from his satchel. He glanced at the young woman and seemed to lose his train of thought. "Zoe . . ."

"You want to mail this?" she asked.

He nodded and handed the envelope to her. "I wasn't expecting you here."

"Letha's sick." She set the envelope on the scale to verify the weight. "Anything else?"

He shook his head, handing her the money.

She stamped the face of the envelope, glanced past him, and saw Remi. "This is your friend from America?"

"Yes," Dimitris said. "Remi Longstreet, my friend Zoe Giana-kos."

"Pleased to meet you," Remi said, shaking her hand.

"Welcome to Fourni." Zoe turned her attention back to Dimitris, her dark eyes looking worried. "You haven't seen my grandfather, have you?"

"No. Why?"

"I'm sure it's nothing. Just that he's been acting very secretive these last few days. He took off very early this morning, saying something about a big job that he expected to bring in enough money to buy a new fishing boat." She glanced at Remi, adding, "He's known for his tall tales around here. This time it's about finding Poseidon's Trident."

"An old fisherman's tale," Dimitris explained to Remi. "Pirates and treasure. A few islanders believe they're descended from the pirates who stole it."

"My grandfather included." Zoe gave a troubled sigh. "I really thought he was over all that. Disappearing for days at a time, searching . . ."

Dimitris took the receipt she handed him. "He'll be fine. The island's not that big. He always comes back."

She nodded, then smiled as she looked at Remi. "I hope you enjoy your visit here."

"Thank you. So far, I'm enjoying it very much."

Dimitris started for the door, then looked back at Zoe. "We're going to Skavos's for coffee before heading out. Would you like something?"

"No, thank you. Do me a favor, though? Ask if anyone knows what my grandfather is up to?"

"I will."

As they left the post office Remi asked, "Have you known Zoe long?"

"All my life. She was my childhood sweetheart. Still is," he said, blushing. "I mean, my girl."

They walked down to Skavos's café. Centrally located on the main street with a partial view of the port, the shade-dappled patio was filled with small tables and colorful ladder-back chairs. They ordered two Greek coffees inside at the bar, then sat outside. When Skavos, the owner, brought the coffee, he placed two demitasse cups on the table. Dimitris took the moment to ask about Zoe's grandfather.

The tall man regarded him for a moment, then stared down into the rich foam at the top of the *briki*. He slowly poured the coffee into each cup, making sure the grounds remained in the pot. Looking back at Dimitris, he shrugged. "Who's to say where Tassos goes? Zoe worries, he always comes back." Remi noted it was said with affection, and he assured Dimitris that he'd keep an eye out.

A half hour later they were boarding the *Asteri* when Remi noticed the camera bag, which she'd left hung over the seat back, had fallen to the deck. The moment she picked it up, she realized it was far too light. She looked inside and her heart sank. "The camera. It's gone."

CHAPTER NINE

Dimitris glanced over as Remi held up the empty bag. "This is Fourni. I can't believe this," he said. "Nothing ever happens here."

"Well, it certainly seems to this time."

He grinned, trying to cheer her. "Maybe it was the murder of crows. Revenge for missing the award-winning shot."

After making a police report—the officer commenting on how rare theft was on the island—the two motored out to the shipwreck. Remi tried to put the stolen camera from her mind.

Dimitris, however, didn't seem too concerned. "It'll turn up. You heard the officer. I assure you, he was telling the truth. Crime out here is almost unheard of. Maybe in tourist season, and even then it's almost unheard of."

"I'll replace the lens. I'm so sorry. I should never have left the bag out in the open."

"You worry too much. Enjoy the sun."

They were nearly to the site when Remi heard her sat phone ringing in her backpack. She recognized the number. "Hello . . . !"

"Remi? It's Sam. I wanted to make sure you arrived safely. And are in good hands."

"The best," she said as she glanced at her dive watch and saw it was after ten in the morning—which meant it was after midnight, his time. "Late night, I see."

"Trying to occupy my time as I pine away."

She laughed. "Sorry. I still can't picture you as the pining type."

Dimitris cut the motor, then glanced at her, mouthing, "Ready."

She nodded, then to Sam, said, "While I'd love to stay and chat, this call's actually being forwarded to my sat phone. A bit pricey on a translator's budget."

"I'll let you go, then. Happy mapping. May the treasure gods be smiling down upon you."

Her phone beeped as he ended the call. She slipped it into her backpack, smiling. The truth was that she'd thought about him, a lot. And she was still thinking about him as she and Dimitris prepared to make their first pass over the remains of the shipwreck, using a side-scan sonar. As soon as they let out the cable for the equipment, Dimitris switched the boat to autopilot. It kept the boat at a speed between three and four knots and was set up with a program that would establish survey lanes of about five hundred feet wide and two miles long, all while recording the data for later processing.

According to Dimitris, trying to triangulate anything on the seafloor was a challenge. One day an artifact might be exposed, the next it was covered in sediment from shifting currents, storms, and even earthquakes, the latter being plentiful in the area. The sonar images would give them a good head start before the archeologists started the actual diving to search for and photograph any artifacts.

Dimitris monitored the screen, pointing out various anomalies that appeared. "See all the amphorae?" The long, terra-cotta jars were scattered across the seafloor, some half buried in silt, most looking intact. "I have a friend who can look at them and tell you exactly from where they originated based on their shape and size or the stamp on some. We'll send him a photo of one of these and he'll know."

Remi was about to comment on how clear some of the images actually were when she heard an approaching vessel. Looking up, she saw two men sitting in a sleek, black speedboat, motoring toward them. "Friends of yours?"

He shook his head. "No."

Something about the way the broad-shouldered passenger braced himself while watching them bothered Remi. "I don't like the looks of that."

"Definitely not."

As Dimitris reached for the throttle, the man stood. He aimed a semiautomatic weapon at them as their boat slowed alongside the *Asteri*. "Don't move," he shouted in Greek. "You," he said to Dimitris. "Shut off the boat."

Remi froze, watching the gunman. Her father, a hobbyist competitive marksman, had introduced her to the sport at an early age, and along with it, gun safety. Which was why she immediately noticed the gunman rested his finger alongside the trigger guard, not on the actual trigger. That, and his stance, suggested military training, or at the very least someone who was well versed in firearms. That meant she and Dimitris were not likely to talk their way out of this.

She eyed the distance to her tote on the seat, then held up her hands as Dimitris turned off the engine. The speedboat kept pace alongside as the *Asteri* came to a stop. As the vessel slowed, the sonar dropped to the bottom of the sea, dragging like an anchor. Remi pretended to stumble against the seat as the boat bobbed in the water. "Sorry," she said in English, gripping the seat back to balance herself. "I'm still trying to get my sea legs."

The driver of the speedboat aimed his gun at them, while the other man holstered his weapon, and boarded the *Asteri*.

Knowing she had just a few seconds, Remi leaned down, pulled the sat phone from the front pocket of her backpack, then pressed the last call received. Sam was half a world away, probably asleep by now.

The kidnapper reached out, grabbed her by the arm, knocking the phone into her bag. Hoping he wasn't going to kill her right there and then, she dug in her heels. "Can someone tell me what's going on?"

Whether or not the kidnappers understood English, she didn't know, nor did she care. The boat driver spoke in rapid-fire Greek, too fast for Remi to catch most of what he was saying, other than the name "Fayez," and "hurry."

Dimitris, standing stock-still, his arms raised, translated. "He wants us to get on their boat."

"Do they want money?" she asked, wincing as Fayez dug his fingers into her arm. Glancing up at the sky, Remi wished it really was dark and said, "Where's the North Star when you need it?"

With a loss of patience, she was forced to board the speedboat behind Dimitris and his reply was covered by the sound of the motor's roar as the vessel surged forward. They barely made it to the seats on the port side. Fayez, sitting across from them, rested his gun on his thigh as they sped off toward open sea.

CHAPTER TEN

S am awoke the next morning to the sound of Blake unlocking the front door to his real estate office, then turning on the overhead lights. "Wakey, wakey!"

"Wakey, wakey? What am I, five?" Sam covered his eyes against the glare of the fluorescents. "You're early."

"Apparently not as early as you," he said, dropping a fast-food bag on his desk. He gave a pointed look at Sam's feet propped up on an empty, overturned trash can, and shook his head. "When I said you could use the office, I thought it was going to be an occasional thing."

"So did I." Sam stretched, his shoulder muscles tight from the hours spent sleeping in the chair. "Maybe renting a room over a garage where budding rock stars live wasn't the wisest move. I figured I'd come in, get some work done."

"You and your project," he said, nodding at the paperwork Sam had spread across the desk, "both need a new apartment. And my office isn't it."

"I'm looking. I swear."

"Not fast enough." Blake pulled two breakfast sandwiches from the bag and tossed one to him. "Any chance you're going to get all of that together in time for your investor meeting?"

"That's my goal," he said as the scent of fried egg and bacon wafted up. "When that day comes, I'll pay you back."

"Should you get rich, remember that I not only found your investors, I gave you office space *and* fed you so you could keep working on—I'm never going to remember the name of that *thing*."

"An argon laser scanner."

"Right. The fancy metal detector."

That *thing*, as Blake called it, was—if all turned out well—going to be Sam's future. Originally, his intent was that it could possibly be used for mining operations, but as he worked on it the possibilities expanded, including archeological purposes. Some days he looked at the plans and felt he would never be ready—not that he was about to let that stop him.

He bit into the sandwich, then checked his phone, surprised to see a voice mail from Remi not long after he'd called her last night. He played it, but all he could hear was the hum of what he presumed was a boat motor in the background. Clearly the call was unintentional. He heard someone saying, "He wants us to get on the boat."

Then after a few seconds, muffled by the sound of the boat, a woman's voice said, "Do they want money?" He couldn't be sure if it was Remi's voice until he heard Remi asking, "Where's the North Star when you need it?"

Beyond that, he heard nothing but the rev of the engine. The call ended soon after. Curious and a bit shaken, he called her number, but it went straight to voice mail.

"Blake," he said. "What's this sound like to you?" He played the message on speaker. "What does it sound like she's saying?"

"That Remi?"

He nodded.

"Sounds like she's on someone's yacht. So call her."

"Already did. No answer."

"But what did she say?"

"Something about where's the North Star when you need it."

"Stop getting all worked up," Blake told him. "I'm sure it's fine. It's Greece, not some third world country."

Even so, he called again, trying to think of something witty to say about the North Star and leaving a message for her to get back to him.

But he couldn't shake the feeling that something was wrong. After all, he had told her the North Star would lead him to her. Two hours later, he called her again. This time, a man answered with something that sounded like "*Yes sas.*"

"Is Remi there?"

"No. Who is this?"

"I'm a friend of hers. From California. She called me—"

"You heard from her? When?"

The urgency in his voice worried Sam. "Not directly. She left a strange message on my phone. I wanted to make sure nothing was wrong."

There was a long pause, then, "I wish I knew. Dimitris is with her. We found their boat but not them." At least that's what it sounded like. The man's accent was so thick, Sam wasn't quite sure.

"To whom am I speaking?"

"Nikos Papadopoulos. Dimitris is my son. You say Remi called you? What did she say?"

"I don't think she was talking to me. If that was your son with her, he said something about getting onto a boat. She asked if they wanted money."

There was a muffled sound as though Nikos was moving the phone, then a hurried conversation in Greek with someone else. A moment later, "Thank you. I'll inform the police. I'll call you once I hear something."

"Something wrong?" Blake asked once Sam disconnected.

"It's looking that way." He stared at the phone, his mind spinning with possibilities, all of them bad.

"She's an American citizen. Won't the FBI get involved?"

"Maybe." While he assumed that the Greek authorities would notify the U.S. that a citizen had been kidnapped, thereby triggering an investigation by the FBI, he couldn't be certain. He did, however, know someone who would know—his friend Rubin Haywood, a CIA agent—and he immediately called him.

They'd met almost seven years ago at Camp Peary, during covert operative training bootcamp. Sam was there as part of an experimental program as a DARPA engineer. DARPA's belief was that it was in their best interest to give their top engineers the same real-world, hands-on training that the CIA agents received, which would allow them to design even better technology. As a result, Sam was trained in everything from hand-to-hand combat to bypassing complex alarm systems. While the training had been intense—and definitely worthwhile in its application to designing high-tech gadgets for the various national security agencies—after he left DARPA for civilian life, Sam doubted it was anything that he'd ever personally use.

He was beginning to rethink that with each passing ring of the phone.

Rube finally answered. "Tired of California already?"

"I need your help." Sam told him about the call from Remi's phone and then his conversation with Nikos.

"Forward that voice mail to me. I'll get someone to translate it."

"Thanks."

"And Sam? I know you can handle yourself out there, but officially, I'm telling you to stay out of Greece and let the government do its job. It's possible there's a logical explanation. Wait to hear what's going on."

"Unofficially?"

"Good luck and safe travels."

The moment Sam disconnected, he opened his laptop, searching for airline tickets.

Blake leaned over, looking at Sam's monitor, whistling at the price of the last-minute one-way ticket. He shook his head. "That's a lot of money for a woman you just met."

"I didn't just meet her."

"Oh, okay. Like, two whole weeks ago."

"A lifetime."

"Never. What about your investor meeting? That's a once-in-a-lifetime opportunity."

Blake was right. Sam looked at the jumble of paperwork covering the desk, thinking about all the years of work he'd put in just to get his argon laser to the point where he could finally present it as a viable idea. He hesitated at the thought he was possibly giving up what had been a dream of his for as long as he could remember—investors of that type didn't come along every day.

Then again, neither did women like Remi Longstreet.

CHAPTER ELEVEN

Samos, Greece

Life on the smaller Greek islands, Sam quickly discovered, ran at a much slower pace than anywhere else. He was lucky that he arrived in Samos after his flight from Athens in time to catch the one ferry that stopped off at Fourni, since there wasn't another until two days later. He boarded behind a group of young men and women, all dressed for hiking, following them up the stairs to the outside deck, willing everyone to hurry and the boat to move.

Finally, the ferry pulled out, and he leaned against the railing, the salt-tinged air blowing through his hair as the boat picked up speed. Had he been there as a tourist, he might have enjoyed the sight of the picturesque port of Pythagorio and the masts of the various sailing yachts moored within it. Above him, billowing white clouds in a blue sky accentuated the white houses terraced upon the hill, overlooking the water, where, farther out, several fishing boats headed in with the day's catch. Sam, however, paid little attention. His mind was on his last conversation with Rube, whose preliminary investigation failed to turn up anything significant—other than confirming that Remi and her friend Dimitris were both missing. The Greek translator had only been able to pick out a few words on the voice recording, one of the men insisting that they needed to hurry. Another CIA analyst determined that the engine heard in the background belonged to a high-powered boat. They all agreed that a woman did say, "Where's the North Star when you need it?"

None of that was enough for anyone to confirm that a kidnapping had actually taken place, though they had notified the FBI's International Violent Crimes Unit. According to Rube, Sam's only recourse was to let the local authorities conduct their own investigation.

Not that he was about to stand by and do nothing. Sam was glad to know Dimitris's father felt the same. He'd already started his own search and welcomed Sam's offer to help.

"Excuse me?"

Sam looked up to see a blond-haired woman from the tourist group standing beside him. She tried asking a question in halting Greek.

"American," he said.

"Sorry. I figured you were a local. The backpack." She nodded at the bag slung over his shoulder.

Sam nodded toward a small carry-on tucked under a bench. "Quick trip," he said.

"Have you been to Fourni before?"

"My first time."

"Oh. Well, I guess that means you don't know the best place to eat lunch once we arrive."

"Sadly, no."

She held out her hand. "Emma," she said, then cocked her head at the man on her right. "My husband, Geoff. With a G."

"Nice to meet you," he said, shaking her hand. "Sam. With an S."

She smiled, then moved to the railing, next to him, taking in the view. A few minutes later, her husband joined them, pointing to a large yacht floating in open water between the islands. "Someone important," he said, lowering his sunglasses and looking out over the rims.

"And rich," Emma replied. She pointed to a smaller yacht in the distance. "If we win the lotto, *that's* the type of boat I want. Much more manageable."

"That little thing? No. Definitely the big one," Geoff said. He nodded to a long, black speedboat. "What do you suppose that costs?"

Sam glanced up as the sleek Omega 41 zipped past, then pulled up to the superyacht. "About four, five hundred thousand dollars."

Emma laughed. "Sorry, Geoff. You'll have to win the lotto twice at that price. Guess it comes as a set."

Sam listened with half an ear as the couple discussed other vessels they'd buy with their imagined lotto winnings. His mind, however, was solely on Remi Longstreet and the odd call from her phone, hoping it was all one big misunderstanding. Surely they'd joke about it when he got there, she pointing out the fact he didn't speak Greek, and how could he ever have imagined anything was wrong?

His hopes for an alternate reality were dashed when the ferry docked an hour later. Emma and Geoff waved goodbye as they followed their group down the ramp. As the crowd thinned, Sam noticed a man wearing a blue ball cap, standing off to one side on the dock. Recognizing the logo on his hat as being from the Fourni Underwater Archeological Preservation Society, Sam approached. "Nikos?"

The gray-haired man gave a grim smile. "Sam Fargo?" They shook hands. "Do you have luggage?"

He held up his backpack. "Just the carry-on. I travel light."

"Thank you so much for coming out. Still, I don't know what good it'll do," he said, his thick accent much easier to understand in person. "The port police assure me they're doing everything they can. Remi's parents have been in touch with the FBI. Beyond that . . ."

"Have the police told you anything more?"

"No, nothing. That's why I worry. Their belief is that my son and Remi may have fallen off the boat, or perhaps went diving. But their dive gear is back at the office. And Dimitris would never dive without someone on the boat. He is very experienced."

Sam, hoping for a miracle, asked, "What do you think happened?"

"I don't know." He drew his gaze from the water, his dark eyes troubled. "If they were kidnapped for ransom, surely they would've made a demand by now?"

"Possibly," Sam said. "In the meantime, maybe we'll see something that stands out to help the police with their investigation."

Nikos gave a doubtful nod as they walked from the port, past the group of people lined up waiting to board the ferry. He led Sam up a narrow street paved with gray flagstones. It was lined on either side with mulberry trees, their trunks painted white to guard against the harsh summer sun. The Fourni Underwater Archeological Preservation Society was located about halfway up the street on the right. At the office, Nikos led Sam into a room with a table and several chairs set around it. A large map of Fourni was tacked on the wall. "Can I get you anything to eat or drink? We have nothing here, but we can go to one of the cafés."

"I'm fine. Thank you." Sam studied the map, noting grid marks drawn in various places in the water around the island, some in black, some in red. "What are these?"

"Shipwrecks," Nikos said, joining him. "The red areas are where we're currently mapping. The black are documented wrecks that we'll get to in the future."

"Where were Remi and Dimitris when you last saw them?"

He tapped an area in the lower left quadrant of the map. "Here.

You actually passed by it on the ferry. It's where we found the *Asteri*," he replied. "Another reason I know they weren't diving. The sonar wasn't reeled in. My son knows how important this site and the equipment is to our group. He would never treat it so carelessly."

The office door opened. Both turned to see a petite woman in her early thirties walk in. Her shoulder-length wavy brown hair was pulled back in a ponytail, her cheeks pink from the wind. She paused just inside the doorway, regarding them with her bright blue eyes. "Sorry we're late," she said.

"We only just arrived," Nikos replied. "Where's Manos?"

She glanced behind her as a bearded man walked through the door a moment later.

"Good, good," Nikos said, waving them in. "Manos Mitikas is responsible for helping start the documentation and preservation of all the Fourni shipwrecks. His girlfriend, Denéa Buckingham, is from Australia. They're helping with the search." After Sam shook hands with both, Nikos looked at the young couple expectantly. "Any news?"

"Not yet," Manos said. "We're heading back out after lunch."

Nikos gave a brief nod, then turned to Sam, his face looking haggard and drawn. "Where were we? Ah, yes. The boat . . ."

"Where is it now?"

"Docked. We passed it on our way in. The port police examined it, but maybe you'll see something?"

"Can't hurt."

CHAPTER TWELVE

Sam and Nikos boarded the *Asteri*, which was, as Nikos said, empty. No blood, nothing to indicate anything violent had happened. "Who discovered the boat?" Sam asked.

"One of the local fishermen found it not too far from where they were working. The only thing left on the boat was an empty camera bag, and Remi's backpack. That's where we found her sat phone."

"What about where Remi was staying? Has anyone taken a look there?"

"Not that I know of. She was staying in one of the cottages down in Kampi."

They took Nikos's car, a small white Suzuki sedan, which was parked at the port. The village of Kampi was to the south of Fourni, less than five minutes away. The main road turned off to the right, then veered sharply on the steep road, ending in a cul-de-sac about halfway down the hill. Nikos parked, then led Sam down a long, narrow staircase into the small beach community.

Remi's cottage was located at the far end of the beach. A jingle of bells caught Sam's attention and he looked up to see several goats grazing on the low shrubs sprouting from the otherwise barren rocks that jutted out next to the cottage.

Nikos, seeing the direction of his gaze, smiled. "Goats. You'll see them everywhere on the island." He opened a low gate into the courtyard of a small white house with dark turquoise trim around the windows and door. "This was Remi's."

Sam checked the door. Locked. "Do you have the key?"

He dug a ring from his pocket and opened the door.

Everything seemed in order. Assuming Remi had been the last person in there, the bed appeared slept in, but neatly made. A carry-on and two larger suitcases were stacked in a corner by the bed. Yup, that's Remi, prepared for any occasion. In the closet, he saw a neat row of sandals, boat shoes, and barely-worn hiking boots. There was even an evening dress and fancy strappy red shoes with high heels that women love to wear. They walked out to the kitchen. A table and two chairs were set up before a window that looked out over the quiet bay. An empty coffee cup sat in the sink. Other than that, everything seemed to be in its place.

So much for his detective skills. If there were any clues to be found, he wasn't having any luck.

Outside, Nikos led Sam across the courtyard to a set of stairs that led up onto the roof, giving him a view of the entire beach. A boy sat on a wooden dock to the left, fishing. A half-dozen moored boats of various sizes bobbed in the water just beyond him. "What about Dimitris?" Sam asked. "Where was he staying?"

"At home. With me. Unfortunately, no one saw either of them after they left. I'm not sure if you knew, but Remi's camera was stolen. My nephew, Ares," he said, nodding to the boy at the end of the dock, "was fishing from a skiff that morning. He told us that there was a strange boat in the area. Sadly, he didn't see who was in it."

"Do you mind if I talk to him?"

"Of course not. His English is not so good. But he's learning."

They walked to the end of the dock to talk to the boy. Nikos introduced them, adding, "Remi is Mr. Sam Fargo's friend. He's worried about her, and wants to know what you saw." He repeated it in Greek, then translated the boy's response, saying, "A speedboat driving away from the *Asteri*. He's never seen it before . . . They're not from around here."

Which didn't help. "Do you know what kind of boat?" Sam asked.

The boy drew his pole back, then flicked it forward in a perfect cast as Nikos translated. "Long and fast. For racing. There was a name on the side, but it was not written in Greek, so he couldn't read it. Which," Nikos added, "there are many of around the islands."

Sam thanked Ares for his help. About to leave, he looked back at the boy. "Any chance you could draw the boat you saw?"

Nikos asked him, then nodded. "Maybe."

Ares secured the hook upon the reel, tightened it, then set his pole on the dock. When they reached the beach, he jumped down into the sand, smoothed out a portion with his hand, and traced an outline of the boat, saying something to Nikos, who said, "It was long and dark, like this."

Which didn't narrow it down any, Sam thought, watching as the boy made a circle on the side of the boat, along with a few scribbles. As he drew, he spoke to Nikos, who in turn, said, "This is where the name of the boat was written. And the numbers."

He drew the letter *O*, then poked his finger where the rest of the letters were, Nikos saying that he couldn't recall the name. Then he added the numbers *1* and *4*.

Sam did a double take. "What color was that boat?"

Apparently the boy understood that, because he said, "Black."

Sam, wondering if he could have transposed the numbers, crouched down beside him, writing *OMEGA 41* in the sand.

The boy nodded, speaking rapidly.

"That's the name," Nikos said.

"I may know where it is."

Nikos glanced at the crude drawing, then at Sam. "You can tell from that drawing?"

"From the name and the color. It was heading toward a yacht in between here and Samos. Had I known, I would've paid more attention."

"The police will want to know this."

"Let's make sure the yacht's still there before we call. The more information we can give them, the better."

They hurried back to the port. Within fifteen minutes, they were motoring away from Fourni toward the waters of Samos.

"There!" Sam said, pointing at the superyacht he'd seen earlier that day.

Nikos lifted his binoculars. After a few seconds, he handed them to Sam. "If that *is* the same yacht, I'm not sure the police can help. The *Mirage* belongs to Adrian Kyril."

"Why would that make a difference?"

"There are those who believe that the billions the Kyrils have made from exporting olive oil really comes from their ties to organized crime. The rumors are unproven, mostly because no one can get close enough to the Kyrils to prove anything."

Sam studied the yacht through the binoculars. In his mind, a vessel that size had far too many places to hide hostages. And if the Kyrils were, as Nikos said, part of some organized crime family, Sam suspected that once the police boarded—and failed to find Remi or Dimitris—it'd be the last anyone would see of either of them.

He immediately called Rube to update him on this newest detail. "How long until you can get a team out here to rescue them?"

"Through the proper channels? Tomorrow at the earliest. There's a team in Italy. How sure are you that she's on that boat?"

"Does gut instinct count?"

"Between you and me? Yes. To my bosses? Before they commit

any resources, they're going to need some firm evidence to back that up."

"I can give them some once I'm on board."

"Do me a favor? Let me see what *I* can do before *you* do anything that gets you in trouble, which then gets me in trouble."

"Keep them on speed dial," Sam said. "If you don't hear from me by morning, send them in after me."

"Fargo, do *not*—"

Sam disconnected. By the time Rube gathered the necessary intel to put together a rescue operation, their window of opportunity might be gone.

"What did he say?" Nikos asked. "Can he help?"

"He can get a team out here by morning, if we can get evidence they're on board."

"That's a long time from now. And how do we get evidence?"

"Too long, and we get it the old-fashioned way, in person." Sam took one last look at the yacht, then lowered the binoculars. "Which is why I plan on going in after dark."

Nikos nodded. "I'll go with you."

"I'm not sure that's a good idea. If it goes wrong, I'll either end up dead or in jail. Someone's got to make sure to tell Rube what happened. Then, make sure someone follows up."

"But—"

"If I know you're here to do that, I'll be able to concentrate better." He looked at his watch. A little after seven. "We have a few hours to get everything we need. First thing on the list, a *very* fast boat."

CHAPTER THIRTEEN

Remi, hands zip-tied in front of her, had her ear to the door, listening, while Dimitris, cuffed in similar fashion, searched the tiny cabin. Until ten minutes ago, they'd been held down in the tender garage very near the same speedboat they'd been kidnapped in. She wasn't sure why they'd been moved to the small cabin one deck up. She was, however, grateful, since now they had water and a toilet, and no longer had to call out for a guard to escort them to the head.

During their time below, their captors hadn't bothered to give them food or water, which told Remi they probably weren't interested in how they were faring. No doubt their being thrown in this tiny cabin was more a matter of convenience for them, not their prisoners.

After standing at the door, she heard footsteps, then heard one of the guards saying, "Ilya's on his way."

That was a name she hadn't heard before.

"Found something," Dimitris said.

"Someone's coming."

She hurried to her spot on the floor. Dimitris stepped out of the head and sat next to her as the door opened. A guard stepped in, his hand on his pistol. A second stood just outside, his posture straightening as a third man finally walked up and entered the cabin. Several inches taller than the other two, he had dark curly hair, and a thin mustache covering his upper lip. He wore a charcoal gray suit and a white shirt, open at the collar. The sheen of the material told her this was not something off the rack. The fit told her it was definitely custom-made.

Ilya, no doubt.

He took one look at Dimitris and Remi, then spoke to the lead guard in Greek, asking, "Why are they here and not down below as usual?"

"We're short-staffed. It's easier to watch them from here."

Ilya's gaze narrowed and he suddenly switched to Italian—rebuking the man for discussing staffing levels in front of the prisoners.

Remi, who only spoke what she considered passable Greek, happened to be fluent in Italian. She listened impassively, as though she understood none of it—not an easy task, considering that they suddenly switched subjects and were now discussing how best to kill the two of them.

"We could just throw them overboard," the guard said.

"You'd have been better off killing them on their boat. Imagine the inquiries on why two divers were kidnapped, murdered, then dumped. The last thing he needs is to bring attention to the island." Who "he" might be, Remi didn't know. Ilya might be the one in charge here, but it seemed apparent that he answered to someone else, a fact confirmed when he took out his phone and looked at the screen, which lit up with an incoming call. He answered in Greek, saying, "It's being take care of." When he disconnected, he directed his attention to the guard, switching back to Italian. "We'll put out a ransom demand to string them along."

"For how much?"

"Does it matter? The American authorities are already speculating that they've been kidnapped by pirates. In a few days, you can dump their bodies in Turkish waters."

In English, Remi asked, "What do you want from us?" When they ignored her, she added, "If you're going to hold us down here, can you please remove the ties?"

Ilya started to turn away.

"Unless," she added, "you think we can fit through that porthole?" She gave a pointed look to the tiny, round window.

He walked out, telling the guard, "If they make any attempt to escape, shoot them."

The guard closed the door, locking it from the outside. Remi waited until she no longer heard their footsteps. "What'd you find?"

"Manicure kit. We can cut our ties." He slid a small black case from beneath his shirt. Opening it, he showed her a set of plier-style toenail clippers, and a nail file. "I guess they didn't do a thorough search."

"I gathered from their conversation that this cabin isn't normally used as a prisoner hold." When he started to pull out the clippers to cut their zip ties, she stopped him. "Not yet. If they check on us before we're ready, we're not likely to get another chance."

"I didn't think of that." He hid the case beneath his shirt once more. "What else were they saying?"

"Besides that they're going to kill us? Ilya was angry that one of the guards slipped up and mentioned they were short-staffed. Too bad. We might have had a better chance of escaping through the tender garage." She eyed the cardboard cases of cola stacked on the lowest berth. "The good news is that we won't die of thirst."

"Cola or lemon-lime?"

"Cola. I can use the caffeine."

He tore open one of the cases, gave her a can, then took one for himself.

She sank to the floor, cracked open her soda, and took a long sip, the room-temperature carbonation bubbles burning her dry throat. "There's got to be some way we can get out of here. I have someone waiting for me in the States."

She stopped, surprised by what just came out of her mouth. *I'm an independent woman with a career, a future for myself. And now I'm longing for someone who would find me because the North Star is always there.*

"They're going to murder us and *that's* what you think of?"

"What about you and Zoe? Aren't you thinking of her? I saw it in your eyes."

"Well, I heard it in your voice."

She stared down at the open can in her hands. As odd as it was for them to be discussing her future love life, it was exactly what she needed to stay calm, keep her head, and not let the stress overtake her. "I at least want a chance to find out if he's the one."

"What makes him so special?"

"Good question." It wasn't the way he'd raced into the water to rescue that surfer. If anything, his actions that afternoon seemed . . . daring, even reckless. Definitely not the sort of man she'd ever dated before. It was just two weeks that they had dated. But what a two weeks it turned out to be. Spur of the moment. To places she'd only dreamed of. And at a pace she could hardly keep up with. Helicopters appearing out of nowhere. Kelp diving off Catalina. Long walks on the beach. The cliff top. Where he'd said *they* would build their home.

"He's sharp, witty, loves the ocean. And if you ignore the fact we come from two completely different worlds, almost a perfect match."

"Almost?"

"I'm reserving judgment." Her parents definitely wouldn't

approve. That brought a smile to her face. As much as she loved them, she'd felt stifled by their carefully orchestrated attempts to keep her firmly entrenched in Boston society. It was the main reason she'd taken the lower-paying translator job in California, when there was a higher-paying position with the same company in Boston. And now, faced with the threat of death, wondering if she'd ever see her parents again, she didn't regret it at all. Well, maybe just a little bit.

"What about you?" she finally said, her voice cracking. "Tell me more about Zoe."

He smiled. "We have always been together for as long as I can remember. But she is devoted to her grandfather and I'm afraid that as long as she is taking care of him she won't marry me."

"Have you asked her grandfather for permission to court her?"

"Not yet. I'm not sure I would like the answer. What about you? Do your parents know about . . . ?"

"Definitely not." Considering her sheltered East Coast upbringing—her physician mother and architect father making sure she was exposed to only the finest members of Boston society—Sam was an anomaly. A dreamer who wasn't caught up in the trappings of social standings or privilege. Someone who would take a chance. Even a risk. And if that didn't work, he'd come up with Plan B.

That's it. That's what she needed. A Plan B. Wait a minute, first she needed a Plan A.

She took another sip, then looked over at Dimitris. "It's settled then. As soon as it's dark, we're cutting these ties and getting out of here. And when we do, you're going to find Zoe. And I'm going to find my North Star."

"Remi?"

"What?"

"Exactly how are we getting out?"

She shifted around, eyeing the cases of soda behind them. Until this afternoon's visit with Ilya, they'd seen only one guard at a time tasked with watching them. She hoped that arrangement wouldn't change. "We could hit a guard over the head with one of those cases. Between the two of us, we can take him down." She looked over at Dimitris and outlined her Plan A.

CHAPTER FOURTEEN

Sam was heartened when he learned that Nikos's cousin Valerios actually owned a cigarette boat and was willing to let him borrow it for the night—as long as he promised to take good care of it. About twenty minutes later, plans made, they walked out to the dock to find Valerios disembarking from the oldest, most derelict-looking cigarette boat Sam had ever seen. Sam could only stare, wondering how it could still be seaworthy.

"She is a beauty, yes?" Valerios said, his accent even thicker than Nikos's.

"She's definitely . . . unexpected."

"I take the engines out and put them together myself. Good as new. Better than new."

Judging from the shape and condition of the hull, *new* had to have been a good thirty or more years ago, Sam thought.

Valerios, not noticing his reaction, grinned. "Wait until you see her fly across the water. You will never believe it, I promise."

Had the situation not been so dire, Sam might have shared in Valerios's enthusiasm over what he could only assume was a labor of love. Anyone who knew anything about boats could surely recognize that it had been, a long, long time ago, a thing of beauty.

"Exactly how fast can she go?"

Valerios shrugged. "Eighty? Probably ninety. Who's to say. I never go that fast. Come, come. I'll show you."

Sam hopped in, putting his hand on the cracked leather seat back, hoping to get a look at the engines. But before he had both feet in the boat, Valerios was turning the key. Fully expecting the engine to sputter and die, the twin engines gave a low rumble. Then they roared like a lion.

Valerios clapped Sam on the back. "Like I say, she will fly."

Approaching the *Mirage* unnoticed in the borrowed old but well-loved cigarette boat had taken Sam far longer than he'd anticipated. The larger vessel was anchored a few miles offshore, the bow facing inland. Two guards took turns making periodic rounds before meeting up again. In the hour that Sam and Nikos had been watching them, both seemed more concerned with looking for threats coming from the island than from the open sea. To make sure their attention stayed toward the shore, Nikos enlisted a few of his friends to drive their boats in a manner that deserved scrutiny so that Sam could approach the yacht from behind.

So far it had worked, and when he was within hearing distance Sam cut the motor, allowing his boat to drift forward until he reached the swim dock at the stern of the *Mirage*. He tied the boat to the rail, climbed aboard, then made his way up the aft steps, coming out on an upper deck with a Jacuzzi, a bar, and plenty of plush chairs filled with colorful cushions for guests to take in the view.

Hiding behind the bar, Sam waited for the guard to make his rounds. From his observations, the guard made regular ten-minute checks on something located mid-deck on the starboard side.

Anything in there warranting that sort of attention was exactly where Sam wanted to investigate first.

He waited for the man to resume his rounds. The moment it was clear, Sam crossed the deck, and headed down the stairs into a narrow hallway. After guesstimating it as the potential location on the boat to keep captives, he worked his way down the hallway checking doors until he reached the last one. It was secured with a slide-bolt lock.

He listened and, hearing nothing, slid the bolt, then partially opened the door, whispering, "Remi . . . ?"

The room was dark and Sam opened the door wider to investigate. He whispered again, "Remi." From the corner of his eye, he saw something large and square flying down at him. The object squarely struck his head, then exploded. Cans burst out, clattering to the floor, and he right along with them. At the same time, someone came at him from the opposite direction. Dazed, his hand shot out, blocked the blow, catching Remi by her wrist, holding tight. "It's me," he said.

She stared in shock. "Sam?"

Dimitris threw on the lights. "Who are you?"

"It's Sam! Sam? Sam, it's me, Remi. You can let go."

"Remi?" He looked from her to Dimitris, then to the open door. "Get the door closed before anyone comes down the hall. We must have made a racket." Dimitris pulled the door shut while Remi kneeled beside him.

"Is it you? Where did you come from? It is you."

"Geez, Remi," Sam said, rubbing the bump on his head. "You did say the North Star."

"Wait." Dimitris stared. "Is this the guy from the bar?"

"I can't believe it. Oh, where are my manners? Dimitris, this is Sam. Sam . . ."

"Really, Remi. This is no time for small talk." Sam looked up. "Nice to meet you, Dimitris."

"I can't believe it. You got my call."

"Yes, now help me up. We better get going before someone decides to investigate all this noise."

"Sam, I can't believe it. It's you. The North Star. It worked."

"Is she always like this?"

He took Remi by the hand and led her and Dimitris out. Then he bolted the door behind them, hoping that'd be enough to make the guards think their prisoners were still inside. He'd already used up too much time recovering from the attack and corralling Remi. "Okay, now, quickly and quietly," he said, directing them to the stairs. So far, no one was coming. "To the right. All the way down, then to the right again. Hide behind the bar."

He waited until they were safely past before he followed, rounding the corner, coming face-to-face with one of the guards.

The startled guard reached for his gun. Sam stepped in, drove his right fist into the man's gut, then shot his left hand out, catching the guard's hand as he frantically tried to draw his pistol. When he couldn't free it, he headbutted Sam. The blow knocked Sam back into the bar. Blindly reaching behind him, he grasped a full bottle of alcohol. As the guard drew, Sam brought the bottle crashing against his gun hand. The weapon fell. Sam swung again, slamming him in the jaw.

He slumped to the ground, groaning, his eyes fluttering. Sam recovered the gun, then searched the guard in case he was carrying a backup weapon. Finding zip ties tucked in his pocket, he secured the man's hands behind his back, then his feet together at the ankles. As they dragged him out of sight, he came to. Sam grabbed a washcloth from beneath the bar and shoved it into his mouth.

"Someone's coming," Remi whispered, ducking behind the bar with them.

Sam pressed the gun barrel against the guard's temple, and Dimitris kneeled on his legs to keep him from moving. He struggled against them.

"I have a Plan B," Remi said. Then, pulling a slim object from her pocket, she held it against the guard's neck, saying something to him in Greek.

The man suddenly stilled. As the footsteps neared, Remi pressed harder. His gaze widened.

Curious, Sam leaned over, saw Remi pressing toenail clippers against the guard's carotid. Sam couldn't help but smile and turned back, aiming the gun, grateful when the footsteps passed by without incident.

When it was clear, he motioned Remi and Dimitris to head down the stairs. Sam took the clippers from Remi and kept them wedged against the man's neck, buying them precious seconds to get away. Sam waited until they were on the stairs before following them down.

"What'd you say to him?" Sam asked once they reached the lower deck.

"That I had a very sharp knife and if he made one noise, his throat wasn't the only thing I'd cut." She glanced at Sam as they climbed over the railing into the cigarette boat. "I let his imagination do the work."

Dimitris untied the rope and pushed off as Sam started the engine, then immediately opened it up, full throttle. Sam hoped the old boat was up to the task, but Valerios had said that her twin inboard engines could do at least eighty miles per hour.

There was no doubting the moment their escape had been discovered. He looked back, saw the internal dock door open. Within moments, a searchlight swept across the water, over them, then backtracked, lighting up their vessel.

Sam concentrated on steering the boat.

They were midway to shore when he glanced behind him, saw the muzzle flashes coming from the speedboat chasing them. "Guns!" he shouted.

Remi and Dimitris ducked.

He drove in a zigzag pattern, worried they'd be overtaken before they reached the shore. He looked over at Remi, shouting, "How good of a swimmer are you?"

"Why?"

"A wild idea," he called out. "You two jump off the back. I draw them away. Keep to a breaststroke. They won't see you in the dark."

"How?" she asked. "We're going too fast."

"Technique," Sam shouted. "Not quite a back dive. More like a mummy in a coffin. Body straight, arms crossed tight on your chest, feet together. Just make sure you land on your butt and back, not your feet."

Remi glanced over her shoulder at the heavy wake trailing after them, then at Sam, her eyes filled with uncertainty.

Dimitris took her arm. "Better than getting shot."

She looked back at Sam. "How are you getting off?"

"After I lead them away."

Dimitris tried guiding her to the back of the boat. When she hesitated, Sam said, "Don't worry. You and I have a date. Wouldn't dream of missing it." He waited until they were in position, hoping to keep them out of view and out of the other boat's path. He slowed to about fifty miles per hour. The two poised on the back of the boat. "Now!"

They pushed off. Sam pressed the throttle forward, steered away from them. His slower speed cost him. The Kyrils' speedboat was gaining.

At least Remi and Dimitris were safe.

Not that he was about to give up on his own life. He lashed one of the mooring ropes around the wide-open throttle, started to tie that to the steering wheel, aiming for open water. He was going a lot faster than when they jumped. Still, what choice did he have? About to let go of the steering wheel and make for the back of the boat, he saw the red port-side lights of the Kyrils' yacht.

A much better plan, he decided.

CHAPTER FIFTEEN

Remi ended up about fifteen feet behind Dimitris, finally seeing him once the wake of the passing speedboats dissipated. As Dimitris swam toward her, she looked around. They were at least two miles from shore, the lights of the city twinkling against the ink-black horizon. Turning about, she saw the two speedboats growing more distant. As much as she realized she and Dimitris needed to swim to shore, she felt tethered to the spot, treading water, while her gut twisted inside her.

Dimitris followed the direction of her gaze. "You think he'll jump?"

"Let's hope so." His boat seemed to be slowing, which made her think he already had—until she saw it make a sudden turn toward the Kyrils' yacht. They were too far away for her to see if Sam was still on the boat, but the turn was too deliberate. A barrage of bright muzzle flashes from the pursuing speedboat lit up the night sky.

Sam's vessel continued veering toward the *Mirage*. It hit the swim deck, then hurtled upward, the red and green sidelights spinning like a kaleidoscope. It exploded in a blinding flash, then crashed into the water.

Remi's gut clenched. Her limbs turned leaden, pulling her down.

If Sam *was* in that boat, there was nothing they could do. If he wasn't . . . they needed to get help. She forced herself to breathe evenly, trying to clear her sense of shock. "Let's go."

They started the long swim to shore, covering the first mile in about half an hour by her estimation. Dimitris was a strong swimmer, but paced himself to match Remi, who discovered that swimming a couple miles in a pool was a far cry from the same distance in the sea, when their only nourishment these past two days was the soda they'd found in the cabin. Each time they stopped to rest, Remi looked back, thinking about Sam.

Her only hope was when she saw the Kyril yacht pulling away. That, at least, meant they weren't coming back for them or Sam—if he'd survived.

"He'll be fine," Dimitris said. "We'll send help as soon as we reach shore."

He started sidestroking to the north. Remi followed with a paced breaststroke. After what seemed like an eternity, Remi was certain the lights they were swimming toward seemed farther now than when they'd started. She and Dimitris stopped to rest again. She turned on her back, unable to do more than let the current carry her where it would.

"Remi?"

She didn't have the energy to respond. Instead, she stared up at the sky, trying to find the North Star.

Sam . . .

It'll always lead me to you.

"Remi! Look!"

She mustered enough strength to turn her head in the direction Dimitris was pointing. Either she was hallucinating, or the lights from the shore were moving in their direction. It was a moment before she realized that's exactly what was happening. An entire flotilla of lights.

Dimitris started waving his hands, shouting in Greek, "Over here! Over here!"

Dozens of fishing boats and trawlers were heading their way. Spotlights swept across the surface, one finally landing on them as Dimitris continued waving.

Remi joined in, relief buoying her energy as the boats neared. Someone threw out a preserver. Dimitris swam to it, then brought it back to Remi.

Nikos motored up in the *Asteri*, hugging them both the moment they boarded. As Dimitris told his father about what they'd witnessed, Nikos's expression turned grim. Even so, he radioed the others to start heading toward the Kyrils' yacht.

Or rather, where it used to be.

It was long gone by the time they started searching.

CHAPTER SIXTEEN

The crash had been spectacular, although Sam regretted having to sacrifice the beautiful old boat.

But it had the desired effect. Kyril's men decided to turn tail and run, rather than risk any inquiries from the unwanted attention that the explosion brought to the *Mirage*.

He hoped that meant Remi and Dimitris were safe. Much depended on whether or not they were picked up by one of Nikos's friends or, since they were much closer when they'd jumped, managed to swim to shore.

Sam, on the other hand, was several miles from anywhere. He'd been swimming northeast for the past hour, not sure if he'd made much progress, trying to get to the flotilla of fishing boats heading to where the yacht had been.

Too far away to call out to them, he realized they'd be gone by the time he could get there. His only recourse was to stay put and hope that help came to him.

A good decision, it turned out.

As dawn crept in, one of the fishermen spotted him.

Within minutes, he was pulled aboard and taken into the cabin.

Someone got on the radio. A moment later, he recognized Nikos's voice coming from it. "Fargo! We found them both. They're fine."

Someone led Sam to a seat, wrapped a blanket around him, brought him a hot cup of Greek coffee. It was extra strong, made with three teaspoons of sugar and two heaping teaspoons of coffee. The *vary glykos* warmed him immediately.

He held it between his hands, a mix of emotions coursing through him, and only one thought running through his mind.

Remi was safe.

Within a half hour, Sam rejoined Nikos on the *Asteri*, where Remi and Dimitris were waiting. Both had showered and were dressed in borrowed clothes from the crew, Remi's far too large, the cuffs on her pants and shirt rolled up several times to accommodate her.

Though it was a far cry from the color-coordinated wardrobe he'd seen hanging in her closet, he thought she looked perfect. Even more so when she smiled, and gave him a hug. "Thank you," she said. "I still can't believe you're here."

"Remi, I told you the North Star will always lead me to you."

She wrapped her arms around him and he drew her close. This time the kiss lingered, but ended far sooner than either of them would have liked.

Nikos held up a bottle of ouzo and four ice-filled glasses. "Sit, Fargo. It's time to celebrate." He poured the clear liquid into each glass, then took a small bottle of water, topping each. The moment the water hit the ouzo, it turned from clear to milky white. He lifted his glass in a toast. "Whatever the reason, I'm very glad you came. I thank you for my son's life. For Remi's life. For surviving, yourself."

"Hear! Hear!" Dimitris and Remi joined in.

Sam sipped the alcohol, the taste of licorice heavy on his tongue as he set his glass on the table. As much as he wanted to relax, there were too many questions that needed answers. "I'm all for celebrating, but does anyone have *any* idea why they came after the two of you?"

"Not exactly," Remi said. "Although they did mention something about killing us and not wanting to bring attention to the island. I gathered they're looking for something."

"Whatever it is," Sam said, "it must be worth a lot for them to risk an open kidnapping. Any chance the shipwreck you two were mapping has more to it than a bunch of broken pottery?"

"I have no idea." Remi glanced at Dimitris.

"There are certainly enough amphorae down there," he said. "On the black market, intact pottery can be worth a lot of money."

"Worth kidnapping for?" Sam found it hard to believe they'd take such a risk for a couple of sunken vases.

"No," Nikos said. "The seafloor around Fourni is littered with shipwrecks. Why not go after one of the other sites, where no one is attending?"

"If I'm not mistaken," Remi said, "the Kyrils' yacht was there at least the day before."

Dimitris nodded. "It was. Why bother us now?"

They tossed around several ideas and wild theories, but by the time they finished their drinks, they were no closer to determining why the two of them were targeted. Eventually, Nikos picked up the empty ouzo bottle, shook it, and peering inside gave a sad smile. "I'd say that's our cue to call it a night. Let the Aegean sing you to sleep. I suggest we continue this discussion in the morning." He stood. "Come, I've put clean towels in your berths."

They followed him down to a narrow cabin with two bunks, both with a small towel and a facecloth neatly folded at the foot.

Nikos smiled at Remi. "My apologies. The quarters are tight and the mattresses are stiff."

"We'll be fine," she said, hugging him. "Thank you."

He left them alone.

Remi sat on the lower berth, lying back, closing her eyes. "I'm just going to lie here for a minute. After two nights sleeping on the floor, this mattress is the softest I ever slept on." Then, very quietly, almost a whisper, she said, "Sam? You're here."

He was about to answer, but when he looked over, she was fast asleep.

First thing in the morning, he'd call Rube and let him know all was well. Too tired to do much of anything, he climbed up on the top bunk, thinking about the events that led up to the kidnapping. *Something* had to have occurred to bring Remi and Dimitris to the attention of a man like Adrian Kyril. What that might be, he intended to find out. For now, they were safe. But he doubted Adrian Kyril was simply going to pretend that nothing had happened.

He'd be back—looking for retribution.

CHAPTER SEVENTEEN

Adrian stood just inside the open-air pool house of his cliff-top home, his gaze fixed on the young woman swimming laps in the infinity pool, her long blond hair streaming across her back as she moved. Phoebe, a model he'd picked up in France, had been staying with him these last few weeks. Though he'd long tired of her company, his mother seemed to like her, which made her an asset. Impatient, he finished his drink, set it on the table, then walked out to the glass wall to see if Ilya's boat had arrived yet. He was halfway across the terra-cotta tiles when a red light flashed on the control panel of the lift as someone rode it up to the topmost patio, one of three terraced onto the cliff face. Stone-paved steps led down to each level as well as to the dock built at the base of the cliff, though he couldn't recall the last time anyone but the gardeners had taken the stairs or even gone down to the lower patio.

Today, however, would be different. He needed a place to talk where they wouldn't be overheard by his staff or his girlfriend. Finally, the lift door opened, and Ilya stepped out, his expression grim.

"This way," Adrian said, leading him down to the next level. Both men leaned against the glass balcony. About twenty-five feet below, the azure sea rippled at the base of the cliff. The view had always calmed him in the past. Not now. "What happened?"

"Someone managed to board the *Mirage*. Whoever he was, he overpowered one of the guards and freed them."

"How did he get on the boat without being seen?"

"We were shorthanded. He managed to get in from the swim deck. The good news is that he and the two hostages may not have survived their escape attempt."

"What makes you think that?"

"He lost control of his boat when my men gave chase. There was an explosion when it hit the swim deck."

"Any bodies?"

"No time to look. They were worried about the attention it might bring should anyone decide to investigate the accident."

Adrian gripped the balcony railing, then forced himself to let go. "They should worry about the attention that escaped hostages might bring. You realize what this will do? We left a body on that island with two witnesses."

"Even if they did survive, it doesn't appear that they saw anything. We found nothing on the camera."

"Maybe not. But they were held hostage for two days. On *my* yacht. How do we explain that?" Angry, Adrian looked over at him, trying to read his expression. A shadow on the stairs caught his attention. He turned, seeing his girlfriend walking down, a towel draped over her shoulders. "Phoebe."

Still dripping from her swim, she smiled innocently. "What are you two doing down here?"

"Problems with the early harvest. I'll be up in a minute."

"Hurry," she said. "I don't want to eat breakfast alone." She gave a bit of a pout, but headed back up.

Ilya waited until she disappeared. "Do you think she heard anything?"

"If she did, she's not privy to enough to know what it is we were talking about."

"Never underestimate a woman's power of observation. Especially if it's something she thinks she can use for her advantage."

Adrian looked back at the stairs, glad to see she was no longer in sight. Even so, he lowered his voice. "Back to the more pressing matter. What are we going to do about the escaped hostages?"

"As of now, nothing. We continue with the story that they were targeted by pirates for ransom. The woman comes from a very wealthy family. It stands to reason she'd be targeted."

"Except she escaped and knows pirates had nothing to do with it. They'll come looking for me."

"Not necessarily. Your name was never mentioned, you were nowhere near the *Mirage*—" He nodded toward the top of the stairs. "*And* you have an alibi."

Adrian followed the direction of his gaze, suddenly glad that Phoebe was there. For the first time since Ilya had called him about the escape, he dared to hope that things might work out after all. "Exactly how are you planning to make sure this doesn't fall on me?"

"Because the guard who was overpowered is now dead. I needed someone to blame if the hostages survived that boat crash."

"That's your plan?"

The man's face remained impassive as he stared out at the water. Finally, he looked at Adrian. "Have I ever given you cause to worry?"

He wouldn't have survived this long if not for Ilya's efficiency. "No, but I'm this close to having everything pulled out from under me. I don't need this added stress."

"Speaking of, have you heard anything from your parents' attorney?"

"Not yet."

"Maybe they've changed their minds."

"Even if they have, once they get word about this, it's over."

"I have a plan for that, too."

Adrian pulled himself up straight, took a deep breath, and looked over at him. "Do tell."

CHAPTER EIGHTEEN

Two days later . . .

Y ou're not going to like this," Rube said to Sam when he'd called to update him on the case. "The Kyrils are insisting that their yacht was overtaken by pirates, and that the person they'd hired as caretaker probably facilitated the kidnapping."

"What a ridiculous lie." Sam looked over at Remi and Dimitris. Both stood on the dock, Dimitris instructing Remi on how to use a throwing knife. They took turns tossing it so that it landed point-down in one of the wood planks. The object, apparently, was to move the knife one plank forward with each throw. Remi was starting to get the hang of it. "Did anyone talk to this caretaker?"

"Apparently, he was killed when the kidnappers made their escape."

"So, the only witness to the Kyrils' claim is conveniently dead? Considering we left everyone very much alive, I'd like to know how he supposedly died."

"The Kyrils," Rube said, ignoring the obvious, "have no knowledge of the kidnapping and are cooperating completely with the authorities. They are, however, taking responsibility for not doing a thorough background check on the caretaker. They'd like to formally apologize to both Remi and Dimitris for anything that happened due to their oversight."

"No one actually believes this, do they?"

"Between you and me? I expect they have too many friends in high places, and without hard evidence, this case isn't going anywhere."

"So what happens now?"

"Formally, we add a supplemental to what we have on file, let the local authorities handle it, and move on. It's out of our jurisdiction. Now that your friends are out of danger, and it isn't a national security issue, it goes to the bottom of the pile."

"That's it? They get away with it?"

"I know you don't want to hear this, Fargo, but maybe it's time to call it a day. Return to the States and get on with your lives."

As much as Sam had tried to convince Remi to leave, she had already made it clear that she planned on staying until the police had made an arrest. "I'm not sure that'll go over well."

"Regardless, there's nothing much any of you can do."

"Let's say I decide to do some digging on my own. Any suggestions on how best to go about it?"

"My formal suggestion? Stay far away from this group. They're dangerous." Rube paused and let out a deep sigh. "I know, I'm preaching to the choir. If you do find anything, turn it over to me. I'll add it to the file. Beyond that, I can't make any promises."

Which wasn't much help at all. "I don't suppose you have anyone on speed dial who's discreet *and* can help with some under-the-table research?"

"I might know a few people. Let me check with a couple of my associates. If I come across someone, I'll contact you."

"Thanks, Rube. Appreciate it."

After ending the call, he walked over to Remi and Dimitris. They were about six planks into their game. On Remi's next turn, the knife landed but didn't stick, the blade skittering past its intended mark. "*So close!*" She looked up at Sam as she retrieved it. "What'd your friend say?"

"His first suggestion is to pack up and go home."

She handed the knife to Dimitris, waiting for him to take his turn—a solid hit—before asking, "Why would we do that?"

"To start, it's safer."

Remi glanced over at him, then back to the game, throwing the knife. This time, it actually stuck. "Ha!"

"See?" Dimitris said. "You just needed a little *oomph* behind it. Try it again."

She did. When it stuck with a solid *thwack*, she walked over, pulled it up, then returned to Sam's side. "That can't be all you talked about."

"The Kyrils are blaming the kidnapping on pirates who were given access to the boat by their now-dead caretaker."

"Dead caretaker? You know they're lying."

He eyed the weapon she held. "To be clear, I'm in complete agreement with you. Rube, however, suggests that we return to the States."

"Exactly what my father said," she said, handing the knife to Dimitris.

"In this case, I agree. You should probably go home."

"Me? I thought you said we? I can't just up and go home. Would *you* go home if this happened to you?"

"No, but that's different."

She crossed her arms, her green eyes narrowing. "Why?"

What could he say? He had a feeling she was expecting him to point out the obvious answer, that she was a woman and he a man.

But that wasn't what he'd been thinking at all. Nor had it anything to do with the very real answer that, because of his training at DARPA, he was better suited to remain behind and look into things.

The truth, though, was nothing close to that.

While he wouldn't call it love at first sight, he'd definitely describe it as pretty damned sure—not that he was about to announce that fact. And that knowledge made him terrified that if anything happened to her, he'd never forgive himself. "I work better by myself," he blurted to avoid the truth. That sounded lame even to him. Clearly, he was turning into a lovesick puppy.

Remi crossed her arms. "*I* was the one kidnapped. Not you. I'm staying. *You're* welcome to go home."

"Don't forget, you called me."

"Please. It wasn't like I expected you to personally show up. We had things under control."

"What were you planning to do? Hold the guard hostage with the toenail clippers? The attack on me with a case of soda cans didn't exactly work."

"A shame we didn't hit you harder."

"Hard enough."

"Regardless, we would've come up with a solid Plan B. Right, Dimitris?"

Dimitris pulled the knife from the plank and handed it to Remi. "I think I'll check on my father. Let you two work things out."

Remi ignored him, her attention on Sam. "I'm not leaving."

Sam could almost see her mind racing as though she couldn't help what she was saying and knew he was right. She'd wanted him to show up. They didn't have things under control. There was no Plan B.

Sam broke into her thoughts. "There's got to be some way we can resolve this."

She held up the knife. "A game of planks. Person who wins decides if I stay or go."

"You're sure you want to decide it this way?"

"Positive. You're the one who should worry. When it comes to things with a target, I'm pretty good."

"You just learned how to play."

"I've had half a deck to warm up." She held the blade toward him.

Sam didn't move. "I'm not throwing a knife to decide something this important."

"Worried you might lose, Fargo?" For all her bravado, she couldn't hide the vulnerability in her eyes.

He took the knife. But instead of the plank, he aimed for the pylon about eighteen feet away. It hit. "You were saying?"

Remi watched the handle vibrating from the impact. "How about a game of rock, paper, scissors?"

Sam just stared at her, wondering how anyone could be so confusing. But before he could say anything, Nikos came storming out of the house, Dimitris right behind him.

"My son tells me that the Kyrils are denying that they're behind his kidnapping. Is this true?"

"It is," Sam said. "At least, according to my friend who works for the CIA."

"How do they believe these lies?" Nikos's dark eyes narrowed. "I'll go after Adrian Kyril myself to get the truth."

"Not without me," Dimitris said.

"Me too." Remi looked at Sam. Whatever vulnerability he'd seen earlier was now shuttered. "Are you in? You don't really want to leave the three of us to fend for ourselves?"

CHAPTER NINETEEN

Sam looked at each of them in turn, Nikos, Dimitris, Remi. "If any of you had any idea the sort of danger you might encounter—"

"Considering what Dimitris and I went through, I think we do."

He doubted that very much. But seeing the determination in their eyes made him realize that if left to their own devices, they were likely to go after Adrian on their own. He'd never forgive himself if anything happened to any of them. "Fine. We go together. As long as we do it my way."

"Really?" Remi said, a smile forming on her lips.

"Why are you so surprised?"

"I was afraid you'd say no."

"If I had, would it have made a difference?"

"No." Then, just as quickly, Remi said, "Okay, Fargo, what's our next move?"

"I think our best bet is to do a little armchair recon. I'll lay odds that they've already made sure any evidence left on their yacht is long gone. Let's do our research on the Kyrils. Remi, you start on-line. Niko, Dimitris, hit up any sort of town archives or records you can find."

The web was filled with article after article on the Kyril family, their olive oil exporting business, and how much they constantly donated to the community from their family charity.

After a couple of hours, Remi closed the lid on her laptop. "If I read one more story on how much the people in Greece love the Kyrils, I'm likely to toss this thing across the room."

Nikos shook his head. "I've lived here my entire life. For as long as I can remember, that family has ingratiated themselves into the community. The Kyrils can do no wrong. They might as well be gods living on Olympus."

"What we need," Remi said, "is to find their Achilles' heel."

Sam, who'd been using one of the foundation's computers, leaned back in his chair as he studied the picture of the Kyrils' cliffside home. "What about a trip to this island? If we're lucky, one of the locals will know something."

Nikos piloted the *Asteri* to Patmos, a two-hour boat drive from Fourni. He motored along the west side of the island, then slowed, pointing. "That is Adrian Kyril's villa."

Sam aimed his binoculars, focusing on the spectacular cliff-top home. A boat dock at water level was secured with an iron gate. One could take a lift up to the house, or take the stairs cut into the cliff. From what he could see, there were three levels. The lowest was a manicured garden, the middle was one long patio with a row of lounge chairs for sunbathing, and the third an infinity pool set in front of a two-story house with floor-to-ceiling windows facing the Aegean.

"That family," Sam said, handing the binoculars to Remi, "has some serious money."

She peered through the glasses, then nodded. "That is truly beautiful, except for the one . . . no, three guards patroling."

Sam studied the layout. "Whether we come in by boat or by land, we're going to have a hard time getting into that villa without being seen."

Dimitris pointed to the north of the house. "What if we came in from the side? The neighbor's villa?"

Sam shook his head. The cliff jutted out between both properties, creating a natural rock barrier. "I'd hate to try scaling something that sheer, especially at night." He signaled for Nikos to motor past. The last thing they needed was to be spotted by one of Kyril's guards, especially while piloting the same boat that Dimitris and Remi were kidnapped from.

Back at the Fourni archeological office, they returned to the computers. Nikos asked, "If you managed to get into his house, what exactly would you be looking for?"

"That, my friend, is a very good question." Sam continued looking at the villa. "Those people went to a lot of trouble to make sure Remi and Dimitris didn't escape. We need to find out why. The question is how."

"You're not thinking of breaking in, are you?" Remi asked.

"Only as a last resort."

"I'm not sure that's a good idea. What if you get caught? In a foreign country? There's got to be a way to get in legally."

"I can't think of any offhand."

"Door-to-door sales? Pretending to take a survey? Something."

"First and foremost, it's got to be safe," he said as his phone buzzed with a text message. "It's Rube . . . 'Selma Wondrash' . . . ?"

"Who?"

"Apparently . . . " He read the text. "Someone who works for the Library of Congress's Special Collections Directorate. I asked him for the name of a good researcher."

"Researching what?" she asked.

"The Kyrils."

CHAPTER TWENTY

Sam called the number Rube had provided. "Ms. Wondrash? A mutual acquaintance, Rubin Haywood, recommended you as someone who was good at tracking down obscure information."

"Research is a particular passion of mine," she said, her Hungarian accent thick. "What is it you are hoping to learn, Mr. Fargo?"

"I'm looking for any and all information you can find on someone named Adrian Kyril. Rich businessman, based out of Greece."

He heard the rapid click of a keyboard in the background as she said, "Olive oil exporter. Lives on the island of Patmos in Greece. And you need this information for?"

"He kidnapped some friends of mine—they're fine—but we're worried he may come after them again. I need to find some way to get close to him. Bonus points if I can find a *legal* way to get into his house," he added, feeling Remi's gaze on him. "About payment."

The keyboard clicking stopped. A moment later, she said, "Twenty dollars an hour. So far, you owe me thirty-three cents."

"Pardon?"

"Adrian Kyril is hosting a fundraiser for underprivileged youth in two days at his villa. Casino Couples Night. Tickets are seventy-five hundred for singles, and ten thousand for couples."

"I'll have to get back to you on that."

"Let me know."

He disconnected, telling them what Selma had discovered.

Remi looked suitably impressed. "Do you realize that I spent two hours on that computer and came up with nothing? Whoever she is, you should keep her on speed dial."

"That still doesn't get us in the door."

She took a deep breath. "I could ask my parents for the money."

The hesitant look in her green eyes bothered him. "What aren't you telling me?"

"Nothing, really," she said, making him think it was quite the opposite. "Except that, after the kidnapping, my parents have suddenly become overprotective."

"Understandable."

"Let's just say that they're very good at getting things their way."

"Apparently that runs in the family." He was glad to see the spark return to her eyes. "But asking them won't be necessary."

"But, Sam . . . you . . ." Remi started.

Sam quickly said, "I've got my slush fund for just such occasions."

"This fundraiser," Nikos said. "Even if we do get the money, do you think that's a good option? It might be dangerous. Perhaps we should rethink this."

Sam, hoping Remi would be amenable to calling the whole thing off, since it was someone else suggesting it, said, "Good point. We don't know what to expect."

"But," she said, "it'll be worth every penny if it gets to the truth."

"It'll be cheaper if I go alone," he said, deciding to give one more shot at talking her out of going.

Remi's expression turned skeptical. "Have you ever *been* to a high-ticket fundraiser?"

"Never. But I have done my share of required dinners in D.C."

"Well, then you know, walking in as a couple will be far less noticeable. Especially when at least one of them speaks Greek." She smiled, trying to calm the waters. But she couldn't help herself. "Of course, you're welcome to take Nikos or Dimitris as your date."

As much as he didn't want her anywhere close to that house, she presented an almost indisputable argument on why she was the right choice. A couple *would* blend into the background far better than a single man. "What do you think, Nikos?"

"I agree, going together may be the best way to get in."

Sam called Selma back, saying, "Two tickets, please."

"Under what name?"

He looked at Remi. "I suppose we should pose as husband and wife?"

"Quick courtship?" A spark of amusement lit her green eyes. "Sure."

"Sam and Remi Fargo," he said into the phone.

Again, the rapid keyboard clicking, then, "Credit card?"

Sam reached into his pocket and read the numbers to Selma.

"Anything else, Mr. Fargo?"

"You could call me Sam . . ."

"I'll email you the tickets as soon as they come through."

"Thank you."

"Glad to help, Mr. Fargo. Call if you need anything else."

"How to arrive?" Remi asked as he texted Rube with an update. "We can't take this boat. They'll recognize it."

"I have another cousin," Nikos said, "who owns a water taxi. We can use that to drive you in."

"Looks like we have everything we need," Sam said.

"Except clothes," Remi replied. "You'll need a tux. And shoes. The whole nine yards."

"What about you, Remi?" Dimitris asked.

Thinking back to those strappy shoes and that evening dress hanging in the bungalow closet, Sam said, "Oh, don't worry about Remi. She doesn't travel light. She has all her bases covered, packs for every occasion."

She opened up a website on her phone. "Here you go, Fargo."

He looked at the price, then whistled. One rental tuxedo was by Versace, the other was Ralph Lauren. Where was Jos. A. Bank? Regardless of which one he picked, he'd have to buy the patent leather shoes, dress shirt, and cuff link and stud set. "At least they throw in the bow tie."

"That bow tie is awful. We'll have to buy one," Remi added. "It's the little things that can't be overlooked."

Sam rolled his eyes skyward. "That'll put a pretty good dent into the slush fund."

"Half the battle of getting past the gatekeepers is looking the part."

Two days later, Sam dressed in his rented tux, a Ralph Lauren white double-breasted dinner jacket with a shawl collar, and waited for Remi. When she finally emerged from her room, he stared for several seconds. Her refined elegance, while always there no matter what she wore, shone with a particular brilliance in its simplicity. The hanger certainly hadn't done the dress justice: an understated, floor-length black gown, with red strap stiletto heels peeking out, and a red envelope purse with a rhinestone clasp. "You look amazing."

Her smile reminded him of the first night they'd met. "Thank you."

He held up his bow tie. "I did try."

"Why is it men can never manage to tie their own bow ties?" With a sigh and a few flips of her wrist, it was perfect. "Time to go, double-oh-seven. We've got some super-sleuthing to do."

CHAPTER TWENTY-ONE

Sam and Remi rode to the villa in the water taxi, with Nikos at the helm and Dimitris hidden from view. Between them, the only weapon they had was the throwing knife hidden in Remi's purse.

Before they left, Sam had gone over every eventuality that might come up, including having father and son waiting in the taxi on the other side of the inlet, out of sight of the cliff-top house—just in case anything went wrong. As Nikos motored toward the short pier, Sam repeated the most important direction. "Remember. Three hours."

Nikos nodded. "If you're not back, we call your CIA friend."

Sam helped Remi from the boat, then took her arm in his as they crossed the dock toward the two burly doormen stationed at the arched entry beyond the gate. One of them checked his clipboard as Sam handed over paper tickets printed from the email that Selma had sent.

The man said something in Greek, welcoming them, then handed each a small velvet bag from the basket on the table next to him, while the other opened the massive wood door that led into an arched stone tunnel.

"Our chips for the gaming tables," Remi said as they entered. They walked across a red Turkish carpet that absorbed their footsteps as they passed through the tunnel to the lift that whisked them up to the top level, where the fundraiser was being held.

When the lift door opened, they stepped out onto a tiled patio. Guests mingled around various tables set up between the house and an infinity pool that overlooked the Aegean Sea. Lights strung overhead added to the festive appearance, as did the soft classical Greek music being played by a small ensemble. Uniformed waiters carrying trays of chilled champagne and ouzo approached as Sam and Remi made their way from the elevator to the party.

Sam took two flutes, handing one to Remi as they made the rounds.

She looked over at him, her expression unreadable. "Shall we start with roulette?"

"Roulette it is."

They paused by each table, playing a game or two, all so Remi could listen in on conversations, while Sam took in the lay of the villa. The ground-floor level of the house was open to the guests, the massive floor-to-ceiling glass doors opened wide so that they could come and go from a lounge that faced the pool and the sea view. The upper levels, with the main living quarters, were dark, and the staircases on either side of the vast patio and pool deck were blocked off with velvet rope barriers guarded by broad-shouldered men wearing earpieces.

No doubt in Sam's mind that they were carrying guns beneath the jackets of their impeccable suits.

The soft strains of the classical Greek music stopped, and a moment later, a man's voice sounded. Sam looked around, seeing a large group gathering in front of the pool house. He and Remi wandered up to the edge of the crowd, though neither could see who was speaking.

Several people applauded.

"What's he saying?" Sam asked Remi.

"He's talking about the charity and telling everyone to enjoy the night."

As the applause died, the group parted, revealing the speaker, a man in his early thirties, his dark hair slicked back, his goatee trimmed short.

Remi's breath caught. "I've seen him before."

"Where?"

"The morning we were kidnapped. I saw him in my telephoto lens standing with some other men . . ."

A passing waiter stopped in front of them, holding a tray of stuffed grape leaves. "*Dolmades?*"

Remi declined. Sam took one, biting into the cold, herbed rice hors d'oeuvre, tasting lemon and fennel.

"Excuse me," Remi asked the waiter. "Who is the gentleman?"

He glanced in that direction. "Adrian Kyril."

Sam waited until he left, saying, "No doubt Adrian Kyril Jr. A little young to be the patriarch we were reading about."

"He has to be behind the theft of my camera from the boat. That's the only explanation. Especially considering we were kidnapped a few hours later."

"What were the photos of?"

"Nothing memorable. Birds, landscape. The memory card. I changed it right after I saw them."

"Do you still have it?"

"It was in my pocket when they took us aboard the *Mirage*. As far as I know, it ended up at the bottom of the Aegean after our mummy dive."

"I'd say either you caught a photo of something he didn't want you to see, or they think you did."

"Certainly the obvious answer, but of what? They were just standing there."

"Maybe Adrian Sr. was telling the truth. He really *didn't* know anything about the kidnapping. Junior, on the other hand." Sam watched the man a few moments more. "Let's hope he doesn't make the connection, should you two cross paths tonight."

"I'll definitely avoid him," she said as Adrian set the microphone on the table, shook hands with a few nearby guests, then started walking directly at them.

Worried that he might recognize Remi after all, Sam drew her to him, leaned down, putting his mouth to her ear. He was captivated by her warmth, the scent of her hair and the desire to never let her go. He whispered, "I swear there's a good reason for this."

She wrapped an arm around his shoulders, pulling herself tight against him, wishing they were anywhere else. "I'll bet you say that to all the girls you help rescue from kidnappers' yachts."

"Every one of them."

Adrian continued past, stopping when one of the men wearing an earpiece approached him, holding out an envelope. The billionaire's son looked around, clearly concerned about who might see him. As his glance rested on Sam, Sam lifted Remi's chin, kissing her. The man's gaze swept past, and he slipped the envelope into his pocket, dismissed the guard, then crossed the patio toward the south staircase.

Reluctantly, they separated and Sam led Remi to the craps table, telling her what he'd seen. They positioned themselves with a view of the stairs, Sam saying, "Whatever was in that envelope, he seemed anxious to get rid of it."

Within moments, a light went on in the second-story window to their left. Less than a minute later, it darkened again. When Adrian appeared on the stairs, the guard held aside the velvet rope at the bottom, allowing him to pass. Remi pulled a few chips from her bag, pretending interest in the game. "What do you suppose that was all about?"

"I have no idea. But I'm definitely curious. Are you sure you can avoid him while I get upstairs?"

She looked around, nodding. "There's enough people here to stay lost in the crowd."

He put his hand on the small of her back, looking her in the eye. "No matter what, do *not* go up. If anything happens to me, get out, find Nikos and Dimitris."

"Got it. Stay here, go for help if anything happens."

"Promise me."

She looked up at him and smiled. "Promise."

He leaned down and gave her the swiftest of kisses. After leaving his untouched champagne flute on a tray, he wandered toward the staircase, grateful to see the guard had moved off to deal with some unknown incident. Sam was about to slip past the rope barrier when two men in tuxedos walked toward him. One said something to him in Greek.

"Sorry," Sam said. "American."

"What are you doing here?"

"Looking for a bathroom."

"This way." One of the men indicated Sam should follow, then led him to the pool house.

"Thank you," Sam said. As soon as the man took off, Sam returned to the stairs, hoping something would draw the guard's attention, allowing him to get by. Prepared to linger in the shadows for as long as it took, he was surprised when Remi approached the guard herself. She said something, laughed, then motioned the guard closer, pointing at the gaming tables. With the man's gaze diverted, Sam slipped past the rope barrier, then up the stairs, grateful the door leading into the left wing was still ajar.

He walked through a foyer, then down the darkened hallway, stopping in front of the third door on the left. He pulled a pick set out, a souvenir from his covert op training at Camp Peary. Within a few seconds, he was in, closing the door behind him. Moving to the window, he parted a curtain, looking down at the veranda below. Remi was back at the craps table. Adrian was deep in conversation with two men at the roulette table. Dropping the curtain, he turned back to the room, headed to start his search at the carved mahogany writing desk facing the door. There was only one drawer, locked. He teased the pick in and out until the pins lined up, turned the tension wrench, then pulled it open.

No envelope.

What he did find, however, put the Kyril fortune into a whole new light.

CHAPTER TWENTY-TWO

Remi placed a bet, then positioned herself with a clear view of the window, all the while feigning interest in the game as the man next to her rolled the dice.

"Eleven!" He looked over at her, grinning. "Shall we let it ride?"

She was about to reply, when she glanced over, shocked to see two of Kyril's herculean guards heading toward the same staircase Sam had taken. One of them touched his ear, as though listening through an earpiece, at the same time looking up at the second level. The third window, she saw, was still dark. Even so, those two men looked way too interested. Worried Sam might run into them on the way out—or worse yet, they might catch him up there—she took her phone from her purse and started to text him.

On their way u

Someone in the crowd knocked the phone from her hand before she finished the text. The device skittered across the tiles. When she tried to retrieve it, a man bent down, picked it up, and blocked her path.

Adrian Kyril.

Her heart skipped a beat. She froze, praying he wouldn't look at the phone screen—or recognize her.

He smiled, his white teeth gleaming against his tanned skin as he held it out. "*Kuria*, I believe this is yours."

Recovering, she gave an embarrassed laugh. "Thank you. I was in a bit of a hurry."

His dark eyes held hers. "Do I know you?"

"I don't think so," she said, then leaned in slightly, whispering, "I really do need to find the ladies' room."

"That way," he replied, nodding at the open pool house to the right of the staircase. The two guards had just started up.

"Thank you." She made a beeline to the pool house, sending the text as she walked. The moment she saw Kyril's attention diverted, she changed paths, stepping around the rope barrier, then up the stairs. At the top level, the door was ajar.

She slipped in, her footfalls cushioned by a thick Oriental rug as she entered the foyer behind the guards, who had just started down the hall. "Sam?" she called out in a loud voice.

The two men turned and saw her. "Who are you?" one of them asked.

She smiled, placing her hand on her heart. "I'm so sorry. I seem to have lost my husband. I think he's had *far* too much to drink."

"You shouldn't be up here."

"Yes. I know. I'm just not sure *he* knows." She gave a dramatic sigh, hoping Sam was within hearing distance and taking her warning. "He's probably sleeping it off somewhere, but I'm still worried."

They exchanged glances, one of them saying something she couldn't hear. He then looked directly at Remi, saying, "Guests are not allowed—"

A loud noise from the hallway—something Remi could only describe as a mix between a pig's oink and a goose's honk—caught them by surprise. Both men slipped their right hands beneath their jackets as they pivoted around, prepared to draw.

They relaxed their stance, one of them turning to Remi, asking, "Your husband?"

She peered down the hallway, seeing Sam slumped against the wall, his eyes closed, his legs sprawled out in front of him. He snored softly as one of the guards walked up to him, kicking his foot. "Get up!"

"I knew it," Remi said, marching over and inserting herself in front of the guards. She bent over, opening her purse with one hand, patting Sam's cheek with the other.

He opened his eyes, mumbling unintelligibly.

Remi tried to slip him the knife but couldn't when the guard moved beside her. Instead, she took Sam's hand, helping him to his feet. "I thought we agreed you weren't going to drink any more tonight."

He gave a lopsided smile as he staggered alongside her toward the door. "I only had . . . Don't 'member . . ."

"Let's get you back to the hotel. You can sleep it off there."

Unfortunately, as they neared the door, the nonplussed guards regained their senses and started to follow. "Wait!"

Sam put his hand on his stomach, leaning forward. "I—I don't feel so good."

"Don't get sick in here," Remi said, grateful to see his theatrics had the desired effect. The guards had stopped in their tracks. She led Sam out, then closed the door behind them.

"That was close," Sam said as they hurried toward the stairs.

The moment they turned the corner, she saw a tall, stocky man with dark curly hair standing near the stairs. He turned around, his gaze hitting Remi.

Fayez, one of the kidnappers, she realized.

He immediately dismissed her as any sort of threat. Instead, he reached for his gun, his attention on Sam. Remi, still holding the knife, opened the blade, then threw it. It hit the wall behind Fayez, clattering onto the tiles at his feet.

He looked down, surprised, then at her. In the second of distraction, Sam stepped forward, blasted his fist against Fayez's face. His head bounced back against the wall and he slumped to the ground.

Sam grabbed Remi's hand. "We've got to work on your knife skills," he said, leading her down the stairs.

"Which way?"

"The elevator down to the boat dock." Sam took out his phone, sending a text to Nikos as they walked.

They were halfway across the patio when the elevator door opened and two men stepped off. "Slight problem," Remi said, recognizing one of them. "That's Ilya. One of the kidnappers."

"Roulette table," Sam said. "Get lost in the crowd."

Too late. Ilya saw her, then motioned for a couple of his men to move toward them. To make matters worse, the two guards who'd nearly caught Sam in Adrian's office came down the stairs, found Adrian on the other side of the gaming tables, then pointed in their direction. Remi moved closer to Sam. "What now?"

"Stay calm," he said. "There's a lot of witnesses. I doubt Kyril will do anything stupid." Unfortunately, the partygoers were more interested in their gambling than anything that was happening on the periphery. No one seemed to notice when Kyril's men started moving in on Sam and Remi, effectively cutting off their escape by backing them into the corner of the patio near the table where Adrian had made his announcement earlier that night.

Kyril approached, eyeing Remi, then focusing on Sam. "My men tell me you were found in my private quarters. What were you doing up there?"

"Made a wrong turn," Sam said. "I was looking for the men's room."

"Take them down to the dock. You know what to do."

Remi, worried that once they were out of sight of the guests, they'd have little chance of escape, glanced behind her, saw the microphone on the table. She grabbed it, turned it on, and in Greek, said, "Thank you so much, Adrian Kyril. Is everyone having a good time?"

There was applause.

The guards hesitated, realizing that their group was now the center of attention.

"We're so glad to hear it," Remi continued as she and Sam edged their way around the table. "Please, everyone, take a moment and personally thank Mr. Kyril for this wonderful work he's doing on behalf of the children. And Adrian. If you can give us a few words on what else you have planned?"

More applause as she held out the microphone. The ensemble stopped playing.

Without missing a beat, Adrian took the microphone and waved to the crowd.

The moment he did, Sam clasped Remi's hand, whispering, "This way."

With the guests watching, and the guards momentarily at a standstill with all the undue interest focused in their direction, Sam pressed Remi's elbow, leading her across the patio, hoping to take the stairs all the way down to the dock. Unfortunately, when they reached the lower level, two guards appeared on the stairs below, blocking their exit.

"To the right," Sam said. Remi kicked off her shoes and hiked up her dress as they raced past a row of lounge chairs lined up along the patio to a small retainer wall built along the cliffside. Sam hopped up, then helped her to the overhang on the other side. He looked down, then at her. "You ever see *Butch Cassidy and the Sundance Kid?*"

She peered over the edge at the water below. "You couldn't have picked a different movie? One with a less *ambiguous* ending?"

"I thought it worked," he said, glancing back at the guards.

"We don't even know if they *lived* after they jumped."

"We don't know they died, either."

"There're rocks down there."

"Try to miss them."

She took a step back. "I don't think I can do this."

"Do you trust me?"

She hesitated, then grasped his outstretched hand. "Yes."

A gunshot rang out as they leaped.

CHAPTER TWENTY-THREE

When Adrian saw Sam Fargo and the woman jumping from the cliff, he was close to ordering Ilya to shoot them. Had it not been for the crowd around him, he would have. The majority of guests had found their way to the glass balcony and were leaning over, watching as Fargo surfaced, then swam toward the woman, who was struggling from the weight of her dress.

Just when Adrian was hopeful she'd drown, Fargo pulled her free, and she was able to take a deep breath.

One of the guards raised his gun, ready to take a shot.

"Witnesses," Adrian said to Ilya under his breath.

"Hold your fire," Ilya radioed.

Adrian turned back to his guests, smiling broadly as he raised his hands. "I hope you've enjoyed our extra entertainment!"

The guests hesitated, their gazes straying out to the water as a motorboat sped in and plucked the two from the sea. Laughter rippled through the crowd. Someone signaled the ensemble to start playing, and within minutes they turned back to their gaming.

Relieved, Adrian told Ilya to meet him upstairs in ten minutes, then made a leisurely circle around the tables, stopping to talk, making sure to appear amused at the recent turn of events.

By the time Adrian arrived in his office, Ilya had the video surveillance ready for viewing. He pulled out his chair and sat. "Tell me it's not as bad as we think."

"He didn't get into the safe," Ilya said.

"What *did* he get into?"

"I'll let you see for yourself . . ." He started the video.

Adrian watched, furious at how quickly this Sam Fargo had gotten past his guards, and into his office, by picking the lock. "What do we know about this man?" he asked Ilya, who stood behind him.

"Not a lot. He bought two tickets originating from a computer in the U.S. But seeing this and knowing what my guard observed the night he rescued our hostages, it's clear he's had military training."

Adrian replayed the video, trying to determine the man's purpose. He was definitely searching for something. "What about the woman? What do we know about her?"

"Remi Longstreet. Other than another American, nothing that we've been able to find."

"Except that she made fools of all of us. She was your prisoner for two days. How is it you didn't know she spoke Greek?"

"As far as we knew, she only spoke English. The man with her translated everything. Even so, we took precautions."

"Precautions? What's that supposed to mean?"

"We spoke in Italian around her and the other prisoner."

Adrian took a deep breath, then blew it out slowly, telling himself he was getting worked up over something that was out of his control. This, though . . . He watched Sam Fargo moving about his office. The multiscreen surveillance showed him stepping out into the hallway, pretending to be asleep, while his fool guards walked with the woman. The fact that they fell for such a ruse sent his blood pressure rising again—and he was actually grateful when someone knocked on the door. "Come in."

One of his men entered. "Sorry to disturb you. You wanted to know as soon as your parents got here. They're downstairs."

Adrian tensed.

"Don't worry," he said, seeing Adrian's reaction. "They missed the disturbance."

"I'll be right down." The moment the door closed behind him, Adrian hit play, this time paying particular attention as Fargo went through his desk.

Ilya leaned closer. "What's he looking at?"

Adrian pulled open the file drawer, approximating which folder he'd removed. Not that it mattered. All of these folders belonged to the olive orchards. When his gaze lit on the profit and loss statements, he hesitated. "Why would Fargo be looking into our olive oil business?"

"Crime of opportunity?"

"Maybe . . ." He returned his gaze to the monitor as Fargo looked up suddenly, replaced the folder, and quickly left the office. On another screen, the redhead was busy distracting his guards, allowing Fargo to slip out, then pretend to be sleeping on the floor in the hall.

Having seen enough, Adrian shoved his chair back. "Do whatever it takes to find those two."

"Of course." Ilya shut off the monitor. Adrian was halfway out the door when he added, "Good luck."

"I'm sure there's nothing to worry about." But even Adrian didn't believe the lie.

He found his parents holding court near the roulette table. His mother, her brown hair in an elaborate French twist, wore a sapphire-blue gown. She offered a small smile as he approached. His father, he noted, refused to meet his gaze.

"Adrian," his mother said, turning her cheek to him. "A lovely party. I'm assuming you've received the letter from our attorney?"

"I haven't yet had the opportunity to read it," he said as they walked toward the edge of the patio, away from the other guests. Knowing what it probably contained, he hadn't dared.

She sighed as she turned to her husband. "Darling. Can you get me a glass of champagne?"

He looked relieved to be given the errand.

The moment he left, she rounded on Adrian. "What on earth were you thinking?"

"About what?"

"This business on the *Mirage*."

"Perhaps this isn't the best place to discuss the matter."

She smiled at a passing waiter, ignoring the offer of an appetizer. The moment he was out of earshot she said, "You're putting the entire family name at risk. I won't allow that to happen."

"It's not what you think."

"Then what is it?"

"An investment opportunity."

"Let's hope it's a good one. As of today your name has been removed from the board."

"Mother, please—"

"I love you, Adrian. But I'm not about to lose everything because of your carelessness. If your father were healthier, he'd be the one telling you this."

"Not likely."

"I'm not without heart," she continued. "I've deposited one hundred thousand euros in your account."

It was everything he could do to maintain his composure as he processed her words. "That wouldn't last me a month."

"Then I suggest you make adjustments and spend it wisely." She started to walk off, stopped, turning back to him. "Since it seems you couldn't be troubled to read the letter my attorney sent you, I'll paraphrase. Should I or your father meet an untimely death, the bulk of our fortune will go to charity—well, except for the trust we've set up for Phoebe's child. Whether or not she sticks around is anyone's guess."

"What child?"

"Perhaps you should ask her about that." She sighed, then gave a patronizing smile. "A shame. I had such high hopes for you."

CHAPTER TWENTY-FOUR

Did you find anything worthwhile?" Nikos asked Sam once they were safe, back at his cousin's home.

"I did. Problem is, I'm just not sure how it'll help us."

The three waited.

"The Kyrils have been exporting low-grade olive oil as extra virgin."

"That's it?" Remi said. "We jumped off a cliff for that?"

Dimitris sank back in his chair. "What good will that do?"

"Nothing, yet," Sam replied. "I did notice a couple of names figuring heavy in the books. Hydra Containers and Heibert Lines. When we get back I'll email what I remember to Selma and see if she can find anything. In the meantime, maybe something will come to me in the middle of the night."

Unfortunately, nothing did. The four sat around the table the next morning, drinking strong Greek coffee over the remains of their breakfast, while discussing what to do with the information that Sam had found. "The Kyrils," Sam said, "have been duping the public for a hefty profit. In a business where reputation is everything, theirs could be ruined in an instant, should it get out."

"How do you know this?" Nikos asked.

"I saw the doctored accounting books in Adrian's office. Even if they're importing olives from somewhere else, based on their harvest and their first press last year, they couldn't possibly export the amount of extra virgin oil that they've listed."

Remi gave a frustrated sigh. "But we knew they were crooked. There's got to be something more that we're overlooking. And what about that envelope that Adrian received?"

"That, I don't know."

"Still," Nikos said, "Sam is right. Maybe they can explain away the kidnapping by blaming it on pirates—"

"For now," Sam said, thinking about Ilya's presence on the boat and at the party. Unfortunately, it was Remi's and Dimitris's word against the Kyrils'.

"For now," Nikos echoed. "But their reputation is everything—their name synonymous with quality olive oil. They wouldn't want that to get out. So why not turn that against them? Maybe we can use this olive oil business to show the police that the Kyrils aren't the Olympus gods everyone believes them to be." He gave Sam an expectant look. "You have proof, I assume? You took pictures with your phone?"

"Unfortunately, there wasn't time." Even if there had been, his phone wasn't waterproof.

"Back to square one," Remi said.

"Maybe not. Let me email everything to Selma. Who knows what that might turn up?"

"How does inferior olive oil, my stolen camera, and our kidnapping all connect?" Remi asked.

"Considering Adrian must think you saw him that morning, I'd say the theft of your camera is more than likely connected. Any idea what the missing photos were of?"

She stared into her coffee cup a moment, then looked up at him. "I was trying to get a shot of the birds. Something startled them and they all took off . . ."

"Something Kyril and his men were doing?" he asked.

"After, I remember thinking they probably set the birds to flight. But if so, it definitely wasn't anything obvious the moment I saw them." She gave a slight shrug. "As I mentioned last night, they were just standing there. I've even thought about what was on the memory card that was lost—there's not a shot on it that would explain why they came after us."

"You're sure?"

"Very. I have a near photographic memory. I can recall each of the photos I took, and none of them were of those men."

"She's right," Dimitris told Sam. "If it wasn't for the birds, we probably wouldn't have noticed them at all, they were that far away. And we left shortly after. If they were doing anything, it wasn't obvious to me, either."

"Whatever they were doing," Sam said, "it's clear they think the two of you saw or photographed *something* that they didn't want anyone to see. Maybe a field trip up there is in order. If we're lucky, we'll discover what has them so rattled."

Nikos looked up at the clock. "It'll have to be without me. I have a full crew coming in to start documenting the shipwreck."

"Are you sure it's safe for you to be out on the water?" Remi asked him. "What if Adrian Kyril's men come after you?"

"I have a hard time believing they would be so foolish as to try something again in broad daylight. Especially now that the police are aware. And if that isn't enough to dissuade them, perhaps the presence of nearly twenty divers and archeologists will make them hesitate."

Their first stop before returning to Fourni was to replace the water-damaged cell phones. Once back on Fourni, Sam, Remi, and Dimitris hiked up to the top of the hill, where Remi had stood taking photographs. The offshore breeze swept across the hilltop as they surveyed the countryside. Remi, holding her auburn hair off her face, pointed to her right. "You see that patch of junipers about halfway down the hill? That's where I saw the men."

Dimitris nodded. "And the birds flew up from there. I think if we drive around to the other side of the island, it'll be easier to get to that spot."

Sam pulled his binoculars from his backpack, focusing in on the area. From this vantage point, there wasn't much to see but the rocks and shrubs. "Let's go have a look."

They hiked down to the car, then drove to the other side of the island, having to stop for a herd of goats that crowded the road. Dimitris honked, slowly idling the car forward as the animals took their time crossing the pavement, before disappearing down the east bank in a cacophony of bleats and bells. Once past, he drove a bit farther, then pulled over, parking on the side of the road. Sam saw a number of footprints in the dirt on the side of the road, indicating several people had been there before them. He stopped the other two as they started forward.

"What's wrong?" Remi asked.

"Nothing, yet," he said, crouching down on the ground, eyeing the footprints on the trail leading up to the area. "How many people did you see?"

"Four, but then only three."

"Interesting. There're four sets of prints leading up. And look, over here, only three going back."

CHAPTER TWENTY-FIVE

Remi moved next to Sam, crouching down beside him. "Maybe one set is older."

"Maybe . . . We won't know until we get up there." He stood, moving around the outer edge of the trail. The area was a mix of low scrub and jagged stone angling up the steep hill like steps. It was slow going, but they made it to the area Remi had pointed out, recognized by the odd grouping of junipers around what at first appeared to be a level clearing of flat limestone.

"Wait here," Sam said, then moved closer on his own. He crouched beside a spindly fig tree.

The sun glared down on them, keeping her from seeing what Sam was looking at. "Did you find something?" she asked.

"Possibly an explanation as to what they were looking at." He motioned them to join him, adding, "Keep to the far right. There's a few footprints here."

She and Dimitris picked their way across the same path Sam took. When they reached his side, Remi was surprised to see a yawning, dark hole just in front of him. As she neared, she could feel the cool air coming up from the depths. "How deep do you think it is?" she asked.

Sam found a large rock and tossed it in. She heard it hit four times on the way down. "Deep enough," he said.

Dimitris seemed shocked. "I didn't know this was here."

Remi examined the footprints in the patch of dirt near the cave entrance, seeing what looked like scuff marks, as though one of the persons standing there suddenly pivoted. She stepped across a narrow gap between two rocks on the right of Dimitris, thinking it might have a better view down into the cave. The stone beneath her foot shifted, causing bits of gravel to fall into the hole. She peered down, realizing what she thought was a solid surface was anything but. "Sam . . . ?"

"*Don't* move your feet." He leaned forward, reaching out. "Take my hand."

The urgency in his voice frightened her. She grasped his fingers, her palm sticky with sweat.

"Slowly, step toward me."

She lifted her left foot, hearing more rattling as the limestone turned to sand under her weight. "You're sure it's safe to move?"

"I've got you."

Remi's throat went suddenly dry. As she moved toward him, her right foot slipped out, sending the top stone plunging down into the cave. Sam pulled her to him, wrapping his arm around her. Her heart thundered in her chest. When she was on solid ground, she looked back. The stone where she'd stood was completely gone. A coating of dust and gravel was all that was left in the space beneath.

"That was close." She turned, looking up at Sam, who was still holding her.

"You okay?" he asked.

She nodded.

"You sure?"

She nodded again, but her heart continued to beat loudly.

Finally, Dimitris, with a scuffling noise and a very loud cough, reminded Sam that they were not alone. He held Remi a moment longer, then let go. When he found solid purchase, he turned on his phone's flashlight, aiming the beam downward. It barely penetrated the darkness.

Dimitris kneeled beside him, trying to see in. "I have some gear, but Manos and Denéa are both climbers," he said. "They're out on the boat with my father. I'm sure they wouldn't mind if we borrowed some of their equipment." He nodded at the tree growing on the other side of the rocks. "We could anchor to that."

Sam looked up at the tree trunk, shaking his head. "I don't like the look of these rocks. A few too many cracks for my comfort."

"It looks solid right here." Dimitris patted the rock beneath him. "Remi's light. We could lower her down."

Remi, standing behind both men, thought about her close call, and was glad when Sam nixed that idea. "What about a video camera?" she said. "We could lower it down. Safer than tempting fate."

"That, Remi, is brilliant."

Later that afternoon, they returned with the needed equipment. Sam had managed to rig a small cage that held the camera tilted at a slight angle downward with a flashlight next to it. To keep the contraption from spinning, they attached the cage to two sixty-meter ropes, Sam on one side of the cavern entrance and Dimitris on the other. The basket hit something solid close to the fifteen-meter mark.

"Must be the bottom," Dimitris said.

They lifted the rope a few feet on each side, then moved in a clockwise circle. At one point, Remi thought she saw a flash of white, but the light moved past before she could tell what it was. Finally, they lifted the camera to the surface and removed it from the cage.

The three moved away from the opening, and sitting beneath the shade of the tree, Dimitris opened the control panel of the camera and rewound the video to the start. When he played it back, they saw the rough cave wall as the camera descended. Apparently what it hit wasn't the bottom at all, but a ledge.

"What's that?" Sam said.

"It looks like bones," Dimitris replied, confirming that Remi had indeed seen something white down there.

"No. Not that. A few seconds before."

Dimitris rewound the video and played it back.

Sam pointed to the lower left corner of the screen and Dimitris pressed stop. At first glance it didn't look like much. But Dimitris shaded the screen with his hand, then sucked in a breath. "It's a shoe. Do you think someone's down there?"

CHAPTER TWENTY-SIX

The last murder on Fourni occurred decades upon decades ago. The local police were woefully unprepared to deal with this kind of investigation. They called for the federal police, who sent out a team to recover the body from the cave. Arrangements were made to search the cave for other remains.

Sam stood off to one side as the investigating officer took a statement from Remi and then Dimitris about what they'd seen that morning on the hill. When they were finished, the three waited together as the police raised the body from the cavern, using a stretcher. Two men at the surface guided it up, then moved it away from the cave's entrance.

Dimitris froze when he saw the victim. "Tassos Gianakos."

"You know him?" one of the federal officers asked.

He nodded, unable to speak for a moment. "A friend."

Remi's hand reach for Dimitris's. "Zoe's grandfather."

Sam, seeing how upset Dimitris was, suggested to the police that they allow them to take him home. The investigators could contact them there if they needed anything further.

"Dimitris." Remi took his arm. "Let's go home."

He stood rooted to the spot, unable to pull his gaze from the dead man.

Sam took his other arm. "We should go," he said. "Let the police do their job."

The pair guided him down the hill to the road. He didn't speak, barely even seemed to be aware of his surroundings. He had a hard time understanding when Sam asked him for the keys to the car, then drove them back to Fourni. When they reached his house, Sam led him to a chair, while Remi found a bottle of ouzo. She quickly poured some in a glass, dispensing with any formalities. When he didn't take it, she set the glass on the table next to him. "Dimitris," Remi said. "Look at me. You need to talk to me."

Finally, he focused on her. "I don't understand. Why would Tassos be up there with Adrian Kyril?"

"Is it possible he knew Adrian?" she asked.

"I don't know how."

"Let me get this right," Sam said. "Tassos is Zoe's grandfather. Zoe is Dimitris's girl."

"The same," Remi said. A moment later they heard someone at the door. It burst open. A young woman stood there, her face a mixture of shock and grief. Her gaze landed on Dimitris.

"Zoe," he said, standing.

"Is it true?" When he didn't answer, her eyes welled with tears. She shook her head, backed from the room, then turned around and raced out the door.

He followed her.

Sam glanced at Remi, who didn't seem at all surprised by the interaction. Remi walked to the door, looking out, then back to Sam. "Do you think this will change your friend's mind about having the Kyrils looked into?"

"If this doesn't, I don't know what will." He took out his phone to call Rube. Word definitely traveled fast on the island. Someone must have radioed the *Asteri*, because they saw it pulling into port while Sam was on the phone with Rube, updating him on what they'd discovered. Remi left to meet Nikos, saying something about stopping him before he called her father.

"If it wasn't an accident—" Rube said.

"After everything that happened?" Sam replied. "Obviously it was murder." He glanced out the window to see Remi on the dock. "Which is what worries me. These people are Remi's friends. She feels responsible and guilty. If it wasn't for her taking pictures, none of this would have happened."

"Responsible?" He heard Rube taking a frustrated breath. "The sooner you two are out of there, the better."

"Assuming the police let us go in the middle of a murder investigation."

"You've got that right. Chances are good that the two of you are going to be there for a while. The best thing you can do for her is to tell her to stay close."

"Don't worry. I don't intend to let her out of my sight."

"In the meantime, I'll see if I can find a reliable contact in the Hellenic police to keep you abreast of the investigation."

"Appreciate it."

He disconnected, looking out the window to see Remi talking to Nikos and a policeman on the dock. A moment later Remi walked in. She nodded out the door, where the officer and Nikos stood, deep in discussion. Just beyond them, Dimitris was trying to console Zoe. When the young woman pushed away from him, clearly not ready to talk, Remi glanced at Sam, her eyes holding a glint of tears. "Such tragedy. Thankfully, she has Dimitris. He's a very understanding man." She sighed. "What did Rube have to say?"

"He'd like it better if we were out of here. But that doesn't seem likely with a police investigation."

"Even if we could," she said, looking out the window, "we can't just abandon them."

"It's possible we could be here a lot longer than we anticipated."

"I figured." She turned toward him, her gaze troubled. "Do you think it's safe?"

"I think it's a small island, where everyone knows everyone. We stick together, look out for each other, we should be fine."

She nodded, her attention back on Nikos speaking to the officer. "I hope you're right."

So did he.

CHAPTER TWENTY-SEVEN

The next couple of days were filled with interviews with the port police and the federal police, who, along with Rube, assured Sam that the safest place he or Remi could be during the investigation was right there on Fourni.

Sam, knowing Remi was worried, mentioned what the police said as he, Remi, and Nikos walked up the hill to Zoe's house.

Remi was quiet as they started up the steep stairs leading to the winding path. Finally, she looked over at Sam. "I still think we'd be safer on one of the bigger islands. Like Samos, where there's a larger police force."

"The Kyrils would be stupid to try anything here," he replied, pointing to the police boats in the port. "With the federal police here, too, I'd say it's the safest place to be."

"He's right," Nikos said. "As small as this island is, we'll be the first to notice strangers. Everyone here knows you. They'll keep you safe. On Samos . . . ?" The older man shrugged. "Too many tourists. How will you know who belongs and who doesn't?"

When they arrived at Zoe's house, Dimitris came out to meet them. He'd been helping her notify her extended family and friends on the neighboring islands of the upcoming funeral.

"How's Zoe doing?" Sam asked.

"Okay, for now. Denéa's staying here with her until her cousin gets in tomorrow morning. At least we finished the last of the calls to notify everyone about the funeral." He gave a tired smile. "I didn't think it would be this hard."

Nikos put a hand on his son's shoulder. "As much time as you and Zoe spent together as children, it's no wonder. Tassos practically raised you along with her."

Dimitris nodded, then led them inside. Zoe, her eyes red, the circles beneath dark, brightened when she saw them. Denéa and Manos stepped out of the kitchen, carrying a few dishes that the neighbors had prepared and dropped off. They sat down at the table, Zoe picking at her food, the others eating quietly.

Nikos watched his son pouring more wine into his glass. "What you need is a break. All of you." He gave Zoe a kind smile. "If Tassos were here, he'd agree with me. We declare tomorrow a day of rest. We go out on the boat. Do a little fishing, a little diving. We toast your grandfather on the water. If the police want to talk to us, they can wait."

She looked up at him, quiet for several moments, then nodded. "I think you're right. It's exactly what my grandfather would want."

Dimitris turned a grateful look toward his father. "What time should we meet?"

"Let's all have breakfast at Skavos's café at nine, then head out."

With plans finalized, they finished their dinner, cleared the dishes, then sat around the table, listening to Manos as he told them a story about the time Tassos caught him and Dimitris, both about ten at the time, throwing eggs down the stone stairs not too far from the house. "We hadn't even gotten through an entire dozen," he said. "But he handed us a bucket of water and a couple of rags, and made us wash every step, all the way down to the port."

Remi's brows rose. "Are you talking about the stairs we took to get here? There have to be nearly a hundred of them."

"Those stairs, yes," Manos replied. "And it felt like there were a million."

Dimitris grinned at Zoe, who was laughing. "There was a hole in the bucket," he said. "The water lasted us about ten steps before we'd have to go back up, get more, then lug it down to the next level."

Zoe, wiping tears from her eyes, laughed even more. "I remember him watching you through the window. You realize he gave you that bucket on purpose? He wanted to teach you both a lesson."

"I knew it," Dimitris said. "I always told Manos he'd sabotaged us."

"It worked," Manos said. "We never threw another egg."

After a few more tales, Sam and Remi hugged Zoe good night, then started the walk back. When they reached the stone stairs, looking down the several flights to the street below, they both laughed. "I think I would have liked Tassos," Sam said.

"Me too."

They stood there a few moments, the water shimmering with the lights reflecting from the port, while above them, stars sparkled in an ink-black sky. Remi sighed. "It really is beautiful here."

He looked over at her. "Buy you a drink, Remi Longstreet?"

She linked her arm through his. "There's nothing I'd like better."

They walked down the stairs, then over to the Café Palace, a bar set on the edge of the waterfront. They took a seat at one of the outside tables. A warm breeze swept in from the bay, rippling the red-checked tablecloths. A waiter took their order, brought their drinks, and the two sat there, enjoying the view, talking about Tassos, Fourni, and the beauty of small-island life. Sam, noticing Remi was truly at ease for the first time since his arrival, was reminded of their time in California, before the kidnapping and Tassos's murder.

Remi must have sensed his thoughts. She reached out, grasping his hand. "I'll be glad when this is all over."

"So will I," he said.

"Do you think we'll ever come back here?"

He liked that she was talking about the future. "I hope so."

She smiled, sipped her drink, then looked out at the water.

Sam had eyes only for her.

CHAPTER TWENTY-EIGHT

S am and Remi awoke the following morning to clear weather and calm seas, a promising start to the day spent diving. After they walked into town and ate a leisurely breakfast of yogurt and island honey, they all set out on the *Asteri* to explore one of the more shallow wrecks from the Roman period—much closer to the island than the site where Remi and Dimitris had been that fateful afternoon.

Nikos remained aboard the *Asteri*, as did Zoe and Dimitris, who both insisted that they wanted nothing more than to sit on board and relax.

Sam, knowing Remi was still a novice, stuck close by her as they put on their dive gear and followed Denéa and Manos into the water.

The seafloor was a mix of bare, sandy patches, and areas filled with crustacean-encrusted rocks, all of it teeming with sea plants moving with the current, while tiny striped fish darted about. It was a few moments before Sam realized that what he'd thought were piles of rocks were actually dozens upon dozens of amphorae, some in pieces, some actually whole.

Denéa swam above a stone anchor, then brushed some sediment

from a spot nearby, uncovering a small, intact terra-cotta vase about eight inches in diameter. She pointed it out to Remi.

Remi took the piece, turning it about in her gloved hands, her eyes alight as though amazed that she was holding something over two thousand years old. She showed it to Sam, then returned it to Denéa, who carefully replaced the piece where she found it.

Manos pointed along the edge of the amphora pile, where a moray eel was peering out between some of the pottery. As it disappeared, throwing up a cloud of silt, Sam found an empty, white, conical snail shell. He picked it up, then turned, placing the object in Remi's palm. She put it into her small dive bag.

All too soon, Manos was tapping his dive watch, indicating that it was time to return to the surface. Once on board the *Asteri*, Remi took out the shell, her breath catching at the iridescent beauty of it in the sunlight. She held it up to the others, smiling. "My first souvenir from my trip to Fourni."

Zoe raised her brows. "A snail shell? I think you can find a better one."

"I love it anyway," she said, then leaned over and kissed Sam.

"If I'd known you were this easy to please, I could have saved all that money buying you expensive dinners."

Remi laughed. "Seashells fresh from the Aegean always win a girl's heart."

Nikos opened a picnic basket and they enjoyed a late lunch in the warmth of the sun with friends.

Arriving back at port, the police chief was waiting for them. He was happy to announce that their initial questioning was complete. Sam and Remi would be able to leave Greece.

Sam opened his email to send an update to Rube, and was surprised to find a day-old message from Blake. "I don't believe it. Blake managed to reschedule the investor meeting."

Remi watched him a moment. "Shouldn't you be happier? That's what you wanted, isn't it?"

"The catch is that I have to be home in three days. And we have Tassos's funeral tomorrow," he said.

"Aren't you paying Selma for research? I'd think booking air flight qualifies."

"You're absolutely right. Assuming you're ready to go home."

"More than ready."

He emailed Selma, telling her the date of the meeting, asking her to book them on the earliest—and cheapest—flight to Los Angeles that would get him home in time.

Selma called him back less than five minutes later.

"I have two flight possibilities, Mr. Fargo."

"Call me Sam, please."

"The first flight gets you in at twelve p.m. The second flight is a thousand dollars more. It does, however, get you into the airport just after ten, which should get you through customs and on the freeway well before commute traffic starts up. You could possibly make it with the first flight, but it might be cutting it close."

"If this meeting works out, it'll be worth the cost. Go ahead and book it."

All seemed well, until they arrived at Nikos's house that evening. Dimitris was pacing, clearly upset.

"What's wrong?" Sam asked.

"You're not going to believe this," Nikos said. "They sent an officer to the Kyril home to interview him. He told the police that Tassos was supposed to meet them up at the cave, but never showed."

"When was this meeting supposed to have taken place?" Sam asked.

"The same morning Remi and Dimitris saw them up there."

Dimitris stopped his pacing. "That's why we were kidnapped. Adrian thought we'd seen the murder." He looked over at Remi, his dark eyes narrowed in anger. "They would've killed us if we hadn't gotten away. And they're blaming everything on pirates. We can't let them get away with this."

Remi reached over and grasped Sam's hand, her expression urging him to say something to comfort the young man. "We have to trust the police," Sam said. "They're trained. They know what they're doing."

"Do they? There has to be something else we can do."

"We've done about everything we can. There's Tassos's funeral in the morning. And we leave a couple of days later."

His mouth dropped open as he looked from Sam to Remi, then back. "That's it? You're just giving up? Going home?"

"Please," Nikos said, putting his hand on his son's arm. "We should be grateful for everything Mr. Fargo has done for us. Now we let the police investigate."

Dimitris pulled away. "It might be enough for you. But it's not for me." He stormed out, slamming the door behind him.

Remi started to follow, but Nikos stopped her. "Give him time. When he cools off, he'll know we're speaking the truth."

If he cools off, Sam added silently.

CHAPTER TWENTY-NINE

The following morning, Sam and Remi walked into town for the funeral, meeting Denéa on the way down the hill. When they arrived at the main street, they saw Nikos, deep in discussion with another man.

"I'll catch up with you," Sam said to Remi and Denéa. "I need to speak to Nikos."

"The mayor," Denéa whispered to Remi. She and Remi continued to the main square, crowded with those waiting to enter into the whitewashed walls of the church. Once there, Denéa excused herself to meet up with Manos, while Remi waited by the gate for Sam. A white-haired woman wandered up and smiled at Remi. "Did you know Tassos well?" the woman asked.

"Sadly, I never met him. But I know his granddaughter, Zoe."

"You are American," she said, switching to English. "Your Greek is very good."

"And your English is excellent."

"Thank you." She smiled and extended her hand. "I'm Helena."

"Remi."

The older woman turned her attention to the people gathering at the opened arched doors of the church, then gave a long sigh. "Such a terrible accident. Poor Tassos. Always searching for treasure."

"That's what I heard," Remi said, deciding it best not to mention her involvement, or the true circumstances. "Where do you know him from?"

"We grew up together on Samos. He and my brother were best friends until he fell in love with a girl here on Fourni." Helena gave a sad smile. "Even so, we kept in touch. I was not surprised when I heard what happened. For as long as I remember, Tassos was searching for the lost gold." She leaned in close, lowering her voice. "I suppose one could say he died doing what he loved."

Judging from the conversations Remi had heard the last couple of days, that seemed to be the general consensus. If it gave everyone peace, then she was happy to contribute to the memories. "I'm assuming that's why he was at the cave when he died, searching for Poseidon's Trident."

Helena's gray brows furrowed. "Very odd that he'd be looking on Fourni."

"Why?"

"According to my grandmother and the story she used to tell us at bedtime, Poseidon's Trident is a place, not a treasure. Of course, it broke Tassos's heart when he'd thought he'd found it, then didn't. Still—"

Remi looked at her, surprised. "So, you have heard of the treasure?"

She laughed. "I doubt there's anyone here who hasn't. Do you see that Roman sarcophagus there?" She pointed across the square, where, behind the gathering mourners, a white marble sarcophagus was displayed beneath a tall plane tree. "A farmer discovered that thing buried on his land, filled with treasure. As you can imagine, the discovery added a renewed interest in the legend of Poseidon's

Trident, the treasure, and the pirates who were part of it." Her dark eyes sparkled as she again leaned toward Remi, lowering her voice. "It's a matter of pride for us Samians, many of whom lay claim to their pirate ancestors."

She stopped when she noticed a middle-aged woman waving at her. "My daughter, informing me that I'm wanted elsewhere." Helena turned back to Remi, clasping her hand. "A pleasure meeting you. I'm sure we'll run into each other again. Fourni is not all that large."

"Unfortunately, I'm flying out in a couple of days."

"From Samos or Ikaria?"

"Samos."

"Safe travels, then." She smiled, and joined her daughter. The two walked through the gate into the churchyard.

A few minutes later, Sam joined Remi, taking her hand in his. While they waited, Remi pointed out the sarcophagus, sharing the story the old woman had told. As the service started, those waiting outside grew silent. There were far too many mourners to fit into the church and its courtyard, but someone had placed a portable speaker outside the wall for the overflow crowd to hear.

At the conclusion of the service, Remi and Sam could hear Zoe's voice, painfully soft and strained as she invited everyone back to her grandfather's home to share in food and friendship. Dimitris escorted Zoe through the wrought iron gates of the church, and they slowly made their way home.

By the time Sam and Remi reached Zoe's house, it was already filled with well-wishers. Remi looked around the crowd, thinking that if not for the somber moments of remembrance, funerals were much like weddings, bringing family and friends from faraway places. Neighbors had outdone themselves with tables of food, fruit, and bread, both indoors and outside on the rooftop patio that overlooked the port of Fourni and the island of Thimena just beyond it.

Greek wine was plentiful, and as the afternoon wore on, the remembered stories of Tassos in his youth and as a man were shared by all. Tales of his daring exploits, both as a fisherman and as he searched for Poseidon's Trident and the lost treasure, filled the yard with laughter. Nikos, who was busy pouring wine, raised his glass in another toast. "To Tassos," he called out, then related yet another story.

Skavos, sitting next to Sam and Remi, gave a tired smile as he watched over the festivities. "Tassos would have had a great time today. I know he is pleased." Then he stood, lifted his glass, and in a loud voice said, "May his memory and laughter long be with us!"

A voice from the crowd shouted, "And may he find his treasure in heaven."

"*As ftiáxoume tost me ton Táso.*" Let's toast to Tassos. Skavos smiled. "*The Pirates of Poseidon.* It was a favorite book of all of us, but none more so than Tassos."

Remi was about to ask him what the book was about when Denéa came up the stairs, shading her eyes against the late-afternoon sun as she searched the patio. She spotted Sam and Remi, then weaved her way through the crowd toward them. "Is something wrong?" Remi asked, noticing her look of concern.

"Dimitris sent me to find you. The police chief just arrived and said one of the investigators from Athens wants him to talk to Zoe."

"I thought they were done," Remi said as she and Sam quickly rose and followed her across the rooftop to the stairs.

"So did we, which is why Manos is stalling them. We don't think she should be dealing with the police today, of all days. Definitely not alone."

Denéa led them to a small, private patio at the back of the house, where Zoe and Dimitris were waiting, both looking relieved to see them. Denéa left, then returned shortly with the police chief. He nodded at Sam and Remi, then turned his attention to Zoe. "I hate to bother you, today of all days. I won't take up much of your time. It's about your grandfather."

"What is it?"

"A few questions for the investigators, nothing more."

CHAPTER THIRTY

We found a couple of things in Tassos's pocket that we hoped you might know about," the police chief said.

"What things?" Zoe asked.

"There was a book with a note in it."

"A book?"

"I don't have it with me at the moment. Right now, the Athens investigators are more interested in the note they found. I have a photocopy, if you could take a look?"

"Of course."

He opened his notebook, pulling out a slip of paper and handing it to her. "Have you ever seen this before?"

She studied it a moment, then shook her head. "No, but it looks like my grandfather's writing."

Dimitris looked over her shoulder, reading the note. "A. *Cave.* 9 . . . A has to be Adrian."

"That would be the logical assumption," the chief said before returning his attention to Zoe. "I don't suppose you know what the 9 means?"

Zoe gave a slight shrug. "I can only assume the time of day?"

"It must be," Remi said. "That's around the same time Dimitris and I saw them up on the hill."

"That's exactly when we were up there." Dimitris pinned his gaze on the chief. "That proves he killed him."

"Easy does it," Sam said to Dimitris, earning an appreciative look from the chief. "They're not going to be able to make an arrest based on one note found in Tassos's pocket."

"Mr. Fargo's right," the chief said as Dimitris bristled, his fists tight. "We need more evidence. I'm sure you've heard the term before, but the wheels of justice turn slowly."

Zoe took a ragged breath. "How can it not be enough?"

Remi, seeing her friend close to tears, reached out and clasped her hand. "Maybe we could finish this tomorrow?"

The police chief hesitated, then nodded. "Of course. I apologize for the bad timing, but the investigators from Athens felt this was important."

Zoe nodded, wiping the tears from her eyes.

"I'll walk you out," Sam said to the chief.

Remi hesitated in the doorway after they left, worried more about Dimitris than Zoe. "Are you going to be okay?"

His jaw was clenched as he watched the two men walk off. He gave a sharp nod.

Zoe smiled at her. "We'll be fine. I just need a few minutes to compose myself before we go out."

"Let me know if either of you need anything."

"Thank you. To Sam, too. The both of you have been so much help already."

It was a short while later, after Dimitris and Zoe returned to the gathering, that Dimitris approached Sam. "I need some advice. I don't know what to do about Zoe, how to help her."

Remi smiled at him. "I'll give you two some privacy."

"No, it's fine," Dimitris said. "It's just . . . I don't know what to say to her. I've never been in this situation before. If the police aren't going to make an arrest, what do I tell her? We can't let Kyril get away with this."

"He won't get away with it," Sam replied. "Police investigations like this take time. What you can do is make sure she's surrounded by family and friends. Just knowing how many people love her and loved Tassos will help keep her mind off the frustration over how long it's taking."

Dimitris glanced back at Zoe, who was hugging one of her friends. He looked at Sam. "I'll try."

Remi linked her arm through Sam's as they watched Dimitris return to Zoe's side. "That was pretty impressive, Fargo. I didn't know you could be so philosophical."

"Just repeating what I heard my dad say once."

"Let's hope it helps him. I think he was more upset than Zoe was when he learned the police weren't going to run out and make an immediate arrest."

"That's the good thing about living on Fourni, I suppose. Not too many places he can get into trouble here." He glanced out the window, saw the sun cresting the island of Thimena in the distance, then leaned toward Remi. "What do you say we head up to the rooftop and watch the sun set and give one last toast to Tassos?"

"A spectacular idea."

Several other guests had the same idea, and as the sun dipped below the hilltops of the small island, turning the clouds above a brilliant orange, they lifted their glasses. "To Tassos!"

Silence reigned for a minute or two, then quietly, the others wandered down the stairs, saying their goodbyes to Zoe, then heading home.

Nikos, Sam, and Remi began clearing the glasses and plates from upstairs, bringing them to the kitchen, while Denéa and Manos gathered the empty dishes from inside the house. When Zoe and

Dimitris attempted to help, Remi and Denéa sent them up to the rooftop to enjoy some quiet time.

Remi filled the sink with warm water and soap, washing, while Sam picked up a dish towel, drying each plate and stacking them on the counter. She glanced over at him, pleasantly surprised how easily they worked together, as though it had always been. With goodbyes said, hugs given, they walked hand in hand down the path toward town.

"I hope they'll be okay," Remi said, looking back at the house, seeing Zoe and Dimitris sitting next to each other on the rooftop, silhouetted in the moonlight.

"They need time," Sam said. He drew her to him. "As much as I wished none of this happened . . ."

"I know. But I'm glad you're here."

Neither had eaten a thing at Zoe's, but the tantalizing scent of fresh-cooked food drifted toward them as they took the stairs down. "One last dinner on Fourni?" Sam asked.

"I thought you'd never ask."

They looked down the main street at the square across from the church, seeing the fairy lights strung beneath the plane tree. The restaurant, Platanos, was very near the sarcophagus, candles lit on the patio tables. They dined on grilled fish, dolmades, and eggplant salad, drinking a fresh white wine, then finishing with a serving of watermelon and a glass of dessert wine.

Remi looked up at the leaves rustling in the offshore breeze. A few drifted down from the treetop, then danced across the paving stones. "Do you think they'll be okay?" she asked.

"I think so. Zoe seemed at peace when we left."

"She did. Dimitris, not so much."

"I think he's worried about her. It's understandable."

"Let's hope you're right." She looked at Sam, watching the candlelight play across his face. After a moment, she reached across the table, placing her hand on his. "I wasn't a big believer in fate, until I met you."

He laughed.

"I'm serious. Who else would have showed up because of a voice mail talking about the North Star?"

"You know what I think? That you're brilliant, Remi Longstreet. If we hadn't met, you would've found another way to escape."

"Not so fast, Fargo. Weren't you the one who said my Plan B wouldn't work?"

"Did I?" He pushed the candle aside and leaned across the table, kissing her. "We should probably head back. We're going to need to get up early to haul your luggage up all the stairs in the morning."

Sam paid the bill, then, arm in arm, the two strolled down the main street, until they reached Skavos's café, where Nikos was sitting with a few of his friends. He called them over, and they joined him. "Glad we ran into you," Sam said. "I wanted to double-check the ferry schedule tomorrow. I'm wondering if we'd be better off hiring a boat into Samos to make our flight."

"It might be tight," Nikos said. "But no need to hire anyone. I'm sure Dimitris won't mind taking you." He glanced over at Remi, smiling. "Better he picks you up in Kampi by your cottage. With all those suitcases of yours, it'll be easier to carry it to the dock, instead of up all those stairs."

Sam started to laugh, until he glanced over at Remi. He held up his hands, giving her a mock look of innocence. "I didn't say a thing."

CHAPTER THIRTY-ONE

The next morning, Sam and Remi were waiting at the dock. Sam with his backpack and small carry-on, Remi with her two large suitcases and the biggest carry-on Sam had ever seen. It might be fine in the overhead on an international flight, but he wasn't sure where it was going to fit on the much smaller plane from Samos to Athens. He was about to ask her if she had to pay extra to place it in the hold when he noticed the *Asteri* slowly entering the quiet bay.

It wasn't Dimitris at the helm. It was Nikos. "The *Star Catcher* is missing," he said with a heavy sigh as he and Sam loaded Remi's luggage on board. "Dimitris didn't come home last night."

"*Star Catcher*?" Sam asked.

"The RIB boat that belongs to the underwater archeological society. He sometimes takes it out when he's upset. I know he'd want to say goodbye. Perhaps we'll see him before too long."

"You're sure he's okay?" Remi asked.

"I'm sure. He seems to have settled down a bit these last two days. I think he and Zoe realized that it was better to leave the investigating to the police."

"I had the same feeling, too," Sam agreed.

"Don't worry," Nikos said as he piloted the boat out of the bay. "We'll get you to Samos in plenty of time to make your flight."

Once they arrived at the port in Pythagorio, Nikos received a radio call from Manos. He looked over at them, his brow knit with concern. "Perhaps we're wrong. Maybe Dimitris is taking Tassos's death far harder than we realized. And maybe taking things into his own hands. The *Star Catcher* was seen cruising along the south side of the Kyrils' island between here and Patmos. And Dimitris is not answering his phone or the radio."

"Kyrils' island? Why would he go there?" Sam asked.

"The majority of the Kyril olives are grown on that island." The radio crackled as another transmission came in. This time, he stepped in the cabin and shut the door.

Remi watched him through the window, then turned to Sam. "You need to do something," she said, her green eyes filled with worry. "It's clear Dimitris has gone there to look for evidence on the man he thinks killed Zoe's grandfather. Obviously, he got the idea from you. Which means he's following in your footsteps. That makes it your fault."

It took a moment for Sam to realize she wasn't joking. "My fault? How did you come to that conclusion?"

"Because you're the one who flew all the way out here," Remi said, getting flustered. "Being a knight in shining armor and all."

"Hold up here, Longstreet. Last night you were happy I followed you."

"That's not the point," she said, her cheeks turning red.

Sam couldn't help but smile. "You do realize, that defies all logic?"

"Well, Fargo, why did you come?"

"The North Star. I was worried about you."

"See? Logic has everything to do with this." She took a deep breath and gave him a satisfied smile. While her explanation made no sense to him, what she said next was perfectly clear. "Nikos helped you rescue me. The least we can do is help him find Dimitris."

She was right, of course. He opened the email Selma had sent, found the link to the booking site, and canceled their flight. Remi's return smile softened the sting over the change fee they were likely to be charged. "I'll call Selma and let her know."

She picked up on the first ring. "Mr. Fargo. You canceled your flight. Did your investor meeting get changed?"

As efficient as she was turning out to be, he supposed he shouldn't have been too surprised that she already knew. "Something came up," he said.

"Did you want me to rebook?"

"Not yet. Hard to say when this . . . issue will resolve."

"I see. I assume you'll call or email when you're ready?"

"I will," Sam said. "There is something you can do in the meantime." He turned slightly, lowering his voice. "If I text you the phone number, can you call my friend Blake and let him know I won't be able to make that meeting after all?"

"Would you like me to give a reason?"

"Just offer my apologies. I have a feeling that the truth might be a little hard to believe."

The moment he disconnected, Remi looked at him, her eyes wide with another kind of guilt. "Oh, Sam . . . Why didn't you say something? How selfish of me."

"Remi, stop. It's not that important. You're important."

"Your investor meeting is important. It's your future. You need to go. This is all my fault."

Nikos walked out, overhearing them. "What's your fault?"

There was a moment of awkward silence, then Remi said, "I forgot about Sam's investor meeting."

"Investor meeting?" He looked at Sam for an explanation.

"It's nothing," Sam said. "The good news is, we've decided to stay and help you find Dimitris."

CHAPTER THIRTY-TWO

A look of relief swept over the older man's face after hearing Sam's offer to help. "What about your plane tickets?" Nikos asked.

"If we're lucky," Sam said, "we get a refund. Your son is more important. So, where is this island?"

"Just this side of Patmos. It may be very difficult to find him, though."

"Isn't it harvest season?" Remi asked. "I'd think that'd make it easier. There's got to be enough people on the island who will have seen him."

"Not on this particular island," Nikos replied. "Some areas are very rugged. The only way in or out is by foot or pack animal." In fact, their only option at that point was to head out to the island, find his boat, and hope they could track him from there.

They arrived early afternoon. There was only one port, on the east side of the island. Nikos was certain Dimitris would not have entered from that direction. They cruised around the south, finding the *Star Catcher* anchored behind an outcropping of rock in a narrow cliff-edged inlet, the key sitting in the ignition. Had they approached from the east, they might not have seen it at all.

Nikos moored the boat as close as he dared, suggesting that he and Sam search the island from that point.

Remi, however, objected. "And leave me on the boat alone?"

"She's right," Sam said to Nikos. "If anything comes up, you need to be here, ready. If anything goes awry, you're better able to deal with the authorities. Remi can stay here on the boat with you."

"What if something happens and you need help?" Remi said. "I'm going with you. Don't forget. I have the only sat phone, and by the looks of them there hills, I'd say there's no cell service."

"You're not exactly dressed for the occasion."

She tapped one of her suitcases with her foot. "Lucky for me, I've got a full wardrobe to draw from."

Had he felt he had any say in the matter, he'd insist she stay on board with Nikos. But in the short time he'd known Remi, he'd learned several things about her. Not only was she the most stubborn woman he'd ever met, she was also a capable and worthy partner. Reluctantly, he nodded. "As long as you promise to do what I say and not go rogue."

"Me?" Remi said. "You won't even know I'm there."

Considering how very aware he was of her presence at all times, he doubted that very much.

"In that case," Nikos said, "I have something for you." He opened a cabinet, removing a small black pouch. Unzipping it, he pulled out a holstered .38 Smith & Wesson, which he held toward Sam. "I bought this on a trip to America several years ago. I want you to take it. Just in case."

Sam unholstered the weapon, saw there were six rounds in the chamber, then held it by the grip, index finger along the trigger guard. He aimed it out at the water, testing the balance, the feel of it. Though more compact than what he was used to, the revolver had a nice weight. "This should do," he said.

Remi looked at the gun, then at him. "I hope it doesn't come to that."

"I'm with you," Sam said, returning the gun to its holster. "In this case, though, better safe than sorry."

While Remi changed, Sam and Nikos decided on a suitable in-case-of-emergency plan. "If something comes up," Nikos said, "I can use the ship's radio. If I can't reach Manos at the office, between his cousins and mine, there's bound to be someone within ship-to-ship radio distance."

Remi emerged a few minutes later, dressed in khaki slacks, a safari-style olive-green shirt, and her pristine hiking boots. She looked more like a model about to embark on a photo shoot than someone about to do search and rescue. "Almost ready," she said, kneeling in front of her carry-on bag, searching through it. She pulled out two scarves, both beige, one with large red roses, the other with tiny blue flowers, holding them up side by side as though trying to decide which matched best with her outfit. When she looked at Sam her gaze narrowed slightly. "I sense you don't approve."

"I didn't say a thing. But if you want my opinion—"

"I don't," she said, smirking.

"We're trying not to be noticed." He gave a pointed look at the red-flowered scarf.

She dropped it back in the bag, and tied the other around her ponytail. "Laugh all you want. A good scarf always comes in handy."

"I'll take your word for it." He picked up his backpack, heavier now that it contained a coil of rope, in addition to his binoculars and two bottles of water. He slung it over his shoulder. "Ready?"

"Ready." She smiled at Nikos, giving him a hug. "We'll be back soon."

He nodded, then turned and extended his hand to Sam. "Be careful, my friends."

"We will."

Nikos helped them lower the skiff into the water, then stood at the railing, watching as Sam and Remi rowed toward a small, pebbled beach.

CHAPTER THIRTY-THREE

Sam disembarked, helping Remi out, then looked at the narrow trail leading up between the cliffs. "At least we know he's here," he said.

"Do you think we'll have any chance of finding him?"

"Let's hope." He examined the dry, rocky soil, surprised to see two sets of footprints, one much smaller than the other. "From the look of these tracks, I'd say Zoe's with him."

"What was he thinking, bringing her here?"

Looking over at her, he said, "Imagine a guy letting a girl talk him into doing something he shouldn't."

She crossed her arms. "I was being rhetorical."

"The good news," he said, standing, "is that it doesn't look like either of them are too worried about being followed. If we're lucky, we'll catch up with them before they get into trouble."

About twenty minutes later, the graveled path veered north and inland. It was, as Nikos described, very rugged, and all too soon, Sam lost their trail completely. When the route eventually branched off into more than one direction, Sam suggested they backtrack to make sure he hadn't missed anything.

"Go on," Remi said. "I'll catch up."

He looked back to find her in the shade of a rocky outcropping, kneeling to untie the laces on one of her boots. If he had to guess, her shoes were giving her blisters. She did not complain, he had to give her that. "I'll wait. Just be careful where you choose to sit. An island this remote, there's probably any number of things we wouldn't want to run into."

"Please don't say snakes."

"I wasn't. But now that you mention it."

She turned a dark glance at him.

"The least of your worries," he said, crouching to examine the trail again. "Trust me."

"What could be worse than snakes?"

"Scorpions. Extremely painful. And possibly deadly if you're allergic."

She eyed the ground, her gaze darting from rock to rock. "If this is your way of helping me relax, it's not working."

"Were you thinking about snakes?"

"No."

"See? It worked."

"Very amusing, Fargo." She hurriedly finished tying her shoelaces, then suddenly looked up. "Do you hear that?"

In fact, he did. A sharp breeze rustled the leaves of the surrounding olive trees. As it died down, the scuffing of heavy feet on hard-packed earth grew louder.

"Maybe it's them," Remi whispered.

From the sound of it, far more than two people were coming their way. The olive trees on this side of the island definitely weren't large enough to hide behind. He glanced up at the massive outcropping jutting up from the hillside next to Remi, motioning for her to follow him. They climbed to the top of the jagged rock, about ten feet above the path, then dropped to their bellies, hiding behind a few fragrant patches of sage that grew from the cracks.

Sam drew the little Smith & Wesson, holding it in front of him. A moment later, five men came down the trail below them, two leading pack mules loaded with full sacks of olives.

When they disappeared from view, Remi leaned in close to him, whispering, "What are we waiting for?"

"Making sure no one else is following."

He set his gun on the dirt in front of him, then took out his binoculars, focusing on the beaten path. Their higher position made it easier to see exactly where Dimitris and Zoe had left the trail. Their tracks reemerged about thirty yards beyond that point—something they wouldn't have seen from the ground. "Those men are going in the same direction we need to go."

"We're going to wait longer?"

"Just a bit." A few minutes later, a steady stream of men leading pack mules followed the first group.

The sun beat down on their backs, and Remi shifted, wiping the dust and perspiration from her brow. "Not quite what I pictured when I booked this trip."

"I could think of worse ways to spend the afternoon."

"Really? Name one."

"How about being cooped up in a cubicle?"

"At least the cubicle I work in has air-conditioning. I count that as a plus right now."

"So, camping is out?"

"Unless you're pitching a tent with hot and cold running water, carpeting, and electricity, I'm definitely out. Honestly, what's the appeal of sleeping in a bag with zippers on the hard ground?"

"You realize all sleeping bags have zippers?"

"That's not the point."

"What is the point?"

"Trying to figure out why anyone finds camping appealing."

"It's the totality of the experience, and the company. Especially the company." He glanced over at her. "Being in the outdoors, listening to the rustle of the breeze through the trees, the birds singing, the blue sky above. The beautiful girl beside me . . ." Unable to resist, he leaned forward and kissed her.

When she didn't object, he moved in for a second kiss. She suddenly stiffened, pulling back. "Sam . . ."

"Not quite the reaction I expected."

"Not you. *That*."

Her gaze was on a rather long scorpion crawling out from beneath a rock very close to her right arm. He used the binoculars to flick the insect down the hill. "Nothing to it. At least the great outdoors has a way of letting you know what's dangerous and what isn't."

"Maybe you should be carrying a flamethrower instead of a gun."

"Some of the worst scorpions in the world look like ordinary human beings."

She eyed the rock as though expecting another scorpion to come crawling out. "I don't suppose it's safe to move?"

"I think we're good," he said. Rising, he picked up and holstered his gun, then he offered his hand and helped Remi to her feet. They were almost to the bottom when he heard something in the brush on the other side of the trail to their left. He glanced in that direction, then held out his arm, stopping Remi in her tracks. "Remember when I said there were worse things to worry about than snakes?" He nodded down the trail. "That would be one of them."

CHAPTER THIRTY-FOUR

Ahuge brown boar snuffed through the dried brush. Alongside her, four striped piglets pushed at the dirt with their little snouts. Sam took Remi by the hand and slowly moved her away from the trail.

She craned her head around to look back at them as Sam led her away from the path, making a wide berth around the boar family. "Look at all those cute babies."

"They're cute, until four hundred pounds of mama's pure muscle decides you're a threat."

When Sam drew his gun, Remi's breath caught. "You can't kill a mama pig."

"Trust me. This is only a last resort. I'd rather not give up our position."

The expression in her eyes, when she glanced at the weapon, surprised him. "You don't really think you'll have to use the gun, do you? I thought we were just going in to find Dimitris and Zoe and bring them back."

"Exactly what I was planning on." When he saw a shadow of indecision cross her face, he added, "I don't want you to do something you're not comfortable with. There's still time to go back.

Nikos will undoubtedly appreciate your company if you want to return to the boat."

Since it'd be faster for him and safer for her if she did go back he hoped she'd say yes.

She looked at him for several long seconds, clearly wrestling with the idea, but shook her head. "I want to help find Dimitris and Zoe and bring them home."

He couldn't help but feel pride in her spirit and gumption. "Stay close, then." The trail started winding its way up a steep hill covered with ancient olive trees, their limbs heavy with fruit. The sun angled through the branches swaying with the breeze, casting moving shadows on the ground that made it difficult to distinguish Dimitris's and Zoe's footprints from the harvesters and mules that had trampled across them on the hard earth. Sam crouched to take a better look at the footprints, wondering why the young couple would risk coming here on their own. "Tell me about Zoe's grandfather. Maybe if we can figure out why he was killed, it might tell us what Adrian is after. Did you ever meet Tassos?"

"No. At the post office the morning we were kidnapped, Zoe asked Dimitris if he'd seen her grandfather. So much has happened since then, I'd sort of put that whole conversation behind me." She tucked a strand of hair behind her ear. "Zoe was concerned because her grandfather had been acting oddly leading up to that morning. And said he was excited about a job that was supposed to bring in a lot of money."

"What sort of job?"

"I have no idea. But Zoe thought he'd gone off to look for something called Poseidon's Trident. I remember Dimitris saying it was an old fisherman's tale about pirates."

"Pirates?" he said, losing sight of their tracks again. Hoping that the pair were headed in the same direction as the harvesters, there was little Sam could do at this point but follow the main trail.

"And treasure. But you know that from the funeral and all the stories. Everyone assumes Tassos died looking for treasure."

Sam glanced over at her, surprised. "Exactly what was said about the treasure part?"

"Honestly, it was all rather harmless. You heard it just like I did. Tassos was always searching for gold. I gathered that everyone but Tassos thought the Poseidon's Trident thing was just a tall tale."

"Clearly not that tall of a tale," Sam said, looking down at the path again. "Not if Adrian went to the trouble of killing him."

"It doesn't make sense. The police searched that cave after they recovered his body. Why kill him if there wasn't any treasure?"

"How do we know there wasn't any—?"

A mule brayed somewhere to the north of them. Not wanting to get too close to the harvesters, Sam motioned Remi to follow. Keeping low, they made their way to the top of the next hill. Beyond it, a cliff overlooked a deep gorge, which opened into a narrow valley on their right, where the late-afternoon sun shimmered on the rooftops of a few buildings in the distance. On the opposite side of the gorge, which was lower in elevation, olive trees grew as far as the eye could see.

Sam took out his binoculars, and moved to the edge of the cliff. Seeing the layout from up here made him understand why Dimitris chose the south side of the island to make his entry. The bulk of the orchard grew to the north of the gorge, but the processing facility and port for shipping the olives was down through the valley to the east. The terrain was rugged, the paths from the orchard to the valley below far too steep for anything other than pack mules to carry the harvest down.

In the compound, an empty flatbed truck was backed up to the loading dock of one of the buildings, probably what they used to transport any shipments to the port for distribution. Other than the one truck and a forklift used to move pallets of shipping containers, he didn't see any other vehicles—or any need for one, since there was only the single gravel road that led from the buildings to the port.

Sam turned back to the orchard across the gorge, where a movement in the trees caught his attention. Dozens of workers, some leading pack mules loaded with sacks of olives, were picking their way down the steep trail into the gorge. Sam searched the faces of the men and women, relieved when he saw Zoe and Dimitris. "I found them."

"Where?" Remi asked, crouching next to him.

"Across the gorge." He handed her the binoculars. "See the pack mules heading down that trail? At the end of the line."

"How'd we miss them? They can't have been with the workers that just passed us."

"Definitely not. Zoe and Dimitris had a big head start." He pointed to their left. "The workers we saw are still on this side of the gorge. You can see them through the trees."

She looked, about to comment, when her sat phone buzzed. She handed Sam the binoculars, then pulled the device from her pocket, looking at the screen. "It's Selma."

"Not the best time or place for a conversation. What about not being seen or heard? Hang up."

"I haven't even answered."

"Which makes it even easier."

"And what if it's something important?"

"She'll call back."

"And then we're exactly where we started."

Sam took the phone from Remi and moved farther from the trail, behind a boulder and some thick brush.

"Mr. Fargo," Selma said when he answered. "Thank goodness I caught you. Special Agent Haywood has been trying to reach you. There's a bit of an issue with the Kyrils."

"What sort of issue?"

The sat phone went flying as Remi crawled her way into the scrub after Sam, trying to wedge in next to him. Sam caught the phone before it hit the ground, then put it back to his ear, while Remi leaned in close so that she could hear, as well.

"We're back," Sam said.

"I didn't know you were gone. Hold on." They heard a click.

"Fargo," Rube said. "Why aren't you answering your phone?"

"There's no service on this island."

"For good reason. You need to get out of there. Now."

CHAPTER THIRTY-FIVE

Are you somewhere you can talk?" Rube asked.

Sam glanced down the side of the cliff, then at Remi, who was sitting next to him as he held the phone between them. "Good enough place as any. But we'll need to cut to the core. We're sort of out in the open, where I'd rather not be."

"I guess I don't want to ask. Okay, I'll start at the beginning. We're talking several decades ago. In the early seventies, a Nazi war criminal, Admiral Erich Heibert, assumed the identity of one Bruno von Till, turning Minerva Lines into one of the largest heroin smuggling operations in the Mediterranean."

"Heibert. Minerva Lines," Sam said, not sure where Rube was going with this. "I'm assuming this has something to do with the Kyrils?"

"It does. Admiral Heibert, aka von Till, died without issue. His brother, Kurt, who died in World War I, had a son who was very close to his uncle, and was believed to have actually interned at Minerva Lines, presumably years before the drug smuggling started. He eventually left to start his own shipping company, Heibert Lines. Long story short, he had a son, who then had a daughter, Minerva Heibert."

"Coincidentally named after this defunct shipping line? Or a nod to it?"

"So it seems. In fact, you've met Minerva's son. Adrian Kyril."

"Any chance there's a condensed version of this family saga?"

"I wish there was," Rube said. "I've been in touch with Interpol. The past connection to von Till wasn't lost on them. They've been looking at Heibert Lines for a while. Apparently, they received intel that Heibert Lines has been picking up the slack in the heroin market. Thing is, they don't know how it's being smuggled in or out. Way back when, Minerva Lines used drone subs. That's not the case here. Whatever the Kyrils are doing to get drugs out, they're making it look like a legit operation."

Sam looked out to the valley, seeing the processing facility. "I'll lay odds on it has something to do with olive oil."

"That's their thinking, too. The ships registered to Heibert Lines have been inspected on numerous occasions. The one time that Interpol actually managed to inspect the cargo after it was delivered to suspected dealers, someone set off a charge. It exploded, killing two of their officers."

"We're not anywhere near their ships."

"No. And my goal is to keep you away from them. Last thing you want to involve yourself in is an international drug smuggling ring. Whatever you're doing, turn around, get to the airport, and go home."

"About that. I might need to make a slight detour on my way out."

"I'm serious, Sam. This group is not one you want to mess with. Get off that island."

"If it makes you feel any better, pretend I'm on my way back to the boat. I'll call as soon as I get there." He disconnected, then looked at Remi. "Change of plans. You go back to the boat. I'll go after Dimitris and Zoe."

"No. I'm going with you."

"Remi, you heard what he said. They've already killed a couple of officers. I'm not going to let you be next."

She tucked her phone into her pocket. "And what? You're going to go in like a one-man wrecking crew?"

"I work better by myself."

"That's what you said at Kyril's party. What if I'm the one factor that makes a difference?"

"I'll admit your quick thinking was . . . appreciated, but—"

"Appreciated? Why is it so hard to admit that I might be able to help? Those two guards would've definitely caught you if not for me."

"I don't want anything to happen to you. It's easier to work if I know you're safe."

"That settles it, then. I have to go with you."

"Your twisted logic isn't going to work this time."

"You have no way of knowing that I'll be safe once I leave. I could fall and break my neck on that steep trail. And let's not forget the scorpions, or the four hundred pounds of mother boar protecting her babies." She crossed her arms, then lifted her chin, her expression defiant. "The way I see it, you can worry about me there, or here with you."

"There's nothing I can say that'll convince you to go back?"

"Nothing."

When it came right down to it, he'd rather Remi take her chances with a boar and the scorpions over Kyril's thugs. Realizing he wasn't going to change her mind, he let out a frustrated breath. "Fine. But you have to do everything I say."

"Let me guess. No going rogue. Where have I heard that before?"

Sam rolled his eyes. "She won't take my advice but, 'Oh yes, Sam, I'll do everything you say. No going rogue.'"

Remi arched her brows. "I sound nothing like that."

He looked down over the edge at this side of the gorge. There was about fifteen feet of cliff jutting out, but once they cleared that, it sloped out slightly the rest of the way down—something he thought Remi could handle. "I don't suppose you've ever done any rappelling?"

"Only if you count cliff-jumping at Adrian Kyril's party."

He stood, pulling a coil of rope from his backpack. "Our only hope," he said, taking a knife and cutting off a section, "is to get to Dimitris and Zoe before they get to the processing facility. If we head straight down on this side instead of following the mule trail, we can cut off a good chunk of time. Maybe a couple of hours."

Remi peered over the edge, her brows rising. "I'm going to need you to define exactly what you mean by straight down."

CHAPTER THIRTY-SIX

Sam pointed to the base of the gorge. "As in, we're way up here, and we need to be way down there."

Remi eyed the rope, then the edge of the bluff, wondering if maybe she'd been a bit rash in her decision to accompany him. Once past the twenty feet of sheer cliff, there was at least a hundred more feet of steep slope down to the bottom. "You're sure that's doable?"

Sam finished knotting the length he was working with. "The hardest part is getting down the cliff to where the slope starts. You see that tree growing down on that ledge?"

She carefully peered over, seeing the treetop about twenty feet below. "Yes."

"I'm going to lower you, then I'll follow. We'll rappel down from there to the next tree. And then the next."

She eyed the distance to the bottom of the gorge. "That rope isn't near long enough."

"It's called the Texas Rope Trick," he said, tying the longer length to the much smaller circle. "It's like a giant slipknot. The sling," he said, holding up the circle, "allows us to secure it to the tree trunk. At the bottom, I pull the middle strand threaded through it, bring the whole thing down, and we start all over again."

"You're sure it's safe?"

It wasn't a method Sam would recommend except under the most dire circumstances. "Have I ever led you astray?"

"This from the man who made me jump off the back of a speeding boat? And a cliff into the sea?"

"Rappelling is much safer."

"At least I was landing in water the other two times. That," she said, nodding down to the bottom of the gorge, "looks a lot harder."

"I'll lower you from here. All you need to do is hold on to the rope. Use your feet to walk backward down the cliff. Once we start down the next level, it'll be much easier."

She glanced down, noting that the bottom of the gorge seemed much farther than it had just a few moments ago. "Maybe I should go back and brave the wild boar."

"You already turned down that option."

"You're reminding me?"

He looped the makeshift harness beneath her arms, double-checking the knots he'd tied. "Try to think about something else," he said, sounding very calm about the whole thing.

She was anything but. "Is this the time to mention I had a glamorous life planned out for us?"

He slapped at a mosquito on his arm, then finished securing her into his makeshift harness. "Doing what?"

"After I found that Spanish galleon, I was going to write a book about it."

He helped her over the cliff's edge. "A whole book about one Spanish galleon?"

"It's the thrill of the hunt."

"Off the coast of California? You were there. It's not exactly what I'd call thrilling."

She clung to the rope as he started to lower her. "Regardless, my imagined life didn't consist of belly crawling through scorpion-infested dirt. Or dangling from a cliff. It was going to be martinis at lunch with my editor, who would send me on a fabulous tour, all while my agent sold the movie rights."

"Think how much more exciting this will sound."

She reached out with her foot, but it hit air. The movement sent her spinning. "Sam . . ."

"You're doing great. Easy peasy."

"Sam?"

And then she was there. As soon as her feet touched solid ground, she stopped turning. Slowly, she moved toward the tree, making sure she had something to balance against while she slipped out of the harness.

Sam retrieved the rope, wrapped the sling around the base of the tree, threaded the rope through the ends like an S, turning one strand of rope seemingly into three. He grabbed the first and second strands, tested the strength, and backed to the cliff's edge.

Her heart constricted in her chest as he jumped, free-falling for a second before planting his feet against the cliff, rappelling down. When Sam reached the ledge next to Remi, he pulled. Exactly like a slipknot, the sling and the rope fell to the ledge, kicking up dust as they hit. Sam had a firm grip on the rope as it started to slide past. Stopping it, he looked over at her. "You okay?"

"I'm trying to decide if I was scared to death, or exhilarated beyond anything I've ever experienced."

"You can make up your mind when we get to the bottom."

Once they were both safely on the ground, Sam led Remi along the base of the cliff. With no idea of who might be working for the Kyrils, and who might simply be there as part of the first harvest, Sam took extra care making sure they kept out of sight of the men and women who were leading the pack mules until they reached the trail leading to the bottom of the hill.

"We're going to have to join the caravan to get down to the compound."

"We'll have to pretend to be harvesters."

"Easier said than done." Sam reached over, touching a lock of her red hair. "This might be a bit noticeable."

"Says the man with sandy-brown hair. At least I have a solution." She pulled her scarf from her ponytail and wrapped it around her hair, hiding it from view. "I told you a good scarf comes in handy."

"So you did," he said as they started down the trail. At the next bend, they reached a group of harvesters who'd stopped to rest in the shade. "Keep going," Sam said. He dropped his backpack on the ground, then kneeled to tighten the lace on one of his boots. When he rose, he grabbed his backpack, along with a floppy canvas hat sitting next to it.

Sam caught up with Remi and they continued walking behind the workers who were leading the mules down the trail. A number of men and women had moved off the path to rest. Sam and Remi joined them, waiting for their friends to come down the hill. As Zoe and Dimitris approached, Sam slowly stood and blocked their way and quietly identified himself.

The two stopped, clearly surprised.

"What are you doing here?" Dimitris asked Sam.

"Coming to bring the both of you home."

"No," Dimitris said. "Not until we get what we came for."

"Come sit down with us. We need to talk this through."

"There is nothing to talk about," Dimitris said heatedly.

Remi glanced at Zoe, seeing the worry in her eyes. "Dimitris, please listen. Just sit with us and listen. Sam, tell them what your friend from the CIA told us."

"Short version, we need to get off the island," Sam said. "He thinks they're running drugs."

Dimitris dropped his pack on the ground. "We can't leave."

"Dimitris, please," Zoe said, tears welling up in her eyes. "Sam and Remi are here for us. Maybe—"

"We're almost there," he said. "I just want to get close enough to take some video. I might be able to find something to bring them down."

Zoe put her hand on Dimitris's arm. "Maybe we should listen to Sam."

"There's nothing he can tell me that'll change my mind."

"It's a lot more dangerous than we thought," Sam said. "If they are running drugs, they won't hesitate to kill you or anyone else who gets in their way."

"What do we do now?" Zoe asked Sam.

"We go back to the boat."

She turned to Dimitris. "I think he's right. You know he's right. We need to go back."

He hesitated. "You're sure that's what you want to do?"

"Positive. We should never have come here to start."

"But, Zoe, we came here for your grandfather."

"I know. But I lost him because of these people. I don't want to lose you, too."

He glanced at Sam, then nodded. "Okay."

Remi was glad when they all started up the trail, earning a few odd looks from the harvesters, who were all heading down to the port. At the first bend, Dimitris stopped, looking panicked. "I left my backpack behind. The boat key's in it. I'll just be a second."

Zoe watched him walking down the trail, toward the men and women sitting in the shade of the trees. Dimitris picked up his pack, then stopped to talk to a man who was holding the reins of one of the mules. "This is my fault," Zoe said. "I'm not sure what I was thinking, coming here. Somehow, last night, when we were talking about how easy it would be to take a few videos, and maybe prove how they're counterfeiting olive oil, it didn't seem so crazy."

"The important thing," Sam said, "is that we caught you in time."

"Zoe," Remi said. "Your arm. You're hurt."

She looked down at the dried blood on her elbow and forearm. "I didn't even notice. I slipped when I was climbing up to the trail from the boat."

"The boat." Remi looked at Sam. "Wasn't the key in the boat when we found it?"

"Now that you mention it . . ." They both turned toward the trail, searching.

Dimitris was nowhere in sight.

CHAPTER THIRTY-SEVEN

Dimitris, blinded by his need to exact retribution against the man responsible for killing Zoe's grandfather, had hoped to find some proof that Kyril was counterfeiting olive oil. His plan had been to blend in with the workers during the harvest, take a few photos, then get out of there with no one the wiser. At least that's what he and Zoe had told themselves when they'd concocted this idea.

But now, hearing about the drugs changed everything. Knowing full well that Sam would protect Zoe, the moment Dimitris saw their attention on her hurt arm, instead of returning back up the trail, he slipped down the side of the hill. It was steeper than he'd thought, and he fell twice, scraping his hands and bruising his backside. He earned a couple of odd looks as he weaved his way into a group of men once he reached the lower trail. Twenty minutes later, they neared the warehouses. Here, everything came to a stop as the workers with their mules formed a line, waiting for the scales.

One of Dimitris's cousins owned a much smaller olive orchard, which was why he and Zoe thought they could easily blend in. But on his cousin's farm, harvesting was a family and friends affair. Everyone showed up, picked olives all day, then celebrated at night.

This, however, was something completely different. At first glance it seemed as though the Kyrils had simply taken an old-fashioned business and expanded and updated it with modern technology. He looked into the vast, overhead doors of the building where the olives were milled. Large, gleaming stainless steel storage tanks stood just inside, waiting to receive the newly pressed oil, where it would need to sit for weeks to allow the sediment to settle before it was bottled for sale.

Dimitris looked past the tanks, but didn't see anything that might indicate any improprieties in production. He turned his attention back to the workers. One was leading a mule, its back loaded with full sacks of olives, toward the scales in front of the two warehouses. Those turning in fruit to be weighed had to produce a key card, which was scanned as they unloaded their bags onto a scale. From there, they were directed to another area, given a slip, which they turned in to a cashier for payment, then herded down a long graveled road out to the port to await a ferry that would return them to one of the larger surrounding islands.

It was all very impersonal. Big business.

But now that Dimitris had heard about the possibility of drugs being run, he had a feeling that the key card given to the harvesters was also a way for the Kyrils to know who was where and when. No one except those wearing tan coveralls with the Kyril logo seemed to have access to the milling facility, or the other buildings.

It wasn't until he saw the armed guards in their gray uniforms that he began to regret his rash decision to leave Sam and the others to come here on his own.

But he thought of Zoe. The look in her eyes when she'd come to him after learning that her grandfather had been found at the bottom of the cave.

Even if he and Remi hadn't been kidnapped the same day that Tassos had disappeared, he would've questioned the police theory that Tassos's death must have been accidental. Tassos had spent decades exploring every corner of Fourni, and knew it better than anyone there. He would *never* have put himself in a position that might lead to an accidental fall.

Dimitris knew it.

He intended to bring the Kyril kingdom crashing down. Whether he found evidence of drug running or counterfeit olive oil, Dimitris didn't care. All he needed to do was get inside that other building and find something that proved that Adrian Kyril was breaking the law.

Dimitris, certain Sam would do the right thing and take Zoe back to the boat, paused at the bottom of the hill. After glancing up toward the trail, not seeing Sam, Remi, or Zoe, he worked his way through the men and women who waited in line at the scales. His eye on the warehouse, he saw one of the overseers exiting through a side door, then stop suddenly, the door landing against his foot as he patted his pant pockets. He started to turn back, apparently found whatever he was looking for, then continued out, the door falling shut behind him.

It did not, however, completely close—and the man walked off, never once looking back.

Seeing his chance, Dimitris edged his way out of the line past the hopper, hearing the rattle of olives landing inside it.

Encouraged when it seemed no one noticed him, he walked toward the warehouse door, unable to believe his luck when he reached it. He pulled it open, then slipped in, taking a quick look out before he closed the door behind him.

It took a few moments for his eyes to adjust to the dark surroundings. The only light inside came from a row of windows high up on the north side of the warehouse, but it was enough to see. This building, apparently, was used for storage. Full pallets of cardboard boxes marked ONE LITER were stacked on metal shelving up to the ceiling.

To the right he saw an office built into the corner, its window overlooking the interior of the warehouse.

He decided to start his search there. The door leading into it was locked. He moved around the corner, seeing a window, hoping he might be able to get in. Unfortunately, it was also locked. Cupping his hands against the glass, he looked inside, seeing a desk and chair, file drawers and shelving.

About to turn away, his eyes caught on the desktop, where he saw what at first looked like pencils with wires sticking out. He knew nothing about explosives, but he was pretty sure that's exactly what those things were.

That was the evidence they were looking for.

Pulling his cell phone from his pocket, he opened the camera app, placed the lens side against the glass, and took a photo. He was just about to take a second shot when a motor near the front of the warehouse hummed to life. Light flooded in as the massive overhead door started rolling upward.

Startled, he backed into a telephone mounted on the outside of the office wall, knocking the handset from the receiver. He managed to catch it, returned it to its place, and ducked behind a pallet stacked with boxes as two men entered. The phone on the wall rang. They stopped, one of the men answering it. "Giorgio . . ." He held the phone out.

Giorgio took the phone, then listened. "Yes . . . Right away." He hung up. "They want the tins for the Heibert shipment."

The other man climbed onto the forklift parked near the door, turning the key. It beeped as he backed up, then turned, driving it toward a pallet near the first row of shelving.

"Hold up, Lucas," the gray-haired Giorgio said. "I'm not sure this is the right load." Lucas stopped the forklift as Giorgio walked over, pulled a box cutter from his belt, and slit the plastic binding the boxes to the pallet. He cut open the topmost box, pulling out an empty tin with the green and gold Kyril logo. "Wrong one," he said, dropping it back into the box. He turned and surveyed the row of shelves closest to them, then looked in Dimitris's direction, seeing the pallet. "Why do they keep moving these things?"

Dimitris sunk down as far as he could as Giorgio walked over. The man stood just a few feet away, cutting open the cellophane wrapper securing the cartons. He opened a box, pulling out a tin marked simply OLIVE OIL, without the distinctive Kyril logo. He nodded. "Move it out."

Dimitris's heart started pounding as Lucas drove the forklift toward him, sliding the forks underneath the pallet.

CHAPTER THIRTY-EIGHT

Sam, Remi, and Zoe moved into the trees. Once out of sight of the curious workers walking down the trail, Sam took out his binoculars to search the grounds around the processing facility.

"What's going on?" Zoe asked. "Do you see him? Is Dimitris okay?"

"I haven't found him yet."

He did a quick scan, saw a couple of men in uniforms running from the scales toward one of the open warehouses. Two men in khaki coveralls stood next to a forklift. When one of them moved, Sam saw Dimitris, kneeling on the floor. The two guards ran into the open bay door. One of them pulled Dimitris to his feet, while the other closed the bay door, blocking all view inside the building. "They have him."

"No," Zoe said, her knees giving way. She sat on the ground, closing her eyes. "This is all my fault."

Remi crouched beside her, putting her arm over the young woman's shoulders. She looked up at Sam. "Don't worry, Zoe. Sam always comes up with a plan. Right, Sam?"

When he didn't answer, she cleared her throat, then stared at him with what he was beginning to recognize as her *say something to fix this* look. "Exactly," he said. "I've got a plan. A good one."

"You do?" Zoe asked.

"Absolutely. I just haven't thought of it yet."

"Don't worry," Remi said to Zoe. "He's like that. But he always comes through in the end."

Zoe made a feeble attempt at a smile and then took a deep breath and said, "Right."

Sam turned his attention back to the compound. "We need to find some way to get into the building without being seen."

"Which one?" Remi asked.

"The warehouse on the left." There were three main buildings fanned out in a semicircle facing out to a long graveled road that led to the port. About midway down that road, the ruins of an old stone building sat in the midst of some ancient olive trees. Had it been closer, and on the opposite side of the road, they might have been able to approach from there. Searching for another avenue, he turned back to where the harvesters were unloading sacks of olives from the mules. The fruit was placed into a massive hopper, which separated the leaves and branches from the olives on their way to the first pressing.

Remi followed the direction of his gaze. "Guess we get to be harvesters again." They slipped into the line of workers and mules coming in off the trail, waiting to weigh their loads. The three of them watched as a couple of men in each group unloaded the heavy sacks from the backs of the mules, placing them on the scale. Once the weight was confirmed, a receipt was given to one worker, and they were directed to pick up their payment from a small reinforced cinder-block building with a steel door and steel shutters.

Gun laws in the country were strict, but Sam suspected that the amount of cash on hand probably allowed the Kyrils to acquire permits for some of their guards. He noticed several who appeared to be carrying concealed weapons. No doubt they had even more fire-power in the bunker—which meant he was severely outgunned.

Not that he was about to pull out that little Smith & Wesson un-less he absolutely had to.

He eyed the warehouse where Dimitris was being held. The bay door was still closed, and a guard was now posted outside the entry door. When a uniformed employee walked over, trying to enter, the guard turned him away.

Not a good sign. Clearly they weren't getting in through the front.

"We need to find a way around to the back of that building with-out being seen."

Remi nodded to the pay station. "What about over there? It prob-ably wouldn't be too hard to create some sort of a distraction."

He glanced at the line of harvesters waiting to be paid. "That could work. Can you and Zoe start a commotion by the scales? If we draw enough attention from both directions, we should be able to get around to the back of the building without anyone noticing."

The three continued down the trail until they reached the com-plex. Remi and Zoe broke off toward the men and women waiting in line at the pay station. Once there, Remi began talking to Zoe, then pointing to the scales. Whatever it was the two women were discussing, it seemed to catch the attention of others, as several turned to look at them. A few started asking questions, pulling out their weight receipts, comparing their paperwork with the person next to them. Within moments the agitated workers gravitated to the scales, shouting and waving their receipts. When the guards standing between them and the building started forward, Remi looked at Sam and nodded, as if to say, *Your turn*.

While Remi and Zoe continued stirring up suspicion and angst among the workers, Sam moved to the other side of one of the mules. Drawing his knife, he slashed the ties on one of the full bags. The falling olives bounced on the ground, hitting the mule's hooves. Startled, the beast danced about, trying to escape the torrent of fruit. The commotion drew the attention of the other site supervisors not involved in quelling the protests that Remi and Zoe had instigated at the scales. Seeing it was clear, Sam waved them over, and the three slipped past the guards, hurrying between the buildings.

CHAPTER THIRTY-NINE

Issues with the scales?" Sam asked as he, Remi, and Zoe ducked around the corner to the back of the warehouse.

Remi's green eyes sparkled. "Short-shifting the weight." She looked at the door, her expression sobering. "I don't know how we're going to get in. That looks pretty impregnable."

She was right. There was no way to unlock it from the outside. Judging from the height of the weeds and dry grass growing right to the door, it hadn't been opened in quite some time. He looked up, seeing a row of windows above them that ran the length of the building. A few were cracked open for ventilation. "If you get on my shoulders—"

At the exact same time Remi said, "I could get on your shoulders—"

Sam held out his hand. She grasped it, placed one foot on his thigh, the other up on his shoulder. When she had both feet planted, he stood tall, and moved against the building. Remi leaned forward to take a look inside. After several seconds, Sam asked, "What's going on up there?"

"Looking . . . Hold on . . . I think he's in there."

"Think?" There was a sudden shifting of her weight as she ducked below the window. "What's wrong?" he asked.

"One of the guards just walked in the front door . . . Shhh . . ." Maybe a minute went by before she said, "He's definitely in there." She bent down, placing her hand in Sam's as he helped her to the ground. "They have him in a bullpen. He's tied to a support beam, but he looks okay."

Zoe's frightened gaze landed on Sam. "What do you think they're going to do?"

Not wanting to send Zoe into a panic, since, more than likely, they'd kill him, the only thing Sam said was, "They won't risk doing anything with so many witnesses around. Which means we need a place to hide until everyone empties out."

"What about the ruins?" Remi said.

"If we can get to them."

They moved to the corner of the warehouse. It didn't take long for Sam to realize that was their best option. The roofless stone building surrounded by ancient olive trees sat on the opposite side of the gravel road that led down to the dock. In the short time they stood there watching, they'd seen two guards and dozens of workers walking past on their way to the ferry—none of them seeming to pay any attention to the abandoned structure.

Getting there from where they currently stood would take some care. There were a few scattered shrubs alongside the warehouse, and a stand of trees near the front. Sam led them from shrub to shrub until they reached the trees. From there, they stepped out onto the road, blending in with the workers walking toward the port. As the three neared the ruins, they edged to the opposite side of the road, slipped into the trees, then ducked behind one of the walls.

They watched the building where Dimitris was being held, waiting for the harvesters and, hopefully, most of the employees and guards to clear for the day. The exodus of workers and employees took longer than expected, partly because of the disturbance Remi and Zoe had caused, spreading the rumor that the scales were off. And there were still the stragglers bringing in the last loads of the day.

Eventually, the mules were corralled behind the warehouse, and the last of the workers trudged down to the waiting ferry, their shadows stretching out in front of them. As the ferry took off, the sun dipped toward the rocky hills, then disappeared, casting the entire valley into twilight.

Once it was dark, Sam, Remi, and Zoe crawled to the edge of the ruins. They positioned themselves on either side of what had once been a doorway, giving Sam a perfect view of the complex. As far as he could tell, there were three guards, one for each structure on the premises. The first and smallest building on the left was the cinder-block bunker house where the workers had lined up for payment earlier that afternoon. The middle warehouse was the processing facility, and the third building on the right was the supply warehouse where Dimitris was being held.

As Sam was studying the layout, he heard the rumbling of heavy aluminum panels along with the hum of a motor as the large over-head bay door started rolling up. Light spilled out onto the loading dock as one of the guards walked out, hurried down the stairs, then over to the flatbed truck parked in the middle of the complex. He backed the vehicle against the dock while another guard started the forklift, lifting a pallet stacked with boxes. A steady beep sounded as the forklift backed up, then turned, moving the load onto the truck bed, while the third guard directed the pallet as it was being lowered in the center of the bed.

The three guards climbed onto the back of the truck, two on their hands and knees, examining something at the base of the load. Whatever it was, they resolved the matter, got off the truck, and moved to the loading dock. One walked into the warehouse, turned off the lights, and shut the bay door. A moment later, he exited through the side door, and the three men walked over to the bunker house, two of them lighting up cigarettes.

"Let's go," Sam said, slinging his backpack over his shoulder. He eyed the women as they rose, moving behind him. Had he any choice in the matter, he'd insist they remain hidden here in the ruins. As it was, he was going to need them both to get into the building.

They crossed the gravel road, then ducked behind some low bushes. Sam moved into the trees near the front of the warehouse, and was about to signal for Remi and Zoe to follow, when one of the guards looked in their direction. The man inhaled, the tip of his cigarette glowing orange in the dark. As he blew out a plume of smoke, he pointed to the load on the bed of the truck. The other two men laughed at whatever he said, then all three continued toward the bunker house.

Sam waited a second longer, waved Remi then Zoe over, and they picked their way along the side of the warehouse to the back.

Their plan was simple. Remi and Zoe would boost Sam up to the open window. He'd climb in, free Dimitris, and bring him out.

Remi examined the open window about ten feet above them. "What if there's an alarm?"

"As many times as they've been in and out," he said, holstering his gun and dropping his backpack to the ground, "I doubt it. And if there is one, it's probably turned off."

She nodded, then looked at Zoe. The two women created half a human pyramid, their backs against the warehouse, their knees bent. Sam gripped their shoulders, stepped up onto Remi's thigh, then Zoe's. "Ready?" he asked.

Zoe nodded. "Yes."

"Try not to miss," Remi said.

Balancing, he looked up at the window, gauging the distance, and jumped.

CHAPTER FORTY

Sam pulled himself up and into the window, then dropped down on the other side. Moonlight angled in, casting a blue glow across the concrete floor and the rows of floor-to-ceiling industrial shelving. The pallets of cardboard boxes wrapped in cellophane filled the majority of them.

Sam paused, listening.

Tick. Tick. Tick.

A clock high on the wall somewhere to the left counted off the seconds. Other than that, all was quiet.

He followed along a row of shelving toward the sound of the clock until he reached the chain-link enclosure. A padlock hung in the hasp, securing the gate. Dimitris was, as Remi had described earlier, tied to a metal support beam in the center of an otherwise empty storage area. Blindfolded and gagged, he didn't move. Sam took out his pick and popped the lock open.

Dimitris shifted, bracing himself for whatever might come.

"It's me," Sam whispered. He removed the blindfold and gag.

"Where's Zoe?"

"Safe. With Remi."

"I know what they're doing," Dimitris said as Sam moved behind him to cut the ties. He nodded to the shelves just outside the bullpen. "They're smuggling the heroin out with the olive oil. I have photos of—"

The metallic jingle of keys hitting the door at the front of the warehouse startled him.

"Someone's coming," Sam whispered. He picked up the blindfold and pulled it over Dimitris's eyes. "*Don't* move. I'll be right out there." He left the bullpen, closed the gate, and hung the padlock on the hasp, hoping whoever was coming wouldn't look too close and notice the lock wasn't actually secured.

A door near the front opened. The lights went on as Sam moved behind the next row of shelving, his knee knocking against an open box filled with small glass vials as he crouched. The glass tubes rattled as the guard's footsteps echoed across the concrete floor as he headed for the office. Sam aimed his gun as the guard paused, then walked back to the bullpen to check on Dimitris. Apparently satisfied that all was as it should be, he returned to the adjacent office space, unlocked the door, then walked past the window that overlooked the warehouse. Less than a minute later, he exited, locked the office, and left. The moment Sam heard the exterior door closing, he returned to the bullpen, freed Dimitris, and the two hurried out the back.

Zoe threw herself into his arms the moment he stepped out the door. "I was so worried about you."

"I'm fine."

Sam stood in the doorway. "Let's get out of here."

"What about the heroin?" Dimitris asked.

"Forget the heroin. If they come back and find you missing, we're all in trouble." He started to push the door closed.

"Wait," Dimitris said. "I know how they're getting the drugs out. They're smuggling it in those unmarked olive oil tins."

"What tins?" Sam asked.

"They took out a pallet full of them. I heard them saying it was for the Heibert shipment. It was going out tonight."

"Heibert?" Remi looked at Sam. "That's the name Rube mentioned."

"Regardless," Sam replied, "the last thing he'd want is for us to step in the middle of an Interpol investigation."

"What about the explosives?" Dimitris asked.

Sam, about to shove the door closed, thought about the two Interpol agents who'd been killed because of an IED on one of the Heibert ships. "What explosives?"

"This," he said, accessing something on his phone screen, then showing it to Sam. "I couldn't get in because the office was locked, but you can see them laid out on the desk. Four of them."

Sam took the phone, enlarging the photo. Though slightly out of focus, there was no doubt that he was looking at an assortment of detonators—not what he expected to see in an olive oil production plant. It was, however, something that might come up in the heroin trade. Especially when looking for a way to eliminate any evidence, should one of their shipments fall under suspicion by the authorities.

Zoe eyed the screen. "Those seem awful small for bombs."

"They're detonators," Sam said, then to Dimitris, asked, "Did you see any other explosive devices?"

"No. Just these. But won't that help prove the Kyrils are guilty?"

"Not necessarily." If they had the actual explosive material used to make the bombs, Interpol could test the chemical composition to see if it matched the residue from the incendiary device that killed their investigators. An identical chemical signature would be almost impossible for the Kyrils to explain away.

Had he been by himself, he wouldn't hesitate to go back. Unfortunately, that wasn't the case.

This time, when he tried to close the door, Remi stopped him.

"We can't leave now," she said. "What if this is what finally brings the Kyril kingdom down?"

"It's too dangerous," Sam said. "It won't do any of us any good if we get killed looking for it."

"I'm willing to take the risk," Dimitris said, holding on to the door, refusing to let Sam close it. "It's the only way to stop the Kyrils."

Reluctantly, Sam changed his mind. "I'll need a lookout. You and I can go back in. The women can wait here."

"No," Zoe said, grasping Dimitris's arm. "You can't go. I just got you back."

Remi looked at the two of them, then Sam. "I'll go with you."

There were so many reasons he should have told her no, but the look in her eyes convinced him otherwise. "You're sure you want to do this?"

"Positive."

He turned to Zoe. "You know the trees we hid behind near the front?"

She nodded.

"The two of you wait there. If anything happens, get to the dock. Nikos will be waiting."

"Please be careful."

After he and Remi slipped inside, he heard the clock counting away the seconds. He closed the door behind them, then led Remi to the office, hoping he wasn't making the biggest mistake of his life.

CHAPTER FORTY-ONE

Remi watched as Sam picked the lock on the office door, then opened it. Remi stood just inside, peering out the narrow opening to keep watch, while Sam took a look around. From the corner of her eye, she saw him looking at the detonators, which were laid out on the desk blotter, the wires neatly folded against the small tubes as though someone had recently removed them from their packaging. He picked up one, along with a remote, tucking both into his pocket, then went back to searching. Apparently finding nothing in the desk drawers, he turned around and opened the metal cabinets behind him. He stood there a moment, not moving.

Remi looked back at him. "What's wrong?"

"I was hoping there'd be a safe or munitions box where they might keep the actual explosives."

She scanned the contents of the cabinet. The top few shelves were filled with smaller office supplies, pens, paper clips, and the like. The bottom shelf had an open case of copy paper, ink toner, a large case of Earl Grey tea, and next to that an open box of bubble wrap. She nodded at the shelf. "My money's on the Earl Grey box."

He reached down to pull out the box. "You're right. It's way too heavy for tea." He flipped the lid open, pulling out a thick, gray block in plastic wrapping. "C-4. How'd you know?"

"Besides that there's no mug sitting on the desk? Only a restaurant would keep that much tea around. It doesn't stay good forever." She watched as he unzipped the main pocket on his pack, setting the block of explosive on top of his coil of rope. "Is that safe?" she asked.

"As long as we keep the detonator away from it, very."

Hearing a noise near the front of the building, she looked out. "Someone's coming."

Sam turned off his light, then drew his gun. "Get beneath the desk. Hurry."

She crawled under while Sam moved to the hinged side of the door, his gun in one hand, his backpack in the other. He pressed himself against the wall and waited.

Though Remi tried to even out her breathing, she found it difficult, especially as the heavy footsteps neared. Panic sent her heart racing, the pulse pounding in her ears. Had she listened to Sam instead of siding with Dimitris, they all would've been on their way out to the port, not trapped here in the office.

Breathe . . .

She had to trust that Sam knew what he was doing.

Breathe . . .

The heavy footsteps bypassed the office, continuing on toward the bullpen. The next thing she heard was someone shouting. "He's gone!" Then the sound of running.

"Check the back door," someone else shouted. "I'll check the office."

Breathe . . .

A moment later, the lights in the warehouse turned on. Then someone was at the door, shaking the handle. Remi looked out at Sam, pressed in the corner, his gun out. He put his finger to his lips.

She gave a slight nod.

Breathe . . .

But trying to stay calm wasn't easy. Especially when she heard the sound of a key in the lock. The door flew open, slamming into Sam. He never moved. Remi could see the guard's booted feet beneath the desk, certain whoever was out there surely had to hear her heart pounding.

After only a cursory look inside the office, the guard turned away and raced down each aisle of the warehouse.

"Check out the back," he shouted.

The sound of men running in two directions.

Then nothing but the ticking of the clock outside the door.

It seemed an eternity before Sam stepped forward, reaching for her hand. "Let's get out of here." They stepped out of the office. Sam glanced to his right, then stopped short.

One of the guards was standing outside the open back door, his back to them. Sam led her in the opposite direction. Keeping to the wall, they reached the front door, which stood ajar.

Sam looked out, then drew Remi toward him. "Stay low. Wait for my signal."

She looked to her left, just able to make out Dimitris and Zoe near the trees, hidden behind the shrubs by the road.

"Now."

Remi ducked as she ran. A moment later, Sam followed.

They heard the flatbed truck's engine starting up. One of the guards was driving the vehicle away from the loading dock.

"That's the pallet I was telling you about," Dimitris whispered. "On the back of the truck."

It stopped in the middle of the complex grounds. The driver got out, leaving the door open, the headlights on, and the engine running. He jogged to the loading dock, where the second guard stood, both men keeping watch down the road to the port. They were eventually joined by the third guard, who came in from the back.

Remi stared at the twin beams of light aimed down the middle of the road. The moment they stepped out, they'd be caught. They'd never get to the dock without being seen unless they found a way across the road to the ruins. From there, it was at least a quarter of a mile to the water, but they'd have trees for cover.

"This is my fault," Dimitris said. "I'm the one who insisted on going back in the office."

"No one's placing blame," Sam told him. "Let's figure out how to get out of here."

Dimitris nodded at the unattended truck. "What if we stole that? I think I can get into it without anyone seeing. We can drive that out to the dock before they ever catch us."

Remi eyed the twenty yards of open space between them and the truck. "There's got to be a better way."

Dimitris looked at Zoe. "I love you."

Before they could stop him, he darted out toward the opposite corner of the warehouse.

Sam grabbed Zoe's arm, stopping her from following. As he held her back, Remi glanced at the truck—left so temptingly on its own.

That was when she noticed the red light flashing beneath the pallet.

CHAPTER FORTY-TWO

S am saw the flashing light beneath the pallet at about the same time as Remi. It occurred to him that the guards had a twofold purpose in their placement of the truck. The headlights facing down the road ensured that Dimitris couldn't escape without being seen. Leaving an unattended running truck—with the door open—just about guaranteed that Dimitris would try to use it to escape.

It was a trap set for a single person. And had Dimitris been there on his own, it might have worked.

Then again, it might still work, if Sam wasn't able to stop him.

"Sam," Remi said. "Do something."

The IED could be in any one of those boxes, but it was the detonator that was the key. "Which detonator was missing when we walked in?"

"What?"

"There were four types in his photo. But only three when we walked in. One of those is now wired to that pallet."

He glanced at Dimitris, edging from the corner of the warehouse toward the flatbed—a good twenty yards away. "Dimitris!" he called out. "Stop!"

His warning had the exact opposite effect. The young man ran faster, his attention solely on the truck.

Hoping that he was guessing correctly, Sam aimed his gun at the blinking light beneath the pallet—which left a lot of room for error at this distance.

"Blue lettering!" Remi said. "The one that's missing from the photo."

At the last second, he shot out the tire. The sidewall burst, the weight of the cab shifting onto the rim. The blast of intense heat from the near simultaneous explosion hit Sam in the face as the pallet and all its contents launched upward and out in a flash of light. Dimitris was hurled back, slamming to the ground as flaming debris pelted down around him and on top of the truck.

Zoe screamed, burying her head in Remi's shoulder, while Remi stared in horror. "Is he—?"

Sam tossed his backpack at Remi's feet. "Wait here."

He ran out, dropping to the ground next to Dimitris, relieved to see him conscious, though somewhat stunned. "What happened?" Dimitris asked.

"They set you up. The load was rigged." He reached down with one hand, helping Dimitris to his feet. "Let's get out of here."

They heard a loud click as two halogen lamps on posts flooded the area with light. Sam pulled Dimitris back to the office building, then around the corner as the bunker door opened. One of the guards stepped out, aiming a mini Uzi. "Get back," Sam shouted to Remi.

The gun roared. A deafening *rat-a-tat* echoed between the buildings. A volley of shots hit the corner of the building and the gravel in front of them. The gunman ducked behind the flatbed. Sam gripped his Smith & Wesson, aimed at the blinding lights, and shot both in quick succession. Sparks rained down, then faded into the dark. A second burst of gunfire peppered the ground several feet to

Sam's left. He edged out, fired at the muzzle flash, heard a grunt, then the clatter of the Uzi as it fell to the ground.

One down.

Sam motioned for Dimitris to move to the trees where Remi and Zoe were hiding. He followed, walking backward, his weapon aimed at the bunker where the two remaining guards were holed up. So far, neither had emerged. Sam had a feeling that they were waiting for him to make the first move.

With only two bullets left, and a good quarter mile to the boat dock, he wasn't about to take the chance. They still needed to get across to the ruins and thicker trees. With the truck headlights—although now somewhat askew—glaring down the road, they'd never make it past without drawing fire.

Sam looked over at Dimitris, who was holding Zoe in his arms, the young woman sobbing quietly. Unfortunately, the young man's misguided attempt to save them had actually set them back. Not only did Kyril's men now know Dimitris wasn't alone, they knew exactly where they were positioned.

Time was running out. "I'll stay here and hold them off while the three of you cross over. Get to the dock. I'll be right behind you."

Remi put her hand on his shoulder. "Sam . . . ?"

He reached up with his left hand, grasped her fingers. As intelligent as she was, there was no doubt she realized the position they were in. All he could do at this point was hope to hold them off long enough so that the three of them could—hopefully—make it to the ruins. As he let go, about to tell them to get ready, his foot hit his backpack. Ironic, he thought. Here he was with a block of C-4, a detonator, and a remote, but no batteries to set it off.

But he *did* have a rope.

Simple, but effective.

CHAPTER FORTY-THREE

Remi, her stomach twisting in knots, listened while Sam quickly outlined what he needed them to do. She glanced across the road at the ruins, the moonlight painting the old stones and treetops a soft blue. "Questions?" he asked her.

A million, she wanted to say. First and foremost, how was it that he knew how to do what he did? How was it that he had skills that were beyond those any ordinary man possessed? But all that came out of her mouth was "No."

"Try not to look at the headlights," Sam said to her and Zoe. "It'll ruin your night vision. Once you get to the ruins, use those backpacks to make as much noise as you can. Just keep the trees between you and them." He picked up one end of the rope coiled at his feet, handing it to Dimitris. "Keep this on the ground as you cross. If anything goes wrong, get them to the boat."

Dimitris looked at Zoe, a myriad of emotions flitting across his face. He'd done exactly what Sam had warned against—going it alone—and now they were paying the price. Just when Remi worried that he was going to stand there and beg forgiveness, he took Zoe's hand in his and nodded. "Got it."

Remi, holding Sam's backpack by its straps, started to follow

Dimitris and Zoe, then stopped. She turned to Sam, pulled his face to hers, and kissed him quickly. "Be careful."

He nodded, searching her eyes. "You too."

She took a deep breath, trying to slow her thudding heart. There were so many ways this plan could go wrong, and it seemed each one of them was rushing through her mind. As much as she didn't want to leave him, she let go, moving next to Dimitris and Zoe. "Ready."

They poised themselves at the edge of the road, waiting for Sam's signal. He stepped out, closer to the warehouse. "Hey! Over here!" he shouted, drawing the guards' attention. He fired once.

The three of them burst from the trees, Dimitris dragging the rope through the gravel as Sam fired his last shot. They dove into the ruins on the other side just as the guards returned fire.

Safe for the moment, she, Zoe, and Dimitris crouched behind one of the crumbling walls. Dimitris positioned himself in the doorway and gripped the rope, then nodded. Remi crawled to the edge of the ruins, looking across the road at Sam.

When she gave him a thumbs-up, he pulled the trigger several times on his empty gun, the distinct *click, click, click* audible in the quiet of the night. "Run!" he shouted. "I'm out of bullets!"

And just in case the gunmen didn't understand English, Dimitris yelled out in Greek, "Hurry! To the dock! He's out of bullets!"

Remi and Zoe ran into the woods. They darted from tree to tree, hitting their backpacks on any shrubs they passed. The automatic gunfire sent the adrenaline racing through Remi's veins as she pressed herself against the trunk. But after a few shots, silence descended. The gunmen made no move to pursue them.

Looking over at Zoe, Remi nodded. They ran again, dragging their packs through the shrubs, then ducked behind the next tree, and then the next. Several seconds passed. The only sound was the wind riffling through the leaves on the branches above. If the gunmen didn't make a move, Sam would be trapped on the other side.

Remi edged around the thick trunk, looking back at the compound, seeing the ruins between her and the guards. Apparently they'd played it a bit too safe. Not only could Remi not see the gunmen, they definitely couldn't see her or Zoe, who was leaning against the tree to her right, her chest heaving as she tried to catch her breath.

"We need to find a way to make them follow us," Remi said.

"How?" Zoe asked between breaths.

Remi eyed the tree and shrubs near the road to her left, the area lit up by the flatbed's headlights. To get to it, she'd be opening herself up as a target. "It might be Sam's only chance."

Zoe saw the direction of her gaze. "Remi, no."

She wasn't about to leave him trapped. There had to be a better way to draw the guards out. Gripping Sam's backpack, she thought about the odds as she glanced across the road, where Sam waited. And then it hit her.

"I have an idea."

Untying her scarf from her head, she knotted it to the top of the backpack, then heaved the whole thing toward the bush lit up in the beam of the truck's headlight. As the backpack fell into the branches, the ends of her scarf floated up. Gunfire erupted, the shots ripping through the bush at the decoy.

Remi, her heart in her throat, pressed herself against the trunk. The guards ran out, their heavy footfalls crunching on the gravel.

"Now!" Sam shouted.

She heard the grunts as the two guards tripped over the rope and flew forward.

Sam raced out from one side, Dimitris the other. Sam slammed his booted foot into the ribs of the closest man, grabbed his weapon and aimed it at the other guard. "Drop your gun."

Dimitris repeated his words in Greek.

The second guard released his pistol. Dimitris picked it up, backing away.

"You can come out," Sam called.

Remi and Zoe ventured forward. When Remi reached Sam's side, he handed her the loaded weapon. "If they move, shoot."

Not sure she could ever pull the trigger, she took a deep breath, hoping no one would notice her hand shaking as she held the gun. She pointed it at the man closest to her, while Dimitris covered the other.

One of the men laughed, saying something in Greek.

Dimitris translated for Sam. "He says we'll never escape. They're already on their way."

"Appreciate the warning," Sam said. He gathered the rope, using it to tie both men back-to-back. With Dimitris's help, he dragged them to their feet, led them to the lightpost, and wrapped the remainder of the rope around their waists and the pole, knotting it securely. When he was sure they weren't going anywhere, he picked up the Uzi from the dead guard, realized it was empty, and dropped it. "Let's go," he said.

Dimitris ran back to the truck to pick up a dented tin that had landed a couple of feet from the cab. "It's empty!" He tossed it aside.

"We've got the C-4," Sam said. "If we're lucky, they can match it to the explosion on the ship."

When they reached the dock, there was no sign of Nikos. Now that the immediate danger was over, and the adrenaline had fled Remi's body, her hands started shaking and nausea threatened. She'd never seen anyone killed before. Try as she might, she couldn't shake the echo of gunshots from her head. She turned toward Sam in a panic, when suddenly Zoe pointed to the south. "There," she said.

Remi looked, relieved to see the *Asteri* motoring across the moonlit waters toward them.

CHAPTER FORTY-FOUR

Nikos took off full speed the moment the four boarded the *Asteri*. Relief flooded his face as he looked back at his son and Zoe. Once they'd put considerable distance between them and the port, Nikos engaged the autopilot. "What were you thinking?" he said, grabbing Dimitris by his shoulders. His face crumpled as he pulled his son close. "What if something happened to you? What would I do?"

"I'm sorry," Dimitris said, his voice filled with emotion.

"It was me," Zoe said. "I'm the one who got us into this."

"No," Dimitris said. "I should've stopped you."

"The good news," Sam said, "is that we may have the evidence we need to tie Kyril to the murder of the Interpol agents."

"What sort of evidence?"

"I'll explain on the way. Let's go get the *Star Catcher* and get out of here. The more miles we put between us and them, the better."

They found the RIB boat exactly where Dimitris had left it, moored behind an outcropping of rock in the narrow, cliff-edged inlet. Coming from the east, the boat was effectively hidden in the dark. Nikos maneuvered the *Asteri* next to the smaller vessel, then shifted to neutral. Dimitris climbed down the ladder, stepping into the boat. When he started up the engine, it sputtered and died.

"What's wrong?" Nikos asked.

Dimitris tried again, with the same result. "Just give me a minute. I'll get it running."

Nikos grabbed a small flashlight from the cabin. Turning it on, he aimed the beam at the *Star Catcher* so Dimitris could work on the engine.

It was taking far too long. Sam, thinking about the guard's parting remarks—that someone was on their way—took his binoculars, jumped out of the boat onto the rocks, and climbed up to the top of the cliff. A light breeze swept in off the water, the wind rustling the leaves of the nearby olive trees. He moved to the edge, looking out over the Aegean, his gaze following the coastline on the left, trying to see the port. The moonlight glistened off a wake across the water farther out. It took a few seconds before he saw the boat that was causing it, particularly because he couldn't see any lights. There was no mistaking the sleek dark outline of the Omega 41.

Maybe he should have killed the two guards when he had a chance. The moment Kyril's men landed and found the pair, he knew they'd come looking.

Tracing his steps down the hill to the water, he saw Dimitris was still trying to start the *Star Catcher*. Had there been only one boat hidden in the small cove, they might escape notice if the Omega passed by. With two vessels, they had no hope. "Big problem. Kyril's boat is heading toward the port. It won't be long until they start searching for us."

Dimitris looked up as the engine sputtered. "I've almost got it."

"With the boat they're in, I'm not sure it's going to matter," Sam said. They had less than five minutes to come up with a solid plan. He took a good look around, checking to see if they could somehow make room for the *Asteri* behind the outcropping of rock. The inlet was far too narrow to fit both boats, and they'd never be able to sink the much smaller and nearly indestructible RIB boat in time. "If we only had the one vessel, they'd probably pass us right by."

Remi leaned over the railing of the *Asteri*, watching Dimitris work. "Can't we just let the *Star Catcher* drift away?"

"If they find it empty, they'll still come searching for us. We need to make them think we got away so they leave."

Nikos, still holding the flashlight for Dimitris, looked over at Sam. "What if I draw them off with the *Star Catcher*, like you did before?"

"If I thought there was any chance—" His gaze landed on Remi's suitcases lined up outside the cabin. "You don't have anything with a hood packed in there, do you?" he asked her.

"No."

Dimitris looked up as the engine started. "We have a couple of raincoats on board."

"I'll get them," Nikos said.

"Sorry, Remi," Sam said. "But we'll need your clothes to stuff into them. Make it look like a couple of people."

"You don't think they'll figure out they're dummies?"

"I don't intend to let them get that close. Dimitris, I'll need you to climb up to the top of the hill. Let me know when they're on their way. We may not have much time."

Remi unzipped her largest suitcase, pulling out bulky clothing items. Zoe and Sam kneeled beside her to help stuff them into the yellow raincoats, grabbing whatever was closest.

"Not that," Remi said, pulling a silk blouse from Sam's hands.

"If we fail, that shirt will be the last thing you miss." He finished stuffing the first jacket, then picked up Nikos's much larger coat, realizing for all the clothes Remi had packed, there might not be enough. He nodded at her carry-on. "That'll make a good body for Nikos's coat."

Remi emptied it, then handed it over to him.

"I think we're good," he said, eyeing the stuffed dummies. Grabbing his backpack, he climbed down into the smaller boat, which Dimitris had left idling. "Nikos."

The older man put both dummies into the larger, empty suitcase and lowered it down to him. Sam positioned the dummies on the seats behind the wheel, then opened his backpack.

Zoe's eyes widened as he took out the block of C-4. "That's evidence!"

"Which will do us no good if we're dead."

"You're going to blow up my stuff?" Remi said, looking close to jumping over into the smaller boat.

"If I win the lotto, I'll buy you new everything."

"Ha! Do you know what the odds of that are?"

"A heck of a lot better than us surviving if they find us sitting in this cove." He dug into his pocket, pulling out the remote and the detonator. "Probably a bad time to ask, Nikos. What sort of batteries do you have on board? I need a few triple A's."

Nikos held up his flashlight. "Sorry. All I have is this and a spare nine volt for the radio."

"I'll take one of those."

Nikos ran into the cabin, retrieved the radio battery, and tossed it to Sam. He used his knife to cut open the casing, revealing six triple A batteries inside. He took those batteries and inserted them into the remote and detonator.

"They're coming!" Dimitris shouted.

"Let me know when they're about a minute out!" Sam lashed the dummies in their seats, then set up the detonator and C-4. When Dimitris's signal came, he set the detonator, shifted the motor to

211

forward, then grabbed the ladder of the *Asteri* as he pushed the *Star Catcher* out toward open sea.

The two stuffed jackets looked like a couple of people sitting at the controls. None too soon. The Omega appeared. It kept pace as the *Star Catcher* continued out to sea. One of the men aimed an automatic weapon at the boat.

Sam, clinging to the ladder of the *Asteri*, counted the seconds. The gunman fired, the muzzle blast flashing yellow. Several shots hit the boat, ripping through the air tubes and hitting the dummies. When the smaller decoy came loose, flopping over sideways, Sam pressed the remote. A millisecond later, a blinding explosion rocked the air.

CHAPTER FORTY-FIVE

The *Asteri* pitched from side to side as Sam held on to the ladder. The black speedboat veered away, then idled slowly toward the flotsam and what was left of the *Star Catcher*'s hull. It was still floating, upside down, thanks to the air-filled ribs. As the driver circled the capsized boat, his passenger stood, aimed his weapon, peppering the smaller craft and the water around it. Apparently satisfied there were no survivors, he lowered his rifle and the Omega sped off in the opposite direction.

Waiting until the sound of the 1,400-horsepower twin outboard engines faded, Sam boarded the *Asteri*. He looked up to the top of the cliff, where Dimitris kept watch. Finally, the young man looked over at them. "They're back at the port."

They remained where they were another fifteen minutes after the Omega finally took off again, this time toward Patmos. Once Sam gave the okay, Nikos piloted the *Asteri* out of the inlet, none of them relaxing until they were halfway to Fourni. Sam borrowed Remi's sat phone and stepped outside the cabin to call Rube and update him.

"We're back," Sam said. "I got everyone out of there. In one piece, I might add."

"Do I want to know?"

"Probably not. But I'm going to tell you anyway." He gave Rube a quick version of events. While they spoke, Remi walked out onto the deck and started pacing, alternating glances between the inside of the cabin, where Nikos, Dimitris, and Zoe were having a frank conversation, and at Sam. When she noticed him watching her, she moved to the railing, gripping it tightly while her foot tapped relentlessly. Although she'd been through a lot these last few days, this seemed different. No doubt, seeing someone killed for the first time was not something she'd bargained for, and so he kept his voice low while detailing what happened. "The good news is that we found some C-4 you might be able to match to the residue on that ship explosion."

"Why does it sound like there's bad news to follow?"

"I had to use it to get away. If someone wants to come collect the capsized *Star Catcher*, they might be able to get residue from that. I have a feeling the Kyrils might not keep the rest of the C-4 around for anyone to test. On the bright side, we do have a blurry photo of their detonators."

"Casualties?" Rube asked.

"One."

He heard Rube drawing in a deep breath, followed by a second or two of silence. Then, "In my experience, I see this going down a couple of ways. They cover up the death, or they report it, and shift the blame to you for breaking into their facility."

"If they are running drugs, do you really think they're going to report this?"

"Stranger things have happened. They'll have to come up with some story once the inquest starts. Let me get with my contact at Interpol and find out how best to proceed."

Sam glanced at Remi, then lowered his voice even more. "What are the chances we can hop on a plane and get home?"

"You have to ask?"

"Figured it couldn't hurt."

"I'll get back to you once I hear anything."

Sam disconnected and joined Remi on deck, returning her phone. She didn't move, just stared out to sea, her eyes bright, whether from the moonlight reflecting in them or a sheen of tears, he couldn't tell. "Are you okay?" he finally asked.

She gave a noncommittal shrug. "What happens now?"

"We don't know. Rube thinks there will probably be an inquest into the shooting."

She turned back toward the water, her mouth clamped shut, her nostrils flaring slightly with every breath. After a short while, she looked over at him, the sheen in her eyes even brighter. Definitely tears. "How is it you know how to do all this? The fighting, the shooting . . . everything else . . . ?"

His gut instinct told him that whatever he said next was going to make or break any chance they might have of a relationship. "Boot camp."

Her eyes searched his for several long moments. "I have a couple of friends who enlisted right out of college. None of them learned any of this stuff. And I doubt any of them could commandeer a helicopter because their date was going to miss her flight."

"My training was a little more advanced than the standard."

"How advanced?"

"Very."

"I thought you were an engineer."

"I was. For DARPA."

"Doing what?"

"I designed military systems. In order to know what works best, DARPA sent me to the same training facility that the CIA uses."

"Spy camp?"

"That's probably the easiest explanation."

"Give me the *Reader's Digest* version."

"That is the *Reader's Digest* version. There are things I just can't talk about."

CHAPTER FORTY-SIX

Though it wasn't cold, Remi held her arms protectively across her chest. "Have you ever killed anyone before tonight?" Then, before Sam could answer, she said, "Never mind. Of course you have. You're far too calm." She narrowed her eyes. "Are you really a grocery stocker, or is that a cover?"

"I am a grocery stocker, and it pays the rent while I work on my project."

"The argon laser."

"Yes."

She was quiet for so long, he didn't know what to think.

Finally, he reached out, touched her shoulder. "Remi . . . ?"

She turned away, brushing at her eyes.

All he could do was give her space. He reluctantly left her, and returned inside the cabin.

Nikos, at the helm, looked back at Sam as he entered, then looked at Dimitris.

His son stepped forward. "I wanted to thank you for coming after us. And to apologize for putting you both in danger. I know it was foolish. I only wanted to help Zoe."

Sam nodded. "I appreciate you saying so."

"But maybe what we saw will help?"

"Maybe."

Zoe looked hopeful. "What about the fact they were shooting at us?" she asked. "And the man you killed? That has to mean something."

As much as he wished they could avoid this discussion right now, there was no helping it. "All it proves is that we were there, trespassing on private property. Fortunately, we all survived," he said as Remi walked in.

She strode directly up to him, holding out her phone. "Rube," she said.

He examined her face, unable to tell much beyond the tension in her eyes. Taking the phone, he put it to his ear. "That was fast."

"I got hold of the right person this time," Rube said. "It's a mixed bag. Are you somewhere we can talk? It's not all good news."

Sam, feeling Remi's eyes on him, stepped outside the cabin for privacy. "Give me the good news first. I could use some right now."

"The federal police," Rube said, "are going to investigate the original kidnapping in concert with the circumstances surrounding Tassos's death."

"And the bad news?"

"Don't expect to be going home anytime soon. Which means the two of you need to be careful. You and I both know what happens when the police start dredging up things no one wants exposed."

"Kyril would be a fool to come after us. He'll be the first one they suspect."

"Let's hope he's the logical type."

Sam's glance strayed toward Remi, who stood in the cabin watching him through the window. Despite her show of bravado as she'd accompanied him through the rugged terrain, tracking and rescuing Dimitris and Zoe, that fire he'd seen in her eyes was gone. In retrospect, he should have tried harder to convince her to return to the *Asteri* without him. "Thanks for your help. I'll go break the news."

Sam returned Remi's phone to her. "I just got word that there's going to be an official investigation."

"Into what?" Remi asked.

"Everything. The kidnapping." He looked at Zoe. "Your grandfather's death. And the shooting tonight. That's the good news," he said focusing on Remi. "The bad news is that we'll be needed for the inquest."

"You mean we're stuck here?" Then, as if realizing how that might sound, she glanced at Zoe, Dimitris, and Nikos. "I didn't mean—"

Nikos smiled kindly at her. "Who can blame you?"

"Unfortunately," Sam said to Nikos, "I have no idea how long it will take. But I'd be glad to rent the cottage so you won't lose money on it."

"Rent?" Nikos made a scoffing noise. "You're welcome to stay as long as you need." Outside, the sky turned a deep magenta with the rising sun. He widened his stance as he stood at the helm, his face looking worried. "Red sky at morning . . . From the looks of things, we'll be lucky to make it back to Fourni before the storm hits."

CHAPTER FORTY-SEVEN

The morning rain beat against the windowpanes outside Adrian Kyril's office as he sat at his desk. He picked up the empty Grand Marnier, shaking the last few drops into his coffee cup, torn between searching for another in the kitchen or calling one of the last staff members left on the premises to get it for him. He'd fired all but one maid, the cook, Ilya, Fayez, and three of his men. And if he didn't find a way to get more money soon, he'd have to get rid of them *and* the villa.

"A bit early for that, don't you think?"

He looked up to see Ilya watching him from the doorway. "What do you want?"

"Apparently, you haven't heard."

"Heard what?"

"The incident involving the harvest trespasser. There was a shooting at the orchard. One man dead, two disarmed and tied up."

A dull throbbing started behind his left eye. "What are you talking about? I thought Dimitris's death was supposed to be an accident."

"He escaped. It was one of the guards who was killed."

The pain in his head turned sharp. "Is this going to come back on me?"

"They were trespassing. The guards were merely trying to defend themselves against what they thought was an attack. At least, that'll be the official statement released should there be any inquiries. While we were hoping the escapees were killed in a boating accident, sadly that doesn't appear to be the case."

"Again? You thought that the last time."

"It seems we were a bit too quick to assume—"

Both men looked up when Adrian's girlfriend knocked on the open door. "Where is everyone?" Phoebe asked.

"I told you," Adrian said, his eyes dropping to her belly, failing to see any signs of an impending child. He had a feeling his mother was wrong, but he wasn't about to anger her further and get rid of the woman. "We've had to make some cutbacks."

"How am I supposed to get to the village, then?"

"You'll have to wait or drive yourself."

"In the rain?"

"Yes. In the rain," he replied, having no patience for her theatrics.

Her gaze flicked from him to Ilya, then the phone he held. "I won't be home for dinner, then." She turned and left.

As her footsteps receded, Ilya walked to the door and looked out, apparently making sure she was really gone. "Are you sure you can afford her?"

"I have more important things to worry about than Phoebe. What about Sam Fargo? How do I deal with him?"

"When the weather clears, I'll assign a couple of my men to follow him."

"For what?"

"Maybe we'll learn something we can use. If opportunity arises, we need to be ready."

"Weren't you just asking me if I could afford my girlfriend? How can I possibly afford surveillance?"

"Do you want Fargo or not? A cat doesn't catch the mouse if he doesn't watch the mouse hole. If that's not incentive enough, ask yourself how much you're willing to pay to stay out of jail."

Adrian thought about what little money he had left. Less than one hundred thousand euros. As much as Ilya was one of his oldest friends, he and his men did not come cheap. "We'll fire the maid."

"Not the cook?"

"Unless you know your way around a kitchen, the maid is a better choice. Now show me this video."

Ilya took out his phone and opened the surveillance app.

Adrian watched the footage showing Fargo shooting out the lights before taking out one of his guards. "Does my mother know about this?"

"Not yet."

"Do whatever you can to keep it from her." If she found out, any hope he had of changing her mind about reinstating him into the family business—and access to the bank accounts—would be far more difficult. This wasn't the first time she'd locked him out. It was, however, the first time she'd so severely limited his income. That part was very problematic. His search for Poseidon's Trident had cost a small fortune, and now that he knew this cave on Fourni did not contain the fabled treasure, he was beginning to regret the effort.

His gaze went back to the security video, the feed now showing how Fargo managed to take out two armed guards with a rope. "They know too much. Is there some reason you can't just go to that island and kill them?"

"Besides the weather? No one in, no one out."

That was, unfortunately, one of the hazards of living on the smaller islands. The weather dictated all movement. "I mean after it clears."

"Fourni is far too small. If it's not done carefully, you'll be the first person they investigate for it."

He was right, but that didn't make the news any easier to bear. "There has to be some way we can get rid of these interfering—"

Once again, Phoebe appeared at the door. This time, though, her face was pale, her expression a mix of confusion and fear. "The police are here."

It was only then that Adrian noticed that someone was actually holding her by her arm. Whoever it was pulled her aside. Four uniformed Hellenic officers stepped in, the two in front pointing guns at him and Ilya.

"Adrian Kyril?" one of them said, looking right at him. "You are under arrest for the murder of Tassos Gianakos."

The armed officers stepped aside as the other two approached his desk, one to the left, the other to the right. They each took an arm, lifting him from his chair, one slapping handcuffs on him. He looked at Ilya as they dragged him to the door. "What should I do?"

"Say nothing. I'll call your lawyer."

Adrian refused to make a statement. A parade of investigators came in, each one trying to get him to talk. He wasn't about to make a statement, demanding he would talk only to his attorney. They left him handcuffed to the table for a couple of hours—as if there was any way he could somehow get out with the door being closed and locked each time they left.

"Is anyone there?" he called out after a while. He yanked at the cuffs, rattling the chain that secured them to the bolt on the table, hoping to draw someone's attention. "Hello?"

He wasn't sure how much time had passed, an hour or more, when he heard someone turning a key in the lock, then the door opening. The last person he expected to see walked in.

His mother.

An officer stepped in after her, but only to close the door, leaving the two of them alone.

She stood there, her gaze skimming over him, then landing on the handcuffs. A look of distaste crossed her face as she took a step closer. "Do you have any idea what you've done?" she said after several seconds.

"Me?" Adrian replied. "All I've done is try to protect what is ours."

"Your reckless and rash actions are putting everything we've built at risk. I will not stand by and watch you pull us into ruin."

"I can fix it."

"Can you? After everything that's happened? I don't see how."

"I need more money."

"How much?"

"Enough to pay Ilya—"

"At least he knows how to keep a low profile. You might consider asking him for pointers." She eyed the chair opposite him, but didn't sit. "I don't suppose it even occurred to you as to why I chose to cut off your funds?"

"I can only assume you like to see me suffer."

"I had hoped that you might discover that if you controlled your impulses, stopped to think about what you're doing once in a while, you might actually succeed on your own. For that, I partly blame myself. I probably shouldn't have stepped in and fixed your problems every time you found yourself in trouble. I foolishly convinced myself that you'd outgrow your rash ways." She gave an exasperated sigh. "I really do think you'll be better off."

"In prison? You can't be serious."

"Oh, but I am." She leaned down, kissed the top of his head, then said in a low voice, "I do hope you'll own up to all your mistakes and not drag us into this nightmare that you've made for yourself. You know your father isn't well. I don't think he can handle the stress."

"What do you expect me to do?"

"I'd suggest you listen to your attorney." She knocked on the door. The officer opened it, standing aside for her. She looked back at him, then gave that smile that had infuriated him his entire adult life. "Goodbye, Adrian."

"Mother!"

She walked out.

"You can't leave me here!" He rose, trying to follow, but the handcuffs that were bolted to the table dug into his wrists, forcing him back. "Mother!"

CHAPTER FORTY-EIGHT

S am stood on the rooftop patio, cup of coffee in hand, looking out over the quiet bay. Although another storm was expected later tomorrow, for the moment, the sky was blue, and the warm sun beamed down upon the colorful fishing boats bobbing in the azure waters.

Not that he was at all interested in the view. The weather aside, it had been a rough couple of days. Remi, unable or unwilling to talk about what had happened on the Kyrils' island, was having a difficult time navigating the onslaught of emotions. The few times Sam had tried to get her to open up, she immediately changed the subject. If anything, she seemed to be pulling back from him. He knew the emotional toll that a major traumatic event could take on a relationship. It was the rare couple who survived, and usually only because they'd been together long enough to have built a rock-solid foundation.

While he hated to think that their relationship might not survive, Remi's well-being was far more important. And why he'd invited Zoe and Denéa to stop by this morning. Maybe the change of company would help Remi to open up about what had happened.

He sipped at his coffee, then checked his watch. A few minutes before nine. They should be here any time, and he scanned the shoreline, searching for them. A moment later, he noticed the two young women walking on the sand in front of the Kampi Beach Bar. Zoe stopped by the outdoor tables as Denéa continued on. Eventually, she looked up, saw Sam on the rooftop, and waved. "Good morning," she called out as she unlatched the small blue gate.

"Remi's inside. The door should be open."

She nodded, crossed the patio, knocked on the door, then opened it. "Hey, Remi. It's me."

"What a nice surprise. I was just about to make some coffee."

"Make enough for Zoe. She'll be along in a moment."

He heard the sound of water being turned on, then Remi asking, "How's she doing?"

"Zoe? She's coming along, thanks to Dimitris and Nikos. We were wondering about how you were doing."

"Me? I'm fine."

And though Sam never intended to eavesdrop, he found himself rooted to the spot when Denéa said, "You don't look okay."

"I'm just tired, that's all."

"Have you talked to anyone about what happened?"

"There isn't really anyone."

"There's Sam."

"You don't understand. I—It's just that—" There was a strangled sob.

"I'll get Sam."

"No." Remi's too-quick refusal was gut-wrenching. He stood at the edge of the roof, knowing he shouldn't be listening, but unable to move away. After a few moments, he heard her taking a shuddering breath, and then her words came out in a rush. "I've never been so scared in my life. I—I didn't think we were going to make it back."

"But you did."

"And I keep thinking about the man Sam killed. That's why I can't talk to him. I can't make him feel guilty."

"Guilty? About what?"

"What if that man had a family?"

"Oh, Remi . . ." There was a scrape of a chair, Remi crying, then Denéa comforting her.

That Remi would even think that, spoke to her true character. He doubted the gunman would have given it a second thought had he killed any of them.

"You can't worry about that," Denéa said. "From what Zoe and Dimitris told me, you're all very lucky to be here right now—"

"I know. I have to keep reminding myself of that, if not for Sam . . . It—it doesn't make it any easier."

"Have you told your parents about any of this?"

"Are you kidding?" She sniffed. "They're already overprotective. If they had an inkling, they'd be on the first plane out."

"I suppose you're right. Still, the important thing is, you found Zoe and Dimitris, and you're all safe."

"But . . . the *Star Catcher*. I know that boat was important to the archeological society."

"It's a boat. Totally replaceable." Denéa gave a small laugh. "You have to admit, it was rather genius to blow it up."

He couldn't tell if Remi was laughing or crying. "The dummies," she said. "They flopped over, making it look like they were ducking the gunshots. Even I thought it looked real, and I helped stuff them."

Sam's phone buzzed in his pocket, and he pulled it out, looking at the screen. Seeing Rube's number on the caller ID, he was tempted to let it go straight to voice mail. He wanted to know that Remi was going to be okay, but he also knew Rube wouldn't be calling unless it was very important.

CHAPTER FORTY-NINE

The offshore wind swept across the rooftop, making it difficult for Sam to hear what Rube was telling him. He turned up the volume, certain he'd misunderstood. "Say that one more time."

"Adrian Kyril was arrested. On kidnapping and murder charges."

"That's outstanding," Sam replied. "When?"

"Apparently, yesterday. I only just found out myself. That is not, however, why I'm calling. I've got an Interpol agent on hold. He wants to know a little more about what you saw and heard on that island. If you have a few minutes, I'll patch him through on a conference call."

"Sure," Sam said.

A moment later, he heard a click, then Rube saying, "Sergeant Petros Kompouras, Sam Fargo."

"Mr. Fargo," the sergeant said. "I won't take up much of your time. I was hoping you might tell me anything about the warehouse on the island. What was in it? Anything unusual?"

"Besides the C-4 and detonators? The one you need to talk to is Dimitris. He overheard a conversation about one of the shipments being intended for the Heiberts. That would be the pallet that blew up."

"One of our investigators spoke with him. But, considering your background, I was more interested in your viewpoint."

"Other than an overabundance of security, and automatic weapons that seemed overkill for olive oil production, I'm not sure what I can add. I did see a lot of empty olive oil tins, and boxes of glass vials, which, now that I think about it, seems odd. I understand the Kyrils are involved in drug running?"

"Suspected," the sergeant said. "Are you familiar with the history of Minerva Lines and the late Bruno von Till?"

"A very brief history," he said, recalling the little that Rube had told him.

"Through a now-defunct shipping company called Minerva Lines, von Till ran one of the largest drug trafficking operations, not only in the Mediterranean, but worldwide. Recent information coming through some fairly reliable sources is that Heibert Lines may involve some of the same players. We just weren't sure who or how. When Adrian Kyril's name came up along with their business in olive oil production, it made sense. Private island, no oversight. We're just not sure how they're smuggling it out—or where they're hiding it."

"You'd think they'd have more sense than to store their contraband on their own island."

"Agreed. Unfortunately, our one successful attempt at getting a look at one of their shipments ended with the death of a couple of our officers from an explosion. It was much like the truck explosion that Dimitris described. Any idea of what was on that pallet?"

"I think it was empty olive oil tins. Dimitris actually went back for one that looked intact. Nothing in it."

"Why would they blow up empty tins?"

"My gut instinct? They set up the whole thing to lure Dimitris to the truck. Had they been the least bit proficient in placing the explosive, they might have succeeded in killing him."

"Well, good job taking it out," the sergeant said. "In the meantime, we're gathering information on Adrian Kyril's role. He may be in custody, but there are still a lot of unanswered questions, motive being one of them. I'm not sure a murder charge is going to stick."

"Take this with a grain of salt," Sam said, looking up, seeing Zoe walking toward the beach house. "I don't know what, if any, investigative value this has, but we heard that Tassos was looking for a treasure called Poseidon's Trident. What or where that might be, I have no idea. But it's presumably why he was up at that cave that morning."

"I hadn't heard that. I'll add it to the file. Should you run across any more information that will help in our investigation, we would appreciate anything you can pass our way."

"Of course. I'll let you know immediately."

"And, Rube," Sergeant Kompouras added, "thanks for putting me in touch."

"No problem." There was a click, a second of silence, then Rube saying, "Now you know what I know."

"Which isn't much," Sam replied.

"I expect we'll know a lot more by the time this is all done. By the way, how's Remi doing?"

"I'm hoping better." He moved to the edge of the roof, looking down at Zoe as she entered the gate and walked to the front door beneath him. "This news should help ease her mind. Had the police not required us to stay for their investigation into the Kyrils' olive grove shooting, she'd have been gone by now."

"Let's hope I can help speed things up on this end and get you two out of there sooner rather than later. Keep me informed if anything else comes up."

"I will."

Sam disconnected, then went down the stairs. When he stepped in the door, all three women looked up in surprise.

"Something happened," Remi said. "What is it?"

"Adrian Kyril's been arrested. I just got off the phone with Rube."

Remi sank back in her chair. "Thank goodness."

Denéa reached over, grasping Zoe's hand. Zoe, in turn, said, "That must be why the police chief wants to talk to me. He wants me to stop by this afternoon."

"Could be," Sam said. "I expect there's a long way to go before they finish their investigation." He glanced at Remi to see how she was taking the news. Though her eyes were red from crying, he had to admit that she seemed . . . calmer.

Zoe stood, looking at each of them in turn. "I should probably go see what the police have to say. If anyone wants to come with me, I could use the moral support."

CHAPTER FIFTY

The police chief was surprised to see Sam and Remi standing behind Zoe. Denéa had gone down to the port to try to find Dimitris, since he wasn't answering his phone. "I hope you don't mind that I brought my friends," Zoe said as Dimitris burst through the door.

"No, no. Come in." He beckoned them into his small office. "I'm sorry there isn't more space."

Zoe and Remi sat in the two chairs on the other side of his desk, while Sam and Dimitris stood behind them, Dimitris with his hands on Zoe's shoulders.

Zoe took a deep breath, saying, "I heard that Adrian Kyril was arrested. Is that what this is about?"

"Not exactly. I have a few more questions, and some property to return."

"Property?"

"The book I was telling you about when we spoke the other day." He handed her a manila envelope from the desk. "We found it in your grandfather's pocket—with the note I had you look at. Do you have any idea why he'd have a children's book with him?"

"No." Zoe opened the envelope, finding a small, faded, blue

clothbound book inside. She pulled it out, running her fingers over the cover. "I haven't seen this in so long . . ."

Sam leaned over her shoulder, unable to read the title, which was printed in Greek letters.

"*The Pirates of Poseidon*," she said. "I loved this story when I was little. You could see his face light up when I asked him to read it to me." She hugged the book to her chest as she looked at the chief. "I can take this?"

"Of course. I'll need you to sign for it when we're done. As I said, there are a few more questions I need to ask." He smiled apologetically. "My colleagues in Athens are handling the majority of the investigation, which makes it . . . a bit difficult to coordinate. The one thing they don't yet know is exactly *why* Adrian Kyril killed your grandfather."

"It's not enough that he did it?" Zoe said.

"Not always. The more we know, the better our case. Is there anything else that you can think of? Maybe you remember something more about what your grandfather was doing in the days before he was killed? Or why he was at *that* particular cave?"

"I'm sure he mentioned something about looking for Poseidon's Trident. And he talked about the cave with the bones . . ."

Dimitris looked at the chief. "That has to be it. There were bones in that cave. We saw them. Maybe—"

"Goat bones," the chief said. "I assure you that this is not *that* cave—assuming it even exists." He focused on Zoe. "Did someone actually make an inquiry about Poseidon's Trident? Someone else was looking for this so-called treasure?"

"Or someone was going to help him find it. I don't remember, exactly. So much has happened since then."

The chief leaned back, his chair squeaking. "Try not to take this the wrong way, Zoe. But this is where I'm having trouble with the story. I clearly remember your grandfather claiming to have found

Poseidon's Trident all those years ago. And, if I recall correctly, he was adamant that it wasn't on Fourni. So why take these people to the Vardia cave?"

She looked down at the book, her eyes welling. "Maybe he was determined to make money off the legend. If someone wanted to see a cave with bones, then why not take them to see a cave with bones?"

"He actually found it?" Remi asked. "Poseidon's Trident?"

She nodded. "Not that it did any good. After all that trouble, all that time and money, the only thing he brought back was a single coin. And then—" She wiped her eyes with the back of her hand. "When he took it to have it appraised, he found out it was counterfeit. His friends laughed at him."

The police chief's dark eyes regarded Zoe with kindness. "You do know that everyone here on Fourni loved Tassos. Why do you think so many people came out to his memorial?"

"I know. But it still hurt him. He tried to tell them that that coin proved the treasure was out there, and that he was going to find it. No one believed him."

The chief reached for a tissue box on his desk, handing it to her. "Did he ever tell you where it was? The cave?"

"Never. Only that it wasn't on Fourni." She pulled a tissue from the box, dabbing it at her eyes. "Is there anything else you need?"

"For now, no. If you could, though, at some time, go through his things. There's always the chance that we overlooked something."

She nodded, looked down at the book, then at him. "You said there's something I need to sign?"

He handed her a pen and the property release form. She signed her name at the bottom, then hurried from the office, Dimitris following her out the door.

"I have a question," Remi said. "Now that Adrian Kyril's been arrested, how long will we need to stay here?"

235

The chief glanced at Sam, then Remi. "Hopefully not that much longer. I promise to let you know the moment I hear."

Sam thanked the chief, and they left, finding Zoe and Dimitris waiting for them at the bottom of the stairs.

"Are you okay?" Remi asked Zoe.

She nodded, then motioned them to follow her. Once outside on the street, she held up the small book. "It occurred to me that my grandfather *did* tell me where the cave was."

"Why didn't you say something?" Dimitris asked.

"I had a feeling that if I did, the chief wouldn't let me keep this. It's in here. It's always been in here."

Sam and Remi exchanged glances as Zoe opened the book. She turned to the last page, showing them a pencil sketch of a rather strange face drawn on it. The eyes were angled and angry, the mouth wide open and filled with sharp teeth. Something like a lion's mane framed the entire head, and a long tail-like thing seemed to be growing out of the top.

Sam eyed the face. "What makes you think this picture is anything significant?"

"That's the problem," Zoe said. "I don't know. I only remember him telling me that if I ever wanted to find Poseidon's Trident, *this* is where it was." She closed the book, then hugged it close to her chest. "Before you insist that I turn it over to the police, I was only a little girl when he drew that. I can't imagine it has any significance."

"Actually," Sam said, "I was going to suggest that we all sit down over coffee, then find what, if anything, is so important about this book."

CHAPTER FIFTY-ONE

The four of them, Sam, Remi, Zoe, and Dimitris, walked around the corner to Skavos's café, finding an empty table on the patio. While Dimitris went inside to place their order, Sam brought over extra chairs, then took a seat next to Remi.

"About this sketch . . . ?" Sam said to Zoe as Dimitris returned.

"I only have a vague remembrance of when he drew it. All I recall was that he insisted that it would lead me to Poseidon's Trident." She looked down at the slim volume, running her fingers over the blue cloth cover. "I was wondering what happened to this. That's just so odd he'd have it with him."

"Obviously," Dimitris said, "there's more to the story than we all thought."

"I don't know how." Zoe looked around the café. "There's probably not a person here who wasn't read this story as a child. Most could probably recite it by heart."

Sam glanced at the book. "What's it about?"

"Two boys who were searching for Poseidon's Ear run into pirates burying treasure."

"Poseidon's Ear?" Sam said.

"The Ear was the name of the cave where they could speak

237

directly to Poseidon. My grandfather used to tell me that's where Poseidon's Trident is buried."

Remi eyed the book, then Zoe. "How sure are you that Poseidon's Trident is the name of the treasure?"

"I don't know." After a moment, she gave a slight shrug. "I had always assumed that was the name because of the way my grandfather described it. Why?"

"I was talking to a woman from Samos at the memorial. According to her, Poseidon's Trident was a place, not a treasure. I don't know if that makes a difference, but she seemed fairly adamant about the matter."

"I have to agree with the chief," Sam said. "If the story, or the sketch, is supposedly a map or a hint of where the real cave is, why take Kyril and his men to the one here on Fourni? What do the bones have to do with anything?"

Zoe exchanged glances with Dimitris. "There's a darker version of the tale," she said. "About the two boys having died inside the cave, and their ghosts remaining to protect the treasure."

Dimitris gave a sheepish smile. "I may have used that version to scare Zoe when we were younger."

"You and every other boy on the island," she said. "When I told my grandfather what everyone was saying, he assured me it couldn't be true." She gave a faraway smile. "According to him, that story was proof. It had to have been the two brothers who lived to tell the tale, because the pirates would *never* have given up the location of their secret hoard."

Sam asked to see the book. Zoe handed it over, and he looked through pages, seeing several pen and ink illustrations. The first was of two boys in a small boat. Another was of an ancient sailing ship with oars lining either side, an angry eye at the prow. The writing, of course, was in Greek. "It's about pirates?" Sam asked.

She nodded.

He handed it back to her. "Would you mind translating it?"

Zoe turned to the first page, narrating the story of two boys, Agathos and Xanthos, who set sail in a small boat, their goal to beg the god Poseidon for the return of their father. Unfortunately, before they could whisper into his ear, they were captured by Samian pirates. They escaped when the angry god shook the earth, destroying the island, and killing the pirates. The final illustration was of the two boys in their small boat, the rays of the setting sun shooting up behind them. Zoe closed the book, setting it on the table. "Of course, the moral of the story is that the boys didn't get what they wanted, but got what they needed."

"Don't forget," Dimitris said, "that there's the *unwritten* version. The cave contained the bones of the boys, and that's how anyone would know it was the right location."

"Regardless, everyone—my grandfather included—knows the cave up on Vardia is not where Poseidon's Trident is. Besides, you heard the chief. Those were goat bones. So, no, no treasure there."

"And yet," Sam said. "We have a picture your grandfather drew. Which has to mean something."

Everyone turned to the sketch in the back of Zoe's book as Skavos walked out with their drinks. He eyed the sketch with its round, angry face framed in wavy lines, and said, "That looks like Helios."

"Helios?" Sam said.

"Ancient Greek god of the sun," he said, placing their drinks on the table. "Those could be sun rays."

"Why's he so angry?" Sam asked.

Skavos placed a napkin on the table, setting Sam's beer on top of it. "If you had that thing growing out of the top of your head, you'd be angry, too."

Something about the sketch caught Dimitris's attention. He looked over at Remi. "Do you know what that reminds me of? The Vardia carving. We were looking at it the morning that . . ." He let the words hang as though worried how Zoe might take it. That was, after all, the same morning her grandfather had been killed.

"But that didn't have a face," Remi said. "The carving you showed me looks more like a wreath."

"Think about how many centuries it's been up there," Dimitris said. "Maybe the face wore off."

Zoe reached out, putting her hand on Dimitris's arm. "You know where I *have* seen a face that looks like this? On Thimena. It's carved on a rock overlooking Agios Nikolaos. I know for a fact that there's a cave very near it. I remember finding it one summer when we stayed at one of the fishing cottages."

"Maybe Manos will lend us his boat," Dimitris said. "We could go look for it tomorrow."

Zoe clasped her hands together. "Think how exciting that will be. To finally find Poseidon's Trident." She glanced at Sam and Remi. "You'll come with us, of course?"

Remi nodded, then turned toward Sam. "I'd definitely like to go."

Seeing the way Remi's eyes lit up at the prospect, he smiled. "Wouldn't miss it for the world."

CHAPTER FIFTY-TWO

The next morning, Sam and Remi met Zoe, Dimitris, and Nikos at the port. Manos had lent them the *Lazy Krab*, a RIB boat similar in size to the *Star Catcher*, since it would be far easier to navigate close to shore and in some of the smaller inlets than the much larger *Asteri*.

Dimitris lowered a bag with climbing gear to his father. "Has anyone given any thought to the cave in Thief's Bay just past Skull Rock?" he said. "If you're going to hide treasure, that'd be the place to do it. We're going right past there."

"It's not near big enough," Zoe said. "The cave I'm thinking of is on the north side of the island. Whether or not it's *the* cave . . ." She shrugged. "I think I was ten the last time my grandfather took me there. But I *definitely* remember the carving of the sun face on the rock near Agios Nikolaos."

The wind gusted and Nikos looked up, seeing a few clouds, but otherwise blue sky above. Unfortunately, with another storm expected that evening, the last place they wanted to be when it hit was on the north side of Thimena. "The less time we spend here talking about it, the more time we'll have to look."

Sam eyed the restless water as he helped Remi into the boat. "You're sure we'll be able to get there and back before the weather turns?"

"We should," Nikos said, handing out ziplock bags to everyone on board for their phones. "It won't take us long to get there. Assuming Zoe can find the cave, we should be back well before the rain starts."

"Let's get going."

The boat cut through the water with ease, up until the point they entered the channel that separated Thimena from Fourni. Nikos slowed, telling them, "Hold on. It can get bumpy here."

Dimitris grinned at Remi, who braced herself with each bounce. "This is nothing," he said. "You should see it when it really storms."

"I'll pass," she said.

Sam was glad to see her laughing. It seemed her time with Denéa had done a world of good. Thankfully, the water calmed once they were through the narrow channel and rounded the south of the island, past Skull Rock and Thief's Bay. The rest of the trip was unremarkable, and fifteen minutes later, they were navigating around the north of the island toward the small cement dock in Agios Nikolaos. Other than the blue-domed church overlooking the water, and a few cottages used by the fishermen in the summer, that side of the island was mostly a barren, uninhabited stretch of rocks, low shrubs, and dry grass.

The five of them disembarked, then followed Zoe past the church, picking their way up the hill along a path of limestone rocks jutting out between tufts of dried grass. Goat bells jangled in the distance. Sam looked up, seeing a small herd at the top of the hill. The animals watched warily, then ran off as they neared. At the crest, Zoe stopped to take stock of her surroundings.

"Anything look familiar?" Dimitris asked her.

"Give me a moment to get my bearings."

Sam moved next to Nikos, noticing his attention on the *Lazy Krab* moored far below them. The small boat swept back and forth in the restless waters. Beyond it, the whitecaps rippled across the Aegean, and, to the north, a dark band of clouds hovered low on the horizon.

"This way," Zoe said. "I think we're getting close."

"You're sure?" Dimitris asked.

"Positive. It was just on the other side of this ridge." She turned her back to the wind, her dark hair blowing about her face. "Definitely to the south."

Fifteen minutes later, that dark stretch of clouds was almost overhead. Scattered raindrops fell as they followed Zoe farther along the ridge. Nikos looked up at the sky, his eyes narrowing at the roiling clouds. "It might be best if we left now. The wind seems to be picking up."

"It's not far," Zoe called.

The wind whipped around them. Remi moved in next to Sam, reaching down, putting her hand in his. "I think we should go back."

Sam, agreeing, was just about to suggest it when Zoe suddenly pointed. "There it is. The carving."

She ran down the hill, then crouched before a massive boulder, brushing her hands across the surface. "I knew it was here."

"Where's the cave?" Dimitris asked, picking his way down the hill toward her.

"Just on the other side. I'm sure of it." Zoe looked back at them, her face filled with excitement. "I knew this was the right place."

They followed her, eventually reaching the rock she'd pointed out. There was definitely a face carved on the surface. Admittedly, it wasn't angry like the one Tassos had sketched, but there was no doubt what it was supposed to be.

Zoe continued past the boulder, then down the steep hill, excited. Suddenly she stopped. "Over here! I found it!"

As she turned to look at them, a gust of wind hit her. She stepped back, lost her balance on the steep hill. The limestone disintegrated beneath her feet, and down she went, desperately grasping at the dry brush. One second she was there, the next she was gone.

CHAPTER FIFTY-THREE

Sam and Dimitris raced down the hill.

"Zoe!" There was no answer. Dimitris dropped his gear bag, then started for the edge of the bluff. The ground started crumbling beneath his feet.

Sam grabbed his arm, pulling him back onto solid ground.

"I need to get down there," Dimitris said, his voice filled with panic.

"We'll get to her," Sam said as Remi and Nikos ran up behind them. Sam held out his arm, stopping Remi from getting closer. One more step and she'd hit the same patch of limestone and dried weeds that had sent Zoe tumbling. "We'll need rope." He turned around, examining the area, nodding at the rock with the sun carving. "We can anchor off there."

Dimitris reached for his bag. "I'll go down first."

"Let Sam," Nikos said. "You're too upset."

Dimitris didn't answer. Nikos placed his hand on his son's shoulder. "Think of Zoe. You want someone with a clear head going down to look for her."

The young man nodded, then pulled out the gear. Sam and Nikos checked over each piece, then anchored off the line. When Sam was ready to start his descent, he moved to the edge, kicking at the crumbling limestone where Zoe fell. It slid down toward the cave, gathering speed and gravel like a mini avalanche, some of it disappearing beneath a large boulder that jutted out to the right of the cavern mouth.

Remi watched as he lowered himself over the edge, her green eyes filled with worry.

Sam switched on his headlamp, then started his descent. Because of the approaching storm, the gusting wind swirled down into the mouth, threatening to send him into a spin. The forty-foot cavern dropped straight down. A little more than halfway into his descent, he stopped to take stock. The cavern floor wasn't more than twenty feet wide and completely empty. There was no sense in going any farther. No Zoe, no treasure, just a few jagged rocks that would kill anyone falling from the top.

So, what happened to Zoe?

He began his ascent, this time unable to control the spin as the wind rushed by. The beam from his headlamp bounced off the cavern walls, a dance of light and shadows. When he looked back, he caught a glimpse of a crevice about five feet below the cavern mouth—and Zoe's booted foot just visible between the rocks. Odd, because he hadn't seen her on the way down, and from here, he couldn't see any way into the crevice from the cave mouth. "Zoe!" he shouted.

He wasn't sure if it was the wind or her moaning.

"Don't move. We're coming to get you."

Sam returned to the cliff's edge. He climbed out, then took a slow look around the cavern mouth, again seeing the large boulder jutting out to the right, the same place he'd seen the gravel falling.

"Where is she?" Dimitris asked.

"I think she fell beneath that boulder."

The space beneath the massive rock was dark and narrow. Had he not seen her foot on his ascent, they never would've found her.

Nikos looked down, trying to see. "How are you going to get to her?"

"I think I can slide down under the rock and pull her up. It'll be tight, but doable."

The two men lowered Sam toward the cave and the rock. Once in front of it, he rearranged his harness. "Ready."

While Nikos and Dimitris controlled the tension, he crawled on his stomach, headfirst into the crevice.

"Zoe?" he said as he worked himself beneath the boulder.

"I'm here," came a weak voice.

He still couldn't see her. He maneuvered farther, finally seeing her looking up at him, then closing her eyes as gravel rained down on top of her. She'd slid into the steep crevice, too far to climb out on her own. "Anything broken?" he asked. "You can wiggle all your fingers and toes?"

"No. My right arm hurts and I can't move my hand."

"You've got quite the lump on your forehead."

She touched it with her left hand, then pulled her fingers back. "No blood. That's a good sign, yes?"

"A good sign," Sam said, not sure if she'd been knocked out or just stunned from the fall. "We'll do this slowly. Okay?"

She nodded.

Sam reached down, but when he touched Zoe's right arm she cried out. He called up to Nikos. "Give me about another foot of length." Nikos let out the rope. This time, Sam grasped her around her torso, staying well away from the injured arm. "I'm going to pull you up. If anything doesn't feel right, let me know."

"Okay."

"Ready," Sam called out.

Nikos and Dimitris started pulling on the rope as Sam held Zoe. When they cleared the space beneath the boulder, he helped her onto the small ledge.

She tried to lift her right arm, the pain so sharp she stopped. "I think it's broken."

Sam eyed the lump a few inches above her wrist. "It looks like it." He twisted around and said, "Nikos, drop the second harness." Then, looking back at Zoe, said, "We'll get you up with that."

She nodded, then looked down past the crevice, giving a pained smile. "I found the cave."

"You did at that." He caught the harness that Dimitris tossed down, then helped Zoe into it. Nikos and Dimitris lifted her to the top.

"Zoe," Dimitris said. He started to hug her, then stopped short as she cradled her arm against her chest.

"I'm fine," she said. "Where's Sam?"

Nikos had helped Sam onto the hillside. He was coiling up the rope while Nikos removed the anchor.

Bewildered, Zoe said, "Why are you putting that away? Isn't someone going to look in the cave?"

"It was empty," Sam said.

"How do you know?"

"I was able to look inside," Sam assured her.

"Let's get you off this hill," Nikos said as he and Dimitris each took one side, helping her down the path toward the blue-topped church. A few fat drops splattered on the ground in front of them. Looking out, the rain was dancing across the sea that had been calm but was now darkening, and the clouds were racing toward the shore. In the short few minutes it took for them to get from the top of the hill to the bottom near the dock, the sun had disappeared behind a thick bank of angry clouds, and the cerulean waters had turned black.

The storm was nearly on them.

CHAPTER FIFTY-FOUR

Nikos looked up at the sky. "I don't think anyone expected the weather to turn so soon. Certainly not me."

"It's not your fault," Sam said. "We weren't expecting to be here this long."

They headed into the church to take a better look at Zoe in order to decide their best course of action. As they stepped inside the gate of the courtyard, a particularly large wave hit the six-foot wall, sending a spray of water over the top. Nikos and Dimitris, on either side of Zoe, helped her quickly through the door, where it was still dry. "How are you feeling?" Nikos asked her.

"Other than my arm, I'm a bit dizzy."

Dimitris helped her to sit. She took a deep breath, then closed her eyes. "What about that carving on the rock? It looked like the sketch, didn't it?"

"Yes, it did. But not as angry."

Sam, worried about the hit to Zoe's head, drew Nikos aside. "On top of what looks like a break in her arm, she may have a concussion. We should get her to a doctor as soon as possible."

Nikos glanced back at her. "The sooner we get out of here, the better," he said as the wind whistled beneath the door. "If the storm hits and the boat capsizes . . ."

He didn't finish. He didn't need to. Zoe, with her injuries, would never be able to withstand the choppy seas.

"If you're talking about me," Zoe said, "there's no way I'm getting into that boat with this arm. I'll walk to the town first."

"It'll take an hour to walk," Dimitris said. "We can be home in fifteen minutes."

She started to laugh, then gave a half-sob. "As rough as that water is? Fifteen minutes of pure torture. I'm the injured one. Shouldn't I get a say?"

Sam looked out the door. The cape that normally protected the bay was being smashed on both sides, the waves nearly covering the rocks. Their RIB boat bounced up and down and against the dock as if it were a toy. "Is there anyone here on the island who can help her?"

"She'll need to get her arm set in Fourni. If we can get the boat to the town's port, she'll have an easier time of it. The water is calmer, as it's protected by the two islands. We just have to do it before the storm breaks."

"By land it is. I'll take the boat and meet you all at the harbor in Thimena."

"Just be aware," Nikos said. "The channel can be difficult. It's where the north and south waters converge. You saw how it was when we went through earlier. It's likely to be worse."

Sam, fortunately, had plenty of experience in navigating similar boats in harsh weather. His mother ran a boat chartering business in South Florida, an area that was often hit by hurricanes. "Understood."

Remi brushed her hair back from her face as she looked up at him. "I'm going with you."

"Remi—"

"Who's going to rescue you if you fall out?"

"She's right," Nikos said. "Better with two should something happen."

Sam nodded. "How strong of a swimmer are you?"

"Very. I swam long distance at BC."

He knew it was a lost battle, especially seeing the determination in her green eyes. "Okay. No argument. Let's go."

As Dimitris and Nikos gathered Zoe between them, starting up the narrow trail along the north side of the island, he and Remi walked down to the dock, grateful that it hadn't yet started raining in earnest. He jumped into the *Lazy Krab*, then reached up for Remi, holding her hand as she tried to time her jump when the boat rose. Launching wasn't easy. Sam attached the kill switch to his wrist, hoping they'd never need it.

Remi sat next to him, bracing herself against the roll bar as he navigated over the choppy water. They both relaxed once they were out of the turbulent northern waters, then zipping south along the much calmer west side. That all changed when they rounded the southern tip of the island and neared the channel.

Sam slowed the boat as they approached, shocked to see how vastly different it was from their earlier trip. It had seemed so much wider earlier that morning. Now the three-hundred-foot space between the two islands had turned into a churning mass of white water. "Hold on!" he shouted.

Remi nodded, then wrapped her arms around the roll bar.

Sam took it slow, the boat bouncing from wave to wave. The bow raised then slammed down into the trough as the next wave rose up in front of them. At several points, the wind was so strong, it sent them hydroplaning backward, the ninety-horsepower motor not enough to keep them moving forward. They were nearly through the channel when the tip of the boat hit then breached a wave. As the trough opened beneath them a sharp gust hit beneath the hull. The bow flew upward. Suddenly, they were airborne, the boat sweeping up and around like a roller coaster, tossing them into the water. Sam surfaced to a tornado of whitecaps swirling around him.

Remi was nowhere in sight.

CHAPTER FIFTY-FIVE

Sam heard nothing but the roar of the wind in his ears as he called Remi's name.

A wave lifted him as he treaded water, searching. He glimpsed the boat about fifteen meters away just before he dropped down into a trough. Somehow it had landed upright, and he tried swimming toward it. The current in the channel was too strong. Another wave lifted him. He glimpsed the boat flying toward him. It would likely pass him if he stayed where he was. Swimming to the right, the next wave brought him up, the boat almost on top of him. He reached for one of the handles on the side, feeling the rubber sliding beneath his fingertips. He gave one more kick, reached out with his other hand, grasping the handle. Gripping it, he swung his leg over the side, pulling himself in. The wind gusted, lifting the boat then slamming it down, tossing him into the bottom. He scrambled to the controls, realizing the motor was still propelling the boat forward. The kill switch strapped to his wrist had snapped off when he fell. Small miracle, he thought, putting the engine in neutral, searching the water for Remi, shouting her name.

"Sam!"

He heard rather than saw her. As a wave propelled the boat

upward, in a flash he caught sight of something dark on the surface about a boat's length away.

Remi.

The bow dropped into the next trough, knocking him down. He found a rope, dragged it toward him with his foot, grabbed a life preserver, tied one end of the rope to it, the other end to the roll bar, then pulled himself up on the seat back. The craft rose. He threw the life preserver in the direction he thought he'd seen Remi, losing sight of it in the storming water. The rope sank below the surface. He reached for it, figuring he'd have to make another attempt, when it suddenly went taut.

Linking his arm around the roll bar, he pulled on the rope, finally seeing Remi clinging to the preserver. He managed to get her aboard while the water roiled around them, tossing the boat about. Exhausted, she clung to the seat as he started the boat, navigating through the channel—finally reaching the calmer waters between Thimena and Fourni. As they motored into the port at Thimena to await the others, he looked at Remi, shivering in the seat next to him. "Remind me the reason you were coming?"

"Good luck charm?"

He held up his wrist, showing her the broken kill switch. "Guess it worked," he said, then leaned over and kissed her.

Thankfully, the trip from Thimena to Fourni was much less eventful, the storm holding off until after they'd reached the larger island. Once there, they took Zoe up to the clinic, where they were expecting her. By the following afternoon, the rain had lessened to a light sprinkle, barely wetting the ground. The ferries were running on schedule and life on the island seemed to be back to normal. After the harrowing afternoon the day before, Sam and Remi decided to take advantage of the break in the weather to walk into the village to meet Nikos, Denéa, and Manos for coffee at Skavos's café. As they sat there, a number of islanders stopped by their patio table to talk to Sam, their Greek spoken too fast for him to get the gist.

"They're thanking you," Nikos explained. "For bringing Zoe home."

Sam, slightly uncomfortable under the constant stream of well-wishers, began to realize exactly how tight-knit the community was. "Tell them you and Dimitris did the heavy lifting. All we did was bring the boat."

Skavos brought their coffee, refused to take payment, then added his thanks to the list.

Remi smiled, then turned her attention to Nikos. "How's Zoe?"

"Much better. Dimitris is with her. She wants the four of you to come up for dinner. Apparently one of her neighbors brought over enough food to last her a month."

"She should be resting, not entertaining," Remi said.

"It's just the four of you. She should be fine."

"You're not going?" Sam asked.

"I think I'll enjoy stretching my feet out and doing nothing tonight."

"I'm in," Denéa said. "Manos?" He nodded.

Remi glanced at Sam. "Up for it?"

"And have another chance to sample some home-cooked Greek food? Absolutely."

That evening, Sam and Remi picked up a bottle of Santorini-grown Assyrtiko white wine, then strolled up the hill to Zoe's cottage. As they walked in, the scent of savory meat and spices filled the room.

"Whatever that is," Sam said, breathing in deep, "it smells wonderful."

"Moussaka," Dimitris called out from the kitchen. "Ground lamb and eggplant casserole."

Zoe, seated on the couch, stood up to greet them. Sporting a bruise on her forehead that seemed to be settling down to her right eye, and a cast on her right arm, she looked remarkably spry for someone who'd just taken a good fall down a hillside only the day before. She hugged them both, then offered to help in the kitchen until Dimitris shooed her back to the sofa like a mother hen. Denéa and Manos arrived a few minutes later, bringing another bottle of wine. The men disappeared into the kitchen, opened the wine, then returned and set the table. Surprised that they had talked their way through the first bottle, Dimitris pulled the casserole out of the oven and brought it to the table, the sauce and cheese on top still bubbling. The second bottle opened, and everyone seated, he raised his glass, toasting their safe return.

"To Sam," Zoe said, "for managing to find me."

Sam lifted his glass. "To the moussaka. Before it gets cold!"

They laughed and started eating. Zoe watched Sam as he dished up a hefty serving. "Things are still a bit fuzzy, so you'll have to forgive me if you already mentioned it. But did you see anything at all in the cave?"

"Nothing worth exploring," he replied. "If there was ever a treasure in there, it's long gone."

She sighed. "I was so sure about that marking on the rock."

"It's Greece," Manos said. "There are a lot of markings carved on a lot of rocks."

Remi laughed. Her smile, Sam decided, seemed far more relaxed than it had in several days. Whether it was news of Adrian Kyril's arrest, her talk with Denéa, or their shared experience on Thimena rescuing Zoe, he didn't know. One thing he was certain of, Remi's spirit had definitely taken a turn for the better.

As much as Sam didn't want the night to end, if only because Remi was enjoying herself for the first time in a while, he saw how tired Zoe appeared. "We should probably go."

"I'll get the dishes," Remi said.

"Definitely not," Denéa told her. "You and Sam get a pass for bringing home the *Lazy Krab*. Who knows what would have happened to it. Manos can do the dishes."

"Me?"

"It's your boat." Her blue eyes sparkled with laughter as she got up to clear the table, shooing both Remi and Sam away when they tried to help. It wasn't until he and Remi were on their way out the door that she happened to glance at the *Pirates of Poseidon* book sitting on the coffee table. She stopped to pick it up, looking back at Zoe. "It just occurred to me. Selma seems good at researching. If there're any historical references to Poseidon's Trident, she might be able to find them."

"Not a bad idea," Sam said. "Would you mind if we took photos?"

"Of course not." Zoe turned the pages for Sam as he took a photograph of each. "Imagine if your friend actually discovers that Poseidon's Trident really exists." Her eyes lit up. "That would be a wonderful way to honor my grandfather."

A few minutes later, they emailed the photos to Selma. After saying their goodbyes, Denéa waved a dish towel at them. "We're almost done if you want to wait for a ride home."

Sam glanced at Remi, who shook her head. "It's too nice out not to walk."

He and Remi took the stairs down the hill to the port, then started up the steep, winding road toward Kampi. Because there was so little traffic on the island, there were no sidewalks, and no streetlights. A low stone wall on their right was all that separated them from the sharp drop to the sea, and they could just make out the sound of the waves breaking on the rocks far below.

About midway up the hill, Remi looked back in the direction of Fourni. "Zoe's right. Finding that treasure would be a wonderful way of honoring Tassos."

"Assuming it really exists."

"But if it did, wouldn't it help prove that's why Tassos was killed?"

He stopped, looking down at her. "Remi . . ." Whatever might have been said next was lost when a car came speeding up the hill, its tires screeching as it rounded the curve toward them.

CHAPTER FIFTY-SIX

Blinded by the headlights, Sam pulled Remi to the side of the road against the low wall. The dark blue compact car sped past them to the top of the hill.

Sam, still holding Remi tight, felt her heart beating against his chest. And with good reason. Pressed against the wall, they had only to look down to see the sheer drop on the other side. Before they had a chance to even process their close call, a second vehicle drove up and stopped beside them.

Manos was behind the wheel, Denéa in the front passenger seat. She rolled down her window. "Are you two okay? It looked like they almost hit you."

Sam drew Remi from the wall. "Luckily, we managed to get out of the way."

"Hop in," Manos said. "We'll give you a ride home."

They climbed into the backseat and Manos took off. At the top of the hill, the blue car was making a three-point turn, and the vehicles passed each other, going in opposite directions. The silhouette of two men sitting inside the other car, one tall, one short, was all Sam could see as it drove back down the hill.

"Probably tourists," Manos said. "There's a rental car sticker on the windshield. They're either drunk or lost. Or both."

"Lost?" Denéa laughed. "On Fourni? It's not like there's all that many places to go. Drunk is more like it."

A few minutes later, Manos turned off into Kampi, navigating down the long drive, until they reached the stairs. Sam and Remi got out, thanked them, then took the stairs down. A litter of calico kittens jumped off a low wall, then followed them until they reached the bottom by the Kampi Beach Bar. The cats ran off, and Sam and Remi continued on, hand in hand, along the water.

Remi was surprisingly quiet. When they finally reached the cottage, she stopped him just outside the gate. "What were you going to say up there, right before the car—Before Manos and Denéa picked us up?"

Sam was going to tell her that they might be better off leaving the treasure-hunting alone. But there was something about the way she looked at him, and all rational thought seemed to escape him. "This" was all he managed to say, then took her in his arms and kissed her in the moonlight. He pulled back, brushing a lock of hair from her face. "If that's okay."

Remi, somewhat breathless, nodded. He reached behind her and opened the gate.

By the time Sam and Remi sat down to lunch the following day, Selma called with a report on the photos that he'd emailed to her the night before. "Good afternoon, Mr. Fargo."

"No need for formalities," he said, though he was beginning to suspect she would continue to ignore this request. She seemed to be firmly entrenched in using titles.

"I'll keep that in mind, Mr. Fargo," she said, proving his point, then launching into the purpose of her call. "After receiving the book pages you sent—"

"Hold on," Sam said. He put the call on speaker. "Go ahead. Remi's here with me."

"Working under the assumption that this story is a fictional re-telling of something that really happened, it seems there are a few threads that may actually reference historical events. If the cave entrance was destroyed as depicted in the book, it was obviously an earthquake. Unfortunately, that doesn't narrow down the time period, since the area is and has always been rife with seismic activity."

"So we can strike any historical earthquakes as a reference?" Sam replied.

"Exactly. The next best clue is that the boys want to speak directly to Poseidon. With that reference, we can rule out anytime *after* Christianity firmly took hold in the area—which makes it more than likely the third century A.D. or earlier. The boys' names were somewhat common in ancient Greece, which is no help. One name from the story stands out, primarily because it isn't Greek. Pactyes. The spelling varies, but the name *is* prominent in Lydian history, especially around 546 B.C."

"Lydian?" Sam asked.

"Turkey," Remi whispered, "before it was Turkey."

"How do you remember this stuff?" he whispered back.

She shrugged as Selma continued, saying, "King Cyrus conquered Lydia, invaded Sardis, the capital, and entrusted the Sardis treasury to a Lydian named Pactyes, who was supposed to take the gold back to Persia. Instead, he hired mercenaries to steal it. In short, *if* this Pactyes mentioned in your children's book is the Lydian Pactyes, then it's no wonder someone's bent on killing over the whole thing."

"Why's that?" Sam asked.

Remi's brows went up as she turned toward him. "Surely you've heard the term 'rich as Croesus'?"

"Exactly," Selma replied. "King Croesus was reported as being one of the wealthiest monarchs in history. And, while Pactyes was eventually captured somewhere in the Greek islands by King Cyrus's army, there's no record that the stolen Sardis treasury was ever recovered."

"So, is there a Poseidon's Trident?" Sam asked her.

"Unfortunately, there are very few written records that describe Poseidon's Trident as being anything other than a spear wielded by the god himself. Since the book suggests otherwise, I thought it might be prudent to find an expert who could possibly guide you on ancient children's fables."

"Are you saying you found someone?"

"The closest I could get was the classical literature expert from the University of the Aegean, Professor Pallas Alexandris. If you can get to Samos, the professor is willing to meet you. I've cc'd you on the email. There should be a response waiting."

"I'll take it from there. Thanks, Selma." He checked his email, finding that the professor had forwarded the ferry schedule for their convenience. After emailing back that he would head over that afternoon, he looked at Remi. "I don't suppose there's any use in suggesting you stay here while I head to Samos?"

"You can *always* suggest. I just don't know how much good it'll do."

"We'd better head to the port and pick up our ferry tickets."

CHAPTER FIFTY-SEVEN

Minerva Heibert Kyril let herself into Adrian's office, then took a seat at his desk, leaning back with a tired sigh.

As much as she didn't' like having to see her son locked up like some common criminal, what choice did she have? It had taken her decades to rebuild what had once been a thriving family business.

Her gaze strayed to a painting on the wall of a World War I plane. The *Hawk of Macedonia*, flown by Kurt Heibert, one of her granduncles. She'd found the work of art gathering dust in a basement after inheriting the crumbling Heibert estate from her father. It was her other uncle, Admiral Erich Heibert, however, whom she had been interested in, primarily because her own father had been obsessed when he'd learned about the admiral's history—even naming her Minerva after the now-defunct shipping line the man had been involved with.

Her granduncle's criminal enterprise, run under the name Bruno von Till, was not something that Minerva had *ever* publicly discussed. Certainly not with her husband, and definitely not with Adrian, who had clearly inherited the Heibert propensity for crime.

Poor Adrian. The Kyril men, while handsome, were not known for their intelligence.

She leaned back in her chair, wondering if she'd kept a tighter rein on the boy, would they have avoided this whole sordid mess? Her husband, the senior Adrian Kyril, had always been perfectly content to sit back and let her handle the more important matters of their business. The only reason she had married him was for the capital she'd needed to rebuild the Heibert empire. Adrian Sr.—as the public face of the olive oil business and the charities they headed up, loved by all who met him—had never delved too deeply into her affairs, for which she was grateful. He did, however, want children, which was how Adrian Jr. came to be.

And now she was left to clean up the mess their son had made. Again.

She tapped her fingers on the desktop, eyeing the empty spot where Adrian's computer had been, as well as the empty file drawer to her left—all of it taken by the police in their search of the premises.

A soft knock at the door alerted her to Ilya's arrival. "Come in."

Adrian's friend and security adviser entered the room, closing the door behind him. "My apologies for being tardy."

She waved her hand at him. "I've only just arrived myself. Sit."

He pulled a chair to the desk.

"I'm glad," she said, once he was seated, "that the police didn't destroy the property in their search."

Ilya gave a slight nod.

"What I don't understand," she continued, "is how this started?"

"Your son was looking for Poseidon's Trident."

She was certain she'd misunderstood. When she asked Ilya to repeat himself, she was stunned. "Explain."

"It may be one of the greatest treasure finds in Greek history. Adrian hoped that by locating it, his financial difficulties would be solved."

Another of Adrian's faults. He had no concept of what a budget was. Giving him this home was a last-ditch effort to help him put his life in order. All he had to do was pay for the upkeep and the property taxes, something he should have easily been able to do on the salary he earned sitting on the board of their olive oil empire. Sadly, he couldn't even manage that. Chasing after this Poseidon's Trident, when he was near bankruptcy, was one more example of his lack of common sense. "Why didn't you tell me about this?"

"It seemed like a harmless diversion—one that would keep him out of the business. Who knew he'd decide to kill the man who was helping him?"

"Do you think they'll be able to prove murder?"

"I doubt they'll be able to prove anything there. I saw nothing, and Fayez would never talk. It could very well have been an accident. That he slipped."

"Except the kidnapping," she said. "That sort of negates that it was all innocent." She tapped her fingers on the desktop again. "I pay you good money to keep him out of trouble. I don't understand how things have gotten so out of hand."

"Things were going fine, until Sam Fargo happened."

"Exactly who is this Sam Fargo I keep hearing about?"

"I've made a few inquiries, but there isn't much known."

"Surely you've found something?" she asked.

"Other than he works in a California grocery store as a shelf stocker, no. I do have this, though." He took out his phone and showed her a surveillance video from their olive oil processing facility.

Within a few short minutes, she watched as the man blew up the pallet load on the back of the truck, effecting their escape from the island after killing one guard and taking down the other two. "Show that to me again."

He started it from the beginning, telling her, "Based on what a few of my men have said, he's extremely competent in hand-to-hand combat. His skill set, the way he easily broke into your son's office, and what you see him doing here in the video, suggests he's a very competent adversary. Definitely a good shot. And he also managed to convince the two who came after him that they'd successfully killed him in a boat explosion."

Her brows went up. "Do you mean to tell me that *this* man"—she nodded at the screen—"has a job whose sole purpose is to put things on shelves in a grocery store? I find that hard to believe. He must be a spy. Or a government agent."

"I suppose that possibility exists. But my source tells me otherwise."

Frustrated, Minerva pushed back her chair, then rose, walking to the window to look out. Now that the weather was once again clear, Adrian's latest flame, Phoebe, was in the pool, swimming. The girl was the last hope that the Heibert name might continue on. Perhaps young Phoebe's genes might lend a better mix to the Kyril-Heibert line. "Has she heard about the charges?"

"Not yet. I didn't think it my place to tell her."

"I suppose I should sit down and have a chat with the poor girl." Ilya cleared his throat.

"What is it?" she asked without turning around.

"Are you actually planning to let your son take the blame?"

"He committed the crimes."

"He did."

Minerva looked back at him. "Would you rather it was you or I sitting in that jail cell?"

"No."

"Then Adrian it is. For now." She cocked her head to the window. "Perhaps, if I'm lucky, I'll have a granddaughter to carry on the bloodline."

Ilya's gaze flicked to the window, but he said nothing.

With a sigh, she returned to the desk, sitting. "Where were we?"

"Sam Fargo."

"Yes. Do you think he found anything on our island?"

"No. There was no product there at the time. Containers only. As soon as Dimitris was discovered, they stopped the shipment."

"And where is it?"

"Awaiting your orders."

"We'll have to stop all shipments for now. I expect the police will be watching us even closer." She held her hand out. "May I see that video again?"

He unlocked his phone and slid it toward her.

She scrolled through the video, pausing as the man shot out the truck tire, causing the pallet to explode. "It appears he knew that the explosive was set to go off if the weight shifted."

"I would agree."

That smacked of more than just luck and skill. The man had to have had some sort of training, she thought, watching as he shot out the lights a moment before killing a guard. "I don't suppose there's any way we could use this against him?"

"Not unless you want to explain why they were holding Dimitris against his will."

"I suppose you're right." With a heavy sigh, she returned the phone to him. "As soon as things calm down, I want that heroin out of here. I hate to think I sacrificed my son for nothing. As for this Sam Fargo, what is it you're planning?"

"Already implemented. The men who were following him last night informed me that he and the woman with him are boarding a ferry to Samos."

"Do you know why?"

"I have no idea."

"Find out. Then take care of him. All of them. I can't imagine they'll be able to prosecute Adrian if every one of the witnesses are dead."

CHAPTER FIFTY-EIGHT

After Sam and Remi stored their rented motorcycle and helmets in the ferry's hold, they headed up the stairs to find a spot on the crowded upper deck. The weather was clear, and the waters calm, once the vessel departed, and the two found a couple of seats near the stern.

Sam, his hair slightly damp from the sea mist that sprayed over the side, recognized quite a few of the passengers who were residents of Fourni. Perhaps because of everything they'd been through, he found himself scrutinizing everyone on board. There were two men who caught his attention. He'd seen them talking on the pier as they waited for the ferry to arrive. The taller of the two, wearing a red ball cap and dark sunglasses, seemed familiar, but Sam couldn't place him. It was possible he was simply a Fourni islander. Once on board, the man took a seat inside, and Sam didn't see him again. The second man, however, had followed them out to the deck, and stood not ten feet away from Sam and Remi.

Never once looking their way.

It was that last part that bothered Sam, because he and every other passenger on that boat had nothing better to do than look at each other for the one-and-a-half-hour ferry ride into Pythagorio.

Not wanting to alarm Remi in light of their near miss on the road the night before, he said nothing. Had Manos and Denéa not driven up when they did, he couldn't help but wonder if the car might have made a second attempt at running them down. Of course, it was highly possible that Sam was simply being paranoid—easy to do, considering all that had happened to them.

For now, he kept his eye on the man, hoping he was wrong. Remi, apparently, noticed his interest. "Something going on?"

"You didn't happen to notice that man at the pier, did you?"

She glanced to her left, then looked away, giving no indication that she was at all bothered by his presence. "No. Have you heard back from Selma about where we're supposed to meet the professor?"

He checked his phone, realizing he should have had Selma send a text to Remi's sat phone instead. "No signal. We probably won't get one until we reach port."

As they neared Pythagorio, the red-tile-roofed houses, set high on the hills, overlooked the busy marina filled with yachts and fishing boats. Gulls flew overhead, one calling out as it dropped down, skimming the surface in search of food.

"It's beautiful," Remi said as the ferry backed into the terminal.

Sam paid little attention, his focus on the one man, who hurried inside, getting lost among the passengers filing toward the exit. He and Remi followed, only to find the man lingering near the steep stairs. Seemingly in no hurry to leave, he was focused on his phone screen, glancing up with casual interest as Sam and Remi walked past. He lifted his phone to his ear, speaking to someone on the other end, unfortunately in Greek. The taller man was nowhere in sight.

Sam, following Remi down the stairs to the lower deck, leaned toward her, asking, "You didn't happen to catch any of that conversation, did you?"

"He said hello to his mother and that the ferry had arrived."

Definitely not what Sam was expecting. He glanced up the stairs, seeing the man waving other people past him as he continued his call. "Maybe I was wrong."

"Let's hope so."

His suspicion rose when he noticed one of two vehicles stored in the hold. One was a navy-blue compact car with a rental sticker on the windshield. Though he couldn't be sure, since it had been dark at the time, it was close in size and color to the car that had nearly run him and Remi off the road.

Remi saw him looking at the vehicle. "Please tell me we're simply being paranoid and that's not the same car."

"I wish we were down here when they loaded it. It would've been nice to see who was behind the wheel." Sam handed Remi her helmet, then glanced up in time to see the man in the red ball cap and dark glasses walking past. "There's the other guy. He seems familiar."

"I was thinking the same. Maybe the car's his?"

But the man walked past, disembarking on foot with the other passengers.

"Guess not," Sam said.

Remi put on her helmet, and climbed on the motorcycle behind Sam. He cruised down the ramp onto the pier, weaving around the long line of cars that were waiting to pick up or drop off passengers.

Although Sam could've parked in the lot adjacent to the pier and marina, he decided it might be best to put some space between them and the men from the ferry—just in case. He found a parking space in front of a busy souvenir shop. Leaving their helmets with the motorcycle, they walked down to the waterfront. While Remi asked for directions to Elia, the restaurant chosen by the professor, Sam moved out far enough to watch the people leaving the ferry. The blue rental car was locked in a logjam of taxis and other vehicles that had all converged at the pier, unfortunately too far away to see who was at the wheel.

The man in the red ball cap, he noticed, was well in front of the blue car, strolling through the parking lot, not seeming to be in a hurry at all.

Remi walked up, looking. "I suppose that means we were wrong about them?"

"So it would seem." He glanced at her. "Did you find out where the restaurant is?"

"Elia is at the very end of the marina." She pointed to their left.

Hand in hand, they walked along the stone-paved waterfront past a number of busy restaurants, all with tables set on the patios facing the harbor. Elia was the very last restaurant. A light breeze swept in off the water, fluttering the pale green tablecloths. No one seemed to be waiting for them.

"You're sure we have the right time?" Remi asked.

Sam checked the email. "Elia. Two o'clock . . . According to Selma, Dr. Alexandris looks like a professor."

"Did she really say that?" Remi surveyed the nearby patrons. "Exactly what does a professor look like, in her opinion?"

"She didn't say. Sherlock Holmes? Tweed jacket and a pipe?"

"You're sure you're not thinking of Dr. Watson?"

"Watson doesn't smoke a pipe, does he?"

"'Ship's tobacco,' to be exact," Remi said. "More importantly, what makes you think the professor is male?"

He nodded to their left at a man sitting at a corner table. Early fifties, his brown hair flecked with gray, his attention was on a news-paper as he nursed a glass of beer. "That's got to be him."

"Sam Fargo?" a woman called out from the opposite direction.

He and Remi turned to see a silvered-haired woman in her late sixties sitting at a table on the other side of the aisle. She stood, wav-ing them over.

Remi cleared her throat, her green eyes gleaming. "You were saying . . . ?"

Sam guided her to the table. "Professor Alexandris?"

"You seem surprised," the woman said.

"A bit," he replied, ignoring Remi's catlike smile as he pulled out her chair. He took a seat next to her. "There was a bit of confusion about your name."

She smiled at a waiter who brought two plates to the table, one with bread and olive tapenade, the other with thick slices of white cheese covered with a red compote. She slid that one toward Sam and Remi. "Grilled Halloumi cheese with cherry salsa. I hope you'll try it. It's a particular favorite of mine."

"Thank you," Remi said.

"So," she turned her attention to Sam. "I read the book, *The Pirates of Poseidon*. What is it you're hoping to learn?"

CHAPTER FIFTY-NINE

I don't suppose you heard about the man on Fourni who was found at the bottom of the cave? Tassos Gianakos?" Sam asked.

The professor's brows rose. "These are small islands. News like that travels fast. This morning's headlines announced they'd made an arrest."

"Well, this is about him." Sam dipped his knife into the olive tapenade, spreading it onto the bread. "His granddaughter, Zoe Gianakos, said that he'd spent his life looking for a treasure called Poseidon's Trident. Have you heard of it?"

"No, but I have to imagine there's some connection to this children's story, *The Pirates of Poseidon*, or we wouldn't be having this conversation."

"Zoe believes it has something to do with the treasure mentioned in the story. He had the book in his pocket when he died."

Professor Alexandris reached for the serving fork on the dish of Halloumi. "I have to admit," she said, placing a slice of the cheese and cherry compote on her plate, "this is nothing close to what I imagined when I received the email."

"By any chance," Remi asked, "are you familiar with the story?"

"Very. It was a favorite of my brother's when we were children.

The history of it is uncertain. While I didn't have much time to research before our meeting, I managed to find one scholarly article that suggested the tale was derived from one of Aesop's fables."

"Aesop," Remi said. "That would put it around the same time period that Cyrus conquered Lydia."

"Depending on which historian you want to believe, Aesop probably died a good fifteen or twenty years before. Even so, he suggested that it was meant to be a cautionary tale about looking too far afield."

Sam helped himself to the cheese and cherry appetizer. "I take it you don't agree?"

"I don't. The story's far too long, and most of Aesop's fables are represented by animals."

He bit into the thick, firm goat cheese, the mild flavor accentuated by the tart cherries and sweetened sauce. He slid his plate toward Remi. "You need to try this." Then, to the professor, he asked, "Could *The Pirates of Poseidon* be based on any truth?"

"It could. As you can imagine, though, there's no way to know what was changed, or simply left out, over the centuries. One has only to look at Herodotus as proof."

"Why is that?" Sam asked.

"Herodotus," Remi said, "was known for embellishing tales, and making assumptions."

"Exactly," the professor continued. "Unfortunately, many of these old tales were never written down. The idea of books meant for the masses was still centuries upon centuries away." She gave a pointed nod to the portfolio on the table, no doubt containing her photocopied pages. "There's no way to know how close the modern-day children's book might be to the original story."

Remi sank back in her chair. "Then it could be completely made up?"

"Absolutely. That being said, what makes me think that the tale is based on some kernel of truth is the fact it's so well known in these parts. I doubt there's a child in the Aegean who hasn't heard the story. So, why so popular?"

"Pirates?" Remi suggested.

"And treasure," Sam added.

"Undoubtedly," the professor replied. "And, if the story is based on truth, then someone lived to tell the tale."

"So why not the boys?" Remi said. "That would make sense since the story is from their point of view."

"What about Pactyes?" Sam asked.

"Again, assuming this story has some real connection to history, there's every reason to assume that the Pactyes mentioned in the book is undoubtedly the same Pactyes who made off with King Cyrus's treasury. According to Herodotus, that Pactyes was eventually captured on Chios."

"The only problem with Chios," Sam said, "is that doesn't line up with our theory that the treasure is on one of the islands in the Fourni archipelago."

"I wouldn't discount it," she replied. "As Remi mentioned, Herodotus sometimes took liberties with what he didn't know first-hand. But he also left out large swaths of history. So it's anyone's guess as to what happened in between the theft of the gold and Pactyes's arrest. It could even be that someone made up this tale of Poseidon's Trident to fill in that gap, and the story carried on through the centuries."

"So we have nothing," Remi said.

"Not necessarily. Herodotus being Herodotus, any scholar would wisely try to confirm the man's narrative with other sources. We know that Pactyes hired mercenaries to move the Sardis treasury from Lydia to the coast. With that sort of wealth to protect, Pactyes had the means to hire the best. And that brings us to the Samian pirates."

"Why the Samians?" Sam asked.

"Proximity." She took a bite of cheese, then nodded out toward the marina. "You can see Lydia—or Turkey, as we now know it—from here." They looked out, seeing the hills of the Turkish coast in the distance. "More importantly, Pactyes needed mercenaries who'd be willing to go up against Cyrus. Pythagorio, the oldest man-made harbor in the Mediterranean at the time, was filled with them. And it probably helped that the Samians were the sworn enemy of the Lydians. From the Samian point of view, I imagine the prospect of helping to loot what was left of the Lydian kingdom found great appeal."

Sam glanced at the portfolio next to her. "So you think there could be some truth to this children's story?"

"There's nothing to suggest otherwise."

"Any idea where this cave could be? We've heard conflicting reports, that Poseidon's Trident might be the name of a treasure, or the name of the cave where it was hidden."

"That I can't say. I can tell you this much, though. The cave where your friend's grandfather was found could not possibly be the cave in the book."

"Why not?" Remi asked.

"Quite simply, the boys want to whisper into Poseidon's Ear. He was, after all, the god of the sea, so it would make sense that his ear opens up to the water."

Sam and Remi exchanged glances. "Definitely not the cave on Fourni or Thimena," Sam said.

"The takeaway from your book," she continued, "is that the pirates hid their treasure in a cave that opens up both somewhere on land, and also to the water."

"Any chance you happen to know of any caves that fit that description?" Sam asked.

She laughed. "This being Greece, sea caves past and present were and are somewhat plentiful."

"So much for that lead," Remi said. "I don't suppose you happened to notice the sketch of an ugly sun face at the end of the book?"

"I did." She opened her portfolio, turning the sheets of paper until she found the photocopy of the sketch.

"We were told it might be Helios."

"I suppose that's one possibility." She studied it a moment, then shrugged. "It certainly looks like flames around the face. I have to admit, Helios is usually depicted as being handsome. This," she said, tapping the sketch, "is quite the opposite. If I had to make an educated guess. I'd go with one of the three Gorgon sisters. They're often depicted with broad, round heads, large teeth and fangs."

"Sisters?" Sam said.

"The most common reference is that they're three mythical sisters, Stheno and Euryale, immortals, and their human sister, Medusa."

He looked at her in surprise. "As in snakes-for-hair Medusa?"

"As in turn-you-to-stone Medusa. Because of that ability, their images were often placed upon objects and buildings as protection. You really can't travel through Greece without running into one somewhere."

Remi tapped on the thing growing from the head. "That could be a snake."

Sam was about to agree, when he happened to glance up, seeing two men, one of them wearing a red ball cap, stopping in front of the next restaurant over. The pair stood in front of the menu displayed near the maître d' podium and appeared to be searching the faces of the patrons sitting at the waterside tables. "Remi." Sam tapped her foot with his, nodding toward the patio seating on their right. "The men from the ferry."

She looked over as the one man pulled off his ball cap, running his fingers through his curly hair. "That's Fayez."

The moment she said the name, it came back to him. Kyril's party. He was the man Remi had thrown her knife at—and missed. "Professor. You've been a big help. But . . . something's come up, and we really need to go."

CHAPTER SIXTY

Their only option for a quick exit was a narrow street leading behind the restaurant. Remi had enough time to grab her purse before he led her out, the scent of cooking meat and fresh baked bread hitting them as they hurried past.

"What about the professor?" she asked, looking over her shoulder.

"She's definitely safer on her own. Those two men are looking for us, not her."

"But Kyril was arrested—"

"And you're a witness who will need to testify against him. Get rid of you, go after Dimitris, no trial." Once past the restaurant, they hid behind a delivery van parked nearby. Sam peered out, then ducked back as Fayez came around the corner and stopped on the other side of the vehicle.

He looked around. "Zenos," he called out to his partner.

The other man ran up, slightly out of breath.

Fayez rattled off something in Greek. Zenos took off toward the marina, while Fayez started walking the opposite way.

Sam, holding tight to Remi's hand, waited a minute, making sure they didn't return. "What'd he say?"

"He told Zenos to walk on the waterfront."

Sam rose up high enough to look through the windows of the van. Fayez, apparently, intended to parallel his partner, walking up the street behind the restaurants. Unfortunately, both men were heading in the direction that Sam and Remi needed to go to get back to their motorcycle. "I think if we head up another block, we can parallel the both of them, and keep out of sight."

They made a right turn, walking up a steep street, the cobblestones slippery from being so worn. Keeping the port on their left, the streets and alleys were easy to navigate as they worked their way west, then south. They turned the corner, then stopped, seeing Fayez blocking their way.

"Time for Plan B," Sam said, taking her arm.

"Which is what?"

"We run." He pulled Remi down a narrow, covered street crowded with shops and kiosks. A cacophony of sounds carried toward them, music and the drone of voices. Merchants called out, trying to entice customers into their space, some selling fine linen and Egyptian cotton, others jewelry, souvenirs, and T-shirts. Sam and Remi ran past, then jumped over a dog napping at the entrance of a catwalk between two buildings. The wire-haired mongrel was apparently used to the comings and goings. Sam looked back. "I think we lost him."

Remi, however, was looking in the opposite direction. "Doesn't that remind you of the drawing in the back of Zoe's book?" She pointed at a banner strung across the awning of a ceramics shop on the opposite side of the street.

Sam glanced up as a gust of wind caught at the sign, rippling the material like a ship's sail. When it finally settled, he saw an angry face surrounded by snakes staring at him. He was about to agree when he heard the sound of footsteps echoing somewhere behind them.

Remi looked up at the Gorgon as they crossed the street. "The professor did say Gorgons ward off evil."

"Let's hope she's right," Sam said, then drew her inside the store.

CHAPTER SIXTY-ONE

A young man sat on a stool, carving away at a block of wood, while pale-colored shavings accumulated on the floor at his feet.

His dark eyes regarded first her, then Sam, with mild curiosity as Sam returned to the door, keeping watch outside. Remi, trying to look like a normal customer, eyed the ceramic pieces, many depicting the same angry face as that on the sign out front.

She picked up a mug sitting on a shelf, rubbing her thumb over the carving on the mug. "I'd say this looks far closer to Zoe's sketch, don't you think?"

Sam glanced over. "Definitely in the face. But Zoe's sketch has a head full of hair, not snakes."

He was right about that. Every one of these faces had thick-corded hair with snake heads at the ends. Curious about the origin of the design, she turned to the boy, showing him the mug. "What is this?" she asked in Greek.

He looked up from his carving, his brow furrowing as he glanced from her to Sam, then back. He pointed to his mouth. "To drink. Coffee? Tea?"

She laughed. "I mean the face." She looked about the shop. "It's everywhere. What is it?"

"You like this? Everything here, my mother makes." He called to someone in the back of the shop.

An old woman holding a broom pulled aside a curtain and looked out. She tapped her broom on the floor. Having overheard the conversation, she knew they were Americans and replied in English. "Gorgons. To ward off evil."

"Gorgons," he repeated.

"We should buy one," Remi said to Sam.

"Why?"

"What if it works?"

"You don't really believe that stuff?"

"Who knows?" She replaced the mug and picked up a quart-size blue pot with what she thought was a delightfully ugly Gorgon face on the front. "We might be pleasantly surprised. I do like this one."

Sam looked at her, his brows going up as she pulled money from her shoulder bag to pay for it. "A flowerpot? Why not one of those flat wall plaques? We're on a motorcycle."

"This one called out to me."

"Of course it did." He glanced out the door, then suddenly stepped away from the opening, backing toward her. "While he's wrapping it, you mind asking if there's another way out? And you'd better hurry it up."

Remi took the shopping bag, apologized for the inconvenience, then asked if there was a second way out.

"Remi . . . ?" Sam said, his eye on the front door as he continued backing toward her.

"I have to be polite."

The young man, witnessing this exchange, hesitated, then pulled aside the curtain. "Through here," he said in perfect English.

"Thank you," Remi said.

Sam took her hand. "Our friend seems to have found us," he said as they hurried through. The old woman looked up from her sweeping, yelling at them as they rushed past, scattering dust in their wake. They fled out the back door, their footsteps echoing as they raced down the street. Sam paused at an intersection, looking both ways, then started toward the left.

"Not that way," Remi said.

"We need to go left," Sam insisted.

They rounded the corner, then hit a dead end.

"Why," Remi said, "do men refuse to trust a woman's sense of direction?"

"For the same reason women insist on buying flowerpots at inopportune times."

They retraced their steps. Unfortunately, as they ran past the intersection, Fayez burst out the back of the potter's shop. He followed as they took off in the opposite direction. They turned a corner onto a narrow street, then into an alley, where, up ahead, bright pink bougainvillea vines spilled over the top of a high wall. As they raced past it, they noticed the entrance to an open courtyard filled with potted plants and a wrought iron table and chairs. Backtracking, they ducked inside. About ten feet away, on the opposite side of the alley, a boy sat in a doorway, playing with several gray kittens. He picked up one of the tiny creatures, watching warily as Sam and Remi hid behind the thorny vines that grew on either side of the open gate. Remi set her shopping bag at her feet, pressing closer to the wall. Hearing Fayez's heavy footfalls, she looked at the boy through the bougainvillea leaves and put her finger to her lips.

"Did you see the Americans?" Fayez asked.

The child held out his hand, saying, "You pay?"

Fayez scowled as he dug a coin from his pocket, tossing it onto the ground. It bounced, then rolled along the stones, landing at the boy's feet.

He picked it up, took a step toward the courtyard, then let the kitten go, shooing it inside. "Hurry!" he said, and darted off down the alley.

Fayez started to follow. The kitten mewed, then jumped onto Remi's shopping bag, swiping its tiny claws at the handles. Fayez, hearing the noise, retraced his steps, and drew a dagger from a sheath on his belt.

CHAPTER SIXTY-TWO

The moment Fayez stepped into the courtyard, Sam grabbed him by the collar and swung him around. As Fayez lashed out with the knife, Sam caught his arm, the two struggling for control of the weapon. Fayez brought up his other hand, splaying it across Sam's face, forcing him back into the courtyard, nearly knocking Remi over. Sam pivoted, managed to get his other hand on Fayez's wrist, and slammed it against the wrought iron table, again and again, until the knife clattered to the ground. Remi scooped it up, then circled around the table.

Fayez threw two quick punches, both blocked. Sam landed a blow to his jaw. The man stumbled back, recovered, then rushed, ramming his shoulder into Sam's gut. They fell against the table, shoving it back several feet. Fayez wrapped his fingers around Sam's neck, choking him.

"Sam!"

From the corner of his eye, he saw Remi raising the knife. "Don't—"

She threw. The handle hit Fayez in the side, then skidded out of reach.

Sam gripped Fayez's hands. Unable to pry them from his neck, he dropped his shoulder, using the momentum to throw Fayez to the ground.

Rolling over, Fayez saw the knife, toppling a chair as he strained to reach the weapon. He grasped it, then slashed out, the blade barely missing Sam.

With the advantage, Fayez rose like a cat, thrusting and feinting, forcing Sam against the wall. "Too bad I missed you with my car," Fayez said, his dark eyes gleaming in triumph. "I've got you now."

"You may think so."

"If I don't kill you, Zenos will." Fayez, gripping the knife, took one step toward Sam, then caught sight of Remi's shadow. She slammed her Gorgon flowerpot over his head. The earthenware broke, blue-enameled shards falling to the ground. Momentarily stunned, he turned to her, lifting his knife. Sam grabbed his shoulders, spun him around, pulled him forward, ramming his knee into the man's stomach, then shoved him into a chair. As he landed, Sam pushed the chair back. Fayez landed hard, slamming his head on the ground. Stunned, he rolled and turned to one side, trying to right himself. Sam drove his boot down against Fayez's knee, shifting his entire weight. The bone cracked, and Fayez screamed in agony.

Sam looked down at the broken Gorgon pot as he took Remi by the hand, the two racing from the courtyard. "Guess that thing does ward off evil. Your knife throwing, on the other hand, is definitely not your strong suit."

"At least I hit him this time." She looked back as they ran down the alley. "Shouldn't we call the police?"

"From somewhere a lot safer than here." They stopped at the corner. Sam looked around it, and seeing it was clear, he drew Remi out. They reached the main thoroughfare, thinking there were enough tourists to keep them from standing out. Or so he thought until he saw Zenos at the end of the street.

"To your right," Sam said to Remi. "Our friend from the ferry."

She glanced over. "How'd he know we'd come back here?"

Sam nodded at their motorcycle parked on the opposite side of the street. "We left a giant calling card."

"Tell me you have a plan."

"I might. Depending. There was this time in Cambodia—"

"You're telling me a story?"

"Not a story," he said, pulling Remi quickly across the street and handing her one of the helmets before putting on his own. "It's my plan."

"I hate that plan."

"You don't even know what it is."

She shoved on her helmet, then looked back over her shoulder. "Whatever it is, work on it faster. He's in his car, coming this way."

She climbed onto the motorcycle behind him, wrapping her arms around his waist. He started the bike. The rear wheel skidded out on the smooth pavers.

Remi craned her neck around. "Sam! He's catching up."

Sam drove faster, trying to put distance between them and Zenos. The car gained on them, its reflection filling the rearview mirror. "Hang on," Sam shouted, then opened the throttle wide.

CHAPTER SIXTY-THREE

Remi held tight to Sam while he navigated around the cars, leaving Zenos stuck behind a line of other vehicles. Within a few short minutes, they were out of the town, passing the airport, heading out into the country. She looked in the rearview mirror and saw the blue car in the distance.

Sam never slowed until they reached the small village of Mitilini. A van pulled out from a side street. Sam braked, steered around the vehicle, then continued down the narrow road, having to slow several more times as cars appeared from both directions. After they passed through the village, he picked up speed, continuing on until they reached a small house sitting by itself on the right. He braked, stopping in front of it, studying the road up ahead, then looking back toward the village. Pulling into the drive, he glanced back at her. "Get off. We're not going to outrun him. I need to let him catch up to me."

Reluctantly, she slid off. "What are you talking about?" she asked.

"The Cambodia thing. This road was made for that." He nodded up the hill. The highway stretched out, then curved right before a bridge.

"Sam—"

"Get down. Here he comes."

She ducked behind a bush on the side of the house as Sam sped up the hill, then stopped in the middle of the road, waiting. He revved the engine, watching in the rearview mirror. The blue car finally appeared in the distance. It continued on a short way as though the driver expected some sort of trap. Sam took off, speeding up the narrow two-lane road. He disappeared momentarily as the road dipped down, then rose. Once again, he stopped. Looking back at the car, he gave a taunting wave.

It worked. Provoked, Zenos hit the gas, racing after him. Sam sped down the middle of the two lanes, playing cat and mouse, increasing his speed just enough to keep Zenos from catching him, until he neared the curve and the bridge. Remi's breath caught, her heart thudding in her chest, when she realized Sam was going far too fast. He braked into the turn, his rear tire slipping out from beneath him. The bike went sliding onto the bridge, back end spinning around until Sam was actually stopped, facing the oncoming car. Zenos drove into the turn, tires screeching, back end shuddering. His rear fender scraped against the stone wall leading up to the bridge. Sam started driving toward him. At the last second, he veered the motorcycle to the opposite side of the road and the inside of the curve. Zenos yanked the wheel, trying to hit Sam. The over-correction sent his vehicle spinning. It hit the wall, flipping up, over, and down the embankment. Sam, steering around him, was wrestling for control of his bike. The back end wobbled. Remi wasn't sure if he jumped or fell, but suddenly Sam was on the ground. The last thing she remembered was seeing him rolling in one direction, the bike sliding out in the other.

Remi had no idea that she'd actually jumped up and was racing down the street toward him, until a small pickup from the village came up behind her. The driver pulled over. All she could do was point. "Accident," she finally managed.

"Get in."

Somehow, she managed to climb into the truck. When they neared the bridge, she saw the motorcycle lying on its side. About a hundred feet farther up, she saw Sam sitting on the side of the road. She threw open the car door and jumped out, running over. "Sam!"

He pulled off his helmet, looking down at his torn shirt and a long burn on his right arm. "Could be worse. You think the bike's okay? Something tells me I forgot to purchase the extra insurance."

"Forget the bike. What about you? You scared me to death. I can't believe you're not dead."

"I'm fine," he said, walking over to the side of the bridge, looking down the embankment. The car had landed on its roof. "I don't think he's doing too good."

The man who'd given Remi the ride held up his phone. "The police are on their way. Do you want me to stay here with you?"

"No, thank you," Remi said. "We'll be fine."

After he left, she looked at Sam. "I'm trying to decide if you're insane or a genius. This is that thing you were talking about in Cambodia?"

"Let's just say it worked a whole lot better there. Probably the dirt roads."

Remi wasn't sure if she should laugh or cry. As the adrenaline fled her body, she found her knees giving way.

Sam helped her sit down on the side of the road. After what seemed like an eternity to Remi, they finally heard a siren in the distance.

"I'm not sure if it matters to you," Sam said, "but by the time we get done with the police, we're likely to miss our ride back to Fourni."

"The way I see it, that might work out for the best."

"Why's that?"

Shaking, she let out a deep breath. "After this? I'm going to need time to recover from the copious amount of drinking I'll probably be doing tonight."

"That makes two of us."

CHAPTER SIXTY-FOUR

Sam and Remi arrived in Fourni the following morning, dropping off the motorcycle at the rental shop. It was still drivable, having suffered mostly cosmetic damage. Sam—grateful he'd purchased the extra accident insurance after all—apologized once again for the damage as he and Remi left. From there, they walked over to Skavos's café to meet up with everyone for lunch.

Dimitris, Zoe, Manos, and Denéa were waiting at a table on the patio when they arrived.

"Zoe, you're looking better," Sam said, pulling out a chair for Remi.

Zoe, her right arm in a cast and sling, reached up with the other, touching the lump on her forehead. It and the bruising that had settled down beneath her eye had turned from dark purple to a lighter green tinged with yellow. "And feeling better." She held a photocopy of the sketch from her book, setting it on the table. "What did the professor say?"

"That it was probably a Gorgon," Sam said.

Remi nodded, adding, "We found a store with a bunch of Gorgon heads that had that same angry look. I even bought one to bring home to you."

"You did? I can't wait to see it."

"Unfortunately, I needed it to ward off evil. It broke in the process. But, good news. It worked."

Sam glanced at the photocopy of Zoe's sketch. "I think we can rule out the Gorgon sisters as the model. I don't see any resemblance to snakes or women."

Denéa tapped on the sheet of paper. "What about this thing sticking up from the head? Maybe that's a snake?"

"Why only one?" Manos asked. "That'd make for a pretty sad Gorgon."

"Maybe," Zoe said, "it's a mistake. Or artistic license."

Sam considered the possibility, then dismissed it. The strokes of the appendage on the top of the head were as bold as those on the face. "I don't think it's an afterthought." He studied the photocopy as he drank his coffee.

Remi, however, was distracted by a gray and white cat with topaz eyes that had meandered onto the patio. It hopped up onto a planter, balancing, its tail straight up, the tip of it twitching back and forth as it stared at them.

Sam and Remi watched the cat a moment, looked at each other, then the photo.

"Of course," Remi said. "How did we not see it?"

"I'm blaming it on perspective," Sam said. "The head's blocking everything behind it. That, and it doesn't look like any tail I've ever seen."

Nikos walked up at that moment, scaring off the cat as he pulled out a chair and sat at the table. "What have I missed?"

Zoe turned the sketch toward him. "We think this thing on its head is a tail."

He leaned in closer. "It's not Helios?"

"And not a Gorgon," Dimitris said.

Nikos picked up the paper. "So, it's not the rays of the sun or snakes circling his face. Maybe it's a lion's mane?"

"It could be," Sam said. "But that's definitely not a lion's tail."

"A scorpion tail?" Remi said.

Sam eyed the barbed end. "What sort of creature has a man's face, a lion's mane, and a scorpion tail?"

Remi was already looking it up on her phone. "What if it's a manticore?"

"A what-icore?" Sam said.

"Manticore. A man's face on a lion's body with a venomous tail. More importantly . . ." She read something on the screen, then looked up at them. "I can't believe it was staring us in the face the whole time!"

"Staring us in the face?" Sam asked. "Very funny, Remi. Your levity is appreciated."

"I'm serious, Sam," she answered. "A manticore is a creature that eats its victims whole."

He eyed the picture on her phone. "I'm clearly missing something."

"It particularly likes the taste of humans."

"Of course," Nikos said, "Tassos's cave must be on the islet of Anthropofas. In English it translates to man-eater."

"Does it have a cave there?"

"Yes, it does. The cave holds a natural basin that collects rainwater, which the goat herders use for their animals. Others have explored it in the past. If there had been any treasure, someone would have found it."

"There's only one way to find out," Sam said. "We take a look ourselves."

CHAPTER SIXTY-FIVE

There were actually two islets that shared the name, both about a mile and a half to the south and southeast of Fourni—Megalos and Mikros Anthropofas—Big and Little Man-eater, supposedly named for the number of sailors who drowned after their ships were smashed upon their rocks. Sam wondered if they shouldn't be searching both islets, but Nikos assured him that Mikros Anthropofas was barely a rock worthy of being called an islet, and definitely not large enough to hide a cave.

They set out for Big Man-eater the following afternoon. As was the case on all the islands in the Fourni archipelago, the northern exposure was vulnerable to any sudden changes in the weather. The constant barrage of wind and waves left the rocks devoid of any vegetation. As they approached, the desolate cliffs loomed up ahead, a barren wasteland jutting out from the sea. For now, the water was relatively calm, and Nikos steered the *Lazy Krab* all the way around to the south side of the islet, where a small bay would protect them from the north winds.

While there was no beach, someone had embedded an iron hook in a flat rock, turning it into a makeshift dock. As they neared, Nikos cut the motor, allowing the boat to drift forward toward the rock. Dimitris, holding the mooring rope, tied it around the rusted hook, then pulled himself out, reaching for the bag of climbing gear that Sam lifted out to him.

Once they all had disembarked, the four started the trek up the steep hill through the low, prickly scrub growing on the south exposure of the rocky incline.

They passed a concrete shelter that, according to Nikos, the government had erected for the fishermen and goat herders who occasionally landed on the islet. Just beyond it, the group stopped, seeing two possible routes up. Because Nikos had been told the cave wasn't necessarily the easiest to find—one could walk past it without knowing—he consulted with some of the goat herders, trying to find the easiest route. After listening to the legends and old fishermen's tales, the general consensus was that the cave was on the north side of the islet. Unfortunately, no one agreed on the best way to get there. One man told them to follow the goats, since the cave caught fresh rainwater.

Coming from the west, the wind whipped down from the top of the hill, bringing with it the faint bleating of goats. They headed in that direction. After a fifteen-minute hike, picking their way through the rocks and sparse, prickly vegetation, they finally reached the peak, then paused to take stock of their surroundings. To the north, they had a view of the southern end of Fourni, and beyond it, to the northeast, Samos. Fishing boats dotted the calm waters around the islands. Up above, seabirds floated on air currents, bright white against a blue sky.

Remi stood next to Sam. "Can you smell that?" she asked. "Thyme." She reached down, picked a sprig of the fragrant herb that grew wild on the island. Closing her eyes, she lifted the woody stem to her nose, breathing in the pungent scent, while the wind whipped red strands of hair from her ponytail.

Seeing her like that, it was easy to picture her half a world away, standing on their cliff top at Goldfish Point.

She glanced over at him. "What are you staring at?"

"You . . ."

She smiled. There was no hint of trouble, fear, or worry in that smile, and he wanted to remember it forever.

A moment later, her attention was drawn to the landscape. The island wasn't all that large, but the rocky terrain made it difficult to see anything that might resemble a cave entrance. Remi took a slow turn around. "Going back to the it's-a-place-not-a-treasure, that has to mean something. There has to be a reason for the name."

"Man-eater?" Nikos said. "Given because the sailors drowned."

"No. If Poseidon's Ear is a cave facing the water, what makes someone call a place Poseidon's Trident? A rock formation?"

"Sorry," Sam said. "There's nothing remotely close to a trident up here."

"But in the story, Poseidon shook the ground in anger. So, what if that earthquake knocked his trident to the ground?"

Definitely an idea with merit. Sam examined the rock formations, trying to imagine if any of them appeared as though they might have, at one point in time, been standing up. Near the northwest edge of the islet, he saw one rock formation that angled across another. He pointed at it. "That sort of looks like it could have fallen from an upright position."

Remi glanced around. "But where's the cave?"

She was right. From where they stood, there didn't appear to be one at all. As they started to walk toward it, they heard the tinkling of a bell, then saw a goat's head pop up from the ground just a few feet from the rocks. The creature scrambled out and ran off.

Nikos laughed. "My friend did say to follow the goats."

"That he did." They approached the formation, which very much appeared to be a massive spire of rock that had fallen upon another. And there, in front of it, the gaping mouth of a cave.

CHAPTER SIXTY-SIX

Minerva Kyril sat aboard the *Mirage*, when Ilya finally walked in the stateroom. "Please tell me we finally have word?" she asked.

"They've apparently landed on an islet just south of Fourni, Megalos Anthropofas."

"Why would they be there? More of this Poseidon's Trident nonsense?"

"That would seem the most likely reason. The islet is a barren piece of rock. My men can pick them off before they ever realize they're targets. I've ordered the helicopter readied."

A fitting end. Because of her son's obsession with that godforsaken treasure, bringing unnecessary attention to her island, she'd had to suspend all operations in the face of the federal police investigation.

Her phone rang. She checked the caller ID, saw her attorney's number, and answered it, turning it on speaker. "Leon," she said, placing the phone on the table. "Please tell me there's some good news?"

"The best I can give you is that it's not all bad. Since your men are unwilling to testify that he pushed the old man into the cave, and the two witnesses didn't actually see anything but your son standing there, the police don't have a case for murder."

"Small miracle."

"That being said, they do have a good case for kidnapping. If it goes to court, we're likely to find ourselves in the midst of an ugly inquest. I have a feeling that none of us will survive it."

The mistake had been hers. She should have cut Adrian from the family business years ago. He was reckless and there was no talking to her son once he set his mind to something. Sadly, his narcissistic personality clouded all sense. He knew better than anyone, refused to listen to reason, and blamed everyone else for his inept handling of whatever the task at hand. "So how do we stop this . . . nightmare from happening?"

"Short of murdering your son in his cell?" Leon said.

Ilya's expression darkened. "I don't find that amusing."

"I agree," Minerva said. While Ilya might work for her, he had an unwavering loyalty to her son.

"I meant no harm," Leon replied. "It was merely an unfortunate figure of speech. The prosecutor has offered a plea deal, which is why I'm calling."

"A plea deal?" Minerva said. "To what?'

"Kidnapping," Leon said. "My suggestion is that Adrian will admit to organizing the kidnapping in his misguided attempt to protect the family olive oil business, after the old man slipped into the cavern. The sentence for that is far less than anything else they're likely to offer."

The idea had merit. But her son wasn't the only problem they were dealing with. There was also the shooting at their processing facility. Ilya had suggested that they may have to sacrifice a few guards for the good of the organization, adding a well-thought-out letter of confession to go along with their suicides—not that she was about to suggest such a move to her attorney. Right now, though, her son's situation was more important. "Can I give this some thought and get back to you later this afternoon?" she asked Leon. "We have something in the works."

"Unfortunately, I need to let the prosecutor know before we appear in court this morning. Otherwise the deal is off, and we're faced with a trial."

Minerva looked at Ilya. "How long do we need?"

"As I said, they're readying the helicopter now."

In the end, her decision wasn't that hard. Adrian was going to have to pay for his misdeeds. Unless she found a way to even the playing field for him—and eliminating Sam Fargo was at the top of her list. She picked up the phone and turned off the speaker. "Hold off on that deal until you hear from me."

"Very good."

"Is that wise?" Ilya asked her once she disconnected.

"Until I know every one of those people is dead, I'm not willing to take a chance that my son will spend the rest of his life in prison."

"I understand. I'll call you as soon as it's done."

"You won't need to. I'm going with you."

Ilya, the man who usually seemed so calm, suddenly stood, looking alarmed. "I wouldn't advise it. You need to be here. Besides, there's not enough room."

"They'll have to make room." She walked out, crossed the deck, then took the stairs up to the helipad, the sound of the rotors beating the air growing louder.

Ilya followed her. "Mrs. Kyril . . ." he shouted as he followed her up. "It would be best if you stayed here. By the phone. I'll call you as soon as it's done."

She rounded on him. "Every single time I've relied on you to make sure things get done, your men have failed. Perhaps it's time for someone else to ensure this is handled properly."

The pilot and two men carrying assault rifles were already

aboard. When she climbed on, the pilot looked over at Ilya, who waited behind. Minerva turned. "Why isn't he boarding?"

"Not enough room, Mrs. Kyril," the pilot shouted. "Four seats, four passengers."

She waved her hand. "Let's go. Maybe this time we can get it right."

He gave a slight nod, then took off.

CHAPTER SIXTY-SEVEN

Had Sam and the others not seen the goat leaving the cave, they might have missed it altogether. Between the glare of the sun, and the shadows cast upon the ground, not to mention the large rocks in front of it, they were lucky to have even seen the goat from where they stood. With smaller rocks and scrub cleared, it was hard to believe anyone could miss such a wide opening.

Remi stood at the entrance, looking down. "I guess I thought it'd be covered with more rock. Wasn't part of the story about how Poseidon shook the earth and swallowed the cave?"

Nikos laughed. "You forget you're in Greece. With all the seismic activity over the centuries, it's not surprising that what at one time covered the cave is no longer there."

When everything was ready to go, Sam stepped up to the cave mouth, turning on a flashlight. Remi moved next to him and looked in. The cave sloped diagonally into the interior of the islet and the light hit the walls about thirty feet down. There was a definite dark shadow below. Beyond that, Remi couldn't see.

"It doesn't look too deep from here," she said.

"It's hard to say until we get in there," Sam replied.

He double-checked Remi's harness, making sure the fit was right. "You'll be fine. It's a lot easier than rappelling down a cliff."

"And what if something bad happens? Who's going to call for help if we're all down there?"

Dimitris smiled at her as he adjusted his helmet, grabbed the rope, then started down. "Zoe knows we're here. She'll send someone to come looking for us."

The first part of the descent appeared easy. The stone rock formation made natural steps down into the shaft, and the rope was used more for balance.

Nikos went next. When he reached the bottom, Sam looked at Remi. "Your turn."

She buckled her helmet's chin strap, then peered into the cavern. It wasn't getting down there that was the hard part. It was *being* down there. She wasn't a fan of deep, dark places. "You sure you don't want me to stay here and chase the goats out?"

"Something tells me we'll be fine from any marauding wildlife."

He held out his hand. She took it, stepping down into the cave, and grasping the rope, let it slip through her hands as she picked her way down the stone steps. At the bottom, she dropped the rope, waited for Sam, then crossed the cavern floor toward Nikos and Dimitris. The two men stood near a pool of water, the surface reflecting the light from their headlamps.

Nikos crouched down in front of it. "Runoff from the rain," he said. "Undoubtedly why the goats visit." He stood. "It would have been too much to ask that the treasure was in there."

They worked their way around the edge of the pool, where, just a few feet beyond, was an opening in the floor leading down into another chamber. Dimitris took a coil of rope from his pack, looking for a spot to anchor it.

Remi eyed the rope, then the cavern below. "That looks pretty dark."

Sam reached over and switched on her headlamp. "Better?"

She looked down, the beam of light bouncing off the cavern walls but failing to reach the bottom. "Definitely not better. Exactly how deep is it?"

He picked up a large rock and tossed it down.

Clunk, clunk, clunk.

"About that deep," he said.

She moved away from the edge. "If you find anything good, you can come back and get me. Or, even better, I'll see it when you bring it up. To the surface. Where I'm going."

Dimitris looked up from the knot he was tying. "What if we find something?"

"Something tells me I'll be one of the first to find out. Good luck."

Dimitris descended first, and Nikos followed. Sam grabbed on to the rope, then looked over at her. "It's not too late to change your mind. You'll be missing out."

"I'll take my chances," Remi said as Sam rappelled down after them.

When their lights disappeared, she climbed back up to the cave's mouth, walking to the cliff's edge, looking out across the water toward Fourni. So much had happened since she'd arrived here. And then there was Sam . . .

They were completely mismatched. She meticulously planned out every aspect of her life and her future. He acted on impulse. All that aside, when it came right down to it, what did she really know about him? Sam Fargo was an enigma.

Deep in thought, she drew her gaze from the water, aware of the faint sound of a helicopter coming from the south. She smiled at the memory of how Sam had called in a favor to someone high up in the military to secure her a ride back to Long Beach, all so she wouldn't miss her flight to Greece . . .

Turning, she watched the helicopter as it neared, curious, because it seemed to be headed straight toward them.

As the noise of the rotors grew louder, curiosity turned to alarm when the craft seemed to slow, then hover over the south side of the island. There was only one reason someone would send a helicopter here: they were looking for them. Remi backed toward the cave, seeing Dimitris's gear bag sitting near the mouth. She shoved it underneath a rock, then grabbed the rope, lowering herself into the cave entrance. "Sam!"

No answer.

She started down.

The slope wasn't too steep near the opening. "Sam!" she called out again as she extended her foot behind her, trying to find a good toehold. Suddenly she was sliding, the friction from the rope heating the palms of her gloves as she pulled herself to a stop.

"Don't move, Remi. I'm coming up."

She looked back, catching a glimpse of Sam's headlamp somewhere near the bottom. "There's a helicopter out there. I think they're trying to land on the island."

Sam climbed up, then helped Remi to a ledge on the side. "Wait here."

He pulled himself out of the mouth and crept toward the outcropping of rock that shielded the cave from view. The beating of the rotors grew louder as the aircraft rose from the south side of the island.

Sam, crouched behind the rocks, watched for a moment, then called back at her. "Do you have your sat phone?"

She pulled it from her pocket, looking up Zoe's number as the helicopter moved in, hovering. Glancing up, she caught a glimpse of the pilot, a woman, and two other men leaning out, looking down at them.

"Get down!" Sam shouted. He pressed back against the outcropping.

Remi ducked as one of the men pointed an assault rifle. Bits of rock and dirt jumped as he peppered the ground in front of them.

Sam drew the little Smith & Wesson, fired once, then ran to the cave as the helicopter banked away. He holstered his gun, then held his hand out to her. "We need to go down."

Remi craned her head upward, saw the helicopter rising, whipping the dirt and dried brush. She shoved the phone in her pocket, took Sam's hand, stepped off the ledge, balancing one foot on the cave wall as she grabbed the rope, then started down.

Dimitris and Nikos shouted from below as the helicopter thundered above them. Sam was still near the top, holding the rope with one hand, the pistol with the other.

The helicopter rose over the rocks and cave entrance, one of the gunmen leaning out, aiming his rifle into the cave.

Sam aimed for the pilot and fired. Again and again. Blood splattered across the windshield. The gunman twisted, grabbing the rail before falling to the ground as the chopper rose, spun around, then hit its tail on the massive rocks. Sam rappelled to the bottom. He grabbed Remi's hand, pulling her behind him as the pilot lost control and the helicopter slammed into the huge rock above them.

CHAPTER SIXTY-EIGHT

It sounded like an explosion echoing through the chamber, the walls rumbling around them. Sam shielded Remi from the falling rocks. Dust filled the air. They pulled up their shirts and covered their mouths and noses, trying not to breathe in too deep. Nikos and Dimitris found them, after they climbed up to the entrance of the lower chamber. As their coughing subsided, Sam heard the hiss of gravel and sand that slid down the cavern walls.

He glanced at Remi, who was patting her pockets. "Are you okay?"

"I'm fine. But I think I dropped the phone."

"It won't do us much good now. Nikos? Dimitris?"

"We're fine," Nikos said.

Sam turned back in the direction of what had been the opening of the cave. "Let's see if we can't get up there and dig our way out."

The beams from their headlamps lit up the particles floating in the air. Sam looked over at the pool, where rainwater had collected, the surface rippling from the debris falling from above. They followed Sam past the pool. The cavern entrance was blocked, the spire of rock having fallen right over the mouth. The rope they'd used to make their descent was still there.

"Should we try it?" Dimitris asked.

Sam tugged. It held firm. "Let's do it." He looked back at Remi and Nikos. "Stay over there. In case anything else falls."

He held on to the rope, using it to climb over the rocks that had landed at the base. His foot slipped, knocking one of the larger pieces. It caused a small avalanche, making it more difficult to see. Dimitris waited until it settled, was about to step over, when he glanced at the rubble. "That looks like red clay." He picked up a rather large shard of thick pottery. There were many pieces scattered with the rock. "Something definitely broke down here."

Nikos, watching from the other side, said, "Maybe one of the goat herders dropped a jar when they brought it in to fill with water."

Sam, hanging on to the rope, looked down, the beam of his headlamp hitting the pile of rocks. What he noticed was that some of the shards were sitting on top of the rubble pile. As though they'd fallen from above. He looked up. Pieces of the narrow ledge that Remi had been sitting on near the top had sheared off from the force of the helicopter's impact.

So why were the shards sitting on top?

Dimitris must have thought the same thing. His gaze followed Sam's. "Do you think . . . ?"

"Whatever it is, it's going to have to wait. Let's find a way out."

"Sam's right," Nikos said. The man's dust-covered face was tense, his expression mirroring Sam's. Worried. "We can always come back."

A moment later, Sam felt the rope moving below him as Dimitris began climbing up the scarred slope. Side by side, they balanced on what was left of the stairs carved into the shaft, their headlamps shining on the rock that now covered the opening. Sam and Dimitris reached up and pushed. It felt solid.

That was both the good news and the bad.

It didn't look like it was going to come crashing onto them

anytime soon. For now, there was no getting past it. No loose corners that they might dig out, freeing up enough space to get through.

Sam and Dimitris returned to the bottom.

"Let's move out of here," Sam said. They walked past the pool of water to the opening leading to the lower chamber.

"Zoe will send someone," Dimitris said.

Sam had no doubt. Though Zoe might not sound the alarm for a few hours, since they weren't expected back right away, someone was bound to have seen the helicopter crash. "We don't want to waste battery power. Until then, I'd suggest we find a safe place to sit in the dark while we wait." He moved next to Remi, who sat on a flat rock jutting out, while Nikos and Dimitris sat on the cave floor opposite them.

They each switched off their headlamps, the dark turning absolute. Sam reached over, grasping Remi's fingers in his. She leaned against him, resting her head on his shoulder. Perhaps because of the absence of light, the sounds around them seemed to magnify, and he listened to the calm breathing of Remi next to him.

After a minute, maybe two, she suddenly sat up. "Do you hear that?"

"Hear what?" he asked.

"Rhythmic."

"The air's moving," he said. "It's like putting your ear to a giant seashell. Which is good for us. We won't suffocate."

Remi let go, then stood, moving away. "Quiet . . ."

"I hear it, too," Dimitris said.

"Hear what?" Nikos asked.

"The sea," Remi and Dimitris said together.

CHAPTER SIXTY-NINE

Sam switched on his light, finding Remi pointing to his feet. "It's coming from under there."

He crouched, his headlamp shining into a foot-high crevice beneath the ledge that seemed to go back quite a distance. Closing his eyes, he listened. Whether it was actually the sound of the sea or simply the sound of air moving through the narrow passage, he wasn't sure. "I'll go see where it leads."

"I'm going with you," Remi said.

"So are we," Dimitris said.

"I'm being outvoted by all of you now?"

Remi crossed her arms. "Really, Sam?"

"Guess that means I am outvoted."

Sam went first, belly-crawling through the tunnel, the space so low in some spots he smacked his helmet whenever he tried to raise his head enough to see in front of them. The progress was slow. He stopped, looking behind him, squinting against the glare of Remi's headlamp.

She reached up and switched it off.

"Everyone okay?" he asked.

"A-OK," she said.

"Fine," Dimitris called out.

A moment later, they heard the *clunk* of plastic hitting the top of the tunnel from much farther back, then Nikos muttering loudly in Greek.

Remi shifted behind Sam. "Any chance you need that translated?"

"I think I got the gist." He turned back, eyeing the long stretch of tunnel in front of them, wondering if it was ever going to end. "Onward."

After several minutes of elbow-scraping, head-banging progress, they emerged into a slightly taller, dome-shaped chamber, almost two feet high at the center and at least ten feet in diameter.

What Sam didn't see was any possible way out, beyond the tunnel they'd crawled through.

The other three entered the chamber, Remi moving beside him, looking around in disbelief. She let out a breath, dropping her head to her arms. "All that to end up here? I can't believe this. I could've sworn that sound was the sea. I can still hear it."

He glanced over at her, seeing the disappointment on her dirt-covered face. "It was worth a try." Reaching up, he switched off his headlamp. The others did the same.

"We should go back," Dimitris said. "At least in the other chamber, we can stand."

Nikos sighed. "Give me a minute or two. I'm not looking forward to the trek back."

"It wasn't that bad," Dimitris replied.

"Don't forget, my bones are twice as old as yours. And my knees twice as bruised."

As his son's laughter echoed through the dark space, then died, Sam's gaze caught on the low roof at the far end of the chamber. For a moment, he thought it might be his imagination, his eyes playing tricks. "Look. Straight ahead."

Remi shifted beside him. "At what? There's nothing there but the end of the cavern."

"Exactly," he said, crawling in that direction. "So, unless we've suddenly developed extreme night vision, there's no way we should be seeing it." Somehow, light was seeping in, too faint to reach the entire chamber, but enough for them to notice, now that their eyes had adjusted in the absence of their headlamps.

Had they not waited in the dark for Nikos to rest, they might have missed it entirely.

As Sam neared the end of the chamber he saw that the domed ceiling dropped sharply to their right, a faint glow leading the way. Once again, he had to crawl on his belly. When he stilled, he thought he heard the far-off cry of a gull. Or the wind whistling through the opening somewhere above him.

He reached out, holding his hand toward the space, not only able to see each of his fingers in the diffuse light, but able to feel the air moving.

Turning onto his back, he looked up. The ceiling rose about four feet, into a narrow, angled shaft. Though it was somewhat brighter at the top, and plenty of fresh air sweeping down, it clearly didn't lead straight out.

He glanced at Remi, who'd crawled into the space behind him. "I'll go first," he said. "If I knock anything loose, you don't want to be beneath me."

She nodded, then moved back.

"Is it a way out?" Dimitris asked.

"Let's hope so," Sam said. He climbed into the passageway, dislodging bits of rock as he dug the soles of his boots into the walls, trying to find purchase. Eventually, the tunnel angled up like a narrow chimney. Light filtered in at the top about ten feet above him. He emerged onto a narrow ledge and looked over the edge. The waves broke against the rocks about thirty feet below. The sun was low in the sky to his left, and Fourni was straight ahead to the north. He saw a few fishing boats out in the far-off distance, but none close enough to signal to. Still, they were free. He called down to Remi. "Definitely the way out. Come on up."

A few moments later, her head popped out of the shaft. Dimitris, then Nikos, followed. While they settled themselves onto the ledge, Sam was looking at the rocks above, trying to find a way up. There was enough of a ridge to their right that they could carefully navigate across the face of the cliff to work their way up to what looked like a possible path to the top. "We have two choices. Wait here and hope someone sees us before nightfall, or climb to the top, and hope no one survived the helicopter crash."

Nikos eyed the cliff, then Sam. "You really think anyone survived?"

"They were fairly close to the ground when the helicopter hit the rocks."

"I vote we go up," Dimitris said. "Better than waiting here."

Nikos nodded in agreement.

"Remi?" Sam asked.

"I'm going with you."

They slowly made their way along the ledge. Close to the top of the almost vertical cliff, the ridge they were using narrowed to just a few inches wide. Sam found a solid crack about shoulder height, wedged his fingers into it, then reached out with his right foot. The rock crumbled beneath his weight, his foot slipping.

Remi's breath caught.

"I'm fine," he said, pulling himself up. He extended his foot farther, hitting the ridge just beyond the break, relieved to feel solid rock beneath. He looked back at Remi and held out his hand. She grasped it, stepping over the break. "You've got it," he said, watching her foot hit solid rock.

Once Remi was safely past that point, she edged her way closer to Sam. "And here I thought it was going to be a stress-free day."

"Weren't you the one who wanted to write a book?"

"About a shipwreck. In California."

When she reached the top, she rolled onto her back, both exhausted and exhilarated.

Sam looked over at her. "You have to admit, this beats sitting in a gray cubicle."

Dimitris and Nikos climbed up behind her. As the four of them rested on the top of the boulder, they looked down, seeing the crashed helicopter about fifty yards to their south. And a man using a rifle to sift through wreckage. They quickly ducked out of sight, and Remi looked over at Sam. "Between you and me? Unless you can come up with a good plan, that cubicle's looking pretty good."

CHAPTER SEVENTY

Grateful they hadn't been spotted, Sam shifted to where he could see between the rocks. The gunman was still using the tip of the AR-15 barrel to poke through the wreckage.

Remi moved beside him. "What do you think he's searching for?"

"Sat phone, maybe?"

Sam wasn't sure why the man hadn't taken off in the *Lazy Krab*. The only explanation was that he didn't know it was there, or they'd shot it on their way in, to make sure there was no chance of escape. "As long as he's out there, we've got a huge problem."

Remi's eyes were filled with worry. "Why can't we just wait here until help comes? You know Zoe's going to call someone when we don't come back."

While the last thing he wanted to do was instill a sense of panic—especially after everything they'd been through—Remi needed to know what they were up against. "Whoever shows up here looking for us, he'll kill them the moment they step foot on this islet."

"He's right," Nikos said. "We need to do something."

"What about your gun?" Dimitris asked. "Can't you just take him out?"

"Empty. Used up the ammo shooting at the helicopter. Still, we have one very big advantage. He thinks we're buried beneath a ton of rock. Which means I'm the last person he's going to expect."

Remi reached out, touching his arm. "There's already dead people in that helicopter."

He had no idea if she was telling him to be careful or to not kill the other man. Figuring it was both, he said, "Let's hope my idea works."

His plan was simple. He would approach the gunman from behind, his goal to disarm the man. Unfortunately, it meant he'd have to go back down the cliff face to the tunnel entrance and come up the other side. Still, he was an experienced climber, and it was much easier on his own without having to worry about the others. Within minutes, he was pulling himself over the ledge, just a dozen yards behind the man, using the large rocks to hide behind and work his way closer.

The gunman crouched, picking up something too small for Sam to see. Sam moved out from behind the boulder toward him. Less than five feet to go, Sam stepped on a piece of brittle rock. It cracked beneath his weight. The gunman heard the snap, looked up, swinging his rifle toward Sam.

So much for that plan. Sam froze, raising his hands.

"Hey!" Remi shouted. "Over here!"

The gunman turned toward her. Sam rushed him, slamming one hand at the rifle barrel, pushing it up, while grabbing the stock with his other hand. The two struggled for control of the weapon. Sam, holding it tight, brought his knee up into the man's groin, then wrested the rifle from his grasp. He drove the stock into his gut, stepped back, swung the barrel around, aiming. The man held both hands palms-down, then suddenly reached for something at his waist.

Sam fired. The gunman fell onto his side, his dark gaze staring at nothing. Sam, his ears ringing from the high-velocity round, kept the AR-15 aimed as Remi and her friends climbed down from the rocks, racing toward him. Remi stopped just short of the fallen man, her mouth dropping open as she looked at Sam. He could see it in her eyes, the questioning look.

Nikos kneeled beside the man, placing his fingers on his neck, and shook his head. He started to rise, then stopped, rolling him over, revealing a handgun in the dead man's grasp.

Remi eyed the weapon, then took a deep, shaky breath. "I think I need to go sit down."

Sam started to follow her, but Nikos stopped him, then nodded at Dimitris. "Go with her." After the two left, he turned to Sam. "I know you want to help, but I think giving her space will be the best thing for her right now."

"Why does it feel as though everything that's happening is drawing us apart?"

"Because it is," Nikos said as he and Sam walked toward the wreckage. "I have no idea what your background is, but it's clear you're no stranger to any of this. But for someone like Remi—even the rest of us—this is all more than we're used to. It will take time."

Sam glanced over at Remi and Dimitris, who'd taken a seat on an outcropping of rock near what had been the cave entrance. "I hope so."

"If she is able to get past this, she'll let you know."

"And if she isn't?"

"She'll let you know."

Sam knew he was right. It was bad enough Remi had seen a man killed on the Kyrils' island. Here, with the helicopter crash, there were four deaths, Sam directly responsible for each of them.

And no cover of darkness to hide the fact.

Finally, he turned his attention to the downed helicopter, looking through the shattered windshield into the crushed fuselage, seeing the dead pilot, the other gunman, and the woman beside him, their bodies crumpled on the floor of the cabin.

Nikos shaded his eyes, peering in. "Minerva Kyril," he said.

"You're sure?"

"Positive."

"I guess that answers the question about who was behind all of this." Sam pulled out his phone and took a few photographs, intending to forward everything to Rube once they were back on Fourni with cell phone service. When he finished, he and Nikos walked over to where Dimitris and Remi sat.

Remi was staring at what was left of the cave entrance, now covered by the fallen rocks. She stood, walking over to it. "It would have been nice to actually see if that broken amphora really was part of Poseidon's Trident."

"We could," Dimitris said. "By going in through the same way we got out."

"Right now," she said, "all I'm looking forward to is getting back to Fourni."

CHAPTER SEVENTY-ONE

The first person Sam called once they were back on Fourni was Rube. "Minerva Kyril's dead."

"What? How?"

"I may be indirectly responsible. Directly if you count that I was the one who shot at the helicopter she was riding in."

"Holy—" Rube drew in a deep breath. "Is everyone okay? Where are you?"

"We're fine, in Fourni, and Nikos is with the police chief now." Sam gave him a quick version of what happened.

"How's Remi taking this?"

"Shaken at first," he said, glancing at Remi and Dimitris. The two sat silhouetted in the dark about twenty yards away on the low wall at the entrance of the port parking lot, both looking out over the water. "I'd say she's doing better."

"Good to hear. Let me get with Interpol and see what the next step is."

Apparently, the next step was sending a parade of Interpol agents and Hellenic police investigators to the island of Fourni to take statements, and crime scene technicians to the islet to gather evidence and retrieve the bodies. The process was exhausting for all.

Sam, being the shooter, was questioned last. Sergeant Petros Kompouras, the Interpol agent whom Sam had spoken to about the explosives and Kyril's olive oil facility, had borrowed the Fourni police chief's office. "Good to finally meet you in person," he said, shaking Sam's hand.

"Likewise."

"Just to let you know where we're coming from, Adrian Kyril has decided not to plead guilty to the kidnapping and assault charges. Apparently, he changed his mind once news of his mother's death reached him. I'm afraid that means you and Miss Longstreet will probably end up having to return for the trial."

"What about in between now and then?"

"More than likely, as soon as we finish here, she can go home. I expect no more than a couple of days or so. You, on the other hand . . ." He shrugged. "I'm afraid it's going to be a bit longer. I hope no more than a week or two for us to wrap up all the loose ends. Four deaths here, one on the Kyrils' island, and if I'm not mistaken, a vehicle accident on Samos." He gave Sam a grim smile.

"It is what it is," Sam said. "I'm willing to do whatever it takes to assist you in your investigation."

"Very good. Let's get started."

It took about three hours for them to finish up their interview, Sam relating what happened, Sergeant Kompouras stopping him every now and then to clarify details or refer to the diagram Sam had drawn of the islet and their positions as the helicopter assault took place. Finally, Kompouras looked at his watch, almost midnight. "It's been a long day. As I mentioned to the others, I would like to finish up the interview with the four of you tomorrow on Megalos Anthropofas. I can't imagine that will take very long, but I would like to see this cave. I wasn't there very long before coming over here. The evidence techs were just cordoning off the site and removing the bodies. They hadn't been able to locate the cave opening."

"Understandable. It wasn't easy to find even before it was blocked."

Remi, exhausted, had immediately fallen asleep. Sam, however, had lain awake most of the night, thinking about her. Her emotions had to be running the gamut.

The following morning, she was quiet, but she appeared well rested, not like she'd been the morning after their escape from the Kyrils' island. She even seemed close to her normal self when they walked into town to meet Nikos, Dimitris, and Zoe for breakfast at Skavos's café.

At ten, they met Sergeant Kompouras at the port, Nikos taking the *Asteri*, since the *Lazy Krab* was out of commission after the helicopter attack. Once everyone was aboard, Remi braced herself against the railing as the boat took off. Sam moved beside her, the two simply sharing the space in what he hoped was companionable silence. About midway there, when Remi made no move to speak, he asked, "Are you okay?"

She nodded. "I think so."

". . . Are we okay?"

"I'll be glad to get home."

Which wasn't an answer at all. Sam decided not to press the matter. "The sergeant said that if everything works out, you may actually get to leave as early as tomorrow."

"Not you?"

"Not for a while. He was thinking a week or more."

She stared out toward the water, her gaze on the islet as they approached. "I really have to think about all of this . . . us . . ."

The finality of her words caught him by surprise. "If it helps, I'm willing to wait as long as it takes."

She drew in a deep breath, reached over, and put her hand on his. "I know. I think that's what makes this all so bearable."

It wasn't much, but it was enough for Sam, and they remained there, side by side, as Nikos motored into the quiet inlet. Within minutes, they were hiking up the rocky hillside to the top. As before, they heard the bells tinkling from the small herd of goats that lived on the island, a few watching warily as they neared the crest, then approached the wreckage. While the bodies were gone, the crumpled remains of the helicopter's fuselage was a stark reminder of their narrow escape from certain death.

Sergeant Kompouras pulled his small notebook from his pocket. "Where, exactly, is this cave?"

Dimitris walked over, standing on the rubble. "Beneath this rock."

Kompouras moved beside him, then looked at Sam. "This is what fell when the helicopter hit?"

"It was. Remi and I were just inside when they attacked."

"And how was it that all of you escaped?"

"Remi found a tunnel leading out," Sam said. "It opens up on the north side. We climbed to the top and then . . ." He glanced in the direction of where he'd killed the lone gunman. "This way. I'll show you."

Kompouras followed him to the cliff's edge, overlooking the Aegean and Fourni in the distance.

"You see the crevice about twenty yards down? That's where we came out," he said, pointing to the rocks on their left.

"You're telling me that you scaled that cliff all the way over there?"

"We did."

"I'm not sure I would have dared it."

"We didn't have much choice."

Dimitris moved beside them. "What's really sad is that we may have actually found evidence that the treasure called Poseidon's Trident exists. Now it's buried under a couple of tons of stone."

The sergeant crouched at the cliff's edge, using his phone to take a few photos. "What puzzles me is why Minerva Kyril would have been here. You were looking for some mythical treasure. She was allegedly trying to protect her drug empire." He glanced over at Sam. "If I had to guess, her son's obsession with Poseidon's Trident brought too much unwanted attention to the family business. Especially when the four of you ended up on the Kyrils' island."

"Not that we found much there," Sam said, "other than a few trigger-happy guards."

He looked up from his phone. "But you did mention the glass vials you saw in the warehouse. I meant to ask you about that. By the time my team arrived on the island to investigate the shooting, the glass vials were gone."

"You think they're important?"

"We're not sure yet. What makes it worth looking into is that we found bits of glass in the debris from the explosion that killed one of our agents. No one has found any explanation for it. Especially when the shipment was supposed to be nothing but olive oil, tins, wood, and plastic wrap around shipping cartons."

Sam recalled seeing the boxes of vials, but at the time, his focus had been on finding and freeing Dimitris. "Had I known . . ."

"Yes. That old hindsight, twenty-twenty." The sergeant eyed the cliffside, then stood, glancing at Dimitris. "You really think there's some evidence of this treasure down there?"

"I found some shards from a broken amphora."

"It couldn't have been from one of the goat herders?"

"I suppose it could."

"Except," Sam said, "we didn't see the shards until after the helicopter crashed. The impact caused part of the cave wall to shear off."

Sergeant Kompouras slipped his phone into his pocket. "Any chance you would be willing to take another look? If we prove Poseidon's Trident really exists, it will be one more piece of evidence against Adrian Kyril."

Dimitris gave a firm nod. "Count me in."

"Yes," Nikos said.

Sam, recalling Remi's reluctance to enter the cave from the beginning, asked, "How about it?"

"I think I can go in."

"Let's do it," he said to the sergeant. "The more evidence, the better."

CHAPTER SEVENTY-TWO

Once Dimitris retrieved the gear bags from the *Asteri*, they were able to find a solid spot to anchor their rope almost directly above the cave's north entrance. Before they started, though, Sam pulled Remi aside. "You don't have to go down there."

Remi's gaze searched his, and for a moment, he was certain she intended to back out. He could see the hesitation, even a moment of fear in her green eyes. But then she took a deep breath, and nodded. "Yes, I do. I am not going to let that man win. And if I have to go back into the cave to take him down, so be it."

"I'll be right there with you, every step of the way."

Sam went first, testing the route, deciding it wasn't too difficult for the novices—Remi and the sergeant—to scale. Once everyone had descended safely, Sam lowered himself into the chute, shimmying down. Remi went next, the others followed, with Dimitris bringing up the rear.

When Sergeant Kompouras made it into the low cavern, forced like everyone else to move about on his belly, he took a good look around. "Tell me it gets better than this?"

"It does," Sam said. "But not before it gets worse. Whatever you do, when we get to the tunnels, keep your head down." As they cleared the domed section and started into the long tunnel, he heard several clunks from plastic helmets hitting the low ceiling. Finally, they emerged into the large cavern, and from there, climbed the rope to the upper chamber. Kompouras moved next to Sam, using his phone to take photos, the flash lighting up the space with each shot. "I'm not sure I wouldn't have gone into a total panic if I'd been trapped in here." He glanced down at his screen, then at Sam. "So, where are these shards you found?"

"Over there. To the right of that pool."

At the base was the pile of rubble where Dimitris had found the shards. Sam shined his light on it, seeing several more. Remi reached down and picked up an elongated piece of terra-cotta, something that looked like it might be the handle of an amphora.

She traced her finger over a distinctive rectangular marking. Sam noticed Greek letters in the middle of it. "What is it?" he asked her.

"Possibly the stamp of whoever manufactured it."

Nikos took a closer look. "That's quite the find. They may be able to date the piece based on that."

Dimitris, digging through the pile of rubble just a few feet away, stood, excited. "Look what I found! An ancient Greek sat phone!"

Remi laughed as he handed the device over to her. She pressed a button. "Battery's dead, but it looks pretty good otherwise."

Sam turned his attention up toward the now-blocked cave entrance. The rope still hung down, and he gave it a good tug, then climbed up. "This," he said to the sergeant, "is where we came in."

There wasn't much left of the outcropping that Remi had been sitting on right before the helicopter crashed. The impact had caused a cascading effect, shearing off the ledge, and sending the pieces crashing into a pile of rocks and dust. What had once been a narrow crevice between the cave mouth and the outcropping of rock was now over two feet in width.

A hollow area had opened behind where the ledge used to be—one he hadn't seen after the crash because of all the dust in the air. Now that everything had settled, there was no doubt the area was quite large.

"What is it?" Dimitris asked.

"Looks like a pocket opened up." He glanced at the rubble on the cave floor, noticing the largest pile was directly beneath this hollow, exactly where Remi and Dimitris had found their pieces of terra-cotta. Gripping the rope, he slung one foot across, straddling the crevice, testing his weight on the opposite rock wall. Rope firmly in one hand, he reached into the hollow, brushing some of the debris and dust away, seeing a large orange-red terra-cotta piece. No doubt about it. He was staring at the bottom half of an amphora lying on its side, the top having been crushed and covered by the fallen rocks. Just beyond it, he saw another broken amphora, also on its side. He jumped back, hooked up his harness to the rope, then straddled the space again, this time using both hands to sift through the rubble of the broken amphorae, feeling mostly rocks, but then something smooth, thin, and round. "I think I've got something. It feels like a coin."

He ran his hands through more of the broken amphora. "Make that several."

"Photos, Sam," Remi reminded him.

He left everything where it was, then pulled out his phone to take pictures. It was the flash from the camera that lit up what appeared to be a third and intact amphora, lying on its side behind the broken two.

He tucked his phone in his pocket, then reached out, his fingers brushing against it. He stretched farther, grasping the handle, at the same time trying to pull himself into the opening. As he leveraged himself, the neck split open. Coins spilled from the jar's mouth, revealing rocks beneath.

"You're not going to believe what I found," he said.

"The treasure?" Dimitris said. "Poseidon's Trident?"

"Don't get too excited. Unless you think a jar full of rocks is worth everything we've been through." He grabbed a couple, holding them out for the others to see. "But there is a layer of coins covering the rocks."

"You're sure?" Kompouras asked.

"Very." Once again, he used his phone and took photos of the amphora, the gold coins that had spilled from it, and the rocks clearly inside. He stuffed two of the rocks and several coins in a pocket, tucked his phone away, then started down. At the bottom, he dug the coins from his pocket, handing them to Nikos. They certainly glittered like the real thing, and the lion's head stamped on the face certainly made them look authentic.

The older man looked them over, then sighed. Sergeant Kompouras plucked one of the coins from Nikos's hand, holding it in the light. "This one's been gouged," he said, making the same conclusion that Nikos had made. "You can see the lead."

"If I had to guess," Sam said, showing them the photos from his phone so that they could see the rocks contained in the intact amphora, "whoever hid the treasure went to a lot of trouble to pretend they were hiding a hoard of gold."

"So, we have nothing?" Dimitris said. "All this trouble. For what?"

"History," his father said. "We found a piece of history."

Sergeant Kompouras seemed to be the only one who wasn't disappointed. "You do realize what this means? It proves that the legend behind the gold is real, even if the gold isn't. It's a direct connection to Tassos, and from there to Adrian Kyril." He looked at Remi. "In fact, I'd say that we have about everything we need, and you should be able to go home. You, on the other hand," he said to Sam, "will get to enjoy our Greek hospitality for a while longer."

CHAPTER SEVENTY-THREE

At the counter of the Samos airport, Remi handed over her passport.

"Any more luggage?" the clerk asked.

"No. Just the carry-on," she said. It sounded odd. She wasn't used to traveling so light, and briefly wondered if she could actually learn to travel this way.

Probably not.

The woman printed up her ticket, then slid it and the passport across the counter. The ticket was only to Athens, the first leg on her flight back to the States. Picking it up filled her with an immense sadness, no doubt due to the man standing next to her. Sam had insisted on escorting her in, making sure she got her ticket, then made it safely to security.

In all likelihood, she was never going to see him again—not after everything that had happened. They were polar opposites, she and Sam. He deserved someone more suited to his lifestyle. She couldn't picture herself with someone who could simply pull a gun and kill a man, then carry on as though nothing had happened.

"That's it," Sam said. "Looks like you're all set."

She started to reach for her oversized carry-on, but he picked it up. "Thank you," she said when they reached the line for security.

He set it down at her feet. "It's light."

"I mean for everything. For coming all this way. Helping me and Dimitris . . . I'm sorry I ruined your chances to get investors." She smiled at him, feeling equal parts guilt and relief. "I guess this is it. Thank you."

"That sounds so final when you say it like that."

She hesitated, not wanting to leave him with any sense of false hope. "Maybe if we'd met at a different time in our lives, things might have been different."

"So, my timing was off?"

"That's not what I meant."

"It's the argon laser, right? The moment I bring it up, the women run," Sam said, a forced smile on his face and sadness in his eyes.

"No, no, I wish you good luck with that." She blinked back her tears. "I'm sorry we didn't find that treasure. You could have in-vested in yourself."

"You never know. Maybe I'll win the lotto. Which reminds me. When I do, I owe you a new wardrobe."

"Don't you have to buy a ticket?"

"I knew there was a catch. Buy me one when you get back to the States?"

She laughed, then stood on tiptoes to kiss his cheek. "Goodbye, Sam Fargo."

He placed his finger beneath her chin, lifted it slightly, and kissed her on the lips. "Goodbye, Remi Longstreet." Then, kissing her once more, he let her go, his brown eyes somber. "Safe travels."

Remi, feeling as if there was so much more she should've said, watched him walk off. When he looked back, she tried to wave, but a crowd of tourists rushed into line behind her, blocking her view. With a sigh, she entered the line for security.

A white-haired woman in front of her turned a knowing gaze in her direction. "So hard saying goodbye to someone you love."

It took a moment for Remi to realize she was talking to her. "Oh, we're just friends."

"Are you?" The woman's eyes held a hint of disbelief. "I'm not sure he knows that."

A much younger woman glanced back, and in Greek, said, "*Mána*, mind your own business." Then, in English, to Remi, said, "If you haven't guessed by now, my mother likes to insert herself into everyone's lives."

Recognition hit as Remi looked from the younger woman to her mother. "You were both at Tassos's funeral. Helena?"

The older woman smiled. "That's the beauty of these smaller islands. We're always running into someone we know." She glanced over her shoulder. "I should probably catch up with my daughter."

The younger woman had already turned away, putting her carry-on and her mother's onto the conveyor. Remi did the same, then passed through the metal detector, collecting her bag and purse on the other side. Items in hand, she looked for a quiet spot to call her own mother.

"You're actually at the airport?"

"I'm heading to the gate now."

"It's probably a good thing. I'm not sure this young man you've met is someone you should be spending so much time with."

"What are you talking about?"

"Sam Fargo. Olivia told me he followed you to Greece."

Remi wasn't sure who she was more upset with. Olivia for telling her mother, or her mother for inserting her opinion into Remi's relationships. "Well, then. You should be happy. We broke up."

"Oh . . . Remi. I'm sorry. Let me know if you want to talk about it. In the meantime, your father and I were thinking, why don't you just come back to Boston? We'll have your car shipped, your furniture put in storage, and you won't have to worry about anything but flying home. I probably should have asked, but I changed out the colors in your room. It's so much brighter."

It was moments like this that reminded her why it was she'd moved all the way out to California in the first place. Their idea of how her life should run differed vastly from hers. "Mom. I'm not moving home."

"Yes, yes. You say that now. Don't worry, dear, we'll talk about it when you're back in the States."

Trying to discuss anything with her mother once she'd set her mind on something was futile. "Boarding the plane now. Love you, bye."

She disconnected before her mother had a chance to interject anything else.

At the gate, Helena saw Remi, and walked up. "I recognize that look," she said.

"What look?"

"The same one my daughter gives to me when she doesn't like something I tell her." Her dark eyes sparkled as she reached out, clasping Remi's hand. "You'll make the right decision. I see it in your eyes."

Helena's daughter walked up at that moment. "Ignore her. When we get on the plane, she'll find a new friend to torment." Then, in Greek, added, "*Mána*. Don't do this at the wedding. Please."

Remi glanced at the woman, who seemed unfazed by her daughter's mild rebuke as she gathered her bag, then followed her to two available seats in the waiting area.

With almost an hour to go until her own plane boarded, Remi settled back in her chair to wait. The longer she sat there, however, the more she heard the woman's parting refrain: *You'll make the right decision.*

What decision? Definitely not about moving home. That was never going to happen. Thirty minutes later, a loudspeaker overhead announced her flight. She got in line, handed over her ticket, then walked out the door to her plane.

CHAPTER SEVENTY-FOUR

Once Remi was safely on her way, Sam spent the next several days being interviewed by Interpol agents about every aspect of the case involving Adrian Kyril—from the time Sam arrived on Fourni after receiving Remi's call to the moment they were trapped in the tunnel on Megalos Anthropofas after Minerva Kyril's helicopter appeared.

At least there was some good news. With the death of Minerva Kyril, and the cooperation of her husband, not only were the Greek authorities finally able to shut down the drug empire, but they'd figured out how Minerva, the brains behind the operation, had managed to transport the heroin. The key had been those glass tubes Sam had reported seeing in the warehouse. The heroin was sealed inside the tubes, then placed inside the tins, which were filled with olive oil. That, in turn, made a nonpermeable barrier around the drugs, preventing them from being detected. So, while her husband was running the legitimate olive oil business, she had been smuggling drugs right beneath his nose.

After more than a week, with the close of the investigation, they informed Sam he was free to return home, with the stipulation that he and Remi would both need to return to testify when the case went to court.

None of that mattered to Sam. His mind had been on Remi. After she'd left, the cottage, the island, everything seemed far too quiet. It gave him too much time to think about what he might have done to change the way things ended between them, or what he might have said that would have made a difference. He'd called a couple of days after she'd departed, just to check up on her. When she didn't answer, he left a voice mail asking her to call back. Two days later, after no response, he decided to send a text: Did you make it home?

She texted back two words: Yes. Thanks.

His instinct was that he needed to let her be. And so he did. Remi had his number. She'd call or she wouldn't. The choice had to be hers.

When the day finally came for him to leave Fourni, he slung his backpack over his shoulder, grabbed his carry-on and walked down to the port. Though he shouldn't have been surprised, he couldn't help but feel a sense of sadness when he saw Manos, Denéa, Zoe, Dimitris, and Nikos waiting for him on the dock. He shook hands with Manos, then smiled at Denéa. "Thanks for all your help and with Remi."

She smiled and kissed him on the cheek. "We'll miss her. And you."

Dimitris gave a sheepish smile as he held out his hand. "If not for you . . ."

Sam shook the young man's hand. "Glad I could be there for you. Take care of Zoe."

"I will."

"And you," he said to Zoe after giving her a hug, "take care of Dimitris."

She nodded, blushing as Dimitris put his arm around her.

Nikos clasped Sam's shoulder. "I can never thank you enough, my friend."

"No thanks needed." He reached into his backpack, pulling out the holstered Smith & Wesson, handing it to Nikos. "For such a small handgun, that thing packed a good punch. I liked it better than I thought I would."

"You should take it."

"As much as I'd love to, I can't accept such an expensive gift. I am honored you trusted me with it."

"There's no one else I'd trust more. I'll mail it to you."

"Don't—"

"Too late. Maybe you'll save another life with it." He smiled. "Take care. If you're ever out this way again . . ." Nikos grabbed him in a bear hug. "There are no words. You are my friend and there is always room at our table."

Sam nodded, started to walk toward the ferry, when Dimitris elbowed Zoe.

"Wait," she said. "I almost forgot." She held out a small pouch. "For you."

"What is it?"

"Some of the counterfeit coins. A souvenir of your time here." She placed the pouch in his hand, then pulled him into a hug. When she stepped back, her eyes were glistening. "Thank you. For everything."

His arrival back in the States was the exact opposite of his departure from Greece. No one was waiting for him when he walked out of the airport, or when he finally walked into his apartment. There were, however, over a dozen messages on his answering machine. Two from his old supervisor at DARPA, and the rest from his boss at the supermarket, wanting to know when he was coming back. It was the final message, only yesterday, that got to him. Someone from the supermarket chain's human resources department saying that, since they hadn't heard back, they were terminating his employment.

He erased them all, took a long, hot shower, then went to bed.

All the while, trying not to think about Remi.

No way was that going to happen. It was as if the stars had lined up, putting them both in the right place at the right time at the Lighthouse Cafe. And then those same stars seemed to conspire against them. If she hadn't taken her ill-fated trip to Greece, would things have turned out different for them? They would never know.

As much as he wished otherwise, he wasn't fine with the way things had turned out, Remi going her way, him going his. He kept trying to convince himself otherwise as he finally drifted off to sleep.

Sam was jarred awake to the sound of his cell phone buzzing on his nightstand. He picked it up, saw the *R* through sleep-hazed eyes, then quickly answered. "Good morning."

"You have *no* idea what time it is, do you?"

"Rube . . . ?"

"Who were you expecting?"

He glanced over, saw the late-afternoon sun angling into his bedroom window. "Sorry. Jet-lagged. What's up?"

"Apparently, you've impressed a lot of bigwigs over at Interpol."

"Trust me. That was the last thing on my mind."

"Regardless, word gets around. They want you back at DARPA."

"I know. They left a couple of messages on my machine." A truck rumbled past on the busy street outside, shaking the windows of his apartment. Back less than a day, and he already missed the peace and quiet of Fourni. "So, why are you calling? Is DARPA that desperate they're paying you to recruit for them?"

"After all the news came in from Interpol, one of my bosses thinks you should come work for us."

"The CIA?" Sam laughed. "I may be unemployed, but I'm not desperate."

"I told him you'd say something like that. He asked me to call anyway."

"Pass on my thanks. But I'm declining all job offers at the moment."

"Don't be so quick to discount the offer from DARPA. You never know. Maybe you can negotiate your own lab time."

"There's a thought." Sam felt a slight vibration in his phone from an incoming text. He pulled it away from his ear, seeing Blake's message on the screen. "I'll get back to you. Blake's texting that I need to call, A-SAP." The moment Rube disconnected, Sam returned Blake's call.

"What're the chances you can get to my club, say, in the next two hours or so?"

"Why?"

"I just got done playing nine holes with three of the guys I was hoping might want to invest in your laser thing. If you can make it here by the time we finish the next nine, I think they'd be willing to listen to your pitch."

"I'd have to go by your office and pick up the portfolios first."

"Whatever it takes. Just do it fast. This may be your last chance."

Sam flung the covers aside as he got out of bed. "I'm on my way."

CHAPTER SEVENTY-FIVE

Blake met Sam outside the clubhouse, his brows going up at the unusual sight of Sam in a suit and tie. "Don't screw this up, Fargo. You have no idea how hard it was to convince these guys that, A, you're not going to flake out on them again, and B, your idea is worth their time and money."

"It'd be nice to think I wasn't wasting my time, either."

"Just go in there and sell it."

The two men walked in together, Blake moving to a chair in the corner, Sam to the center of the room. Three men in their fifties, all dressed for golf, sat on one side of a long table, watching Sam as he approached. He placed his phone and the portfolios on the table, shook hands with each of them, pulled out the chair, and sat.

The man sitting on the right said, "I understand you're working on some sort of a laser . . ."

"Argon laser." He picked up the folders, about to pass them out, saying, "I've put together some information—"

"Save it," the man said. "Just tell us."

"It detects mixed metals and alloys from a distance."

"A metal detector?"

"Not exactly."

"Explain."

"Typically, the properties and ratios of argon are used to determine the age of rocks. By adjusting the laser that detects argon in the earth's surface, I've discovered that age is only one quality it can detect. The other is the type of metal. For instance, the elements—"

The man in the middle raised his brows. "Type of metal? As in gold?"

"As in *any* metal. Gold, silver, platinum, palladium."

All three leaned forward with interest. "Go on . . ." the first man said.

"As mentioned, the gist is that it works from a distance. Whether you're searching underwater or on land—" His phone screen lit up with a text from Rube: Just received word. Kyril to plead guilty. Will let you know.

"Mr. Fargo?"

"Sorry," he said. "Where was I?"

"Detecting metal beneath the ocean's surface. Definitely something I could invest in."

"Right. The ocean . . ." For some reason, after seeing Rube's text about Kyril, all he could think about was the conversations he'd had with Remi. She thought he should be building the laser on his own, not teaming up with a bunch of investors.

Which made him wonder why on earth he was rushing into this.

He glanced at Blake, then the three men sitting at the table, and finally at his phone. There was absolutely no hurry. "I'm sorry. I . . . have to apologize for wasting your time."

They looked at one another, then at him. "Excuse me?" one of them said.

Sam slipped his phone into his pocket and picked up the portfolios. "This was a mistake."

Blake shot up out of his chair. "Sam—"

"Sorry, Blake. I appreciate all of this. I really do. It's just . . ."

What was he supposed to say? That a woman who had broken up with him felt it was a bad idea for him to put this out to investors? "I've rethought the whole thing."

"Mr. Fargo," the first man said. "If you walk out that door now, you're done." His expression, like that of the other two men, barely concealed his annoyance.

Not that Sam could blame any of them. "I realize that. And I thank you for agreeing once again to see me, but . . . Enjoy the rest of your day."

Blake followed Sam out the door into the hallway. "What the—? Do you have any idea how long it took me just to get those three in the same room as you? I promised them you weren't going to flake out."

"I'm not flaking out. I just don't want to give up control to a bunch of investors."

"Wasn't that the whole idea? Let someone else front the cash so you can work on this thing?"

"It was," he said when they reached the lobby. "But once I do that, it's no longer mine. It's theirs. I'm just the guy who's putting it together. I do all the hard work, they reap all the benefit."

"I don't get you, Fargo."

"Nothing to get." He pushed open the heavy glass door, striding out into the parking lot, Blake on his heels. "I'm going to fund it myself."

"How?"

"I've got that empty lot at Goldfish Point. How much can I get for that?"

"Are you kidding? I could sell it tomorrow for double what you paid."

"Do it. Doesn't get much easier than that."

Blake halted in his tracks. "Wait. What about Remi? And the house?"

"Not in the cards," he said without stopping. "Might as well put the money to good use. Funding my laser."

"Exactly where are you planning to do this?" Blake asked, catching up with him. "I love you like a brother, but I really need my office back."

Sam opened the door of his Jeep, tossing the portfolios he'd prepared onto the passenger seat. Sliding in behind the wheel, he looked over at his friend. "The quicker you sell it, the faster I'm out of your hair. And your office."

"You're really going to leave?"

He thought about that last text from Remi. No hint of a future together. "Can't think of one good reason to stay."

"And go where?"

Until that moment, he hadn't really given it much thought beyond that he couldn't stay here. There were too many reminders of Remi. "DARPA wants me back. I think I'll give it a go."

Blake stood in the way, preventing Sam from closing the car door. "Forget I said anything about my office. Take as much time as you want."

"Can you sell the lot or not?"

"In a heartbeat."

"Let me know when it's done." He pulled the door closed, then drove off.

CHAPTER SEVENTY-SIX

"Miss Longstreet, Olivia on line two."

Remi glanced up at Marla, the blond-haired receptionist standing in the entry of her cubicle. Olivia, no doubt, was calling about the dinner party tomorrow. Covering the mouthpiece of her headset, she whispered, "Tell her I'll call her back."

The young woman gave her a thumbs-up, then left.

"*Lo siento, Señor Gonzales,*" Remi said into the mic. "*¿Por favor repita eso?*" She listened while he repeated the order, double-checking the invoice to make sure the shipment was as he'd requested. Satisfied that Mr. Gonzales had everything he needed, she thanked him, then disconnected.

Leaning back in her chair, she looked around her cubicle, which, after her time away in Greece, seemed so gray and claustrophobic. As much as she loved the people she worked with, each nine-to-five day felt like a lifetime—and this after only two weeks back.

With a sigh, she started to pull off her headset, when the phone line lit up. Olivia was clearly impatient. She pressed the button. "Don't forget to pick up the cake. Wear something nice. Your brother will be there. I know. I know."

There was a second or two of empty air, then, "Remi? It's Sam."

"Oh . . . Sam."

"That excited to hear from me?"

"Sorry," she said, belatedly realizing what she'd just rattled off to him when she answered the call—as though she'd neatly picked up her life, while his was still on hold. "I thought you were Olivia. She's worried I'm going to blow off this party tomorrow."

"With her brother."

"It's a birthday thing."

"No worries. How are you?"

"I'm fine." Her gaze strayed to her desk blotter and the dozens of scorpion doodles populating it. She and Sam hadn't spoken since he'd left her at the airport in Samos a little over two weeks ago, and she was unprepared for the jumble of thoughts and emotions that swept through her on hearing his voice. "Is everything okay?"

"Fine, actually. Which is why I'm calling. Good news, in fact. You won't need to return to Greece for the trial. Adrian Kyril pled guilty."

Remi leaned back in her chair. "When?"

"Apparently yesterday. Rube just called to confirm. He also mentioned that they confiscated the *Mirage* along with the rest of Adrian's and his late mother's assets. Ill-gotten gains from the drug trade."

"That's got to be a blow."

"Doubt he'll find it of much use in jail. Anyway . . . I just thought you might like to know."

"Thank you, yes."

An uncomfortable stretch of silence was made more noticeable when both tried speaking at the same time. They stumbled over their words, until Sam said, "Go ahead. You first."

She decided on a safe topic. "Did you ever reschedule your investor meeting?"

"Last week, in fact."

"How'd it go?"

"In the end, I decided it wasn't for me."

"I'm sorry."

"Don't be. Besides, I got the idea from you."

"What idea?"

"To try to do this myself without the investors. The good news—for Blake at least—is that I'm finally moving out of his office. He's having a goodbye shindig for me at the Lighthouse tomorrow for lunch . . . I know it's a last-minute invite, but if you're free, you should drop by."

"I . . . have that party tomorrow afternoon. Promised I'd help get everything ready."

"Right. Olivia's brother."

"I promised." It sounded so hollow to her. "Maybe if we finish early enough, I can stop by?"

"Don't worry about it. It's no big deal. A bunch of guys drinking a bunch of beer, watching the game. I should probably go finish packing up my boxes before Blake calls off the whole thing."

"Well, it was good talking to you."

"It was—I mean, talking to you. Take care, Remi."

The dial tone sounded and an immense sense of loneliness swept over her. She pulled off her headset, laying it on her desk—trying to ignore the regret and guilt she felt by convincing herself she was doing the right thing in making a clean break from Sam.

They had completely incompatible lifestyles, a fact she was reminded of when she walked into the kitchen the following afternoon, where Olivia and her brother Keith were discussing the sorry state of college football.

"I'm telling you," Keith said, "I could do a better job of coaching and for a lot less money."

Olivia laughed. "Don't quit your day job. You might regret it." She glanced at Remi, then at her brother. "Look who's here."

"Remi." The blue-eyed, brown-haired Keith crossed the room, his smile sincere. "So good to see you."

"Likewise." They clasped hands, then kissed cheek to cheek. "How's the law firm?" she asked.

"Still there." He poured a cup of coffee and slid it across the countertop toward her. "I heard a rumor that you were involved in some kidnapping and murder in Greece?"

"Not a rumor at all."

"You're okay, though?"

"I am now. I just found out that the man pled guilty. Which means we won't have to go back to testify."

"What happened to the guy you were over there with?" he asked.

Olivia shook her head, as if to say she couldn't believe he brought up the subject.

Remi ignored her friend, saying, "A lot happened in that short time we were together. On the one hand, I've never been so scared to death. On the other, I've never felt more alive." She gave a slight shrug. "I guess when it came right down to it, it was just a bit more than I could handle."

"Sam Fargo," Olivia said, "is rash and reckless. Do you know he killed a man like it was just another day at the office? That's why I think Remi needs to date someone like you."

"Olivia, shut up," Keith said, his gaze on Remi. "It's not your decision to make."

His words caught Remi by surprise. No doubt it was mere coincidence, but she couldn't help but think about that old woman at the airport, and her parting words: *You'll make the right decision.* "I'll be . . ." Remi laughed. "She's right."

"See?" Olivia gave a catlike grin.

"Not you. Helena." Remi smiled at Keith. "Thank you."

"For what?"

"I'm not really sure. Listening, maybe? And I need to go."

"Go where?" Olivia asked.

"The Lighthouse Cafe."

CHAPTER SEVENTY-SEVEN

S am loaded the last of the things into the back of his Jeep, then
realized he'd forgotten the package that Blake was holding.
Nikos had sent it from Greece—the promised Smith & Wesson. He took the small box, tucking it into the cargo hold with the
others. "I think that's it."

Blake stepped up onto the curb. "Hate to say it, Fargo, but it's not
going to be the same without you hogging half my office."

"Enjoy your newfound desk space."

"You sure you want to do this?" he asked as Sam rearranged a
few of the boxes, then closed the tailgate.

"Positive."

"Maybe you should give it a cooling-off period. Wait until tomorrow to sign everything like you said you were going to. Who knows?
You might feel different in the morning."

"Doubt it." Sam looked back at Blake's office building, mentally
going over everything he'd packed. "If I forget anything, put it in the
mail."

"What about the party?" Blake asked.

"You really think anyone cares whether I'm there or not?"

"Of course they do. I do."

"You might be the only one." Sam opened the driver's door, eyeing his friend, not surprised by his look of concern. Blake had spent the last few days trying to convince Sam to stay—all to no avail. "All they care about is the free food and booze."

"Which begs the question, why bother having a party if you're not going to be there?"

"Pass out a few business cards, tell them what a great real estate agent you are, then write it all off on your taxes." He clapped Blake on his shoulder, giving him a grim smile. "Besides, you're making a second whole commission off this deal. And I get to make my laser. Win-win."

"Why does it feel like lose-lose?"

"All in the perspective, my friend." As upbeat as he tried to sound, there was a hollowness about the words. It didn't matter how many times he convinced himself that he was doing the right thing, he always came back to one thought. Everything felt empty without Remi. "I'll be fine. I promise."

"Look, I'll be the first to admit I thought you were jumping off the deep end for someone you barely knew, but after hearing everything that happened, I think she deserves to know how you feel. She deserves a call at the very least."

"Already did."

"Did you actually explain things to her? In detail?"

"There's nothing to explain. She's moved on with her life. Time for me to do the same." Sam smiled as he held out his hand.

They shook.

Blake stepped back, watching as Sam slid into the driver's seat, turning the key in the ignition.

Apparently, the man wasn't willing to let it go. He banged on the window, walking alongside the Jeep, keeping pace. "I'm kind of rethinking the whole wanting-my-space-back thing. I've gotten used to you working there."

Sam, worried that Blake intended to follow him all the way out to the street, hit the brakes. He sat there a moment, both hands gripping the steering wheel.

As much as he appreciated everything his friend was trying to do, there was no way he could begin to describe the impossibility of reversing this course of action.

Remi had made her choice—and whatever her plans, they didn't include him.

"I'm okay with this," he said, seeing the concern etched on Blake's face. "You should be, too. Besides, you're making a ton of money."

"You know I don't care about the money."

"Somehow I don't think you'll turn it down, either."

"Well, it'd be stupid to let it go to waste."

"Better hurry or you'll be late to the party." Sam waved, then drove off.

He stopped at the first gas station, filled the tank, then glanced at his phone sitting in the center console. He picked it up, tempted to call Remi's number, when a car pulled up behind him, the driver honking the horn.

Sure, he could call Remi again, but he wasn't sure what good that would do. She had his number. She could have called him back at any time, but she hadn't.

He was fine with that.

Right.

As long as she was happy.

CHAPTER SEVENTY-EIGHT

Remi walked into the Lighthouse, seeing Blake at the bar with a few of his friends, laughing at something. Sam was nowhere in sight. She approached, tapping him on the shoulder.

He turned, saw her, his smile fading. "Remi . . . What are you doing here?"

"Looking for Sam," she said. "Do you happen to know where he is?"

"He took off about an hour ago for San Diego."

"Oh . . . He told me he'd be here. The finally-getting-out-of-your-office party."

"You have no idea, do you?"

Though it was a question, it seemed more of a statement. "No idea about what?"

"We should probably discuss this outside." He set his beer on the bar, then led her to the exit. When the door fell shut behind them, he studied her a moment, his expression a mix of concern and curiosity. "How long has it been since you two have talked?"

"He called yesterday. To tell me Adrian Kyril pled guilty. Why?"

Blake took in a deep breath, then let it out slowly. "I'm not sure how to tell you this."

"Tell me what?" she asked, feeling her heart start a slow thud in her chest.

"He packed up. Leaving."

"Leaving? To where?"

"He's taking his old job with DARPA. They're interested in giving him lab time to work on that laser. And . . . Well, you know how much he wants to finish that project."

None of that made sense. That was the one thing Sam was sure about, finishing his argon laser on his own. He'd told her he'd lost the funding. But not that he was going back to DARPA.

This was all her fault. Had he not followed her halfway across the world, he wouldn't have missed his investor meeting that Blake had set up for him.

Blake, apparently, must have guessed what she was thinking. "Look. Sam could've agreed to this other deal for the funding. Everything was lined up. The money was there. The timing was off, is all."

"Because he was in Greece. Helping me."

He gave a slight shrug. "*C'est la vie.*"

Maybe for someone else, but Remi was certain that Sam shared her feelings. Life was what you made it. If something happened, you made it work. Hadn't they proved that over and over again in Fourni? "What's he doing in San Diego?"

"Meeting with a notary to sign the papers for that empty lot."

"He's selling it?" A light breeze swept in from the ocean. Remi barely noticed the cold. "The cliff top? At Goldfish Point?"

Blake, wearing a short-sleeved shirt, shoved his hands in his pockets. "When you think about it, buying such an expensive piece of property without the funds to build was sort of a risk. Luckily the market's on an upturn. The guy made a fortune off of it. So did I, for that matter."

"But he loves that lot. I have to stop him." She took out her cell phone and called Sam's number. It went straight to voice mail. She looked at Blake. "You need to call him."

"I doubt it'll do any good," he said, digging his phone from his pocket and trying himself. He held it out so Remi could hear. Voice mail. "I'm not sure what happened between you two, but ever since, he's sort of dropped off the radar. I think the only reason he's answered my calls was because I'm handling the sale." He shrugged.

Remi looked at her watch. "La Jolla's what, two hours from here?"

"What are you going to do?"

"Stop him."

He gave her a sympathetic smile. "By the time you get there, it'll be too late. As soon as he finishes up with the notary, he's heading back east."

"I have to try." She hurried out to the parking lot, calling again as she rushed to her car. As before, it went straight to voice mail. "Sam. Remi. Call me."

She made several more attempts on the drive down. The traffic was thick, but by the time she passed San Clemente it had cleared considerably, and she kept one eye on the mirror, watching for the highway patrol as she sped south.

Regardless of what Blake said, this was her fault. Sam had put his life on hold, given up his dream, because of her. But his financing for the laser was only a small part of it—no, not even part of it. She'd been so wrapped up in her own emotions, she'd failed to see the obvious. After everything she and Sam had been through together, how could she ever go back to her old life? How could she ever have a life without him? She gripped the steering wheel, trying to picture the gray void it had become since her return to California—and it had nothing to do with sitting in a cubicle, day after day.

The cubicle she could handle. Not having Sam in her life was unbearable.

Checking her rearview mirror, she saw a police car speeding up behind her, its red and blue lights flashing. "Not now . . ." She put on her signal, then moved over to the slow lane, hoping it would continue past.

It did not.

The uniformed officer approached. She rolled down her window. "License and registration, please."

CHAPTER SEVENTY-NINE

Remi leaned over, opened her glove box, and pulled her registration out, handing that and her license to the officer.

"Do you know how fast you were going, Miss Longstreet?"

"Eighty-ish?"

"Eight-seven."

"Guilty. I don't suppose we can skip with the formalities and get to the ticket part? I'm in a hurry."

He looked over the top of his sunglasses at her. "You realize your being in a hurry is exactly why you're being stopped?"

"I know. And I do apologize. But the guy I love is in La Jolla. He's leaving for a new job, and if I miss him, I may never see him again . . ." Remi saw no show of emotion from the man. She decided a different tack was in order. "No disrespect, but please, if we can hurry up with the ticket, I'll promise to drive at a reasonable speed the moment you let me go."

The officer walked back to his patrol car. Remi watched in her rearview mirror as he clipped her license to the top of his ticket book, then started writing. Two minutes later, he was back, giving her the narrow clipboard and a pen. She signed the ticket, and he ripped off the pink copy, handing it over. He did not, however, return her license right away.

Holding on to it, he looked her in the eye. "I'm going to be taking that next exit up there, which means there's a very *long* stretch between here and San Diego without any patrol. Do me a favor? Drive careful."

"Thank you."

He returned her license.

Remi pulled out, then drove off, making sure she kept to the speed limit. A moment later, the patrol car passed her, and, true to his word, the officer took the next exit. She sped up, though not as fast as before. Twenty-five minutes later, she found the real estate office. It was closed, the doors locked.

Why she expected him to be there when he had at least an hour head start, she didn't know.

She tried his number again, then tossed her phone onto the seat of her car. Finally, she called Blake. "He's not here. Have you heard from him?"

"Sorry, no. They must have gotten through that paperwork fast."

"Where would he go?"

There was a stretch of silence, then, "You know, he said something about staying in that hotel just down the street on the beach. You might try calling them."

"Thanks."

Sam's car wasn't at the hotel, and when she checked at the desk, he wasn't registered as a guest.

She returned to her car. Frustrated, she stood at the door, holding the handle, at a complete loss at what to do. Looking back at the hotel and then the beach brought back the memory of their weekend and the afternoon he'd told her about his dream of building a house on the cliff top.

Their house, he'd said. Without thinking, she found herself on the beach, walking toward the bluff. The sun was dipping behind the clouds as it made its late-afternoon descent. She looked out over the Pacific as the rays of the setting sun broke through, shooting upward. The sky and clouds turned a brilliant orange, and her breath caught.

Not at the sunset, but at the distant silhouette of the man standing on the edge of the cliff.

Sam.

He stood there a moment, then reached down, picking up something from the ground. A rock, perhaps. A moment later, he threw it over the edge, the tension and frustration evident in the way he held himself.

Her heart constricted at the sight.

"Sam!" Her voice was lost as the offshore wind whipped in from the coast, drumming in her ears. Remi raced back to her car, knowing she had to get there before he left.

As she walked across the bluff, he stood stock-still, his back to her, the waves crashing below. When she reached his side, he simply held out his hand.

She clasped her fingers around his.

They stood there in companionable silence for a minute or so, until Sam finally turned to her. "I thought you had a party?"

"Changed my mind." A few more seconds of quiet, then Remi saying, "I missed you at yours."

"Trying to get an early start on a long trip."

The wind swept across the bluff, the low shrubs and long, dry grass bending beneath it. "So, this was where we were going to build our house?"

"That was the plan."

"Can we buy it back?"

His smile was bittersweet as his eyes met hers. "That would be difficult. Never got to the real estate office."

"You didn't sell?"

"How could I?" He looked back out over the water. "This is where we were going to build our home."

"We don't have to build anything. I've warmed to the idea of camping. Who needs hot and cold running water, carpeting, and electricity? The appeal of sleeping in a bag with zippers has grown on me."

"I have a tent in the Jeep."

Before she had a chance to comment, he took her in his arms.

CHAPTER EIGHTY

Georgetown, Washington, D.C.
The present day

S am, Remi, and St. Julien Perlmutter had long since finished
dinner, retired to the library, and settled in front of the fire,
each with a glass of port.

"Sorry," Perlmutter said when they finished telling their story. "I
seem to have gotten something in my eye." He blinked a couple of
times. "What an extraordinary tale. And then you married?"

"We did," Remi said. "Though it was a bit of a compromise. My
mother, firmly entrenched in Boston society, wanted at least a year
and a half to plan."

"Whereas I," Sam said, "wanted to get married the next day."

Remi smiled at him. "We were married six months to the day
after we met."

"That's astounding," Perlmutter said, stroking the head of his
dachshund, Fritz, who rested comfortably on his ample lap. "What
about the Poseidon's Trident treasure? Neither of you ever went back
to look for it?"

"Not officially," Sam said. "Although we did go back to visit our friends a few times over the years."

"They haven't given up the search," Remi added. "Which is what has us worried."

"I can well understand. And both of you are certain the coins you found at the bottom of that cave were counterfeit?"

"Positive." Sam set his glass of port on the table. "We have to assume the gold was emptied from the amphorae before they ever made it into the cave. If that's the case, then we think it was still on the pirate ship that carried it there."

Remi nodded. "Selma, of course, has continued to research it over the years. Surprisingly, it was the rocks found with the counterfeit coins that actually brought us here. She arranged to have some of them sent out to historians, museum curators, geologists, basically anyone who might be able to give us insight. A throw-the-spaghetti-at-the-wall-and-see-what-sticks sort of a thing."

"Apparently something stuck?"

"Definitely. First, the rocks found among the broken amphorae in the cave weren't indigenous to Megalos Anthropofas, they were from Samos. More importantly, it was suggested that it might be ballast from the pirate ship. This offered one interesting possibility—" Remi glanced at Sam, then back at Perlmutter. "Someone switched out their ship's ballast for the gold before they ever brought it to the islet."

"You're saying Pactyes double-crossed the pirates?"

"Or, he was in league with some of the pirates. Either way, someone double-crossed someone."

"It's the only thing that makes sense," Sam said. "A layer of counterfeit coins over the top of the rock found in the one intact jar? I'll bet the other jars were exactly like that before they broke."

Remi nodded. "There's a reference from Herodotus about King Cyrus sending an army after Pactyes to bring him back. I expect the pirates wouldn't have been too thrilled to find out Cyrus was after them."

"A good point," Perlmutter said. "It's highly unlikely the pirate ship would have survived if Cyrus's navy attacked. They would have rammed the vessel, sinking it."

"Exactly what we thought," Remi replied. "Unfortunately, Selma wasn't able to find any specific references about Samian pirate ships going down in that area around that time period. Which is what brings us to you."

"I do love a good challenge. Samian pirates. Archaic period?"

"Five forty-six to be exact."

Perlmutter lowered his port glass to the table, scooped up his dog, then rose from his chair with surprising quickness for so large a man. "I have a vague recollection of a Samian naval ship that went down around that time. Some skirmish with the Persians. It might very well fit the bill."

"We're fairly certain," Sam said, "it was a pirate ship. Samian pirates."

"Back then, it was often the same thing. It merely depended on who was financing the operation, and what they were paying the Samians for." He set Fritz on the carpet at his feet, then began searching his bookshelves. "I'd hazard a guess that might be why your researcher failed to find anything . . . Give me a moment . . . I believe the particular volume I need is in a different room. I'll be right back."

Perlmutter returned just a few minutes later with a thin leather book and a pair of white gloves, which he set on a desk. "This," he said, putting on the gloves, "is a very rare volume of the history of the Mediterranean, transcribed by the Benedictine monks in the thirteenth century from the original, which, sadly, is no longer in existence. I was fortunate enough to acquire it at auction a number of years ago." He sat down and opened the book, turning the yellowed pages with care as he scanned the spidery, flowing script.

Suddenly he smiled. "Here it is . . . Just as I remembered. A report of a naval vessel going down in that very area."

He finished translating the Latin passage, closed the book, then stood, walking over to the map on the wall, studying it a moment. "Ancient trade routes often brought ships along this route," he said, tracing his finger along the map from Turkey, past Samos to Fourni. "If I were the one looking, this is where I'd start."

CHAPTER EIGHTY-ONE

Twenty-four hours later, Sam and Remi boarded their private jet, then set their course for Samos. Sam had sent a message to Dimitris and his father, Nikos, letting them know of the new information Perlmutter had given them. Nikos had immediately contacted the Greek Ephorate of Underwater Antiquities in Athens, which lent the Fourni team the necessary equipment to do preliminary searches, scanning, recording, and measuring with techniques called photogrammetry and photo-mosaicing. In essence, once the wreck was found, they'd be taking pictures with underwater cameras and strobes, creating a 3-D model of the site.

Everything from this point worked in slow motion. Should they find the wreck, a documenting of this magnitude could take five to ten years to process, and millions of dollars. As far as Sam and Remi were concerned, the cost to supplement the Greek Ephorate on behalf of the Fourni crew was worth it.

Returning cultural treasures to the rightful countries was the reason for the Fargo Foundation's existence—of course, had anyone bothered to ask Sam or Remi, they'd be the first to admit that they'd gladly have paid double that amount just to be involved in the recovery.

Their luggage unloaded from their jet, they hired a taxi to drive them into Pythagorio. Dimitris, Zoe, and two dark-haired boys were waiting for them at the port when they arrived. After warm hugs, Remi turned to the boys, seven-year-old identical twins with curly brown hair and large brown eyes. They'd both grown several inches since their last visit. "How do you tell them apart?"

"Tassos," Dimitris said, placing his hand on the shoulder of the boy on the right, "always has his nose in a book. And he's an inch taller." He ruffled the other boy's head. "You'll have to ask Manos about the time he threw some fish in the bathtub to try out his new speargun."

Zoe laughed as she took the hands of each boy. "One thing they have in common is they both inherited their father's love of the sea."

Little Manos nodded. "Especially when we get to go out with Uncle Valerios. It's the fastest boat anywhere!"

Nikos's cousin, Valerios, had been the one who'd lent Sam the cigarette boat that he'd used to rescue Remi and Dimitris all those years ago. Sam had never quite gotten over the guilt of blowing it up when he rammed it into Kyril's yacht. Replacing it with a brand-new cigarette boat was one of the first things he and Remi did after they sold their argon laser scanner. "You've been on that, have you?" Sam asked.

Zoe stopped, looking at both boys, then at Dimitris. "You better not be on that boat. That thing's way too powerful and you're way too young."

Dimitris gave a sheepish smile, then nodded toward the port. "We better hurry if we want to catch the ferry. These two have school in the morning."

Tassos, the older of the two, looked up at his father. "We want to go on the boat with you."

His brother nodded. "Please? You promised we could help."

"In the summer," Zoe said. "After school gets out." She looked at her husband, raising her brows as if to say, *See what you started?* The idea of renewing the search for the fabled treasure had been a point of contention between the young couple. In fact, Zoe had asked Dimitris to back out, if not for her, for the sake of the children. She was worried that Adrian Kyril's early release from prison—not to mention his obsession with Poseidon's Trident—might pose a danger to them.

But it was that very real possibility that had caused Dimitris to reach out to Sam and Remi, asking for their help. As far as he was concerned, the sooner that treasure was found and turned over to the government, the safer they'd all be. Not that Sam and Remi were about to embark on this quest without taking precautions. They'd hired a private investigation firm to tail Kyril, keeping tabs on his movements while they conducted their search. Dimitris, knowing this, gave his wife a reassuring look before addressing his boys. "Your mother's right. Besides, we have to find it first. And that's the boring part. Who knows how long that could take?"

Two weeks later, their enthusiasm waning, they figured they hadn't identified any wreck that could have been the merchant ship. In a last-ditch effort, Sam suggested they try another video consultation with St. Julien Perlmutter. That night, he, Remi, and the Fourni crew, Dimitris, Nikos, Manos, and Denéa, gathered in the galley around the iPad. Perlmutter's face filled the screen. "How far past the coordinates have you searched?" he asked Sam.

"At least ten square miles."

Perlmutter turned, looking at the map on his wall. "Logic would state that the pirates would've headed straight back to Samos. And yet . . ." He faced the camera again. "King Cyrus undoubtedly knew the dangers of giving chase to a Samian ship. When you look at the extent of his expanding kingdom, it's obvious he was a brilliant strategist. He likely would have sent more than just the one ship, blocking their return to Pythagorio, and forcing them into open waters." He rose from his chair, tapping on the map southeast between Fourni, Samos, and Agathonisi. "I'd say extend your search in this direction."

"We'll give it a try," Sam said.

Perlmutter peered into the camera. "No sign of . . . ?"

"Adrian Kyril? None so far. Not that we're letting down our guard any. My investigator says he's still tucked away in his father's house on Patmos. Though admittedly in less luxurious surroundings than he was used to before his arrest."

"Good to hear. And good luck with the search. Remember a shipwreck is never where you think it should be and it's never found until it wants to be found."

Nikos reset the coordinates, then steered the *Asteri* to the southeast. Though it took another week, they found and identified the remains of not one but two wrecks about sixty meters down.

CHAPTER EIGHTY-TWO

With both shipwrecks identified, scanned, the images recorded and sent to the Greek Ephorate of Underwater Antiquities, Sam, Remi, Nikos, and Dimitris decided to begin the long and tedious process of mapping, while Manos and Denéa manned the *Asteri*.

As they approached the seafloor, Remi marveled at the outline of what promised to be the nearly intact hull. It was buried beneath enough silt to protect most of it from the sea worms and harsh salt water that would have, under ordinary circumstances, rotted the wood. Of course, none of this meant it was *the* wreck. Or that someone else hadn't looted it long ago.

Remi, like the others, was equipped with a full face mask with underwater radio capabilities. She hit her talk button. "Amazing," she said.

Dimitris nodded.

An octopus darted out from a nearby large rock, apparently disturbed when they ventured too close.

They both watched, enjoying the antics of the marine creature, until their attention was drawn to the sound of an approaching vessel.

The pair looked up, Dimitris pushing his talk button. "Archeological society?"

"Looks like it," Manos said, his voice much clearer, coming from on board the *Asteri*.

The government archeologists would be working in tandem with the Fourni team, which meant the crew would have access to more equipment and resources.

"Remi . . ." She turned at the sound of Sam's transmission. He was swimming about twenty yards to her left. "Look at this . . ."

She swam toward him, as did Dimitris and Nikos. The three of them gathered around Sam, who was holding the handle of a broken amphora, aiming his wrist-mounted flashlight at it. The maker's mark on the handle was the same as the one they'd found in the cave all those years ago. And while that helped prove the connection to both locations, it wasn't, surprisingly, what Sam had called them over for. He aimed the beam of his flashlight onto the seafloor.

The light glinted off a small sickle-moon-shaped object. Remi reached out, brushing off the sand, revealing a lion's head on the crudely stamped gold coin.

As exciting as that was, they still had a few centuries of silt to remove before they could verify that it was the ship they were looking for, or that their theory was correct, and that Pactyes hid the stolen treasure in the hold.

Nikos, unable to wait until they surfaced, radioed up to Manos and Denéa. "Gold lions!"

"Perfect timing!" Denéa radioed back. "The *Odysseus* is pulling up now. I'll let you know as soon as we're ready."

"Zoe should be here," Dimitris said as he used his brush to carefully dust the silt from the same area.

Nikos paused from his photo taking, nodding at his son. The *Odysseus*'s motor shut off, and they were surrounded by silence, until the radio crackled oddly, Denéa's voice saying, "There's something wrong with the—"

The four waited. Finally, Nikos pushed his talk button. "Denéa?" After a few seconds, he radioed a second time.

Still no answer.

Dimitris gave a thumbs-up. "I'll go check," he told them.

"I'll go with you," Remi said.

He nodded, as did Sam, still aiming the light on the treasure, while Nikos went back to taking photos of their initial find.

As much as Remi wanted to stay and see what else they might uncover in their initial search, she also wanted to be there at the briefing of the national archeologists. It was important to her to make sure that they not only planned to give the proper credit to the much smaller Fourni crew, but that they also would let them lead the expedition—not that she doubted they wouldn't comply, since the Fargo Foundation was sponsoring the search.

She was about to follow Dimitris, when Nikos tapped her leg. She looked back, saw him holding the gold coin toward her. He reached for her dive bag, slipping the coin inside, then said, "Zoe."

She nodded, then started her ascent, pacing herself with Dimitris. When they reached the first decompression stop, she glanced down, saw Sam and Nikos working away below. It was remarkable how far they'd come since their first visit to the Mediterranean and the Fourni archipelago all those years ago. This find would mean a lot to Dimitris and Zoe as well as their children, not only because of what the finder's fee would bring to them, but also realizing what had been a lifelong dream of Zoe's grandfather.

Finding the treasure.

She had to imagine that Tassos was looking down, cheering them on.

Remi and Dimitris both checked their watches, then continued their ascent to the next level, seeing the hulls of the boats above them. The much larger *Odysseus* was moored right up against the *Asteri*, while a much smaller speedboat was tethered behind the former vessel. When they finally broke the surface, Remi half-expected everyone aboard to be watching for them. Cheering, even. After all, this was the find of a lifetime.

Even Dimitris was surprised. He removed his face mask, looking up at the boat. "Rather anticlimactic."

"*Very*," she said.

"Let's get that radio fixed so we can have a proper celebration."

They swam to the ladder. She took off her BCD and tank, handed them to Dimitris, then removed her fins, holding them by the straps as she climbed the steps. About to throw them on the deck, she happened to look up as a gray-haired man stepped out of the cabin.

Adrian Kyril.

And he was pointing a gun directly at her.

CHAPTER EIGHTY-THREE

Before Remi could warn Dimitris, he hefted her gear onto the deck, making a loud clatter as he hauled himself up next to her.

As Adrian's attention shifted from her to Dimitris, she pulled her dive knife from its sheath, slid it between her fins, then dumped the sheath into the water. When Adrian's focus rested on her once more, she said, "You're the last person I expected to see. It's been a while."

"Isn't it a pleasant surprise?" He smirked.

"What are you doing here?"

"I'd think that'd be obvious, Remi Longstreet."

"Fargo," she said, resisting the urge to throw the knife at him right then and there. She carefully set the fins and hidden blade onto the deck.

"Fargo. Of course. You'd think I'd remember, considering I've spent the last decade reading about the two of you."

"I'm flattered."

His nostrils flared as he scrutinized her, his dark gaze narrowing. "You don't seem to have aged at all."

"And you look at least ten years older." She glanced past him and saw Fayez and Ilya. "Where's Manos and Denéa?"

"Aboard the *Odysseus*. Safe with the other archeologists. When can we expect your husband?"

"I have no idea," she said, her eye on his two men as they moved out of the cabin, Fayez walking with a definite limp.

"Check her tank," Adrian said. "I want to know how much air her husband has."

Remi sensed Dimitris bristling beside her. "They both have plenty of air down there. Don't expect them anytime soon."

Ilya walked over and checked the gauge. "Less than half a tank. As deep as the water is, I doubt they can stay down longer than ten minutes at that level." He glanced over, saw the knife strapped to Dimitris's leg, and removed it. He looked over at Remi. "Where's your dive knife?"

"I don't use one."

Fayez laughed. "For good reason. She's likely to hurt herself."

"How's that knee of yours?" she asked.

"Enough!" Adrian said. He motioned with his gun toward the open door of the helm. "I've never been a patient man. Which means I'm going to need you to convince Fargo to make an appearance."

"Good luck with that."

Ilya, his expression never wavering, raised his pistol, pointing it at Dimitris's chest.

Adrian, however, never took his eyes from Remi. "If you want your friend to live long enough to see his father again, you'll do as I say. Bring your husband and Nikos to the surface."

"Don't do it, Remi," Dimitris said. "He's going to kill us anyway."

Of that, she had no doubt. Especially when she noticed two men in wet suits and scuba gear, each carrying a speargun, standing on the swim deck of the *Odysseus*. She looked at them, then Adrian. "What's going on?"

"Let's just say I was anticipating your refusal to be cooperative.

Either Fargo comes up, or those two go down." His smile was chilling. "The question you might want to ask yourself is if you'd like to see your husband one more time before you all die."

"Not a very generous choice. Fine. I'll do what you ask."

"I thought you might."

She glanced at Dimitris, then down at her tank and vest. He knew how much air Sam and Nikos had left. Getting her gear into the water might be their only chance. She rested her hand on his shoulder, then squeezed it. "I'll be fine," she said.

He gave a slight nod.

"Enough," Adrian said. He pushed her into the cabin.

Remi stood in front of the underwater radio, which had been switched off. She glanced out the window, past Adrian, saw Ilya picking up her tank and moving it away from the opening, then ordering Dimitris out of his gear.

So much for that idea, she thought, picking up the microphone.

Adrian stepped back, raising his gun. "Choose your words wisely, Mrs. Fargo."

She took a deep breath, then keyed the mic.

CHAPTER EIGHTY-FOUR

S am, holding the light for Nikos, heard a slight crackle on the radio, then Remi's voice on his internal speaker. "How's it going down there?"

He pushed the talk button. "We're making progress."

"You need to come up."

"Is something wrong?"

He heard her clearing her throat. "Nothing. Most of us are here on the *Voreio Asteri*."

"Be there shortly." He checked his air, saw he had about ten minutes left, and signaled to Nikos that they needed to head up.

The older man nodded, then went back to dusting. He'd uncovered at least a dozen more gold coins very near the location where they'd found the first coin that he'd given to Remi, and was, undoubtedly, eager to find more.

That the Samian ship survived the centuries in the Aegean waters at all was a miracle in itself, but not unheard of. The partial hulls of even older ships, from the late fourteenth century B.C., had been found by sponge divers off the Antalya coast of Turkey in similar depths just east of them. Sam thought that this find would possibly rival that, if nothing else due to the historical connection to Cyrus the Great—never mind Pactyes, the man who'd stolen the gold, then hired the Samian ship to carry it from the mainland.

If this was the fabled Poseidon's Trident treasure, there was a lot more than these few coins to be found. Other than the one Remi had taken up, they weren't about to remove anything before they mapped it. A site this significant, the government archeologists would continue to keep the location secret, and be living on-site until the wreck was completely salvaged of the important and valuable artifacts.

Unfortunately, as much as Sam—and no doubt, Remi—would love to be involved every step of the way, the entire excavation could take several years. They'd have to leave the majority of that work to Nikos, the Fourni crew, and the governmental archeologists, who were no doubt setting up shop above them even now.

Sam, seeing that Nikos had no intention of stopping, tapped him on the arm, then touched his dive watch, indicating that they needed to return to the boat.

And, once again, Nikos nodded, then continued dusting the artifact. The water clouded as the particles rose then settled away, revealing the curved edge of a rather large object just visible beneath the sand. Nikos ran his finger against it, revealing something long, round, and encrusted. Too large to be a plate, too small to be a shield. Maybe a serving platter.

Finally, Nikos put away his brush, then signaled that he was ready.

Sam hit the talk button. "On our way up."

There was a click, as though someone quickly grabbed the radio to acknowledge his transmission. For some reason, that brought to mind Remi's earlier transmission. While there was nothing outwardly wrong, it struck him that something was off. Not her voice—that had sounded normal.

It was something to do with the boat.

Sam's Greek was far too rusty. He reached out, tapping Nikos, then picked up his slate board, writing: *What is "Vorayo Asteri"?*

Nikos eyed Sam's phonetic spelling, then nodded, taking the pen, writing:

"*Voreio Asteri*. North Star."

Sam's blood turned to ice.

Remi was in trouble.

He scrawled Adrian Kyril's name on the board, then pointed toward the surface. As they started their ascent, Sam saw two divers silhouetted above. Both carried what, at first glance, looked like metal detectors, something that members of the archeological team might carry.

Except if he was right about Remi's warning, they weren't archeologists—and those were not metal detectors.

They were pneumatic spearguns.

He grabbed Nikos's arm, pulling him back toward the bottom, then pushing him toward a rock about a yard wide. The octopus they'd seen earlier scuttled out and darted across the rounded edge of the platelike object Nikos had been dusting. Sam reached down, grasped the edge, tugging it from the sand. A cloud of silt swept up as he freed the object. It looked like a large round platter encrusted with centuries of buildup.

Sam held it with both hands as one of Kyril's men stopped swimming, then aimed. The spear shot through the water, hitting the platter. Bits of concretion broke off, floating to the seafloor. The second diver aimed before Sam had a chance to move. He swung his makeshift shield, the water slowing its path. The spear glanced off it, almost knocking the plate from Sam's hands.

The two men started to reload. Sam, seeing his chance, shoved the plate toward Nikos, then swam toward them. He reached the first diver, who was struggling with his speargun. Sam gripped the end of it, trying to pull it from the man's grasp. The diver kicked out, then fired, as Sam jerked the barrel upward, the shot going wide. Sam wrested the speargun, dropped it, then grabbed the man by both wrists.

As they struggled, the diver brought up his knees to Sam's chest, pushing out. Sam kept his hold on the attacker and wrapped both legs around the man's waist, squeezing tight. From the corner of his eye, he saw the other man, his speargun loaded, aiming it at them. Sam held his thighs around the diver, then, twisting, forced him around. The man jerked, then suddenly went limp, the spear piercing through his side.

A thin cloud of blood drifted outward as Sam let the body go. He saw the second diver toss the now useless gun. The man drew his dive knife and started swimming straight toward Sam.

CHAPTER EIGHTY-FIVE

Time seemed to fragment as Remi stood on the deck next to Dimitris, counting the minutes after Kyril's men dove into the water to bring up Sam and Nikos. She knew her husband, knew his capabilities, but try as she might, she couldn't control her growing fear that, when she'd left him, he had only about ten minutes of air left in his tank, and he'd now been down there for twenty minutes.

Adrian Kyril, gun in hand, paced the deck, every now and then stopping to look over the side into the water. After another five minutes went by, he turned to Remi. "Tell your husband that if he fails to come up, I'll kill the both of you and everyone on board the *Odysseus.*"

When she didn't move, he grabbed her by her arm, forcing her back into the cabin.

He pressed the gun into her ribs. "It doesn't much matter who I kill first. The choice is yours."

Hand shaking from adrenaline, she picked up the microphone, and keyed it. "Sam . . . Are you there . . . ?" The several seconds of following silence were punctuated by the sound of her pulse pounding in her ears. "Sam . . . ? Come in . . . please."

Adrian grabbed the microphone from her. A few more seconds passed by. "Why isn't he answering?"

"I don't know. Let me try again."

"I'm done with the niceties." He keyed the mic. "Fargo? I have your wife. If you don't make an appearance in the next five minutes, I'll kill her and everyone on board the *Odysseus*, too." He tossed the microphone onto the radio, grabbed her by the shoulder, and pushed her out of the cabin. "You had better hope he comes to his senses."

With Adrian close behind her, Remi crossed the deck toward Dimitris. Although the late-afternoon sun lit up the crystal clear depths several meters down, the sea was too deep to see where Sam and Nikos had been diving.

"Something's wrong," Ilya said. "They should be back by now."

Adrian moved next to Remi. He peered over the railing, then turned toward Ilya. "What should we do?"

Ilya's dead gaze landed on Remi. "We wait."

The *Asteri* rocked gently as Remi leaned over the side, her focus on the turquoise water, seeing nothing but the sun reflecting off the surface. She knew her husband, knew he would survive. Even so, she worried. Both Ilya and Fayez stood ready to shoot the moment Sam and Nikos surfaced.

Five minutes went by.

They should have been up by now.

Adrian gripped her arm. "Where is he?"

Remi glanced at Dimitris. His expression mirrored her own.

"Look!" Dimitris pointed to a froth of air bubbles.

Someone was breathing down there.

A moment later, two dark forms started to take shape, rising to the surface.

Ilya and Fayez aimed their weapons.

Adrian grabbed Remi's arm. "No!" she shouted, struggling to pull away.

The divers broke the surface and the men fired. *Crack! Crack! Crack! Crack!*

Her heart jumped with each shot.

"Enough!" Adrian said.

The two divers floated facedown, Sam's tank bobbing above on the left, and Nikos's, with the Fourni logo, on the right.

Remi's gut twisted, her knees going weak as she stared at the two dead men.

Neither was Sam or Nikos.

Dimitris stared in shock, his gaze moving from the bodies to Remi, undoubtedly realizing the same thing. They'd switched out the tanks. Drawing her gaze from the water, she threw herself against Dimitris, burying her head into his shoulder, trying to appear the grieving wife—until Ilya said, "We can't leave the bodies there. Evidence."

"Fish them out," Adrian said.

That was the last thing they needed. Remi pushed away from Dimitris, facing Adrian. "Aren't you even the least bit curious about what—if anything—we found down there? Poseidon's Trident. That's what you were looking for when you killed Tassos, wasn't it?"

"Did you really think that's why I'm here?" Adrian studied her a moment, his brows rising. "I came back for one reason. I want nothing more than to see your husband decaying at the bottom of the sea, and for you to suffer for it."

Apparently, she and Sam had totally miscalculated Adrian's lust for that treasure.

Somehow, she was going to have to rekindle it. "The gold was never on the island. The pirates who helped steal it were double-crossed by Pactyes."

Adrian, about to turn away, stopped. "Double-crossed by Pactyes? What are you talking about?"

"The pirates," Remi said, "who helped steal the gold from King

Cyrus. They thought it was buried on Poseidon's Trident, but it was on board their ship the whole time." She pulled the mesh bag from her dive belt, then tossed it on the ground at his feet. "It's in there."

He stared at it a moment, as though suspecting some sort of trick. Finally, he bent down, and picking it up, opened it. When he reached in, pulling out the gold piece, and holding it up, his breath caught at the sight of the gleaming golden lion's head. "You found this . . . down there?"

She nodded. "It's the gold from Poseidon's Trident. And there's a lot more where that came from. But you're going to need us to find it."

"She's right," Dimitris said. "It's not out in the open."

"You truly expect me to believe that? When your boat is anchored almost on top of it?" He smiled, tucking the coin in his pocket.

Ilya's phone rang. He answered it, listening, his eyes flicking across Remi and Dimitris, then landing on Adrian. "Gianni wants to know how much longer."

"We're ready." Looking at Fayez, he cocked his head at Dimitris and Remi. "I want those two on the *Odysseus* when we blow it up."

Fayez pulled several zip ties from his pocket and limped over to the young man, securing his hands behind his back. He moved to Remi, pulling her hands behind her back. As he tightened the strap, they heard a thunk against the hull. Fayez and Remi both looked over the side to see that the current had carried the divers closer to the *Asteri*, one now right up against it. Fayez was about to turn away, when the tank clunked again. It shifted, turning the body just enough to show the man's face. Fayez pushed Remi aside, staring for several seconds. "That's not Fargo. That's Kostas." He looked at the other man floating farther out. "And Gregor."

Adrian strode toward the railing, took one look, then rounded on Remi, his gaze darkening with anger. "Where is your husband?"

"I have no idea."

He glanced at Ilya. "Call Piers on the *Odysseus* that Fargo's on the loose." Ilya moved off, and Adrian turned to Fayez. "Zip-tie their feet."

Fayez kneeled with some difficulty. He pulled a zip tie tight around Dimitris's ankles, then did the same to Remi.

Ilya looked up from his phone. "Piers's phone goes to voice mail."

"Fargo." Adrian rounded on Remi, pushed her to the deck so hard it knocked the breath from her lungs. Pain lanced through her hip and shoulder, but when she looked down, she realized she was just a few inches from the knife she'd hidden beneath her fins. Ignoring the pain, she rolled, reaching behind her until she felt the fins. She slipped her fingers between them, touching the knife, then froze as Kyril looked down at her. Finally, as he turned away, she shifted into a sitting position.

Adrian's gaze was on the research vessel. "We need to find him."

"Why don't we just blow it up now?" Ilya asked.

"Because I want to see his face when I tell him his wife is dead."

"Wait," Fayez said as Adrian stepped on the platform behind Ilya. "We're not taking these two onto the other boat? I thought we were going to blow them all up."

"No time. Dump them overboard, they'll drown. I want it to look like an accident."

Dimitris, glancing over at Remi, saw her working her knife. When Fayez looked at the two of them as though trying to decide who to drown first, Dimitris scooted forward, doing his best to kick at him. "Stay away from her."

Fayez stepped back, out of reach. "Or what?"

"You'll see." He shifted forward, kicking a second time.

Fayez seemed amused. "I'm sure she'll love to see you die first." He stepped behind Dimitris, dragging the struggling man toward the ladder. Remi started sawing her knife against the zip tie. The blade slipped from her grasp. She stilled, but Fayez, busy with trying to shove Dimitris into the water, didn't seem to hear. She grasped the blade, again working it against the thick plastic. She cut through as Fayez pushed Dimitris headfirst into the sea.

With her hands free, she cut the tie at her ankles, then jumped to her feet.

"Fayez," Remi called out.

He turned and faced her, saw the knife she held and laughed. "You forget. I've seen you—"

She hurled the blade.

It struck him below the sternum.

Remi darted forward as he slumped to the deck. Fayez stared up at her in shock. "Practice," she said, looking past him, seeing Dimitris sinking into the depths. She yanked the knife from Fayez's chest. Had she not worried that Adrian or Ilya would spot his body, she would've left him there. Instead, she shoved him over the edge, then dove into the water to save her friend.

CHAPTER EIGHTY-SIX

Adrian Kyril, seething with anger, nearly ran into the back of Ilya when the man stopped suddenly on the deck of the *Odysseus*.

Ilya stood there, one hand on the cabin door, looking in the direction of the *Asteri*.

"What's wrong?" Adrian asked, annoyed.

"I heard a splash."

"Fayez dumping the bodies."

"Maybe I should check."

"Leave them. We need to find Fargo. If he's on board, we're all in trouble."

When Ilya hesitated, Adrian pushed past him, pulling open the door. He stepped in, looking around the multipurpose room. Galley on the port side, a couch and two chairs on the starboard side, the room was divided by a long table, where Adrian saw a half-empty coffee cup, an open box of crackers, and Piers's cell phone. He walked over, touched the mug. It was still warm.

Piers, however, was nowhere in sight.

Adrian's blood pressure rose at the thought that Fargo might have bested him once again. He'd had over a decade to nurse his hatred for Sam and Remi Fargo. Because of their interference, his mother was dead, their property and assets stolen by the government, and he was left suffering the indignity of living like a pauper, all while the Fargos pretended to be philanthropists, raking in millions of dollars in the process. Taking a deep breath, trying to calm himself, he eyed the passageway leading below deck.

Fargo would definitely try to save the hostages.

"Check up here," he said, heading for the stairs. Holding his gun close, he started down, stopping at the bottom to listen, hearing nothing. He reached out, opening the first door, pointing his weapon at the four hostages hog-tied to each other. They looked up in fright as he quickly surveyed the room, closed that door, then crossed over and checked the adjoining cabin, seeing the other four there. And no sign of Fargo.

"I found Piers," Ilya called out from above.

Relieved, he closed the door and hurried up the stairs, seeing Piers standing next to Ilya. "Where were you?"

"In the head. Too much coffee."

"Where's Gianni?"

"Right where you left him," Piers said, pointing upward. "Keeping watch."

Adrian, still worried about Fargo, dug the gold coin from his pocket, holding it up. "Half of the treasure to anyone who captures Fargo. I want him on this boat with the others when it goes up."

Piers's eyes widened. "Is that thing real?"

"Very."

Ilya glanced at the coin as Adrian stuffed it back in his pocket. "Half the treasure. You'll have to reconsider the explosion."

"You're the one who said we should make it look like an accident."

"An explosion will only bring the authorities," Ilya said. "They'll find the shipwreck when they send divers to salvage what's left of the *Odysseus*."

Adrian felt his jaw clenching, then forced himself to relax. He strode to the door, pushing it open. "We find Fargo first, move the boat, then blow it up. If he's not on board, he's lurking around it. Maybe we can see him from the upper bridge."

Ilya followed him out. "This might be a good time to cut your losses and leave. I have friends who can get you out of the country."

"I have no intention of living my life a poor man on the run." He crossed to the starboard side, taking the stairs up. At the top, there was a short open deck leading to the open second bridge, where Gianni was sitting in the captain's chair, facing forward.

He spun around as they walked in. "Something wrong?"

"Fargo's out there somewhere."

"So we let him come aboard, and boom!" Gianni held up the remote. "Charges set on the hull, just like you asked."

"Careful," Ilya said, taking the remote from him.

"I'm not an idiot. No batteries." He nodded to a black bag on the bench seat. "They're in there."

"Change of plans," Adrian told him. "We're moving the boat."

Gianni's gaze shifted from Adrian to Ilya, then back. "So we're not blowing up the boat?"

"Not yet. We need to find Fargo."

"He's not dead?"

Adrian slammed his fist on the console, causing Gianni to jump in his seat.

He took a deep breath, trying to tamp down the overwhelming anger and frustration that boiled up each time he thought of how Fargo had managed to escape. "No. He's not dead. He's either already on board, or planning a way to accomplish it." Looking out, they had an almost unobstructed, 360-degree view of the sea. He saw something move in the water on the starboard side, a few feet in front of their speedboat. The sun's reflection prevented him from seeing much more than a quick, dark blur. He decided it was too small to be Fargo.

Adrian's gaze lit on the remote that Ilya had returned to the console. He picked it up, then found the batteries inside Gianni's bag. While he might not share Ilya's confidence, there was one thing he knew with a certainty. Fargo was going to attempt a rescue. And when he did, Adrian would be ready.

CHAPTER EIGHTY-SEVEN

For Sam, killing the two divers, and switching out the oxygen tanks, had been the easy part. Getting up onto the *Odysseus* without being seen was proving to be a lot more difficult. He and Nikos had been just about to board when Adrian and Ilya suddenly emerged from the cabin, both heading up the stairs to the upper bridge.

Waiting until he heard talking on the upper bridge, Sam signaled to Nikos that he was going up. The older man hesitated, then nodded, slipping down into the water to complete the task Sam had given him.

Sam knew his reluctance. The fact that Kyril's men had attacked them and rigged the *Odysseus* to explode told him that, bomb or no bomb, they wouldn't hesitate to kill all of them. Sam wasn't sure how many archeologists were on board, but on a vessel this size, he guessed at least four, not to mention Manos and Denéa. There was no way that Sam was going to leave any of them behind.

When Nikos swam off, Sam reached up, grasped on to the platform's edge, pulling himself high enough to see over the top. Seeing it was clear, he hauled himself onto the platform, leaving a trail of water as he crossed the deck and opened the door. A broad-shouldered man seated at the table, his attention on the screen of his phone, looked up, saw Sam charging toward him. He stood so fast, his chair flew to the floor. As he reached for his holstered weapon, Sam grabbed his shoulder, pulled him forward, and drove his fist into the guard's jaw.

Just Sam's luck, the man was a southpaw, bringing in an upper-cut. Sam was pushed back. Stunned, he regrouped, then threw a right hook. Sam moved in and struck him again, caught him as he stumbled back and swung him around, slamming the gunman's head against the counter. He wavered, his unfocused gaze rolling sideward as he crumpled to the ground.

Sam kneeled next to him, taking his gun, then pulling off the man's belt, using it to bind his hands behind his back. Gun in hand, Sam rose, headed into a passageway, then took the stairs down, opening doors until he found Manos, Denéa, and two government archeologists tied up in one of the cabins. "How many gunmen?" Sam asked, setting the pistol on the floor, then drawing his dive knife to cut their ties.

"Seven total," one of the archeologists said. "Two were already with us, pretending to be journalists, researching shipwrecks. Gianni and . . . Piers."

His coworker nodded. "Five came aboard from the speedboat. They put us all down here."

"What about the *Asteri*?" Sam asked Manos as he cut his ties.

"They forced us here. I only saw two of them suiting up."

"I already met up with those two."

Denéa rubbed at her wrists. "Where's Remi and Dimitris?"

"I'm not sure. Yet," Sam said, helping her to her feet.

Once they were free, he gave Manos the gun, then freed the other four archeologists in the next cabin over. "Can you get to the front hatch?"

One of the archeologists nodded. "Yes, but if anyone's on the upper bridge, how are we going to get out without them seeing?"

"I'll create a distraction. If you can make it to the *Asteri*, cut the lines and go."

"Not without you," Denéa said.

"I'll be fine. Especially if I know that all of you are safe."

The others followed the head archeologist to the hatch, but Manos looked back at Sam. "I'll go with you."

"Someone's going to need to man the *Asteri*. You know it better than they do."

"The gun?"

"Take it. Just in case."

"You're sure?"

"Yes," Sam said. "Remi and Dimitris are probably on the *Asteri*. Now get going."

"But—"

"Do it. Remi will know it's the right thing to do. Trust me."

Manos nodded, then followed the others into the passageway.

As they were opening the door that led to the front hatch, Sam headed back up the stairs. At the top, he saw the man he'd battled with crawling along the floor toward the door. Sam dragged him back, and knocked him upside the head. At the door, he stopped to listen, surprised when he heard footsteps coming down the stairs from the upper bridge. That distraction was going to be a bit sooner than he'd planned.

CHAPTER EIGHTY-EIGHT

Sam ducked around the corner along the port-side passageway, pressed himself against the wall, waiting.

"Gianni. There's water on the deck. Fargo's here."

Sam stepped out, seeing Ilya and a younger man at the bottom of the stairs. Gianni, Sam presumed.

Ilya calmly pointed a gun at Sam. "Check him for weapons."

Gianni made a wide berth around Sam, finding the knife in its sheath. He pulled it out, pointing his own gun at Sam as Ilya moved closer. Ilya, holstering his weapon, gripped Sam's left arm. Gianni, still holding his gun, took the right. As they led him to the rear deck, Sam raised both elbows, and in a one-two motion, he stepped in and struck the gun from Gianni's hand, then rammed his elbow into Ilya's throat. Ilya staggered back, trying to breathe. Gianni reached for the fallen weapon, but Sam kicked it away. The pistol went spinning across the deck, banked off a dive tank compressor, then disappeared down the port-side passageway. Gianni immediately gave chase. Sam followed, hoping to get to him before he saw the escaping archeologists. He grabbed Gianni by the collar, dragged him around, then flung him against the air tanks lined up in a rack. The canisters clattered to the floor, rolling in all directions. From the corner of his eye, Sam saw Ilya drawing his own gun. Sam pivoted, kicked his leg out, whipped it back, slamming his foot against Ilya's wrist. The gun went flying.

Gianni charged Sam, spinning him around. Ilya jumped on Sam's back, crooked his arm around Sam's neck in a carotid hold. Gianni, shoulder down, moved in again. Sam reached up, grasped Ilya's arm, using it to carry his weight, then lifted both feet, driving them into Gianni's gut. Stunned, the man faltered back, tripping over a loose tank and into the tank rack.

Adrian Kyril, obviously hearing the commotion, hurried down the stairs, then stopped about midway. "Kill him," he shouted.

Unable to dislodge Ilya's stocky arm, Sam dropped to the deck, then pulled forward, using the momentum to fling the much larger man over his head. Ilya landed on Gianni. As Ilya struggled to get to his feet, Sam hefted up a nearby dive tank, bashing it against his temple. Ilya collapsed.

Adrian looked at the two fallen men, then Sam. He drew his own gun.

Sam, still holding the tank, pivoted and swung it at Adrian, knocking the weapon from his grasp.

"I'll kill you," Adrian said.

"It's over," Sam replied. "Do us both a favor and give it up."

The man's dark eyes darted about, then relaxed into a triumphant stare.

In the second it took Sam to turn, Gianni reached over, grabbed Sam's ankles, pulling sharply. Sam lost his balance, his temple hitting the deck as he fell. A bit light-headed, he opened his eyes, looking down the passageway, and saw Manos helping Denéa over the railing of the *Odysseus* onto the *Asteri*.

But they were going the wrong direction. And it wasn't Denéa at all. It was Remi. He shook his head, looked again, seeing nothing. By the time the dizziness passed, Ilya had struggled to his feet.

"Yes," Kyril said. "It's over."

Ilya wiped the blood from his cut lip, glaring at Fargo. "I'm looking forward to killing you."

"Not yet." Kyril held up a hand, gloating as he looked down from his perch on the stairs. "I want him to know exactly what happened to his wife."

"What are you talking about?" Sam asked. His gaze landed on one of the fallen air tanks near his feet.

"She's dead. This is what I took from her right before Fayez killed her."

Sam took in a deep breath. He focused, seeing the gold coin that Nikos had given to Remi. "You took it? Or she gave it to you?"

"Does it make a difference? She's dead, and you're next."

Sam glanced at the passageway, seeing Remi just a few feet away on the port-side deck. She smiled, waving at him, her foot on Gianni's gun. Either she was the most amazing hallucination he'd ever seen, or she was very much alive.

CHAPTER EIGHTY-NINE

In the second it took Sam to decide he really did see his wife, he heard the *Asteri* rumbling to life.

"What's that?" Adrian asked.

"That," Sam said, "is the sound of hostages who didn't quite cooperate, like you hoped."

"After them!" Adrian ordered.

Before anyone could make a move, the *Asteri* motored full-speed ahead. They all turned toward the speedboat. It was no longer tethered to the *Odysseus*, and was, thanks to Nikos, adrift.

"You did this!" Adrian Kyril said, his gaze landing on Sam.

"To be fair," Sam replied, "I had help."

Ilya turned to Kyril as he pulled a small remote from his pocket. "What are you doing?"

"What should have been done a long time ago."

Ilya pointed his weapon at Kyril. "I'm not going to die for you, Adrian. I'll kill you before I let that happen."

As Sam kicked the air tank, the clatter drawing everyone's attention, Remi slid the pistol toward Sam. He caught it, dropped and rolled over, shooting Ilya in the head. Gianni reached for Ilya's fallen gun. Sam turned, and shot him square in the chest, then aimed at Adrian.

Holding the remote, Adrian gave a triumphant smile. "You really think you can shoot me before I press this?"

"You sure you want to do that? You're on board and there's nowhere for you to go."

"I'll die happy, knowing I'm taking you with me."

He gripped the remote, then pressed the button.

Nothing happened. He pressed it once more, whacked the device against his hand, then tried pressing it again.

"I doubt it's the batteries," Sam said as he shifted his legs, then stood. "Something tells me it's those two divers you sent down after us. I'm guessing they probably weren't expecting us to live. Otherwise they'd have done a better job hiding those IEDs we found attached to the hull."

The color drained from Adrian's face as Remi stepped around the corner. He glanced at the two dead men on the deck, then glared at Sam, his jaw ticking. "I'll see you in hell."

"Probably not. But I'll definitely see you in court. Nothing will make me happier than knowing you're spending the rest of your life locked in a prison cell."

Sam handed the pistol to Remi, then walked over to Kyril, dragging him down the stairs.

EPILOGUE

Sam had to admit that the feeling of satisfaction on seeing Adrian Kyril taken into custody was well worth the lump on his head, bruised jaw, and sore ribs. After days of police interviews, he and Remi were both grateful when it finally ended.

With Adrian Kyril and his surviving gunman being held without bail, the archeologists and the Fourni crew could finally begin the task of identification, mapping, and recovery of the artifacts.

A week later, they began in earnest. One of the archeologists who recovered the plate that Sam had used to fend off the spears, bemoaned the fact that there was a dent in it.

"It's a small dent," Sam said. "You'd think they'd be happy about all the gold coins they've uncovered so far. I'll try to be more careful next time." He put his arm around Remi's shoulders. "I don't know about you, but I'm ready to head back to California. I was thinking we could do with a little vacation. I know a great spot where we can go camping."

She turned and looked up at Sam. "Any particular reason?"

"Does there need to be a reason?" He tucked his finger beneath her chin, then kissed her. "I happen to know where there's a bottle of Greek wine chilled to the perfect temperature. And the perfect location. A cliff top overlooking the Pacific Ocean."

"Sam, that's not camping. That's our home."

"But . . . I know where there's a tent and a sleeping bag with zippers."

"You kept them?"

He took Remi in his arms, brushing a strand of hair from her cheek, then gave her a kiss.

"Of course I kept them."

She smiled, wrapping her arms around his neck. "That's what I love about you, Sam Fargo. A true romantic."